ALSO BY ROBERT DUGONI

Wrongful Death
Damage Control
The Jury Master

The Cyanide Canary (nonfiction)

BODILY HARM

A NOVEL

ROBERT DUGONI

A TOUCHSTONE BOOK
Published by Simon & Schuster
New York   London   Toronto   Sydney

Touchstone
A Division of Simon & Schuster, Inc.
1230 Avenue of the Americas
New York, NY 10020

First Touchstone hardcover edition May 2010

TOUCHSTONE and colophon are registered trademarks of Simon & Schuster, Inc.

For information about special discounts for bulk purchases, please contact Simon & Schuster Special Sales at 1-866-506-1949 or business@simonandschuster.com.

The Simon & Schuster Speakers Bureau can bring authors to your live event. For more information or to book an event contact the Simon & Schuster Speakers Bureau at 1-866-248-3049 or visit our website at www.simonspeakers.com.

Manufactured in the United States of America

10   9   8   7   6   5   4   3   2   1

Library of Congress Cataloging-in-Publication Data
Dugoni, Robert.
  Bodily harm / by Robert Dugoni.
    p. cm.
  I. Title.
  PS3604.U385B63   2010
  813'.6—dc22   2009046051

ISBN 978-1-4165-9296-9
ISBN 978-1-4391-0061-5 (ebook)

To Sam Goldman,
the "greatest journalism teacher in the West,"
who taught me to love to write and what it
means to live each day to the fullest.

And to my brothers and sisters,
Aileen, Susie, Bill, Bonnie, Joann, Tom,
Larry, Sean, and Mike, for giving me the best
childhood a kid could have ever wanted.

Death is not the greatest loss in life.
The greatest loss is what dies
inside us while we live.

—*Norman Cousins*

BODILY HARM

PROLOGUE

I t hurt to blink.

The light stabbed at his eyes, shooting daggers of pain to the back of his skull. When he shut them an aurora of black and white spots lingered.

Albert Payne had never been one to partake liberally in alcohol; not that he was a complete teetotaler either. He'd been hungover a handful of times during his fifty-six years, but those few occasions had been the result of unintended excess, never a deliberate intent to get drunk. So although he had little experience with which to compare it, his pounding head seemed a clear indicator that he had indeed drunk to excess. He'd have to accept that as so, because he could remember little about the prior evening. Each factory owner, along with the local officials in China's Guangdong Province, had insisted on a reception for Payne and the delegation, no doubt believing their hospitality would ensure a favorable report. Payne recalled sipping white wine, but after three weeks the receptions had blurred together, and he could not separate one from the other.

Coffee.

The thought popped into his head and he seemed to recall that caffeine eased a hangover. Maybe so, but locating the magic elixir would require that he stand, dress, leave his hotel room, and ride the elevator to the lobby. At the moment, just lifting his head felt as if it would require a crane.

Forcing his eyelids open, he followed floating dust motes in a stream of light to an ornate ceiling of crisscrossing wooden beams and squares of decorative wallpaper. He blinked, pinched the bridge of his nose, then looked again, but the view had not changed. A cold sweat enveloped him. The ceiling in his room at the Shenzhen Hotel had no beams or wallpaper; he'd awakened the previous three mornings to a flat white ceiling.

He shifted his gaze. Cheap wood paneling and a dingy, burnt-orange carpet: this was not his hotel room and, by simple deduction, this could not be his bed.

He slid his hand along the sheet, fingertips brushing fabric until encountering something distinctly different, soft and warm. His heart thumped hard in his chest. He turned his head. Dark hair flowed over alabaster shoulders blemished by two small moles. The woman lay on her side, the sheet draped across the gentle slope of her rounded hip.

Starting to hyperventilate, Payne forced deep breaths from his diaphragm. Now was not the time to panic. Besides, rushing from the room was not an option, not in his present condition, and not without his clothes. Think! The woman had not yet stirred, and judging by her heavy breathing she remained deep asleep, perhaps as hungover as he, perhaps enough that if he didn't panic, Payne might be able to sneak out without waking her, if he could some-how manage to sit up.

He forced his head from the pillow and scanned along the wall to the foot of the bed, spotted a shoe, and felt a moment of great relief that just as quickly became greater alarm. The shoe was not his brown Oxford loafer but a square-toed boot.

Payne bolted upright, causing the room to spin and tilt off-kilter, bringing fleeting, blurred images like a ride on a merry-go-round. The images did not clear until the spinning slowed.

"Good morning, Mr. Payne." The man sat in an armless, slatted wood chair. "You appear to be having a difficult start to your day." Eyes as dark as a crow, the man wore his hair parted in the middle and pulled back off his forehead in a ponytail that extended beyond the collar of his black leather coat.

"Would you care for some water?"

Not waiting for a response, the man stood. At a small round table in the corner of the room he filled a glass from a pitcher, offering it to Payne. If this were a bad dream, it was very real. Payne hesitated, no longer certain that his hangover was alcohol induced.

The man motioned with the glass and arched heavy eyebrows that accentuated the bridge of a strong forehead. Dark stubble shaded his face. "Please. I assure you it's clean, relatively speaking."

Payne took the glass but did not immediately drink, watching as the man returned to the chair, and crossed his legs, before again pointing to the glass. This time Payne took a small sip. The glass clattered against his teeth and water trickled down his chin onto the sheet. When the man said nothing, Payne asked, "What do you want?"

"Me? I want nothing."

"Then why are you—"

The man raised a single finger. "My employer, however, has several requests."

"Your employer? Who is your employer?"

"I'm afraid I'm not at liberty to divulge that information."

The woman emitted a small moan before her chest resumed its rhythmic rise and fall. Payne looked back to the man, an idea occurring. "I've been married for more than twenty years; my wife will never believe this."

The man responded with a blank stare. "Believe what?"

Payne gestured to the woman. "Her. It's not going to work."

"Ah." The man nodded. "You believe that I am here to blackmail you with photographs or videotapes of the two of you fornicating."

"It isn't going to work," Payne repeated.

"Let me first say that it is refreshing to hear in this day when more than fifty percent of all marriages end in divorce that yours remains strong. Good for you. But look around you, Mr. Payne; do you see a camera or a video recorder anywhere in the room?"

Payne did not.

"Now, as I said, my employer has several requests." For the next several minutes the man outlined those requests. Finishing, he asked, "Do we have an understanding?"

Confused, Payne shook his head. "But you said you weren't here to blackmail me."

"I said I was not here to blackmail you with photographs or videotapes. And as you have already educated me, such an attempt would not be productive."

"Then why would I do what you're asking?"

"Another good question." The man pinched his lower lip. His brow furrowed. "It appears I will need something more persuasive." He paused. "Can you think of anything?"

"What?"

"Something that would make a man like you acquiesce to my employer's demands?"

"There's nothing," Payne said. "This isn't going to work. So if I could just have my clothes back."

"Nothing?" The man seemed to give the problem greater consideration, then snapped his fingers. "I have it."

Payne waited.

"Murder."

The word struck Payne like a dart to the chest. "Murder? I haven't murdered anyone."

With the fluidity of a dancer the man stood, a gun sliding into his extended left hand from somewhere beneath his splayed black coat, and the back of the woman's head exploded, blood splattering Payne about the face and neck.

"Now you have."

CHAPTER ONE

The call from King County Superior Court Judge John Rudolph's bailiff had sent the Law Offices of David Sloane into overdrive. Sloane juggled his briefcase as he slipped on his suit jacket and hurried down the hall.

The jury had reached a verdict.

"Give 'em hell!" John Kannin shouted.

Sloane rushed into the elevator lobby, cinching the knot of his tie. One of the red triangles above the bank of elevators lit and a bell sounded.

"David!" Carolyn shuffled into the lobby. "Your phone." She rolled her eyes as she handed his cell to him. "I swear you'd forget your head if it wasn't glued to your shoulders."

Sloane wedged his briefcase between the shutting doors. "Have you reached Tom yet?" He and Tom Pendergrass had tried the medical malpractice action against a local pediatrician for the death of a six-year-old boy. Following closing arguments, Pendergrass had gone straight to his athletic club for a much-needed workout.

"A woman at the front desk said she would look for him. How many redheads could be working out on a StairMaster?"

The doors shuddered, and the elevator buzzed. "Tell him to meet me in the courtroom. And tell him not to be late." The buzzing intensified. "You called the McFarlands?"

Carolyn put her hands on her hips. "No. I thought I'd use mental telepathy. Just get going before that thing blows a circuit and plummets. I can't afford to be looking for a new job in this economy."

When the elevator reached the lobby, Sloane jogged across the salmon-colored marble, his mind again churning over the evidence and hoping that the jurors had understood his arguments. Dr. Peter Douvalidis, for forty years a respected Seattle pediatrician, had chosen not to treat Austin McFarland for flu-like symptoms: diarrhea, vomiting, and high fevers. Subpoenaed medical records indicated that Douvalidis had taken a throat swab and sent the boy home with instructions that the McFarlands keep him hydrated and return if the fever didn't break. That night the boy had slipped into a coma and the McFarlands rushed Austin to the emergency room, where the attending doctor took a blood sample and sent it to the lab, suspecting a bacterial infection. Despite the doctor's efforts, Austin died. The next day the throat swab came back negative for the flu but the blood cultures came back positive for septicemia, a bacteria in the bloodstream, usually from an infection in some other part of the body. Sloane would later learn that septicemia manifests itself in symptoms similar to the flu and, as in the case of Austin McFarland, may progress to hypotension and death.

The McFarlands' focus had been on their bereavement. It was not until six months later that they approached Tom Pendergrass, whom they had met through a mutual friend, to determine if Douvalidis was liable in their son's death. Though expert doctors retained by Pendergrass opined that, given the severity of the boy's symptoms, Douvalidis should have immediately treated Austin with broad-spectrum antibiotics for a presumed bacterial infection, Sloane had never felt totally comfortable with suing the doctor. The experts' opinions seemed much like Monday-morning quarterbacking. He had let Pendergrass handle the case, deducing that it would settle. But Douvalidis's medical-malpractice carrier had refused, and on the eve of trial the McFarlands told Sloane they wanted him to try the case.

As Sloane reached the revolving glass doors he heard someone call his name.

"Mr. Sloane?"

Perhaps in his early twenties, the man had the youthful, un-kempt appearance made popular during Seattle's grunge phase in the 1990s, a fad that continued to linger. The tail of his shirt pro-truded over baggy jeans, and an oversize, olive green jacket hung heavily from his shoulders hiding the manila file until the man pulled a document from it, papers spilling onto the floor.

"I have something to show you." He knelt to recover the scat-tered pages.

Sloane had become a fixture on local and national talk shows since his verdict against the government on behalf of the wife of a national guardsman killed in Iraq that had led to the forced resigna-tion of the secretary of defense. His increased exposure had caused his caseload to explode; everyone wanted to hire "the lawyer who does not lose," as one national publication referred to him.

"I'm sorry I don't have time to talk." Sloane pushed through the revolving doors and kept a brisk pace past the rock wall sculp-ture and down wide concrete steps, hoping to discourage his pursuer, but the man hurried along beside him, talking as he con-tinued to fumble in his file.

"This will only take a minute."

"I'm afraid I don't have a minute." Sloane reached the corner of Sixth and University but the light changed to red, and the pedestrians in front of him abruptly stopped. Nobody jaywalked in Seattle. Sloane would have broken the rule, but traffic emptying from the I-5 freeway onto University was heavy.

The din of the cars nearly drowned out the man's voice. "If I could just show you this article it would explain—"

The light changed. Sloane stepped from the curb, leaving the young man searching his file. He made it halfway across when the man shouted.

"The doctor did not kill that boy."

Sloane stopped. Pedestrians maneuvered to avoid him. Walking back to the curb, Sloane saw that the man held a photocopy of an article from *The Seattle Times* reporting on the medical malpractice case.

"How would you know that?" Sloane asked.

"Because I did."

LAURELHURST
WASHINGTON

MALCOLM FITZGERALD EXITED his navy blue Bentley Brookland, a gift to celebrate his recent promotion, tugged the French cuffs of his shirt past the sleeves of his blazer, and adjusted the lapels. His wife had selected the jacket, and had it hand-tailored to accommodate his tall, slender frame. She liked him in blue, which she said better accentuated the gray at his temples and his fair complexion. For the board meeting that morning, Fitzgerald had decided on a simple white shirt with a lavender pinstripe that matched the color of his tie.

He retrieved the wrapped package from the passenger seat

and followed the stone path between English boxwood hedges into a manicured backyard. The lawn spread like a green blanket to the slate blue waters of Lake Washington, the southern view of Mount Rainier's snowcapped summit interrupted only by the 520 bridge spanning east to west.

The wrought-iron bench had been positioned just beneath the vines of a willow tree at the lake's edge, and faced the finger dock where Sebastian Kendall moored his seventy-two-foot yacht and fire-engine red float plane.

Fitzgerald nodded to the male nurse and stepped to where Kendall sat, his eyes closed, his body hunched over the silver horse head mounted atop his cane. Though it had been only a week since Fitzgerald's last visit, Kendall had physically deteriorated. He wore blue hospital scrub pants and a white T-shirt beneath a terry cloth bathrobe, his initials embroidered in gold on the breast pocket. The radiation and chemotherapy treatments had thinned a full head of hair to white wisps. Once a young-looking seventy-two and perhaps 180 pounds, Kendall now looked as if a breeze off the lake would knock him over.

"Sebastian?"

Kendall opened his eyes.

"I'm sorry to disturb." Fitzgerald had arranged the meeting earlier that morning.

"Just resting my eyes." Kendall's voice, hoarse and guttural, had become nearly unrecognizable. He motioned for Fitzgerald to sit beside him. "How is Melody?"

Fitzgerald did not bother to correct that his wife's name was Erin. "She sends her regards, and her prayers."

"And your daughters?"

"Growing like weeds and keeping us both as busy as ever; Sarah has it in her head that she wants to take tae kwon do, but I don't know how with all the soccer and ballet."

"They grow up fast," Kendall said, though he had no children and had never married.

"How are you feeling today?"

Kendall shrugged. "I'm still here."

Fitzgerald did not patronize his mentor by saying things like "You're going to beat this" or "You'll be here a lot longer." They were beyond that. The most sophisticated treatments had failed to slow the metastatic melanoma's destructive path.

Three months earlier Kendall's illness had forced him to reluctantly resign as CEO and chairman of the board of Kendall Toys, a company his grandfather and granduncle had founded in a booth on a Seattle street corner in Pioneer Square. A Kendall had presided over the company for each of its 110 years, with Sebastian holding the position for the most recent 38.

"The board still giving you a hard time?" Kendall asked.

A flock of crows freckled the sky; thousands of the birds roosted nearby on Foster Island in Seattle's arboretum, taking noisy flight over the lake each morning. "When your profits drop for the second quarter in a row after not having dropped the previous thirty-eight years, you expect tough questions. These are difficult economic times and you're a difficult act to follow, but then we both knew that would be the case. Six months from now, when we're still going strong, everyone will relax."

Neither man said it, but both knew Sebastian Kendall would not be alive to witness that revival.

"Any further overtures from Bolelli?" Kendall asked, referring to the efforts by Galaxy Toys' CEO, Maxine Bolelli, to purchase Kendall, a merger that would make Galaxy the number one toy company in the world, supplanting Titan Toys of Chicago.

"Some."

"What is Ms. Bolelli's current tone?"

"Terse. She said she won't wait forever for us to 'get our shit together.'" Fitzgerald had to raise his voice over the din of music blasting from speakers mounted atop the crossbar of a large ski boat carrying teenagers in swim trunks and bikinis from the Seattle Yacht Club. "She wants a response to her most recent offer, and if she doesn't get the answer she wants, she's threatened to go public with the negotiations." Fitzgerald had spent two days in confidential meetings at a resort in Scottsdale, Arizona, to discuss Galaxy's proposal to purchase Kendall. Galaxy did not have an action figure department, and its own attempts to create one had been abysmal failures. Even in a down market, Kendall's revenues continued to top $150 million, putting it squarely in the category of a midlevel toy company.

"She'll do it too," Kendall said.

"I have no doubt."

A duck swam to the water's edge, bobbing in the wake left by the ski boat. Kendall tore a small piece of bread from the chunk he held in his hand and tossed it, but the crumb fell short of the water, landing on the lawn. The duck quickly paddled over, waddled ashore, and gobbled it.

Kendall tossed another piece. "What's her latest offer?"

"Point six shares in Galaxy for every share in Kendall."

Sebastian Kendall nodded. "You would be a very wealthy man at this morning's stock price."

"As would you," Fitzgerald said.

Kendall remained the largest shareholder, owning 31 percent. Fitzgerald held 20 percent, a deliberate number that allowed them to maintain control of the company.

"You can't spend money where I'm going," Kendall said. "What do you anticipate the board will do?"

A light breeze blew the vines of the willow tree. "I'd say sixty-forty against, but Santoro is pushing hard."

Some at the company had thought Arian Santoro, rather than Fitzgerald, would be named CEO and chairman of the board, and it was well known that he and his minions had not been happy with Kendall's decision to endorse Fitzgerald.

"Bolelli will cut the fat and absorb what she deems an asset. Kendall will cease to exist."

"I'm not going to let that happen," Fitzgerald said.

Kendall patted Fitzgerald's thigh. "Sometimes we cannot cheat the inevitable."

Sensing the opportune moment, Fitzgerald lifted the wrapped package he'd set beside the bench and placed it on Kendall's lap.

Kendall's eyes narrowed. "Is it my birthday? My memory isn't what it used to be."

"Who are you kidding? Your memory is better than mine. Open it."

Though his hands shook, Kendall managed to unwrap the package. He held up the box to peer through the clear plastic window.

"Maybe we can cheat the inevitable," Fitzgerald said.

UNIVERSITY AVENUE

SEATTLE, WASHINGTON

A CAR HORN sounded. The light had again changed. Sloane stepped back onto the curb.

"Why would you say something like that?"

The man's light brown hair was matted to his head, and teenage acne had left pockmarks and red spots on his cheeks. "If you would just look at my file you would understand." He held it out.

Sloane tried a different tack. "Listen, Mr. . . . ."

"Horgan. Kyle Horgan."

"Listen, Kyle, I don't know why you would believe you're somehow responsible for Austin McFarland's death, but I can't—"

"Please, more children could die," Horgan said.

Sloane detected the odor of alcohol. He didn't know whether to feel sorry for the young man or to be concerned. Despite his disheveled appearance Horgan looked and sounded sincere, but crazy people often did.

"No more children are going to die," Sloane said. "Dr. Douvalidis has retired."

Horgan again held out the manila folder. "Please, just read it."

EXITING THE ELEVATOR on the ninth floor, Sloane hurried down the marbled hallway. Judge Rudolph wouldn't be happy; the judge had a pet peeve about attorneys not keeping his juries waiting. When Sloane pushed through the tall wood door, Rudolph's bailiff noted his entrance and exited the courtroom through a side door. Apparently Sloane was the last to arrive.

Sloane stepped behind his opposing counsel, who sat beside Dr. Peter Douvalidis at the table closest to the jury box. Douvalidis's head slumped, and he stared at the tabletop. In the first row behind him, the doctor's wife sat alone. Impeccably dressed, she maintained the stern expression she had worn throughout the trial.

The gallery on the opposite side of the room was half full with relatives and friends who had come to support the McFarlands. Tom Pendergrass had managed to beat Sloane to the courtroom and stood talking with Michael and Eva McFarland. Tears streamed down Eva's cheeks. The trial had been an emotional roller coaster that had forced her to relive the death of her son and to listen to others try to explain it. She had fluctuated between despair and anger.

Pendergrass wiped a trickle of sweat from his forehead, still cooling down from his workout. "Where have you been? I thought I'd be late."

"I got detained."

"Is everything all right? You look worried."

Sloane pulled Pendergrass aside. "Has anything about this case ever bothered you?" Sloane had prepared over the weekend before trial and entered the courtroom confident about the evidence, if not about the righteousness. By the end of the first week insomnia had struck, and he'd spent long hours staring at his bedroom ceiling, wondering why the case didn't feel right.

The question caught Pendergrass off guard. "What?"

Sloane shifted his eyes to Douvalidis. "Have you ever had any doubts?"

"You're asking me this now?"

Before Sloane could say another word Judge Rudolph filled the doorframe. A former college football player, Rudolph retained a lineman's build. With a ruddy complexion and a red tint to hair graying with age, he looked like a Scottish lumberjack in a long black robe. Other attorneys described him as a guy you'd drink a beer with, and the eight days Sloane had just spent in the man's courtroom had done nothing to alter that perception.

"Take your seats." Rudolph sat behind the elevated bench, presiding over a room perhaps forty feet front to back and half as wide, which showed its age with scuff marks on the white walls, chips in the linoleum squares, and banged-up chairs and tables. Even a recent oil treatment polishing the front of Rudolph's bench did not hide all of the scratches etched in the wood.

"I've been advised that the jury has reached a verdict. I want to caution everyone in the court that I won't tolerate any disrespect to the jury's decision, whatever that may be."

Everyone nodded dutifully.

Rudolph instructed his bailiff to bring in the jury, and after a moment they entered, maintaining the poker faces they had kept throughout much of the trial. When the final juror reached her seat Rudolph said, "I will note for the record that the jury has advised the bailiff that they have arrived at a verdict. Who is the foreperson?"

A male juror stood. "I am, Your Honor."

Rudolph considered a chart on his desk. "Okay, Mr. Giacoletti, thank you. Has the jury, in fact, agreed upon a verdict?"

"We're not unanimous judge, but we have a quorum."

Rudolph put up a hand. "What do you mean by a quorum?"

During Sloane's streak of twenty-two straight jury verdicts, all had been unanimous.

"Nine of us agree, Judge. Three don't."

"*Three?*" Pendergrass uttered under his breath.

"All right, Mr. Giacoletti, would you please hand the verdict to the bailiff."

The foreman did as instructed, and the bailiff passed the folded sheet of paper to Rudolph. Rudolph took a moment to consider it before handing it to his clerk. "Dr. Douvalidis, will you please stand."

When Douvalidis did not immediately respond, his attorney touched his arm to gain the doctor's attention. Pendergrass and Sloane also stood, but the McFarlands remained seated, squeezing each other's hand.

The clerk started. "In the matter of McFarland versus Douvalidis, we the jury find for the plaintiffs."

Eva McFarland sobbed in relief and immediately covered her mouth. Her husband wrapped an arm around her shoulder, and she buried her head in his chest, her body shuddering.

The clerk continued. "And award the plaintiffs three point two million dollars in damages."

Rudolph asked Douvalidis's attorney if he wished to poll the jury. He declined. With that, the judge thanked the members for their service, made a brief speech about the important function juries play in the judicial system, and dismissed them. Rudolph then addressed counsel, thanking them for their professionalism in his courtroom, rapped his gavel, and left the bench.

Pendergrass tended to the McFarlands while Sloane shook hands with his opposing counsel. Douvalidis's wife had leaned over the railing, rubbing her husband's back and whispering in his ear, but the doctor gave no indication he heard what she was saying.

Pendergrass slapped Sloane on the back, drawing his attention. "God, don't do that again. You had me worried."

The McFarlands hugged Sloane and thanked him, then stepped into the arms of tearful family members and friends.

Sloane looked back to the door, watching as Douvalidis departed the room between the shelter of his wife and his attorney.

As he did, Sloane thought of Kyle Horgan.

CHAPTER TWO

Kendall's board of directors filed into the conference room looking perplexed and anxious. They filled the blue leather chairs around the table and at the back of the room beneath portraits of Constantine and Aristotle Kendall, the two founding brothers, as well as Constantine's son, Sebastian Senior, and his son, Sebastian Junior. Fitzgerald's portrait did not yet hang among the hallowed, and he knew some in the room, congregating at the far end of the table around Arian Santoro, believed it never would.

Earlier that morning, Fitzgerald had received another e-mail from Maxine Bolelli and her tone had become increasingly less cordial as Fitzgerald rejected her advances. She had increased Galaxy's stock offer, which she referred to as a "gift" in light of Kendall's "horrific" third-quarter losses, and demanded that Fitzgerald and Kendall's board of directors respond by the end of the business day.

As the hastily called meeting got under way, Santoro quickly steered the discussion to Kendall's third-quarter losses and the rumors that Galaxy Toys sought to acquire the company. Fitzgerald had not shared Maxine Bolelli's overtures with any member of the board except Irwin Dean, his president of operations, and, of course, Sebastian Kendall. Santoro's knowledge of the confidential discussions, despite those precautions, and the timing of Bolelli's most recent e-mail—just before an unannounced board meeting—further confirmed Fitzgerald's suspicion that he had a mole trenching through his company.

"Galaxy has made an offer," Fitzgerald confirmed, "point seven shares of stock in Galaxy for every share of Kendall."

The revelation, or perhaps Fitzgerald's candor, brought silence—no doubt because every person in the room was at that moment mentally calculating how much money they stood to make if the board accepted the offer.

Santoro wasted little time. "In light of the most recent profit statement, I think we have to seriously consider such an offer." Santoro's strategic decision to sit at the far end of the table was intended to symbolize the chasm between his and Fitzgerald's positions. "It's our fiduciary duty to advise the stockholders of any reasonable offer."

"The losses have to be put in perspective," Fitzgerald replied. "Nearly sixty percent can be attributed to the overprojection of the sales figures for Lupo." He referred to an action figure Kendall had created in conjunction with the summer opening of a major motion picture. The Lupo team, of which Santoro had ultimate oversight, had estimated revenues to top $26 million, but the movie bombed, and they had fallen short by nearly $24 million. "If those losses are backed out, we actually made a slight profit. In light of the continued transition, that is something we can build on."

Santoro scoffed. "Unfortunately, that type of accounting would land us all in jail, along with our accountants." His minions laughed. "If we're looking to back anything out, why not back out our manufacturing plant in Mossylog. Our manufacturing costs remain three to four times higher than our competitors'.."

Sebastian Kendall had resisted shipping Kendall's manufacturing needs to China and South America; his father and grandfather had served in the army, and the Kendalls considered themselves true patriots. Sebastian called it blasphemous to suggest that Sergeant Smash be manufactured by anyone other than American workers. That company policy, however, had recently changed, at least on a limited basis, though no one in the room but Fitzgerald knew it.

Fitzgerald calmly lifted a wrapped package from beneath the table, placed it on the wood surface, and deliberately opened the box, drawing the board members' attention. He stood the ruby red, eighteen-inch figure on the mahogany surface, which he had ordered polished that morning so the overhead recessed lights would dramatically spot the toy.

While protocol would have been to seek director approval prior to creating a new prototype, protocol had been sacrificed with a mole loose in the building. The toy had been developed under a cloak of secrecy at an off-site, non-Kendall facility to prevent a leak that could allow another company to steal the design and beat Kendall to the market with a knockoff. Initial focus groups had also been limited, and their opinions, which had been off the charts, had been provided only to Fitzgerald.

Fitzgerald placed the remote control on the table, and flipped a switch. The action figure came to life, marching forward, turning and marching back, its red eyes flashing. Nobody looked particularly impressed.

Then Fitzgerald said, "Ladies and gentlemen, I give you Metamorphis."

With another flip of the switch a robotic voice said "Meta-morphis," and the pieces of the figure began to swivel and turn as if bewitched, folding under and over one another until the robot had vanished and what remained on the glistening tabletop was a ruby red tank, complete with turret and long gun. Sebastian Kendall had taught Fitzgerald that the toy business was as much about entertainment as it was about toys, and entertainment was about surprising one's audience.

Fitzgerald directed the tank to roll the length of the table, then adjusted the turret until the gun pointed directly between Santoro's eyes. Santoro looked to his minions but their gaze remained transfixed on the toy. The turret emitted a loud *pop!* causing Santoro and several others to flinch. Moments of utter silence ensued, Fitzgerald watching and waiting. Then shouts of jubilation and applause filled the room and directors bolted from their chairs, rushing forward to ask questions. Others, smiling as bright as children awakening to find toys beneath the Christmas tree, surged for the toy box and began arguing over who got the control next.

THE TIN ROOM
BURIEN, WASHINGTON

THE FAVORABLE VERDICT had not eased Sloane's doubts about the case, and not even a phone call from Tina telling him to meet her at the Tin Room, their favorite hangout in Burien, brought him any comfort.

The proprietor, Dan House, stood behind the bar beneath the sign that had formerly hung on the front of the building when it had been a tin shop, one of the oldest establishments in Burien. Patrons filled the barstools, some watching a Mariners game on the flatscreen hanging from the ceiling.

"Don't want to ring the bell tonight," Sloane said, surveying the large crowd and referring to the fireman's bell near the entry to the kitchen. Ring it, and you bought everyone in the restaurant a drink.

House, a former European soccer star with an easy smile, gray curls to his collar, and an infectious laugh pointed to the bouquet of roses in Sloane's hand. "David, you shouldn't have."

Sloane laughed. "Good, because I didn't."

"What's the occasion?"

"No occasion. Just finished another trial." He bought Tina roses after each of his trials, his way of acknowledging that work had interfered with their life, and he had not been the easiest person to live with.

House pointed toward the back of the restaurant, speaking over the music. "Well, she looks like a million bucks tonight. She's waiting on the patio. What can I get you?"

"Beer would be great," Sloane said.

The Tin Room was hopping, as usual, filled with Burien locals looking for a good meal or a chance to have a drink and unwind after work. Sloane pushed through the glass doors and stepped onto the newly added outdoor deck and patio. Getting a table when the summer weather was perfect was not easy, but Tina sat sipping a glass of water. She wore her white summer dress that, but for two spaghetti straps, showed off her tanned and toned shoulders and arms. She stood when she saw him, smiling brightly, wrapped her arms around his waist, and lifted onto her toes to kiss him.

Pulling back, she asked, "Hey, why the long face?" Her eyes widened. "You didn't lose, did you?"

"No. We won."

She sighed. "Thank God. I'm so happy for those poor people."

"Me too." Sloane knew that nothing would bring back the McFarlands' six-year-old boy, but for the family, the jury's verdict at least validated their decision to sue, erasing the silent stigma that they were nothing more than money-grubbing plaintiffs looking to capitalize on a tragedy.

Parting with another kiss, Sloane produced the bouquet of roses from behind his back.

Tina grinned. "For me?"

"Thanks for putting up with me," he said.

Though Tina never complained about the late nights and long weekends, her accepting the roses made Sloane feel as though he was forgiven.

She kissed him again. "They're beautiful."

When they sat she handed him a postcard of the Roman Coliseum. Alex and Charles Jenkins had taken their delayed honeymoon, leaving Charles Junior with his grandmother in New Jersey. Alex had written a thoughtful synopsis of their visit to Rome. Under it, Charlie had scribbled a note.

Send blue cheese dressing. Sick of oil and vinegar.

"Sounds like they're having a good time."

"They're in Venice. I called Alex today."

"Wait a minute. Charlie pays for a fifty-cent postcard and I get a fifty-dollar phone bill. How does that happen?"

House appeared at their table with two menus and Sloane's beer, but Sloane ordered from memory. "Meat loaf," he said.

Tina ordered the crab cakes.

"You want a glass of chardonnay?" House asked.

"Just water," Tina said.

"No wine?" Sloane asked. "I thought we must be celebrating something."

"I have an early appointment tomorrow," she said.

"Hey, that's great. Big job?"

"Just a remodel here in town." Tina's architecture business had been slow with the economy in the toilet, and Sloane was happy she was bidding on a job again.

"How are things at home?" he asked.

She grimaced. "You want the good news or the bad news?"

"I was hoping the phone call was the bad news."

She threw her napkin at him. "Boy, we are grumpy aren't we, Ebenezer?"

"Sorry," he said. "All right, I'll take the good news."

She handed him a manila packet. "Jake's adoption papers came in the mail, and I talked to Frank. He says he'll sign them. Jake's all yours if you really want to do this. He will officially become Jake Andrew Sloane."

They had discussed Sloane's adopting Jake to avoid the constant and predictable confusion each time Sloane tried to sign forms on Jake's behalf, be it for the doctor, dentist, or school administration. Legally, Sloane was not Jake's father or even his guardian. But the desire to adopt was more than just to solve procedural inconveniences. Sloane wanted them to be a family and to remove every boundary, even artificial ones, to that goal. He wanted to be Jake's father as much as he wanted to be Tina's husband. Doing it legally would be the best way to convince Jake that Sloane loved him and would always be there for him. At the same time, Sloane had been emphatic that the decision to change his last name was Jake's alone to make.

"Have you told him?"

"No. I wanted to wait for you."

"Let's tell him tonight."

"Good. We can also discuss the bad news." Tina pulled out another packet of papers from her purse and handed them to Sloane. On the top page, in bright red ink, was a D–.

"Damn," Sloane said, looking over Jake's algebra exam. "I was supposed to help him study last week and I got delayed at the office to do that piece on Channel Five. I let him down." He sighed. "This is not a good start to becoming his father, is it?"

To her credit, Tina did not rub it in. "What can we do to change it?"

"I can begin by keeping my word and better prioritizing my life."

With his busy schedule Sloane and Jake's time together had suffered. They had not been out on the boat to fish since June, and they had put off a summer vacation when Sloane got called to be the keynote speaker at a national trial lawyers meeting. It was about then when Jake had gone back to calling him "David," instead of "Dad."

"Don't be too hard on yourself. It's just the first test, and his teacher said he can retake it to try to improve his grade."

"What did Jake say?"

She made a face and imitated Jake's voice. "'What's the point, I'll just fail again.'"

Sloane took a sip of his beer.

"What's going on? This isn't end-of-the-world stuff. Did something happen at work?"

Sloane was still learning how to share his emotions. When he had lived alone he could brood in his apartment for days. That was no longer an option. Tina gave him space, but only for so long before she sought answers.

Sloane shook his head. "I'm fine. Just a little blue."

She tilted her head, considering him. "Well, maybe I can do something about that."

"I thought you said Jake was at home."

She kicked him playfully under the table. "I meant I have other news. I was going to save it but . . ."

"Good news, hopefully?"

She smiled. "Hopefully."

Sloane sensed her being coy. "So what is it?"

"I was just thinking that when we tell Jake about the adoption papers we might want to add another pro to his list of reasons to change his name."

"And what would that be?"

"Because then both our children will have the same last name."

GALAXY TOYS' CORPORATE HEADQUARTERS

PHOENIX, ARIZONA

LATE IN THE afternoon, Maxine Bolelli sat with her fist pressed against her upper lip to keep from screaming. When Malcolm Fitzgerald finished talking she moved her fist and leaned closer to the speakerphone in the center of the table. "You're making a big mistake, Malcolm."

"You've said that, Maxine."

"No, I said I won't wait forever for Kendall to get its act together. I know you're still juggling a lot of balls, but if you're holding on out of some sense of loyalty or duty to Sebastian your loyalties are sorely misplaced. He will be dead in weeks. We both know it. A bad deal, but shit happens."

"Your sympathy is touching."

At forty-three, Bolelli, raised in a family with five brothers, did not shy away from competition or confrontation, and she did not mince words. Since Hugh Galaxy and the board had named Bolelli CEO, Galaxy's annual revenues had grown to $3.2 billion, putting the company in position to finally challenge Titan for toy world supremacy. Acquiring Kendall Toys, which had a strong action figure department—something Galaxy had never been able to sustain—would be the final step in her quest, and Bolelli wasn't about to let Malcolm Fitzgerald keep Galaxy from its rightful place at the top.

"The two of us never much liked each other in life. Death isn't about to change that. Your obligation is to your shareholders."

"The board has made this decision in the best interests of our shareholders."

"How can you say that?" Bolelli did not try to hide her exasperation. She shifted her gaze to the two people sitting across from her: Brandon Craft, Galaxy's president, and its chief financial officer, Elizabeth Meyers. "Your third-quarter numbers look like a train wreck."

"A blip on the radar."

"That *blip* has been present since Sebastian announced his retirement."

"The board isn't interested, Maxine."

"The offer is off the table when we finish this conversation, Malcolm. Don't bother to call me back."

"What about lunch next time you're in town?"

Bolelli hung up, pushed away from the table, and paced the blue carpet in her bare feet. She'd had the office decorated completely in robin's-egg blue, from the carpeting to the upholstered chairs and the leather couch. She also frequently wore the color. It wasn't her favorite, but robin's-egg blue was the distinctive color associated with Baby Betty, the doll that had put Galaxy on the map and sustained it for more than half a century. Bolelli had been Baby Betty's nanny since Galaxy lured Bolelli from a rival toy company, and even after her promotion, Bolelli refused to hand off the doll, trusting Galaxy's meal ticket to no one else.

"How could they reject it?" Craft asked.

"I don't know how," Bolelli said. "I don't know why. But that arrogant bastard just told me to shove thirty-five million dollars up my ass."

"How do you want to play it?" Craft asked.

Bolelli considered her options but not for long. "Get on the phone with our contacts in the media and on Wall Street. Let's see how he likes it when his shareholders are screaming for his head on a platter."

"How much do you want to give away?" Meyers asked, referring to the Scottsdale negotiations.

"Everything. I want Kendall's shareholders to know how reasonable we've been and how unreasonable he's been. I want him crawling back, begging me to make him an offer."

"We'll be putting Titan on notice of the negotiations," Craft said, tentative.

"You don't think Ian knows everything already?" She referred to Titan CEO Ian Hansen. "I can't go to the bathroom around here without him hearing the toilet flush in Chicago. I'm not worried about Titan. They don't have the cash reserves to make this kind of offer, and if Fitzgerald would turn down the offer I just made him, no way he'd take less. I'm more interested in how a man watching a century-old company disintegrate while he stands at the helm could say no to millions of dollars and sound like Christmas came three months early at the same time." She looked out the windows at a plane on a flight path toward Phoenix Airport. "He has to have something in his back pocket. There's no other explanation. He's banking on something. I can smell it. Why don't I know what that is?"

Neither Craft nor Meyers answered, apparently thinking her question rhetorical.

Bolelli turned on them. "Why don't I know what that is, Brandon?"

Craft stumbled. "I talked to my source this morning. There was a board meeting, and he said no one looked happy going into it."

"Well then something probably happened," Meyers said, stating the obvious.

"Of course something happened. What I want to know is what that was," Bolelli said. "And I want to know now."

THREE TREE POINT

WASHINGTON

TOO EXCITED TO wait any longer, Sloane and Tina decided to have dessert at home with Jake and tell him the news over a bowl of ice cream. Neither was certain how Jake would react, though he had been dropping hints that it might be okay to have a little brother, and maybe a sister, as long as she wasn't the annoying type.

"I'll get the ice cream," Sloane said as they walked in the back door. "I think we better stock up; you might have those midnight cravings for things like ice cream and sardines."

She scrunched her nose. "Ew."

"You go reel in Jake; he's probably down at the water, fishing."

As he retrieved bowls and spoons, habit caused Sloane to look to the granite counter, but Bud did not trot along its edge, purring and looking to be fed. Two months earlier his cat had darted from the house just as the neighbor's seventeen-year-old son sped up the block in his parents' Mercedes, killing Bud. Sloane and Jake had built a coffin, lined it with Bud's favorite blanket, and buried him in the backyard, facing the Puget Sound, so Bud could dream about fish forever. Sloane had cried that day. He and Bud had been alike. Both orphans, they had managed somehow to find a family. Even after two months, Sloane found himself mourning his cat's death, and any discussion of a replacement seemed sacrilegious, though Jake and Tina were making subtle hints about a puppy.

• • •

WHEN SLOANE FINISHED his ice cream he rested his spoon in his bowl. "So, Jake, your mother and I wanted to talk to you about a few things."

Jake had been uncharacteristically quiet, as if he knew the shoe was about to drop and hoped his silence might make him invisible. He raised his focus from his bowl. "I'm sorry," he blurted. "I tried. I really tried, but I don't get it. Please don't tell me I can't go fishing anymore."

Tina raised a napkin to cover her smile.

"Well, since you brought it up, Jake, let's talk about your algebra test," Sloane said.

Jake's jaw dropped. He looked like he wanted to slap his forehead. "You mean you were going to talk about something else? Oh, crap."

"Language," Tina said.

"Actually, Jake, I should be apologizing to you," Sloane said.

"Why, what did you do wrong?"

"I made you a promise and I didn't keep it. I promised to help you with your algebra. A man is only as good as his word. I'm afraid mine wasn't worth much."

"That's okay, David. You'll do better next time." Jake quickly pushed back his chair from the table.

"Hang on a second there, partner," Sloane said. "That being said, we both have some work to do, and we'll start tonight, after dinner. We'll go over your test and find out why your answers are wrong. Then we'll get started on your homework."

"It's not due until Friday."

"Good, then we have plenty of time to get it done right. I don't want you to wait until the last minute and cram on Thursday night."

"That's what you did for your trial."

"What?"

"You told Mom that Tom did all the work, and you had to cram over the weekend and couldn't take her to that garden show."

Tina raised her napkin again. Sloane wanted to kick her under the table.

"You're right, I did say that, but that wasn't because I was off having fun. I was working on other things and couldn't get to it. Do you understand the difference?"

Jake nodded. "Sure, that's why you couldn't help me with my algebra."

Tina had to turn her head and bite her lip to keep from laughing out loud. Sloane decided to retreat. "Now, the next thing we need to talk about, as a family, is that issue about my adopting you. Have you given that some consideration?"

Jake nodded. "I made a pro and con table like you told me." He rushed into Sloane's office, emerged with a pad of paper, and set it on his chair. "Okay," he said, drawing their attention like a lawyer before a jury. "Let's start with the cons." He flipped the sheet of paper. Sloane's heart sank. Jake had listed eight reasons not to change his name. "To begin with, this could become very confusing for my friends. I mean they know me as Jake Carter, and changing my name to Sloane will be hard for them to remember. It will also be difficult for my teachers, although that might not be such a bad thing for Mr. Jackson," he said, referring to his math instructor.

Sloane couldn't help but chuckle.

"Continuing on . . ." Jake went through each of the eight listed reasons, each a valid point against changing his name, each another blow to Sloane's hopes.

"Now," Jake said, "let's look at the pros." He paused.

Sloane felt as nervous as waiting for a jury verdict.

Jake flipped the chart. On the page behind it he had drawn a huge smiley face. "Because I would be stoked!"

Sloane thrust a fist in the air. "Yes!" He gave Jake a hug. "And I'll be stoked too. I promise you, Jake, I'll be there for you. We'll be a family, just as close as if we were blood related."

"Closer even."

"Closer than blood?"

"Sure. I mean, normally you can't pick your family, right? You're stuck with them. But we're actually choosing to be a family. That makes us even closer."

Sloane turned to Tina. "I think Jake has displayed some real maturity tonight. The kind of maturity that should be rewarded, don't you agree?"

Jake's eyes bugged. "I can get a puppy?"

"We were thinking about something else," Tina said. "Something better than a puppy."

Jake looked genuinely perplexed. "Better than a puppy?"

Tina smiled. "How about a baby brother or sister?"

AFTER JAKE WENT upstairs to read in his room, Sloane and Tina pulled on light fleece jackets and stepped outside to enjoy the sunset over the Olympic Mountain Range, a dazzling display of color and beauty. Hand in hand they stepped over the logs to the sand-and-gravel beach, their shoes crunching as they strolled. A chorus of crickets and the occasional deep bass croak of a bullfrog interrupted the rhythmic lapping of waves. Fishing boats tethered to white buoys bobbed just offshore. August and September had become Sloane's favorite months in the Pacific Northwest. The sun rose early and set late, allowing him to spend more time with Tina and Jake after work.

"So, Mr. Sloane," Tina said. "Are you prepared for this?"

"Walking? Oh sure. I've been walking since I was one."

She punched his arm. "I meant the baby."

Sloane joked, but he knew he had not hidden his apprehension well when Tina gave him the news and she had clearly picked up on it. "I guess I better be," he said. They walked on. "Have you told your parents?"

Tina shook her head. Her smile faded. Her mother and stepfather, Terri and Bill Larsen, had never accepted Sloane, and there was no shortage of reasons for their rejection. The Larsens had raised their daughter in an upscale San Francisco neighborhood and sent her to a private school near Presidio Heights where San Francisco's blue-blooded families maintained mansions. They had been elated when Tina married Frank Carter, the son of one of those families, which helped them gain access into that community, and then devastated that she would divorce him, regardless that Frank had turned out to be a spoiled man with little ambition, work ethic, or sense of responsibility who had blown through his trust fund.

The fact that Sloane was a highly successful attorney did not appease them. Catholic, they had declined an invitation to attend the civil wedding ceremony, considering their daughter still married to Frank Carter in the eyes of the Church and God. That their daughter was an adult capable of making her own decisions, or that the state recognized her divorce, was irrelevant. They blamed Sloane for pressuring Tina into an unholy union, making their daughter an adulteress, and refused to acknowledge him as her husband.

But Sloane knew there was another reason as well, unspoken but one with which he had become quite familiar. The Larsens were no different from others who had rejected him throughout his life simply because he had no pedigree. What was he going to say? "I never knew my father but I have a recollection of my mother being raped and murdered, the rest is a blur."

A lone fisherman cast in shadows nodded to them as he reeled in his line, snapped back the reel, and flicked the lure out into the water. Sloane heard a distant plunk. Tina leaned her head against his shoulder. "You'll be a great dad," she said.

Sloane wished he had her confidence. The truth was he had no idea what kind of father he would make. The past two years with Jake had taught him much and given him some measure of confidence, but Jake had come ready-made. Tina had raised a polite, respectful boy before Sloane ever entered the picture, and he couldn't help but feel like the second-string quarterback stepping onto the field after the first string had already built a huge lead. He viewed his job as trying not to screw up too badly.

He decided not to debate it. "So what about you, Mrs. Sloane, how do you feel about all this, since you'll be doing most of the work for the next nine months?"

"Most?"

"Hey, I said I would rush to the store every time you utter the words *ice cream*."

"Don't remind me. I hate the thought of being fat again." Sloane knew she was only half-joking. "I feel like it took forever for me to get my body back after Jake."

"That's not what I remember." He still held a recollection of Tina entering his San Francisco office to interview as his assistant and his being instantly attracted to her dark hair, olive complexion, and tall, toned body.

"You were horny then. You hadn't had sex in years."

"I was saving myself for you."

"Yeah, right." They had reached the Point, where massive boulders had been deposited. At low tide they could walk around it, but now, with the tide in, the water was halfway up the rocks. They turned and started back in the opposite direction, toward home.

"Any thoughts on names? What about David?"

The name had never meant much to Sloane, given that it was not his real name but rather the name Joe Branick gave him when the CIA agent smuggled Sloane out of Mexico and hid him in California's foster care system.

"Joseph," he said.

She stopped walking and looked up at him. "I like it. Any particular reason?"

"I just like the sound of it. 'Joe.' It's a strong name. It would sound good being announced over a PA system at a sporting event." Sloane imitated the echoing voice of a broadcaster. "Starting at quarterback, number twelve, Joe Sloane."

She laughed. "Oh now that's *really* important."

"You have to consider those types of things," he said. "I mean, what if he becomes president? You don't want a name like Oscar for president."

"Didn't seem to hurt Barack."

"Touché."

"Okay, what if it's a girl?"

"So far, anyone I've known with a teenage daughter has told me to move out of the house when she turns thirteen and not to move back again until she turns twenty-one."

"And what am I supposed to do during those eight years?"

"Produce a young woman as beautiful as her mother."

"Don't try to butter me up, you deserter."

As they continued up the beach Sloane saw someone step over the logs in front of their property and walk in their direction. In the dusk he initially thought it to be Jake. When Sloane could make out the man's face he was surprised.

"Tom?"

Tom Pendergrass looked harried, brow furrowed. "Hi, Tina. I'm sorry to disturb you." He looked to Sloane. "I tried to call, but you weren't answering your cell. Jake said you were out taking a walk." Pendergrass lived not far from Sloane, just up the hill in Burien.

"What's the matter?"

"I just heard it on the news," he said. "Dr. Douvalidis killed himself."

TOM PENDERGRASS SAT in Sloane's family room sipping a Scotch and looking pale and sick to his stomach.

"Why did you ask me about the evidence in court this morning?"

Sloane shook his head. He had hoped to avoid the conversation. "It was nothing."

"You asked me if I had doubts. Why?"

"You tried a good case, Tom. The evidence was solid and the jury found liability; you have no reason to feel any responsibility about what happened."

"Did you have doubts?"

Sloane did not want Pendergrass to feel any worse than he already did. "I didn't doubt you, Tom. It was nothing, just regular doubts whenever the jury is out, that's all. But the jury agreed. You did your job. You're not responsible for this."

Before Pendergrass could question him further the phone rang. It was a reporter Sloane knew, asking him to comment on reports that Dr. Douvalidis had been despondent over the death of Austin McFarland. Sloane politely declined and sat beside Pendergrass and Tina to watch the news.

The death of the prominent pediatrician was the first story after a commercial break, and much to Sloane's chagrin, the reporter took little time tying the suicide to the verdict for malpractice, and to Sloane.

After the news, Sloane sent Pendergrass home, and Tina went upstairs to bed. Knowing he would not sleep much, he slipped into his home office, opened his briefcase, and pulled out Kyle Horgan's file.

His inclination had been not to take the file, but there had been something about Horgan's passionate plea, and Sloane's own doubts about Dr. Douvalidis's guilt, that caused him to ignore that inclination. Horgan might turn out to indeed be crazy, but Sloane didn't think so. Odd maybe, but not crazy.

Horgan had doodled on the file cover in blue ink, rough sketches of what appeared to be various appendages of a space-man: a helmeted head in the left corner, a robotic arm in the right, a hinged leg in the center. Inside the file, Sloane found additional sketches, drawn on graph paper and more refined; mathematical calculations accompanied each sketch, with arrows directed to the various body parts. Sloane had taken calculus in college, but the equations were beyond him. Beneath the drawings Sloane found a handwritten document, which appeared to be a copy of a letter from Horgan to a company called Kendall Toys in which Horgan expressed concern that the plastic component parts of something called "Metamorphis" did not meet ASTM standards, which Sloane knew to be an acronym for the American Society for Test-ing and Materials. Horgan suggested that production be halted until the design flaw could be remedied.

All of that was mildly interesting, but what sent a chill through Sloane was a news article beneath a letter that Sloane initially thought concerned the Douvalidis trial, but did not. A four-year-old child had died in Mossylog, Washington, a rural Southern Washington town, after suffering from three days of nausea, diarrhea, vomiting, high fevers, listlessness, and, finally, loss of consciousness—the same symptoms that had led to the death of Austin McFarland, and for which Sloane had prosecuted Peter Douvalidis.

CHAPTER THREE

S loane had slept little, if at all, and he could feel the fatigue as he climbed the three concrete steps the following morning. A brass sign bolted to the bricks identified the Jackson Street Apartments building in Seattle's Pioneer Square District to be a historic landmark. Stepping inside the lobby Sloane saw why: mahogany walls, marble floors, crystal chandeliers—no one could afford to build like this anymore.

Sloane ignored the elevator, climbing three flights of stairs to a narrow hallway dimly lit by wall sconces. The building smelled like a closet with too many mothballs. He stopped outside apartment 3A, knocking twice. No one answered. He knocked again, noting that the door rattled in the jam despite a key slot for a dead bolt. He waited, knocked a third time, and tried the knob, which turned. He hesitated, then called out as he pushed open the door.

"Mr. Horgan?"

A wedge of light spilled through the lower pane of a southern-facing window, illuminating clutter spread across a twin bed and spilling onto the wood floor. Plastic action figures had been ripped from their boxes and scattered about the room along with comic books and dozens of sketches like the ones in Horgan's file.

Sloane walked carefully through the debris, trying not to crush anything and wondering what the person who made the mess had been looking for. A small Formica counter and a four-by-four-foot piece of orange linoleum delineated a cooking area with a microwave and a single-burner heating plate. Above the counter a cabinet had been emptied of plastic glasses and plates. The door to a small refrigerator had also been left open. But for a few condiments, it was also empty.

"Who are you?"

Sloane wheeled, his left arm rising instinctively to ward off a blow, causing the thin man standing just inside the doorway to flinch and step back.

Sloane caught his breath. "You scared me."

"What are you doing in here?" The man wore a long brown bathrobe. His teeth were stained from too much coffee and too many cigarettes.

"I'm looking for Kyle Horgan." Realizing his predicament, Sloane added, "The door was open. The room was like this."

If the man was concerned with the condition of the apartment he did not let on. "What do you want to talk to Kyle about?" He sounded more skeptical than concerned.

"He came to see me the other day, but I was in a hurry."

The man started for the hall. "I'm calling the police."

"Wait." Sloane pulled out a business card and handed it to him, but it only served to make the man sound even more skeptical.

"An attorney? Why would Kyle go to see an attorney?"

"He gave me this." Sloane pulled Horgan's file from his brief-case and held up the scribbled cover. "Like I said, the door was unlocked and the apartment was this way."

"I know. I came by earlier for the rent. I went to call the police and came back to lock the door, since God knows how long it will be before they get around to getting here."

"Do you own the building?" Sloane asked.

"I wish." He smirked. "I'm the manager."

"You sound surprised Mr. Horgan would come to see me."

"Yeah? Well, don't take it personally. I'd be surprised if Kyle went to see anyone. He spends most of the time in here, working on his sketches and his computer."

Sloane looked about the apartment but did not see a computer. "Does he have a job?"

The man pointed to the clutter. "That's his job."

"He designed these?" Sloane asked.

"He collects and sells them. He's designed some things though. There's a toy store a couple blocks away he sells to."

"When's the last time you saw him?"

The manager shrugged. "About a week."

"Any idea where he might be?"

Another shake of the head. "But if Kyle did come to see you, I can tell you it must have been something real important."

"How well do you know him?"

"Well enough. I look out for him, try to anyway. Remind him to pay his rent, pick up some groceries when I go, things like that."

"Is he handicapped?"

The man seemed to give the question due consideration. "He's not dumb, if that's what you're getting at. He just doesn't function too well around people." He nodded to the debris scattered about the floor. "He's going to be pretty upset about this. This looks just mean-spirited."

Not to Sloane. To Sloane it looked like a deliberate act. Somebody had come to Horgan's apartment to find something.

• • •

THE DOOR TO the apartment closed, ending what portion of the conversation he could hear between the building manager and the man who had come to talk to Kyle Horgan.

He removed the earpiece and watched the entrance from the car, waiting several minutes before a well-built man, perhaps six two with broad shoulders, exited the building carrying a briefcase that undoubtedly held whatever it was Horgan had given him. An attorney. His employer would not be pleased. He contemplated following, but there was no need. The building manager hadn't guessed the visitor's occupation out of the blue. He'd been handed a business card.

The attorney crossed the street and continued north on First Avenue, presumably in search of the toy store to which the manager had made reference. He pushed open the door, waited for a vehicle to pass, and then crossed the street, shuffling up the steps. Inside the building he found the manager's apartment, considered the hallway in both directions, knocked twice, and held up the folded newspaper to block the view through the peephole.

The manager pulled open the door. "Yeah?"

He lowered the paper. "I'm inquiring about the apartment you have listed for rent?"

"You have the wrong apartment building, mister. We don't list any vacancies in the paper. Just put it up on the sign outside."

He rattled off an address.

"That's the building next door, and a lot nicer than this place if you can afford to live there."

"My mistake. I'm sorry to have disturbed." He turned as if to leave.

As the manager stepped forward to close the door the man

swiveled and thrust his right palm hard against the wood. The door sprung inward, crushing the manager's face and sending him sprawling backward into the apartment.

He checked the hall in each direction, stepped in, closed the door, and turned the dead bolt. He found the attorney's business card in the pocket of the manager's bathrobe.

BETHESDA, MARYLAND

ALBERT PAYNE SLAMMED his fist on the table. Plates rattled, his daughter startled and screamed, and his son knocked over the milk carton. Without another word, Payne pushed back his chair and stormed from the room.

For a moment neither child moved nor uttered a word. Their mother stood holding the frying pan with bacon grease in one hand and the tin can in the other.

"Is Dad okay?" Michael asked. "Why is he so mad all the time?"

She put the pan back on the burner. "Beth, cook the eggs. Michael, get a sponge and clean up the mess."

Mary Payne found her husband in the den, staring up at the family portrait over the mantel.

"Albert? What's going on?"

He raised a hand without turning around. "Don't start with me."

"Is it work? Is it the report you're trying to get done for the Senate hearing?"

"All I wanted was a little peace and quiet," he said. "I don't want to hear about her boyfriend or argue about why he can't go to the mall with his friends when we're sitting at the breakfast table to eat. Is that too much for a man to ask?"

"You're scaring the kids."

He turned. "Maybe they need to be scared. Maybe if I blow off some steam now and then people will realize when I'm god-damn serious."

"You don't need to swear."

He shook his head. "No one takes me seriously. No one respects me."

"Is it something at work? Is it Maggie Powers?"

He walked toward the front entry. "It's not work, okay? Work is fine. Don't start badgering me about work."

"I'm not badgering—I just want to help, Albert. You've never been like this. We've always been able to talk about things. Please, tell me what's wrong. Is it the stress? What did the doctor say about your rash?"

He grabbed his jacket from the hook beside the front door and picked up his briefcase, opening the door. "It's a rash. It's just a rash. It's not like I'm dying," he said and slammed the door closed behind him.

HALF AN HOUR later, Payne slipped the small white bag with the prescription cream from his briefcase and shoved it in the upper drawer of his desk. He could now add to his list of maladies, which included elevated cholesterol and blood pressure from being overweight, a rash that itched liked hell and dried out his skin until it flaked. The doctor said it was stress related.

No shit.

Payne already knew from the lump of reddish brown hair in the bathtub drain each morning and the ever increasing streaks of gray in what was left on his head and his beard. He adjusted his glasses and considered the drab walls of his office, his first after nearly two decades in cubicles. The director of investigations had once been one of the Product Safety Agency's highest-profile posts, overseeing all agency investigations and enforcement actions against manufacturers of defective products. But with the prior administration's mandate of deregulation, Payne's staff had been cut by nearly 70 percent, with those having the most seniority, and therefore the highest salaries, pruned first. Given the continuing recession, they had not been replaced, which pretty much ensured no new enforcement actions, despite the change in administrations. Actions that had been under way came to a screeching halt, or settled with the manufacturer paying a token fine and promising to do better.

The latest joke circulating the office was that the agency walked small and carried no stick. Manufacturers had little to fear.

Sitting at his desk, Payne regretted his morning outburst, one of several since his return from China. He'd pick up some flowers on his way home. Maybe take everyone out for pizza. Screw the doctor.

He shut his eyes and massaged the headache at his temples, but the memory of the bloodied mess on the hotel room pillow forced them open, and he had to take a moment to catch his breath. He picked up the dual picture frame with the photograph of his smiling wife on the right and of his son and daughter on the left. The man had been clear about further consequences should Payne not follow his instructions precisely.

Payne removed the bottle of aspirin from his desk drawer and just as he popped two in his mouth his office door opened and Maggie Powers stepped in. "How was your trip?"

Payne choked down the pills. "Sorry," he said. "Something stuck in my throat. You'll have my report by the end of the week."

Payne's trip to inspect Chinese manufacturing plants had sprung from public outrage over a series of product recalls and reports of serious deficiencies in the Chinese manufacturing facilities that more and more American businesses favored. Public outrage had led to the predictable congressional grandstanding, which led to inquiries about what the PSA would do about the problem, which was nothing, given the agency's skeletal staff.

Powers stuck her reading glasses on top of her head, using the frame to keep her shoulder length, auburn-tinted hair out of her face. "Don't be so official all the time, Albert. I saw you earlier and you looked like you got some sun. I was hoping it meant you allowed yourself a little play time."

Payne forced a smile, not about to tell Powers his red glow was a rash. "They kept me pretty busy," he said.

"I wish I could have gone." Dressed in a cream-colored pants suit, open-toe shoes, and a strand of pearls, Powers looked very much like the wife of a successful McLean, Virginia, attorney. "But a son only gets engaged once." She rolled her eyes. "Hopefully. From the looks of the in-laws, I wouldn't put a lot of money down on this one going the distance."

Payne didn't know how to respond. He and Powers had never discussed their personal lives, and the two were not exactly close, given that Powers was the primary reason Payne had so much free time. The former president's appointment of Powers as a director of the agency had been a further step in that administration's persistent efforts to deregulate American business. Powers, once a lobbyist for the Toy Manufacturer's Association, had somehow managed to survive a contentious Senate hearing, and her arrival at the agency had been like the first domino in a falling line. One of the remaining two directors, Harvey Schoenstein, promptly resigned in protest, and the other, Larry Triplett, threatened to do so until certain members of Congress convinced him to be the good soldier and remain. Agency action could not be taken without majority approval. With Schoenstein's resignation leaving an empty chair, Triplett could at least block Powers's actions.

Of course Powers could also block the initiation of enforcement actions against manufacturers. Until the new president replaced Schoenstein they were at a stalemate, and things were not about to change overnight. Any new appointee, whenever appointed, couldn't rush in with a regulation sledgehammer, not with American retailers continuing to suffer in a down economy and American manufacturers already shipping much of their work overseas to reduce costs.

Powers sat and crossed her legs. "So, what's your initial assessment?"

Just when Payne thought he might get a nice quiet summer, the reports of significant injuries and fatalities from products manufactured in China began to surface throughout the nation. What was now referred to as the "summer of recalls" would culminate in a congressional inquiry to be led by California Senator Morgan Tovey, chairman of the Senate subcommittee with jurisdiction over the agency. Tovey had subpoenaed Powers to report on Chinese manufacturers' compliance with U.S. regulatory standards, as well as to educate the committee on emerging technology that could potentially be dangerous to American consumers. Indiana Senator Joe Wallace had joined Tovey to coauthor a bill that would dramatically increase fines on manufacturers who put defective products on the market, toughen reporting requirements, and provide the agency with a much-needed budget boost to hire more investigators. Wallace had then worked behind the scenes to ensure Payne was part of the delegation to China.

"There are always a few problem areas, but for the most part it appears the Chinese have really cleaned up their act," Payne said, trying to sound convincing.

"You see?" Powers smiled. "That's exactly what the threat of losing billions of dollars in business will do. It just proves that the best regulator is the market itself. Wallace and Tovey need to understand that we can't effectively dictate to Chinese manufacturers any more than we can dictate to American manufacturers. No matter how many regulations we put in place we can't effectively enforce them. They have to police themselves."

"I'll have my report to you a week before the Senate hearing," Payne said.

"Thanks for the reminder." Powers grinned. "Actually, I'm starting to look forward to it now. I just love proving other people wrong."

PIONEER SQUARE

DEE'S HOUSE OF TOYS

THE BELL ABOVE the door jingled as Sloane stepped onto a landing and looked down a staircase upon a winter wonderland. Ornate white handrails bordered the three steps leading to a burgundy carpet and seven-foot candy canes with green street signs directing shoppers to aisles stocked with action figures, dolls, stuffed animals, trains and cars, and books. Toy soldiers stood sentry at archways, and overhead, kites and toy models hung from fishing line, as if suspended from a blue sky. A plane flew in circles, its propeller humming.

As he made his way to the counter, Sloane wondered what it would be like to see his own son's or daughter's eyes light up when they walked through the door. An attractive brunette rang up a sale on an old-fashioned cash register, though Sloane also noticed a laptop computer below the counter. Apparently even Santa was now online.

After the customer departed, the woman turned to Sloane. "Can I help you?"

"I'm looking for the owner; I'm assuming that would be Dee?"

The woman smiled. "You'd be correct." She offered a hand. "Dee Stroud."

The name Dee had caused Sloane to envision a matronly aunt with an apron, not the woman in blue jeans with a figure an aerobics instructor would envy.

"David Sloane," he said.

Her eyes narrowed. "The attorney? I saw you on TV."

Sloane cringed, but Stroud explained that she had recently seen Sloane providing legal commentary on a local news station. "What can I do for you, Mr. Sloane?"

"I'd like to talk to you about Kyle Horgan."

Her eyes widened. "You know Kyle?" She sounded as skeptical as the building manager.

"Is there a place we could sit and talk?"

"Is Kyle okay?"

Sloane did not want to alarm her. "He came to talk to me the other day. I was just hoping to ask you a few questions about him."

Stroud smiled. "I was just craving a mocha latte. Let me get my assistant to cover the front. Do you drink coffee?"

STROUD COVERED HER ears as an odd-looking vehicle that carried tourists and could apparently travel on land and water drove past, the driver's amplified voice blasting from a speaker.

"I hate that thing," she said. "It goes right past the store all summer."

Sloane and Stroud walked among a throng of tourists dressed in T-shirts and shorts, the maple trees and three-story brick buildings shading the Pioneer Square sidewalk from the bright summer sun. "How long have you owned your store?"

"Sixteen years. I opened when my daughter was five. People thought I was nuts."

"Why?"

"Because at the time most toy stores were closing, not open-ing. The chains were taking over, and they can buy in volume and sell at prices independents can't touch. Most of my friends thought failure was inevitable."

"But you opened a store anyway."

Stroud flashed an impish grin. "I have a hard head." She knocked on it twice and then fingered a gold chain around her neck as they walked. "The simple answer is I needed to make a living after my divorce, and toys are really all I've ever known. My father owned a toy store in Michigan, and I had always envisioned taking it over, but then I got married and my husband's job moved us out here. Eventually Wal-Mart and Toys "R" Us drove my dad and just about everyone else out of business."

"Well, it looks like you've succeeded."

She stopped, this time to knock on a tree trunk. "Don't jinx me. I'm surviving. Like all retail at the moment, the toy industry is in a slump. Kids don't know how to play like they used to. They all want the video games and cell phones and iPods."

Stroud stepped into an establishment called Kahili Coffee. "My friend Kelly owns it," she explained. "He's got a second store in downtown Kirkland near where I live; I like to support him when I can. Coffee companies have their own struggles, especially in this city."

Sloane treated her to a mocha latte and ordered himself a cup of black tea. They agreed to share a blueberry scone and took a table along plate glass windows. The walls and floor were painted a burnt orange and tastefully covered with prints of coffee plants and leaves.

"What is it about Kyle you wanted to talk about?"

Remembering the building manager's surprised reaction, Sloane asked, "That strikes you as odd, doesn't it, that Kyle would come to see me?"

"*Curious* is a better word. Kyle doesn't talk to many people."

"When he came to my building to see me the other day I was in a hurry and didn't have much time to talk to him. He seemed very concerned about something." Sloane decided to leave the specifics vague. "I just went to his apartment, but he wasn't there." Again, Sloane chose to leave out the details. "The building manager indicated Kyle sold some of his toys to you. I was hoping you could tell me more about him."

"I really adore Kyle," Stroud said. "He's a sweet young man with an incredible imagination, and he can design just about anything." She shook her head, her look becoming compassionate. "But he's also a social misfit, probably manic. He can't hold down a regular job. I feel sorry for him. I think he's starting to drink. The last time he was in I smelled it on his breath."

"Are his designs any good?" Sloane asked.

"He's brought me several things over the years. I usually buy them because they're different, not what you're going to find in the big retailers. And they sell. But he also shows me designs that are just too far beyond what I'm capable of doing."

"What do you mean?"

"He's into action figures. He's probably a genius. But he needs to have them mass-produced to make them affordable."

Sloane stirred a packet of sugar into his cup. "When was the last time you saw Kyle?"

She crossed her blue jeans and thought for a moment. "He came to the store to show me a design for an action figure that he said a child could build from plastic pieces, but that would also change into different shapes on its own. He tried to explain it to me, but I told him I couldn't afford to have it manufactured. He needed a bigger toy company with more resources to finance him."

Sloane opened the file and showed her one of Horgan's drawings.

Stroud didn't take long to consider it. "That's it. He was very excited about it. I told him to get himself an agent and take it to Kendall. Maybe that wasn't the best advice."

"Why do you say that?"

"Sebastian Kendall recently had to step down with cancer, and Kendall's profits have nose-dived. It was just in the paper." She sat up straighter, as if struck by an idea. "Maybe Kyle wants you to represent him."

"Represent him?"

"As his agent."

"There is such a thing?"

"Don't scoff. It can be lucrative." Stroud chuckled, revealing perfect white teeth. "You wouldn't think so, would you? I mean we're talking about toys here, right? Then again, people spend five billion dollars a year on their pets. Well, the toy industry does about five times that amount."

"And these toy companies buy designs from people like Kyle?"

Stroud explained that independent toy designers like Horgan were becoming as rare as the independent toy shops. "There's less opportunity. The big companies buy the smaller ones, and many have their own design departments. It's cheaper to pay them a straight salary than to pay a commission and royalties. Maybe cheaper isn't the right word. There's less risk."

"Risk of what?" Sloane popped a piece of scone into his mouth and sipped tea.

"Having a toy bomb. Even with market research, nothing is certain. Kids are fickle; nobody really knows what is going to sell big and what's going to tank. It's a crapshoot. Do you remember Beanie Babies?"

"Vaguely," Sloane said.

Stroud advised that the inventor of Beanie Babies, H. Ty Warner, couldn't get a toy company to even consider the stuffed animals, then kids went crazy for them, and Warner shot into the *Forbes* list of the World's Richest People.

"But how often does that happen?" Sloane asked, skeptical.

"Not often. But the toy industry is like the lottery. Everyone thinks, Why not me? Why not my toy? No one thought a purple dinosaur would sell, but Barney did, big time. And you probably don't remember Cabbage Patch Kids, but they were initially rejected as being too ugly. Then they generated more than a billion dollars in revenues for Coleco in two years."

Sloane considered the information. "And the risk is that a company could pay a designer a lot of money and have the toy flop?"

"That, and there's always the possibility of another manufacturer putting out a knockoff before the toy even reaches the market."

"They just steal the idea?"

"Hey, if you're not stealing someone's ideas in this business, you're not trying."

Sloane thought of Kyle Horgan and his ransacked apartment. The building manager said he hadn't seen him in a week.

CHAPTER FOUR

The proverbial shit had hit the proverbial fan. Following through on her threat, Maxine Bolelli had issued a press release revealing Galaxy's bid and Kendall's rejection of that offer. Bolelli had also sent a letter to Fitzgerald and each member of Kendall's board of directors, berating them for ignoring their fiduciary duty to Kendall's stockholders. In New York, Wall Street analysts were expressing bewilderment that Kendall would turn down the offer, describing Fitzgerald as stubborn and short-sighted, and opining that the rejection was out of misguided loyalty to the Kendall family heritage—words obviously planted by Galaxy's media people.

The morning before, Fitzgerald had walked from the conference room with a bounce in his step, confident about Kendall's future. Now he was back in the same room feeling flat-footed and anything but certain.

"How bad is the fallout?" Barclay Reid asked. Kendall's outside counsel, Reid was the managing partner of one of Seattle's largest law firms, Reid, Matheson, and Goetz.

"Half a dozen faxes and e-mails," Fitzgerald said. "The most polite have called me an idiot."

"At least two lawsuits have been threatened," Irwin Dean, Kendall's president of operations, added. "Including one by Clay Mayfair."

Everyone in the room knew Clay Mayfair, the infamous New York attorney who made a living suing corporations and their boards for breach of their fiduciary duty to shareholders.

"If Bolelli is serious, her next move will be to buy as much Kendall stock as she can," Reid said, pacing an area by the windows.

The only time Fitzgerald had ever seen the woman sit was in court. At just a shade over five feet, Barclay Reid was nearly always the shortest person in the room, but after seeing her in front of a jury, Fitzgerald knew height was not an issue. In her late thirties and a type A personality, she was a perpetual ball of energy, always thinking, always moving. Her looks were equally deceiving. At first glance she appeared ordinary—drab brown hair cut in a bob, eyeglasses without frames nearly invisible on an attractive face despite no outward attempt at glamour. She wore no makeup or jewelry but for a cross on a gold chain about her neck. Her dark gray, off-the-rack summer suit and plain white blouse did nothing to accentuate her shape, though Fitzgerald had seen her in shorts and a tank top on the golf course and recognized a figure honed by daily workouts. And yet, despite her understated appearance, every eye in the room followed Reid as she paced the floor. She had that intangible ability to command attention by her sheer determination and earnestness in defending her clients. The law's gain had been some ministry's loss; Reid would have been dynamic at a pulpit.

"But so long as you and Sebastian maintain your interests, she can't gain control."

"She could pressure the hell out of us, though," Dean said anxiously. "Any alternatives?"

Reid pressed her palms together beneath her chin as she paced. "Kendall could make its own offer, buy back stock from disgruntled shareholders, but that's risky. The news has already sent the stock up two and a half points. It's inflated. When it drops, you'll be stuck."

"Besides," John Feinstein, Kendall's CFO, offered, "we'd have to spend nearly all of what remains of our cash reserves to do it. In this economy, I don't recommend that."

Fitzgerald expected as much. Feinstein's idea of a gamble was eating an unrefrigerated cheese sandwich. He sat forward. "I like the idea. It's bold. It lets everyone know that Kendall is confident about its future. Let's get the word out to all of our media contacts. I want the financial world to know that Kendall is preparing for the holidays."

"This is an all-or-nothing play, Malcolm," Dean said.

Fitzgerald nodded. "If Bolelli wants to play chicken, let's play chicken and see who flinches first."

U.S. HIGHWAY 12
SOUTHERN WASHINGTON

SLOANE GLANCED FROM the road to the manila file on the edge of the passenger seat and wondered if Kyle Horgan had hit upon the next "It" toy. If he had, Horgan's scribbled drawings could be as valuable as a Rembrandt, according to Stroud. And that changed everything.

Money always did.

The letter in Horgan's file indicated he had sold his design to Kendall. If that were true, it could not have come at a more opportune time for the toy company. Just that morning *The Se-*

attle Times had run an article reporting that, despite apparent financial difficulties, Kendall had rejected overtures from Galaxy Toys, the second-largest toy manufacturer in the world. Speculation was that Galaxy would now make a play to obtain the company through a hostile run on its stock. Analysts were criticizing Kendall's declination as a poor business decision, but Seattleites applauded the move by a local institution and employer of thousands in the region.

Following the directions Sloane had plugged into the car's GPS system, he made a right turn on State Street and drove through the heart of town, no more than a couple of square blocks of stucco buildings that looked to have been built in the 1950s. On the outskirts he drove past manufactured homes, well spaced, with metal barnlike structures in the yard and freestanding canopies under which the occupants had parked tractors and other pieces of equipment. Barbed wire on wooden fence poles pastured horses and cattle. But what caught Sloane's attention was a large metal building that loomed over the town like Mount Rainier over Seattle. Intrigued, he decided to find out what it was.

At a T in the road he turned and drove to a gated entrance. A ten-foot Cyclone fence with three strands of barbed wire enclosed the building and a parking area surrounding it, a white sign fastened to the chain link.

KENDALL TOYS

Now this was getting interesting.

A car passed Sloane and stopped at the gated entrance, the driver talking to a guard in the booth before the gate pulled aside to allow entry. Sloane saw few cars inside the fence. Most of them were parked in a large paved area outside the compound with a footpath leading to a pedestrian entrance.

He made a U-turn and the GPS directed him to one of the cookie-cutter manufactured homes, plain beige, with an older model Volkswagen Jetta parked in the gravel driveway. A four-foot-high Cyclone fence enclosed a simple yard with a swing set on a neatly mowed grass lawn.

It was warmer than it had been in Seattle, but Sloane slipped on his sport coat as he walked to a small porch littered with shoes: work boots that would fit a grown man, women's tennis shoes, children's shoes, and rubber boots. He knocked twice. A Hispanic woman pulled open the door and gave him a curious look.

"Good morning," Sloane said. "I'm sorry to bother you. Are you Mrs. Gallegos?"

The woman looked past Sloane to his Jeep parked along the road. "Yes."

Sloane offered a business card, which the woman accepted tentatively. "My name is David Sloane. I'm an attorney from Seattle and I was hoping for a moment of your time?"

The woman looked up from the card, suspicious. "What is this about?" She had a Hispanic accent but her English was strong.

A very difficult topic, Sloane thought. "I recently had a case in which a young boy got sick. His parents thought it was the flu and took him to the doctor, but he never got better. He got worse. By the time they brought him to the hospital it was too late. He died."

The woman stiffened and took a step back from the door, her ponytail swinging as she turned, shouting in Spanish, but which Sloane understood. "Manny, there is a man at the door asking about Mateo."

A Hispanic man, short but well built through the shoulders, appeared to the woman's right, and she handed him Sloane's business card as she told him in Spanish what Sloane had just said.

Manny looked to Sloane, hands on his hips, the Seattle Seahawk helmet on his blue shirt sticking out. "What do you want with Mateo?" His accent was thicker than his wife's.

"I was telling your wife that I represent a family who also has lost their son. He died of symptoms very similar to the symptoms the newspaper reported your son suffered. I was hoping I could ask you a few questions."

The man shook his head. "No. We do not talk about it."

"I know it must be incredibly difficult—"

Manny shook his head, already closing the door. "We do not talk about it."

"Please, just one question, not about your son."

Manny hesitated, hand on the edge of the door.

Sloane removed Horgan's manila file from his briefcase and pulled out the best sketch of Metamorphis. "Have you ever seen this before?"

Manny shot his wife a side glance and appeared about to answer but his wife stopped him, again speaking Spanish.

"No. The attorney said we cannot say anything, that it will be very bad for us. Do you want us to raise our children in Mexico? There is nothing for us there. Mateo is gone. We cannot bring him back."

Manny lowered his head. "No. We do not see before," he said. Then he stepped back and shut the door.

PRODUCT SAFETY AGENCY
BETHESDA, MARYLAND

ANNE LEROY HAD come to work excited, as she had each day for the past three months. With her degrees in engineering and product design from Georgetown University, her friends thought she was nuts when LeRoy told them she was going to work for a government regulatory agency. She could make three times her salary in the private sector. Call her naïve, but at twenty-four LeRoy didn't want to be making life decisions based on the almighty dollar. Hadn't that been the new president's message? If people believed they could make a difference, they would, and that was the best way to ensure change.

And now LeRoy was about to prove him right.

She knocked on the open door and stuck her head in the office. "You wanted to see me."

Albert Payne diverted his attention from his computer screen and looked up.

LeRoy paused, taken aback. Dark bags sagged beneath Payne's eyes, accentuated by a pasty white complexion with pronounced red splotches on his neck. He looked as though he had aged ten years in the three weeks he had been gone. She wondered if he had picked up the flu on his trip to China, or food poisoning.

"Come in and sit down," he said.

She made her way to one of the two chairs across from him, placing the two-inch-thick document she carried on her lap. "How was your trip? Is it as bad over there as everyone says?"

Payne cleared his throat. "I want to talk to you about your investigation."

LeRoy immediately perked up, as she had that fateful morning when she fielded a cold call from a preschool teacher in Shakopee, Minnesota. The woman told LeRoy that a child in her care had swallowed a magnet no bigger than an aspirin from a broken toy and she was concerned enough that she had called the parents and suggested they take the child to the doctor. Although the doctor had assured the parents the child would be fine and would excrete the magnet, the preschool teacher remained upset. She said the toy came in a box that did not advise of a choking hazard, or even that the toy included these magnets, which she said were very powerful.

LeRoy put the draft of her report on the edge of Payne's desk, flipping through the sections. "Wait until you read what the doctor in Cleveland had to say," she said.

Starting with leads from ASTM International, LeRoy had made calls to different experts around the country. The magnets, manufactured mostly in China, were called neodymium magnets. Comprised of a metal alloy and artificially magnetized, they were many times more powerful than typical iron magnets, so much so that the attractive forces could be a potential danger, such as to people with pacemakers. Despite this, LeRoy was astounded to find just a single report, funded by the Toy Manufacturer's Association, that concluded the magnets were safe. Her own investigation had revealed that no one had actually done any tests to confirm the findings, or to determine what might happen if a child were to swallow more than one of these magnets, or a magnet and metal ball, for instance. She also found evidence that the China Toy Association knew that the plastic used for the toy that had broken was a problem but had not reported the problem, and that some American toy manufacturers had been complicit in the cover-up, fearing product recalls or, at a minimum, consumer restraint.

"I'm afraid I'm going to have to pull the plug, Anne."

LeRoy continued to flip the pages, searching for the section in which she quoted the expert from Cleveland. "He was extremely helpful—"

"Anne."

LeRoy stopped flipping the pages and looked up. Specks of dry skin and dust covered the lenses of Payne's glasses.

"More budget cuts have left us with just no money to be doing independent investigations."

"What?"

"I'm sorry."

"But . . . but you told me to do it. And I'm nearly done. All I have to do is finalize it."

Payne shook his head.

"The expert in Cleveland said the danger isn't in a child swallowing one magnet. The danger is if they swallow more than one. He said—"

"I need you to work on a potential enforcement action against TBD."

LeRoy knew TBD to be a manufacturer of detergent, and that there had been recent reports of the product causing chemical burns.

"TBD? That's a waste of time; it will go nowhere." She caught herself, not believing what she had just said to her boss.

But if Payne was upset he didn't reveal it. He looked almost bored. "Nevertheless."

"I'll finish it on my own time; I'll write it up at home."

He shook his head. "I know you worked hard on this investigation."

"Hard? I've spent three solid months on it. I thought it was going to be part of the congressional hearing? How can you just pull the plug? What about Senator Tovey?"

"It's out of my hands, I'm afraid."

"Is it Maggie Powers?"

"I'd like you to provide me with all of your research and any drafts you have on your computer. If we get the funding in the future perhaps we can pursue it further."

"But it will be too late. The problem is already out there, and the Senate hearing will have passed. Most doctors don't even consider X-rays because eighty percent of the things a child swallows will just pass through their system. But when you have two—"

"I'm sorry," he offered again.

She became more adamant. "Don't you want to hear what the doctor in Cleveland said? There is a significant danger to American consumers, to children."

"I'll need all of your files on my desk by this afternoon."

"We could take it to the media."

Payne pounded the desk, a burst of anger that caused LeRoy to jump back in her seat.

His gaze focused and his face had flushed an even darker shade of red. "You will do no such thing. Do you understand me?" He tapped the desk with his finger as he spoke. "You work for me. That means you do what I tell you. Your work here belongs to this agency. It's proprietary. If you release an unauthorized report I will see that you are fired and that the Justice Department prosecutes you to the fullest extent of the law. Do you understand me?"

LeRoy's lower lip quivered, but she fought back the tears. A stabbing pain pierced her, exactly where she would have expected, just between the shoulder blades.

LEROY HURRIED BACK to her cubicle and began to dump the contents of her desk drawers into the cardboard box she found in the supply closet, pausing briefly to dab her eyes with a tissue. She wasn't bothering to organize her belongings. She didn't care. Pens and pencils mixed with paper clips and scraps of paper. She grabbed the picture frame with the photo of her former boyfriend, over which she had drawn a bull's-eye in permanent marker, and tossed it in with a snow globe from Fort Lauderdale. A tear trickled from the corner of her eye but she quickly wiped it away, not wanting to give anyone the satisfaction.

"You're upset, Anne. Take a minute to think about this." Peggy Seeley stood outside her cubicle, alternately trying to calm LeRoy and to ask her further questions.

"There's nothing to think about. This is a waste of my time."

"Did he say why he was pulling the plug?"

"He said they didn't have the funds."

"Well, that's probably true," Seeley said.

LeRoy stopped what she was doing. "Then why did he bother to have me pursue it at all?" she countered. "What a colossal waste of time. It's exactly as everyone said it would be."

"Calm down. Don't make any rash decisions."

LeRoy didn't want to hear it, especially not from Seeley, who didn't even like to order food in a restaurant unless she could see the cook making it. The two had little in common except their jobs. Seeley was overweight and didn't care. LeRoy worked out daily to try to keep her weight at an even 120 pounds. At twenty-nine, Seeley wore no makeup, wire-rimmed glasses, and did little but brush her light brown hair that extended to the middle of her back. LeRoy wasn't a fashion princess by any stretch of the imagination, but she did take a few minutes each morning to apply basic makeup. She suspected their friendship would fizzle after she had left the agency.

"'Rash'? The only rash decision I made was taking a job at this shithole in the first place."

"Thanks for that."

"We don't get paid squat. We're not appreciated, and he just confirmed that we serve no purpose. What's the point?"

"This isn't exactly the best economy to be out looking for a job."

"I don't care. I'll work in a restaurant again before I stay here another day."

"Give it a day or two. Maybe he'll change his mind."

"Trust me; he's not changing his mind. When I pushed him on it he pounded his fist on the desk and—"

"*Albert* pounded his fist? Are you sure you were in the right office?"

The staff had often joked that Payne's bland demeanor and passive nature were the result of twenty-five years of boredom that had desensitized him. The man had to be desensitized to put up with all the bureaucratic bullshit for so long. LeRoy wasn't about to suffer the same fate. Though she had been optimistic about the new administration, she wouldn't sit around and wait to find out if things really would change.

"He looked like a thermometer popping out from a cooked turkey. I thought his head was going to explode."

LeRoy pulled out a memory stick from her backpack, shoved it into a UBS port on her computer, and sat at the keyboard.

"What are you doing?" Seeley asked.

"I'm not done with this, not after all the time I've invested."

"You can't take your work; it's proprietary."

"They're not going to get away with this."

"Who?"

"The agency, Powers, whoever is behind pulling the plug."

"You're going to get yourself in trouble, Anne, and for what? Didn't you learn anything working around here? You just said it, people don't care. Nobody cares."

"I care."

Seeley's eyes widened. "Well, whatever you're going to do, you better do it fast because Payne just walked around the corner in this direction and he's bringing a security guard with him."

LEWIS COUNTY COURTHOUSE
CHEHALIS, WASHINGTON

PERPLEXED, SLOANE DOUBLE-CHECKED the spelling with the article clipped in Kyle Horgan's file and retyped the name, but the computer again indicated no match.

He approached the clerk's window of the Lewis County Courthouse, located about twenty minutes from Mossylog. A middle-aged woman with reading glasses dangling from a colorful beaded chain around her neck sat behind the glass.

"I was wondering if you might be able to help me. I'm a bit of a computer dinosaur," Sloane said.

"I'm with you," the woman replied, smiling up at him. "But I can try."

"I'm looking for the name of the attorney who represented a young boy who recently died in Mossylog."

"Mateo Gallegos," the woman said without hesitation. "It was in the papers. He got an infection from a rusted nail. It was so sad. Cute little guy."

"A rusted nail?"

"That's what I heard. The family didn't have insurance, so they waited to bring him to the hospital, and by that time it was too late. We get that here with the migrant workers."

The information puzzled Sloane further. "So do you know if there was a lawsuit?"

"I don't think so," she said, "but I heard that Dayron Moore was their attorney."

Sloane retrieved a pen attached to a chain glued to the counter and wrote down the name. "Darren?"

"Day-ron." She wrote the name on a slip of paper despite three-inch-long red nails adorned with stars and moons and handed it to him. "Day-ron."

"Interesting name."

"Wait until you meet him."

"You know him?"

"Everyone knows Dayron around here. He's here so often he could do my job."

"He files a lot of lawsuits?"

"He files his share."

Which made it even more perplexing that Moore had apparently not filed a lawsuit in this particular instance. "Does he handle a lot of personal injury cases?"

"Dayron does anything that walks in the door, has a heartbeat, and can pay fifteen hundred dollars up front."

Sloane pointed to the computer terminals. "So I gather that if I type in his name it will bring up a list of his cases?"

The clerk smiled back at him. "Sure. But be prepared to sit there for a while."

HALF AN HOUR after leaving the courthouse, Sloane got out of his car and walked the block but could not find the address on State Street in Mossylog. He stepped into Smokey's House of Billiards on the corner to ask for help. The man behind the bar pointed to a small sign on the wall at the back of the building that said LAW OFFICE. A bent arrow directed anyone interested up a narrow staircase. Dayron Moore likely didn't get many walk-ins.

As the clerk had warned, Sloane's search using the attorney's name pulled up a long list. Scrolling through the cases, Sloane had quickly deduced that most of Moore's clients had Hispanic surnames. Clicking on a few of those particular cases he found a paucity of pleadings after the initial complaint. That meant Moore routinely settled, and quickly, which gave Sloane a pretty good idea about Dayron Moore the lawyer.

At the top of the stairs Sloane stepped into an office and instinctively ducked. He estimated the rectangular tiles and fluorescent lighting to be about a foot lower than a standard eight-foot ceiling, though it felt just inches from the top of Sloane's head and made the man who stood from his seat behind a laminated wood desk look even more peculiar. Perhaps five six and dressed in a light blue, short-sleeved polo shirt and black slacks that bunched at his shoes despite being hitched well above his waist, Dayron Moore was as round as a Kewpie doll.

"Can I help you?" Moore looked and sounded surprised to see someone in his office. He spoke in a high-pitched voice from behind a bushy white mustache that extended over his upper lip.

After confirming the man to be Dayron Moore, Sloane said, "I'd like to speak to you about a potential legal matter."

Rather than offer Sloane a chair, Moore asked, "You from around here?"

"Seattle, actually."

Moore ran a hand through a shock of white hair, wisps of which stuck out over his ears. "What brings you down here, Mr. . . . ?"

"Sloane, David Sloane." Sloane motioned to a chair. "May I?"

Moore's eyes narrowed, but he wobbled back behind his desk, much of which was taken up by an antiquated computer screen that matched the office decor, which had not been upgraded since the 1960s. The desk, credenza, and walls were a cheap wood laminate, and Sloane sat in one of two matching lime green cloth chairs. Two diplomas hung framed on the wall behind Moore, but Sloane did not recognize either school.

"I hope I'm not catching you at a bad time," Sloane said. He detected a recently applied coating of very strong aftershave which, along with blotchy red cheeks and a bulbous nose traced by several broken blood vessels, indicated Moore had just drunk most of his lunch and likely did so often.

"What can I do you for?" Moore asked.

"I have a client in Seattle who has something in common with one of your former clients," Sloane said, telling the truth.

"You're an attorney?" Moore sounded immediately deflated.

"Your client was Mateo Gallegos."

Moore's eyebrows inched closer and the suspicion returned to his voice. "What about him?"

"My client's son recently died after running a very high fever and suffering flulike symptoms. The family kept the boy home and tried to hydrate him, but by the time they got him to the hospital the kid had a massive infection and died."

Moore offered no condolences. "What'd the coroner say?"

"There wasn't an autopsy. The boy was older than five so the state didn't mandate it."

"Was the body cremated?"

"No."

Moore sat back, rubbing his mustache but offering nothing further.

"I just spoke to Mr. and Mrs. Gallegos," Sloane said, continuing to tell the truth. "I wanted to talk to you about Kendall Toys."

Moore flushed beet red. "They weren't supposed to say anything about that. All of that is confidential."

Sloane had played a hunch and Moore's response confirmed that the lawyer had settled the Gallegos case without ever even filing a lawsuit. Sloane had no idea why Kendall would settle a suit in which a boy had fallen on a rusty nail, but then he had been skeptical of the clerk's understanding of the case. Recalling something else the clerk had told him, Sloane said, "I'd be willing to put up a retainer if that helps. I just want to see the family taken care of."

Moore calmed at the mention of money. "You don't want to represent them?"

"It's not really my area of expertise. Besides, I don't even know if they have a case; it sounds like you've already gone down this road."

"Did they get one of the toys?"

The question caught Sloane momentarily off guard but he recovered to ask, "Metamorphis?"

"That's the one." Moore perked up considerably, retrieved a business card from his desk drawer, and held it across the desk. "Have the family give me a call to set up an appointment. Ordinarily I work strictly contingency, but for this I'll need a ten-thousand-dollar retainer."

Sloane whistled. "That much?"

"This is a big case."

"You think?"

Moore nodded. "Of course you know that I can't breach the confidentiality of a settlement agreement."

"Of course."

"But if this is what I think it is, they'll get back five times that amount, minimum."

Sloane acted impressed. "No kidding?"

"Let's just say the defendant will be very motivated to make this go away."

"Kendall Toys?"

Dayron raised a hand. "I can't say. You understand."

Sloane nodded. "I wouldn't want you to do anything unethical."

THE PUMP HOUSE
GEORGETOWN, WASHINGTON, D.C.

AS SHE POLISHED off the remnants of her second beer, Anne LeRoy checked her BlackBerry. She was about to call when she saw Peggy Seeley walk from the slatted sunlight into the bar's dim atmosphere and waved her over.

"Don't ever do that to me again," Seeley said even before she sat on the adjacent barstool. "I've been a nervous wreck all afternoon." Seeley pulled LeRoy's memory stick from beneath her blouse, slipping the strap over her head and slapping it on the counter. "I don't want anything more to do with this."

"I'm sorry," LeRoy said. "I couldn't think of anything else to do." When LeRoy saw Payne and the security guard marching toward her cubicle, she tossed the memory stick with the downloaded report on magnets to Seeley, who shoved it down her blouse.

The bartender approached. "I'll have a beer," Seeley said, "whatever she's drinking. She's buying."

"Why am I buying? I'm unemployed."

"Too bad, that was by choice."

As the bartender tipped the tall cylindrical glass under the tap Seeley gave a nervous giggle. "I still can't believe what you said to him."

After suffering the indignation of having her personal belongings searched, LeRoy had picked up her backpack to leave when Payne said, "And might I remind you—"

LeRoy had interrupted him. "No, you can't. I don't work for you anymore." Then she stared down the guard until he too backed away. It had been one of those rare moments in life when she had said exactly what she wanted. The retort had just rolled off her tongue. But it had been born more of desperation than bravado. She wanted Payne and the guard out of there before they got the idea to search Seeley as well.

"He was stalking your cubicle most of the day," Seeley said. "He had the IT people clear it out."

"They took the computer?"

Seeley nodded as the bartender put her beer, with a healthy head of foam, beside the memory stick, which LeRoy slipped in her backpack.

"What are you going to do with that?" Seeley asked.

LeRoy had thought about all the reasons she went to work for the agency in the first place rather than taking a job in the private sector. "I don't know. Probably nothing, but it's the principle of the thing. This was a good investigation. Those magnets are dangerous. The public has a right to know that before someone gets seriously hurt, or dies."

Seeley did not respond, drinking her beer.

"Do you think he would do it?" LeRoy asked, with a little less conviction.

"Do what?" Seeley asked.

"Go to the Justice Department. Prosecute me."

Seeley shrugged. "It sounded like he would."

LeRoy lifted the glass to her lips, lowered it. "They really took my computer?"

THE LUNCH BUCKET

MOSSYLOG, WASHINGTON

SLOANE SHIELDED HIS face with a menu as Manny Gallegos walked into the diner, looked about with uncertainty, and sat in a booth close to the door. A waitress filled his coffee mug, but Gallegos shook his head when she offered him a menu. He tore open four pink packages and stirred in the granules while looking out the restaurant windows at the parking lot like a Labrador in a car awaiting his master's return.

Sloane set down his menu, slid from his booth, and approached Gallegos from behind, waiting to allow another man entering the diner to pass and take the booth across the aisle.

When Sloane slid into the booth, Gallegos sat up straight and glanced at the parking lot.

"He's not coming."

Gallegos's eyes narrowed.

In a brief telephone conversation Sloane had told Gallegos he was calling from Dayron Moore's office, and that Dayron wanted to meet immediately to discuss the possibility that Gallegos had breached the settlement agreement with Kendall Toys. Gallegos had become defensive on the phone and Sloane regretted manipulating the man, but he hoped that if he could get him away from his wife, Gallegos might open up about what had happened to their son.

"I'm sorry," Sloane said, speaking Spanish. "But it's important I speak to you."

"I can't," Gallegos responded, also in Spanish. "I can't say anything about it." He started from the booth.

"I already know about Kendall," Sloane said.

Gallegos stopped and looked over his shoulder at Sloane. "Then why are you bothering me if you know about it?"

It was a good question. "I only need you to confirm a few things. You don't even have to talk. Just listen. If anything I say is wrong, you can get up and leave. If what I say is right, you stay and you still won't have told me anything. Okay?"

Gallegos remained seated at an angle, and Sloane was uncertain whether the man would stay or go. His chest expanded and deflated.

"You can't get in trouble for listening," Sloane said.

Gallegos hesitated, then turned back into the booth, his gaze fixed on his coffee mug.

"I know that your son became ill and that you did your best to try to help him. I know that you took him to the hospital, but by that time it was too late; that he had lapsed into a coma and died."

Tears pooled in Gallegos's eyes. "We should have taken him earlier," he whispered.

"You're in the country illegally."

Another nod.

"And you were afraid that you could be deported if someone at the hospital found out."

Gallegos fought back his tears. "We could have saved him; Mateo would still be alive."

"Do you work at the Kendall factory?" Sloane asked.

Gallegos nodded.

"How did you get a job if you're illegal?"

"I used my cousin's name and Social Security number."

"Your name isn't Manny Gallegos?"

"Here I am Manny Gallegos. In Mexico I am Manny Gutierrez. When you come to my home, my wife, she thinks maybe you are from immigration. Mr. Moore, he says that if we don't take the settlement, Kendall will find out I am not Manny Gallegos and we will be deported. He said he negotiated so that I can keep my job."

"Mr. Moore represents a lot of Hispanic workers in this area, doesn't he?" Sloane asked.

Gallegos said Moore did, as the waitress returned to refill their cups.

"Do you want something to eat?" Sloane asked.

Gallegos declined and the waitress departed. He reached for the ceramic container but it was empty. Sloane leaned across the aisle, talking to the man in the adjacent booth. "Excuse me? Could I get a couple packets of sweetener?"

The man handed Sloane the entire container, which Sloane slid to Gallegos. "Can you tell me what happened to Mateo?"

Gallegos opened three more packets. "It is as you say. He got the fever. We think it is the flu and give him medicine from the store. But Mateo, he did not get better. He continues to throw up and have the fever. He did not eat. One morning I go to wake him and he don't wake up. His forehead . . ." Gallegos wept. "His forehead was so hot but his body was cold. We take him to the hospital, but the doctor, he said it was too late."

Again Sloane gave the man time to compose himself. "Was there an autopsy?"

Gallegos nodded. "The police come to our house. The doctor called them. And they send a woman to look to see that we don't have any other bad things."

Sloane shook his head. There had been no autopsy of Austin McFarland, and it was not lost on him that the hospital in Southern Washington had likely called the police because the Gallegos were low income and Hispanic and therefore, by stereotype, not as fit to parent, or more likely to have neglected or even abused their child, than the middle-class, Caucasian McFarlands. But that did not answer the question as to what the coroner found that compelled him to call the police, or why the police had then likely alerted Child Protective Services to inspect the Gallegos home.

"Do you know what the autopsy showed?"

"Not so much."

"Can you read English, Manny?"

Gallegos shook his head. "A friend of ours, he tells us to hire Mr. Moore. He talked to the police and the doctors. He handled it all for us."

"What did Moore say the autopsy showed?"

"He said something about magnets making Mateo sick, but also that Mateo, he fall on a nail and the rust poisoned him."

"Magnets?"

A shrug.

"Where did the magnets come from?"

"Mr. Moore, he says he cannot prove it."

"Can't prove what, Manny?"

"That maybe the magnets they come from the toy that Kendall gives to Ricky."

"Is Ricky Mateo's brother?"

"Yes."

Sloane pulled out a sketch from Kyle Horgan's file. "Was it this toy?"

Gallegos nodded. "But Mr. Moore, he says he cannot prove it."

"Did Mateo play with the toy?"

"No, only Ricky."

"What else did Mr. Moore say?"

"Just that maybe Mateo dies from an infection when he falls on the nail."

"Why would Kendall pay you money if Mr. Moore couldn't prove the magnets came from the toy?"

Again Gallegos shrugged. "He just says that Kendall does not want the bad news."

"You mean bad publicity?"

"He says Kendall's lawyers want to go to the court but he convinces them that they will not like the bad publicity. He tells us to take the money because Kendall is very big and has very much money to go to the court. He says that I could lose my job and be deported."

"Did you sign an agreement to get the money?"

"Mr. Moore says we have to sign, so we sign."

"How much did Kendall pay you?"

Gallegos didn't respond.

"Okay. If the number I say is right, take a sip of coffee."

Sloane remembered Moore's statement that the family could recover five times a $10,000 retainer. "Was it fifty thousand dollars?"

Gallegos took a sip of coffee.

"How much did Mr. Moore keep?"

"Thirty thousand."

Sloane seethed. Moore's fee should have been one third, at most, and given that the man had not even filed a lawsuit, he would have had virtually no costs to be reimbursed. He had one more series of questions for Gallegos.

"How did you get one of the toys?"

"Kendall gives it to me to take home because I work hard and they pay us fifty dollars for Ricky to play with and say what he likes and does not like."

"Do you still have the toy?"

"No. We must return it after the meeting."

"What meeting?"

"They have a meeting to watch Ricky play with the toy and ask him questions."

"Were there other children who played with the toy?"

"Two boys and a girl, I think Ricky say."

A focus group, Sloane thought. "What did your son think of it?"

For the first time since Sloane sat down, Gallegos smiled. "He loved it. He loved it more than his other toys. But some of the pieces, they crack, so they say they are doing more work and the real ones will be better."

Sloane could only hope that Gallegos was right, but at the moment he could only think of his conversation with Dee Stroud. If Kendall was about to launch a new "It" toy for the holiday season there would soon be millions on store shelves.

"More children could die," Kyle Horgan had warned.

NEARING THE END of the workday, Sloane returned to the billiard parlor, about to climb the narrow staircase when he saw Dayron Moore in the corner of the room near a green felt pool table. Moore chose a pool cue from a rack on the wall and chalked the blue end, about to break, when Sloane approached the opposite end of the table. Moore straightened. "You still here?"

"I just had a late cup of coffee with Manuel Gallegos."

Moore gave Sloane a sideways glance. "What for?"

Sloane opened his briefcase and pulled out the document he had hand-drafted and Manny Gallegos had signed in the diner. He handed it to Moore and watched the man's face turn the color of a traffic light as he read it. The document directed Moore to provide Sloane with Gallegos's entire legal file, though Sloane knew Moore's file would be slim. What he wanted was the release of all of Mateo's medical records in Moore's possession, including the autopsy report.

"He can't do that," Moore said.

"He already has. My office will be faxing you a signed Substitution of Attorneys tomorrow morning."

"The case is over."

"The case never got started."

"They signed a binding settlement agreement."

"You coerced them into signing a settlement agreement under threat Manny would lose his job and they'd be deported if they didn't. You also lied about the autopsy report."

"I did nothing of the sort. I just told them the facts."

"You can tell that to the bar association if the Gallegoses have to file a complaint."

"Now wait a minute, Mr. Sloane. I don't know what he told you, but I can assure you—"

"He told me that you took thirty thousand dollars of a fifty-thousand-dollar settlement, Dayron. Given that the case did not proceed to trial, your percentage should have been thirty-three percent at the most, and since you didn't even file a complaint I can't imagine your expenses were more than the gas you spent rushing this settlement agreement back to Kendall's lawyers as fast as you could."

Moore's mustache twitched and his nostrils flared. "Fine. I'll send the file over tomorrow."

"No." Sloane did not want to give the man any time to alter

the file contents. "You and I are going upstairs to your office and you're going to provide me with the file, including the medical records."

Moore stood his ground, either because he was defiant, or about to wet his pants. "I don't have it. It's already in storage."

"Then we'll go get it."

"It isn't open now."

"Mr. Moore," Sloane said. "Do you really want the bar association looking into the files of your past clients as well?"

Moore lowered his eyes. After a brief hesitation, he placed the pool cue onto the table and, without uttering another word, shuffled toward the staircase at the back of the room.

THREE TREE POINT
BURIEN, WASHINGTON

"OH MY GOD," Tina said.

Sloane had just explained the findings of the doctor's autopsy, which he had read in the car before leaving Mossylog. Mateo Gallegos had been taken to the hospital in a coma and, like Austin McFarland, when initial treatment was ineffective, further blood tests were taken, but too late. The throat swab had come back negative for the flu virus, but the blood cultures confirmed the boy had septicemia, commonly referred to as blood poisoning. The word had nearly leapt off the page when Sloane read it. Could it be coincidence that two boys who presented with symptoms of the flu, both died from a very aggressive bacterial infection seemingly caused by an infectious source somewhere in the body? Sloane didn't think so. And while Mateo Gallegos did show physical signs of having suffered a puncture wound to his abdomen, likely from having fallen on a rusty nail, the autopsy had also revealed perforations in his intestinal walls, perforations caused when several powerful magnets attracted one another and pinched the lining, cutting off blood supply to that area.

"Something bothered me, but I couldn't put my finger on it. It was just a gut reaction that Douvalidis did not do anything wrong."

They sat in silence, thinking of the consequences.

Tina said, "Well, it doesn't mean he *wasn't* negligent, right? I mean shouldn't he have diagnosed it, or at least had X-rays taken?"

Sloane knew Tina was trying to ease his conscience, but the two-hour drive home had given him time to think through the implications, and it had done nothing to make him feel better. "Douvalidis had no reason to suspect Austin swallowed anything because there were no signs he had choked, and even if he had suspected it, eighty percent of the things a child swallows are excreted. I'm going to have to check, but I'm fairly certain this is not something that has been heavily documented in the literature. These types of magnets are relatively new and untested."

"What are you going to do?"

"I don't know. They've buried their son, Tina. Eva said the verdict would be a new start for all of them. How can I make them go back? How could I even bring up the subject again?"

AFTER TINA DRIFTED off to sleep Sloane knew he would not be as fortunate. He sneaked downstairs, made a cup of chamomile tea, and stepped into his office to reconsider the Gallegos file in greater detail. He also took out the newspaper, which he had shoved in his case that morning without reading. He started to set the newspaper aside when a headline caught his attention.

BUILDING MANAGER
BEATEN TO DEATH
Latest Pioneer Square Attack
Has Residents on Edge

The headline was above the fold, the article below it. He flipped over the paper and felt the air rush from his lungs.

Seattle Police went door to door yesterday seeking information in the death of a Pioneer Square building manager. Edgar Paterno, 53, was found beaten to death in his apartment on Jackson Street, in a building he managed. Detectives would release little information, but witnesses said Paterno was discovered by the building owner, who had gone to collect the rent. What the owner found instead was something he described as a "horror."

"Interesting reading?"

The voice startled him. Not Tina. Not Jake.

Sloane sprung from his chair, heart in his throat. A man stood just inside his office door. Sloane didn't wait to ask questions or to determine the man's intent. He took two quick steps and bull-rushed him, but grabbed at air. The man sidestepped him and turned his body, then lowered an elbow into the small of Sloane's back, driving him to a knee. Grimacing, Sloane rose, turned, and arced a left hook at the man's head, but with the element of surprise gone the man raised his right arm, blocked the blow and countered, knuckles striking hard against Sloane's rib cage. The force of the punch, and Sloane's momentum, sent him crashing off-kilter into the file cabinet and he again fell to his knees. Back on his feet, fighting to catch his breath, ribs aching, he spun and started for the intruder, but the man now held a gun, aiming a long cylinder screwed onto the end of the barrel directly between Sloane's eyes, stopping his advance.

He had produced the weapon as fast as a card trick.

"Do you know the problem with being famous, Mr. Sloane? It makes it so easy for someone to find information about you. What you do . . . Where you live . . . Who lives with you."

Sloane's side felt as though it had burst into flames, and he fought to regain his breath. The implication that the man had been researching him brought greater alarm, but there was something else more disturbing—a feeling that Sloane knew the man, though he could not immediately recall how.

Sloane contemplated the gun he kept in his upper desk drawer but saw no way to get to it.

"People think using P.O. boxes will keep their address confidential, but there are all those applications out there to the bar association, health clubs, school records, wine clubs, and now they're all online. Just about anyone motivated to do so can violate the sanctity of our personal privacy."

Well-muscled, the man had a dark complexion and shoulder-length hair pulled into a ponytail. But that was not the image of the man Sloane continued to try to pull from the recesses of his mind. The image formulating was of a man wearing a baseball cap pulled low on his forehead.

"People don't think twice about divulging their home addresses and telephone numbers to the school nurse," the man continued. "You really can't be too careful with all the crazies around today."

The image cleared. The diner in Mossylog. The man had entered as Sloane went to Gallegos's booth and then had sat across from them. Sloane had asked him for sweetener.

The man picked up the paper from Sloane's desk, considering the article. "Some people just have no respect for the laws of society," he said.

There was something dark about the man's demeanor, something perverse and unnatural in the calm he projected. Most men, no matter how brave, no matter how lopsided the odds in their favor, would have shown some reservation, some hint of nerves at an impending encounter. But dressed in a black sweat suit and gloves the man looked like he had just finished a casual jog along the beach. This was no amateur.

Sloane needed to find a way to get the man out of the house, away from Tina and Jake.

"What is it you want?"

"You're a bright man, Mr. Sloane. I think you know why I'm here."

"No, I don't think I do."

He sighed. "I came for Kyle Horgan's file."

"I don't have it," Sloane said. "It's at my office in Seattle."

The man moved the newspaper to the side and looked down at the file on Sloane's desk. "Don't worry, Mr. Sloane, I have no interest in your wife or son. I even waited until you put them both to bed. I was hoping you had gone to sleep. I didn't expect you to be awake. Insomnia? That explains the chamomile tea. I also avoid caffeine."

Sloane maintained eye contact though he thought again of the gun. If he was going to die, he was going to do so fighting to stay alive.

"All right, there's the file. Take it and go," he said.

"As I said, that had been my intent, but I'm afraid you've seen me, and . . . well, I can't have that in my line of work."

Sloane raised his hands. "I don't want my wife and kid to see this. Okay? Let's go outside."

"Very noble, Mr. Sloane. As you wish."

The man motioned with the gun and Sloane started for the door. Footsteps descended the staircase, and it brought a wave of panic.

"David?"

The man diverted his eyes to the sound.

"Tina, run!"

Even as he yelled, Sloane had already turned, stepped, and leapt toward his desk, hearing the gun explode. His thigh burst in searing pain. He cleared the desk and barrel-rolled onto the floor behind it. Somehow he had managed to grab the drawer handle as he fell, pulling it from the desk, its contents spilling about the floor.

"David!"

Sloane fumbled through the debris, grabbed the butt of the gun, and rose from behind the desk. The second bullet hit him in the shoulder, knocking him backward and causing his reflexes to squeeze the trigger, firing twice, though well off aim. From his back he watched in horror as the man's arm swept toward the staircase. Tina leaned over the side, looking down at them, eyes wide. Sloane struggled to his knees, blood seeping from the wounds in his thigh and right shoulder. His right arm dangled useless at his side. He fought to raise the gun, but his hand no longer held it.

Sloane grabbed the side of the desk, pulling himself to his knees. The man glanced back over his shoulder, and smiled.

"NO!"

Instinct caused Tina to step away from the rail. The bullet shoved her backward against the wall then she fell, arms splayed, her body impacting against the stairs, seeming to bounce, and hit again. At first she did not move, then, slowly, her body slid down, coming to rest on the landing. The man walked to where she lay, standing over her, watching, seeming to delight in the fear and shock etched on her face. Sloane reached out, but his leg would not move, and he toppled forward, facedown onto the wood floor. He raised his head, watching. Tina spit blood, choking, struggling to breathe.

The man reentered the office, bent to a knee, and placed the barrel of the gun to Sloane's temple. "Ask for mercy, Mr. Sloane, and I may grant it."

Sloane grimaced, struggling to speak. His eyes fixated on Tina.

"No jokes? No funny puns?"

He shifted his focus, looking up. "I'm going to kill you . . ." he sputtered.

The man shook his head. "As a lawyer, Mr. Sloane, I think you would agree with me that the current state of the evidence makes the chances of that occurring highly unlikely." The man glanced back at Tina. "As I said, I did my best to avoid just this kind of scenario. It seems you are not the only one with insomnia. The wrong place at the wrong time, I'm afraid."

"Mom!" Jake thundered down the stairs to the landing, dropping the phone as he did. It clattered onto the hardwood.

"Jake, run!"

But the boy fell atop his mother, his face a mask of pain and agony. "Mom! Mom!"

"Doesn't anyone in this house sleep?" The man stood from his crouch.

Sloane grabbed the man's boot, but he had no strength, and it pulled free of his grip. Sloane sat up, reaching out, watching as the man took aim at the back of Jake's head.

"No."

A siren wailed, close.

The man turned his head to the sound, then to the phone on the ground. He picked it up, considering the last dialed number. "Nine-one-one. Smart boy."

He replaced the gun inside his jacket and stepped back into the office, seemingly undisturbed by the now howling sirens or the flash of lights reflecting on the office windows. He retrieved Kyle Horgan's file, flipping through it.

Voices sounded outside.

Closing the file, he slipped it under his arm, and looked again at Sloane. Then he glided out the French doors, past Jake and Tina, and blended back into the darkness.

HIS FEET SLIPPED in the trail of blood seeping from his wounds, but somehow he found the strength, pulling with the fingers of his one good hand, pushing with his one leg, inches at a time, his only focus reaching her. Nearing, he grabbed for the banister, but the blood caused his hand to slip from the rail, leaving a red smear on the white paint. He struggled forward another inch, gripped the wooden pole, and pulled himself the final distance.

Jake lay over his mother's body, sobbing.

Banging on the door reverberated throughout the house.

Jake raised his head, his face streaked with his mother's blood.

"Dead bolt," Sloane said, gasping for air. "Go."

Jake rose and ran from the room.

Sloane bit back the pain and pulled himself next to her. Tina lay with her head on the bottom stair, eyes open. Her chest fluttered as it rose and fell.

"Tina?"

He lifted himself so she could see his face but her eyes stared absently, pupils dilated.

"Tina?"

Mouth open, she began to moan, a haunting, staccato sound.

"I'm here," he whispered. "I'm right here."

Her chest rose, each breath becoming more shallow.

"No," he cried. "Tina. Please. Don't leave me. Stay with me."

Her limbs stiffened, her chest trembled, rapid breaths, eyes wide.

"Tina! Tina! No. Don't go. Please. Please. Don't go."

He heard the sound of people rushing into the house, toward them.

She blinked, and for a moment her pupils fixated on him.

"Stay with me," he said. "Stay with me."

HIGHLINE COMMUNITY HOSPITAL

BURIEN, WASHINGTON

LIGHTS BLURRED OVERHEAD, blinding him and creating halos of light around the faces hovering above him.

"Forty-seven-year-old male. Gunshot wounds to the right leg and right shoulder, likely forty caliber. Extensive blood loss at scene. Patient is awake. No loss of consciousness."

A different voice. "Pressure's eighty over fifty. Heart rate a hundred and ten, respirations twenty-five with oxygen saturation of ninety-two percent."

"Get a dopamine drip started, run it open. Prepare to intubate."

"Dr. Tressel is in the OR."

A mask pinched Sloane's face. Needles punctured his arms. Tubes led to bags hanging overhead. He heard the sound of his own breathing, but he could not speak, could not ask anyone the one thing that mattered.

Where is she?

He had promised he would stay with her. He had promised he would not let her go.

"He's lost a lot of blood."

"His pressure is dropping."

He felt cold. He had never felt so cold.

"On my call. Go."

The overhead light brightened, blinding. He felt hands lifting him up before placing him back down. Others cut the clothing from his body.

"Do we have X-rays yet?"

Hands touched his chest and abdomen. He felt the cold on his back. "Patient has gunshot wound entrance site in right upper shoulder and right midthigh. Log roll him."

They rolled him onto his side. Fingers touched the back of his thigh and shoulder. "Exit wounds in upper thigh and right scapula."

"Can you move your foot? Can you move your foot?"

Sloane wiggled his toes.

"Possible neurological damage. Likely pneumothorax. I'll need a chest tube."

"What about an air-evac to Harborview?"

"He won't last that long."

CHAPTER FIVE

Malcolm Fitzgerald nodded to the security guard in the brick booth, and the crossbar raised, allowing his Bentley access into the gated community. Located just a few miles east of downtown Seattle, the homes in the development started at just over $2 million, even in the still depressed housing market. For that price you received gated entrances with security guards at two locations, a private golf course, pristine streets swept regularly, manicured lawns and yards, and a whole host of regulations about what you could and could not do with your property. No basketball hoops at the end of driveways or mounted over garage doors. No bikes left forgotten on front lawns. No cars parked in the street. Garden lights were to be subtle, like the light from the streetlamps, evenly spaced to account for safety, and tempered so as not to destroy the ambiance.

Despite the turbulence at work, Fitzgerald had left the office early, which for him meant while it was still light out. He turned into the driveway of his two-story brick house. With white wood trim, dormers on the roof, and a burgundy-red front door, he thought it looked like a fraternity house on Greek Row. It was certainly big enough to house a fraternity. Their real estate agent had told them not to concern themselves with the front of the houses she showed them, rationalizing that they would only see it coming and going. Fitzgerald thought the woman had a valid point, but his wife had not been so easily placated.

He parked in the garage and listened to the automatic door rattle closed, the noise probably a violation of some home-owner regulation. The short porte cochere led to the mud-room, where he replaced one of his daughter's stray shoes next to the match on the built-in cubbyhole professionally labeled ADRIENNE'S SCHOOL SHOES. Fitzgerald couldn't decide what was worse, the fact that his wife was anal enough to separate the shoes into categories, or had enough free time to make the labels. Then again, time was a luxury he could afford for her, along with the three-million-dollar home and the $55,000 Mercedes station wagon she needed to cart the girls to and from private school, piano lessons, ballet, and the seemingly never-ending soccer practices.

Footsteps sounded in the kitchen. Fitzgerald hid behind the doorjamb. As Sarah slid around the corner, her socks gliding over the freshly waxed floor, he surprised her from behind.

"Boo!"

She screamed and jumped.

Adrienne followed a split second behind her sister, yelling. "You cheated."

"No I didn't."

"You didn't say 'go.'"

"I said three."

"You still have to say go."

"Hey, hey, hey." Fitzgerald stepped between them, hugging them both. "Why don't we just call it a tie?"

"No way," Sarah said. "She always cries when I win."

"That's because you cheat."

"All right," Fitzgerald said, "no more calling anyone a cheater."

He hugged them again, and they followed him through the kitchen into the living room, where Adrienne sat quickly at the piano bench.

"Want to hear my recital piece?"

Before he could answer she began to play. Growling like a monster, Fitzgerald chased Sarah from the room and down the hall where she ran past her mother, who stood outside the master bedroom and stepped into his path. "Hold it, Frankenstein." She pointed to her lips. "Plant one."

Fitzgerald did, and she followed him into a bedroom as big as a hotel suite.

"It's after nine," Erin said to Sarah, who had hidden beneath the bed covers. "You should be in your own bed with lights out."

The covers muffled her response. "I heard the garage door."

"I'll call someone to get it fixed. I'm afraid it might disturb the neighbors," Erin said.

Fitzgerald shook his head. "It's a garage door. Garage doors make noise, just like kids make noise. Are they going to outlaw kids too?"

"Don't start again." She pulled down the covers on the bed, exposing Sarah. "To bed," she said, leaving the room. Fitzgerald heard her issue the same orders to Adrienne. He carried Sarah to her room and tucked her in, then returned and pulled off his tie. He threw his shirt in the basket labeled DRY CLEANING, kicked off his shoes, and left them there, a tempered protest against the cubby in his walk-in closet labeled WORK SHOES.

Erin walked back in. "You get them riled up and I'm the one who has to settle them down again. Did you eat? I saved you a plate."

"I grabbed something."

"I heard about Galaxy on the six o'clock news. How bad is the fallout?"

He shrugged. "Tepid. There's still some shareholders pushing for my head, but the board isn't too concerned, with the stock climbing."

"Anyone pushing to take the offer?"

Fitzgerald shook his head. "Nobody wants to be the next Larry Reiner."

Everyone in the toy business knew the story of Larry Reiner, the twenty-nine-year-old inventor of G.I. Joe, who had rejected a one percent royalty payment on every sale of the toy and taken his agent's recommendation to split a $100,000 one-time payment. Over the next forty years Reiner had lost an estimated $40 million in income.

Erin sat on the edge of the bed. "Do you really think Metamorphis could be like that?"

Fitzgerald shrugged. "It's always a gamble, but yeah, I do."

The tone of her voice changed. "Do you think it's worth it?"

"What?"

"The gamble."

Thirty-five-million dollars' worth of worry lines creased her forehead, which was the amount Fitzgerald stood to make if he sold his stock when it was riding high. Fitzgerald couldn't do that to Sebastian Kendall, or to himself. His ego wouldn't allow him to concede defeat.

"Bolelli has a track record for purging the fat from companies she acquires. She'll fire all of Kendall's executives, consolidate manufacturing, and lay off a majority of Kendall's workforce."

And then what would he do, stare at the front of his house all day?

"I'm just saying nobody wants to be the next Edward John Smith either," she said, referring to the captain of the *Titanic*.

HIGHLINE COMMUNITY HOSPITAL
BURIEN, WASHINGTON

CHARLES JENKINS HAD taken the first flight home after Sloane's secretary, Carolyn, called to deliver the news. When his plane landed at Seattle-Tacoma Airport, Jenkins and Alex had driven straight to the hospital and he had maintained a vigil there ever since. For the first four days Sloane had lain in a drug-induced coma intended to limit his pain and prevent him from thrashing about in bed, possibly pulling out the myriad of tubes stuck in his body. Still, Jenkins had refused to leave. When visiting hours ended he took a blanket to the waiting room. The hospital staff gave him a hard time; hospital rules only allowed relatives to spend the night. Jenkins told them he and Sloane were brothers. Since he was black he didn't expect to convince them, but he hoped to emphasize the strength of the bond between the two men, as well as his conviction to stay. The staff relented. Alex had brought him clothes, food, and reading material, unable to convince him to leave even to take a walk.

"I need to be the one," he had told her. "I don't want him to hear it from anyone else."

When the doctor finally removed the breathing tube, Sloane choked uttering his first word.

"Tina?"

Jenkins shut his eyes, unable to hold back the tears that spilled down his face. "I'm sorry." He shook his head. "I'm so sorry."

The words had hit Sloane like the blows of a jackhammer. His chest shuddered, then his back arched, his body becoming rigid as a plank. The doctors and nurses fought to keep him from tearing the IVs from his arms and rupturing the bandages covering his shoulder and leg wounds, but they could not prevent the primal scream of agony and despair that ripped from his soul and rumbled down the hallways. Only a sedative silenced him.

For the next three weeks, Jenkins remained in the chair beside the bed; Tina's parents had flown to Seattle and taken Jake back to San Francisco with them, along with their daughter's ashes for burial. Jenkins didn't try to talk to Sloane, who spent most of his time staring out the window in his own induced coma, numb to the world and everyone in it. When the doctors and nurses asked Sloane questions, he did not answer them. When they put food in front of him, he did not touch it.

According to the doctors, the gunshot wound to Sloane's thigh had broken his femur and caused soft tissue damage to his muscles, but it had missed his femoral vessel. Had it not, Sloane would likely have bled to death, or lost his leg. Surgery on the leg indicated some neurological loss in his foot that the doctors said could cause him to walk with a limp the rest of his life. The bullet to his shoulder had fractured his clavicle, but as with the shot to his leg, the doctor explained that it had missed the subclavian artery, which could have killed him. It had nicked a lung, collapsing it, and the doctors were concerned about pneumonia, particularly if Sloane did not get up and start walking soon.

His surgeon told Sloane he was lucky to be alive.

Jenkins knew Sloane didn't feel that way.

"DO YOU NEED anything for the pain?"

Sloane opened his eyes and looked to his friend, who remained in the chair by the bed. He shook his head. There was no point; his physical pain paled in comparison to the ache in his heart. Sloane had never felt such anguish—a sharp pain that caused him to double over in agony with each recollection, each memory.

● ● ●

THE REAL ESTATE agent had called early on a Saturday morning.

"I have the house for you," she had said.

Sloane was pessimistic. He had told the woman he wanted to live on the water, as he had in Pacifica, where he found the sound of the waves comforting. The agent had interpreted that desire to mean Sloane wanted one of the luxurious homes on Lake Washington, along with their matching price tags and her commission. But that was not what he and Tina had been looking for, though neither could express exactly what it was they sought.

"The owner just passed away," the agent explained as they descended the winding road into Three Tree Point. "He and his wife raised their family here. They lived in the home for fifty-two years."

When they turned the corner she stopped the car so they could gaze at the back of the white clapboard home. It had not been spruced up to sell. It needed a paint job and a new roof. Sloane looked to Tina and could tell she too had a good feeling. That feeling increased when the agent unlocked the door and they stepped inside. This was not a house that came ready made. It was not a monument to wealth and success. It had been functional, serving a purpose, a home for a family that had watched television together and ate meals at the dining room table. The children had slept in the rooms upstairs and bounded down the stairs in their socks and pajamas. They had fought and played and left nicks and scars on the hardwood floors and walls. One of the windows in the kitchen had been pierced by an errant BB, and several tiles on the counter had cracked.

Sloane knew instantly this was what he wanted and why the others had not been suitable. He didn't want a house. He wanted a home.

Tina stood on the enclosed porch, looking out the plate glass windows at the Puget Sound. Jake had already rushed to the water's edge, skipping stones across the surface.

When Sloane joined her she rested her head on his shoulder.
"I think we're home," she had said.

SLOANE HAD NOT seen or spoken with Jake since the night of the shootings. When he tried to call, Bill Larsen told him Jake was seeing a child psychiatrist to deal with his trauma and that the psychiatrist had recommended against Sloane and Jake speaking. Then he hung up. Subsequent attempts by Sloane had been no less productive, and the Larsens had stopped answering the phone. Sloane was in no condition, physically or geographically, to force the issue. He missed Jake terribly, but that battle would come soon enough. He could only imagine what the Larsens had told Jake.

Jenkins walked into the room carrying a white bag and a cup of coffee in one hand and a stack of cards in the other. "How're you feeling?"

Sloane shrugged.

"I brought you a bagel." He held out the bag, but when Sloane did not take it Jenkins set it on the tray beside the bed.

"What did the doctor say?"

Sloane had asked Jenkins to find out when he could leave the hospital. His leg was no longer in a cast and they had him up doing physical therapy. He suffered through it because he knew it was the only way they would consent to release him.

"A few more days." Jenkins sat and sipped his coffee. "People are asking about a service."

"I'll hold a service when I get my son back. I'm not doing it without Jake. Did you call the cemetery?"

Jenkins nodded. "It takes about six weeks."

Tina had wanted to redo the kitchen countertops in a blue marble, but that would never happen. Sloane had been given no say in the Larsens holding his wife's funeral and burying her ashes, but he would not allow them to choose her headstone. He wanted something that would stand out from the traditional gray and black, as Tina had stood out in life. He wanted her to have her blue marble. Jenkins had handled the arrangements.

Jenkins handed him the stack of sympathy cards. Sloane put them on the windowsill with the other unopened envelopes. "There's one more card," he said. Sloane looked, but Jenkins's hands were empty. "He wanted to deliver it in person."

Sloane shook his head, uninterested in visitors, but Jenkins was already moving toward the hospital room door. Before Sloane could protest further, Jenkins had departed and Detective Tom Molia stepped into the room.

Sloane smiled at the familiar face. Tears welled in his eyes. "Tom."

Molia walked in and handed Sloane a card, then bent and hugged him. Four years earlier the West Virginia police detective had helped Sloane track down the men responsible for killing his mother, but not before they had endured an ordeal together. The experience had bonded them, and the two men had stayed in contact despite living on opposite sides of the country. Sloane still kept the photograph of Molia's green Chevy—on which the detective had written *Does not have air-conditioning*—beneath a magnet on his refrigerator door.

Molia did not try to hide his emotions. Tears rolled down his cheeks. "You know us Italians," he said stepping back. "We're criers."

"How did you get here?" Sloane asked, knowing that Molia feared flying.

"I drove. It was time to come out and spend some time with my mother in Oakland," he said. "I brought Maggie and the kids with me."

"You drove the Chevy?"

"In this heat, without air-conditioning, are you kidding? Maggie would divorce me."

The detective pulled up a chair and sat. "I heard about it on the news and called. Charlie filled me in. I thought I'd give you some time. I'm so sorry, David. I'm so damn sorry."

Sloane nodded. What was there to say?

"I ran some checks through the normal channels and asked a friend at the FBI for a favor, but I didn't find anything useful. Without a name or a fingerprint, something . . ."

Sloane shook his head. "I appreciate the effort."

"I also ran a check on the company, Kendall Toys, and the guy, Malcolm Fitzgerald. Both came up clean too. Not even the hint of cheating on their taxes. And I put out an APB for Kyle Horgan, but so far nothing."

Charles Jenkins's research had also revealed nothing on Horgan's whereabouts. There was no activity on his bank account and no record of a credit card. Horgan had never gone back to his apartment and Sloane had to presume that the young man was dead, his body someplace where it would never be found.

"I just wish I had something for you," Molia said.

The two men spent an hour together then Molia stood. "I better let you get some rest," he said. "If there's anything I can do, you call me, you understand."

"I know. Thanks, Tom. It means a lot to me."

"You just promise me one thing. When you do find this guy, I want to be there."

SLOANE SLEPT MUCH of the afternoon, but it had been fitful, filled with images of Tina in a cream-colored wedding dress, standing on the lawn at Three Tree Point. She slipped the gold ring onto Sloane's finger, her face radiant, her eyes focused only on him as the minister asked her to repeat her wedding vows. But as she started to speak blood trickled from the corner of her mouth, a small dribble that increased in volume until she began to choke on her words and blood spewed down her chin and the front of her dress. Sloane awoke in a start, gasping, his hospital gown drenched in sweat.

Charles Jenkins sat in the chair beside the bed, reading glasses on the bridge of his nose and a book in his lap but his focus was on Sloane. Sloane took a moment to catch his breath.

"The detectives are back," Jenkins said. "The doctor told them you could talk if you feel up to it. I've already sent them away a few times. This time they decided to wait."

Sloane knew he could not put off the meeting forever. "Let's get it over with."

When Jenkins returned, a man and a woman dressed in suits followed him. The man, somewhat overweight, introduced himself as Detective Spinelli. The woman was his partner, Detective Adams.

Spinelli thanked Sloane for taking the time to talk to them and offered his condolences. He spoke from behind a neatly trimmed mustache. Heavy, with jowls, he reminded Sloane of a walrus.

The detective opened an envelope and handed Sloane black-and-white photographs. When he considered them, Sloane felt an adrenaline rush that caused his jaws to clench. Though the images were grainy, the face was clear enough, one that Sloane would never forget.

"You recognize him?" Spinelli asked.

Sloane put the first picture behind the stack and went through the others, studying the face, trying to commit each distinct feature to memory.

"Yeah," he said. "That's the guy."

"You're sure, take your time."

"I don't have to take my time, detective. That's him. Who is he?"

"We don't know." Spinelli reached for the photographs.

Sloane put a hand to his throat. "Could I have a glass of water?"

Spinelli turned and picked up a plastic pitcher from the tray beside the bed and motioned to Adams to grab him a cup from the counter. She was a good foot shorter than her partner and further dwarfed by Jenkins. Spinelli filled the cup and handed it to Sloane, who exchanged it for the envelope of photographs.

"Where did you get the photographs?" Sloane asked.

"Do you know a Kyle Horgan, Mr. Sloane?"

The question caught Sloane off guard. "Not personally. He came to my office building one morning but I didn't have time to talk to him. Why?"

"Was that the only time you met him?"

"I didn't meet with him. I had just finished a trial in superior court and I was hurrying because the clerk called to say the jury was back. Judge Rudolph isn't the patient type."

The two detectives shared a look and a grin. "We've been there. Rudolph used to be on the criminal calendar. He's a ball-buster for punctuality. You'd never met Mr. Horgan before he came to your building?"

"No."

"Did you ever see or talk to him again?"

Sloane suspected where the conversation was headed, and it raised another question. "Are you investigating my wife's murder?"

Spinelli shook his head. "No, Mr. Sloane, that's being handled by the King County Sheriff's Office."

"I don't understand."

"We're with the Seattle Police Department. Could you answer my question?"

"No, I never saw him again. But I did go to his apartment building in Pioneer Square." Sloane wanted to ask if they had found Horgan's body somewhere, but that would only make the detectives question why Sloane thought Horgan could have been the subject of foul play.

"Why did you go to his apartment?"

"When he came to see me, Mr. Horgan said that a doctor I had just tried the case against wasn't responsible for the death of a young boy. He said he was."

"*He* meaning Horgan?"

"That's right."

"So you did talk to him."

"That was the extent of our conversation."

"What did you take that to mean?"

"No idea. I guess I initially thought he was crazy."

"So why then go to his apartment?"

Sloane took a moment. "Because he said it with such conviction and it was such a random comment for someone to make that I thought it best to give him a chance to explain himself."

"But he wasn't there."

"No, he wasn't."

"Did you speak to anyone else while you were there?"

"The building manager."

"What did he tell you?"

"He said he hadn't seen Mr. Horgan in a week."

"How long did you and the manager talk?"

"Not long. A few minutes. Listen, detective, what is it you want to know?" Sloane knew the connection but did his best to play it out. "Where did you get the photographs and what relationship does that man have to Kyle Horgan?"

"The photographs were taken from a hidden video camera at Mr. Horgan's apartment building. It seems the owner was having trouble with burglaries, people stealing tenant mail. He installed the camera about a year ago. You were also on the tape."

Spinelli did not tell Sloane they thought the man was responsible for the building manager's death but Sloane already knew that.

"I don't understand. What was he doing at the building?"

"We don't know. We thought you might."

Sloane shook his head.

"You don't know anything more about him, what business he might have had at that building?"

Sloane shook his head. "What did Mr. Horgan say?"

"We don't know. We haven't found him yet."

"He's missing?"

"Appears that way."

"Do you know anything more about this man, his name, anything?"

Sloane knew the detectives could run a person's name, fingerprints, DNA, or picture through a crime lab to determine whether there was any match with records stored in the system. He also knew from his conversation with Tom Molia that the man who killed Tina was not in that system, further confirming the man was a professional killer, not a random criminal.

"Not yet," Spinnelli said. "But we'll keep you posted."

Spinelli handed Sloane a business card. "If you think of anything else . . ."

Sloane took the card and waited until the two detectives had excused themselves and exited the room. Then he sat up and disconnected the IV drip from his arm.

"What are you doing?" Jenkins asked.

"Getting out of here."

"The doctor won't release you. He said another few days."

Sloane pulled out the photograph from beneath the covers, the one he had slipped there when the detective turned to get him a glass of water. Part of his sense of helplessness had been not knowing who the man was, or having any way to find out. Now they had a chance, and that was all the motivation he needed to get better.

He handed Jenkins the photograph. "Find him for me, Charlie, whatever it takes."

"Why not let the police know? Tell them what you know; maybe they can find him."

Sloane pulled the clear tape off his arm. "He's not in their system or they wouldn't have been here asking me questions. If I tell them I think there's a connection between this man and Horgan and Fitzgerald, they'll question Fitzgerald, and that will only make him more guarded before I can get to him. I want Fitzgerald to think he got away with this. I want him to make a mistake." Sloane pointed to the photograph. "Just like he made a mistake. And I'm going to make him pay for it, just like I said."

Jenkins nodded.

"But first I'm going to get my son back."

MONTGOMERY STREET
FINANCIAL DISTRICT
SAN FRANCISCO, CALIFORNIA

THE DOCTORS HAD strongly recommended against Sloane leaving the hospital, but he could not be deterred, just as Jenkins could not be deterred from accompanying Sloane to San Francisco. Sloane had wanted to surprise the Larsens, but Jenkins had convinced him to call ahead.

"Jake's been through enough," he said. "The last thing he needs to see is a confrontation between you and his grandparents."

Sloane compromised by calling Frank Carter, Jake's biological father. The two men had always had a cordial relationship, though Carter seemed uncomfortable around Sloane, which could have been due to any number of reasons, not the least of which was that Carter had never fulfilled his financial or emotional obligations as Jake's father. Sloane sensed Carter to be even more sheepish than normal during their conversation, but he said he would try to arrange a meeting with the Larsens. It took more than an hour before Carter called back. When he did, he provided Sloane with a Montgomery Street address that turned out to be not far from the Transamerica Pyramid building in the heart of San Francisco's financial district.

Inside the building lobby, Sloane confirmed the address to be an attorney's office, the suite occupied by the Law Offices of Harper, Peters, and Cominos. Sloane stepped from the elevator into a modest reception area with dated furnishings and uninspiring prints hanging on the walls. He didn't have to give his name to the receptionist; he could see Bill and Terri Larsen sitting at a conference table in a glass-walled room just behind the desk. Frank Carter had positioned himself at the opposite end of the table, and Sloane wondered if that was symbolic. At the head of the table sat a man in a button-down shirt, bow tie, and suit jacket who Sloane guessed to be either Harper, Peters, or Cominos.

Leaning on his cane and already beginning to feel exhausted, Sloane limped into the conference room, bringing the conversation to an abrupt halt.

He addressed his in-laws. "Bill, Terri." Neither responded. "Frank."

Frank Carter nodded. "Hi, David."

The suit approached, hand outstretched. "Mr. Sloane, I'm Jeff Harper. Thank you for coming. Can I get you a cup of coffee or glass of water?"

Sloane declined.

Harper had a high-pitched voice and a ring of gray hair on an otherwise bald head. Sloane estimated him to be in his midsixties, about the same age as the Larsens, and probably either their personal attorney or a family friend. The man's breath had an acidic odor Sloane associated with nerves. He'd smelled it before on attorneys during trials. Harper likely spent the majority of his time behind a desk and not litigating in the courtroom.

"Why don't we all take a seat," Harper said, though only he and Sloane stood.

Sloane sat opposite the Larsens. Harper returned to the head of the table.

"We have some things to talk about," Harper said.

Maybe it was the throbbing pain in his leg and shoulder, but Sloane had already tired of the charade. "I don't know you, Mr. Harper. We don't have anything to talk about." He looked across the table. "You can't talk to me directly, Bill? Terri?"

The Larsens could barely raise their eyes from the mahogany tabletop. When they did, their focus found Harper.

"My clients would prefer that all communication go through me."

Sloane sat back. "Fine."

"As you know, the deceased set up a trust and placed funds in that trust for the well-being of Jake."

When Sloane and Tina married, she had a modest savings account and the equity from the sale of her flat in the Sunset District of San Francisco, real estate she had purchased with the financial help of her parents. When she sold it, Sloane encouraged her to place the funds in a trust for Jake, to be distributed in installments at various points in his life.

"I'm aware of that."

"And you are the executor."

"I am."

Harper handed Sloane a document, which he quickly identified as a personal note. "Tina obtained the money for the down payment for her San Francisco flat from her parents. This is a note requiring that she repay those funds."

Sloane couldn't hide the smirk. "You want the money back," he said.

The Larsens did not answer.

"Legally—" Harper began.

"I'm aware of the legal significance of the note, Mr. Harper. I'll write your clients a check within twenty-four hours."

"There was accrued interest," Harper said.

"I'll pay it all: interest, penalties, whatever you want. Send me an accounting."

Harper glanced at the Larsens, as if uncertain what to say but pleased by the result. He paused and cleared his throat before moving onto the next subject. "The deceased also had a last will and testament in which she expressed her desire that should any-thing happen to her, you would receive custody of and care for Jake."

Sloane did not like Harper's tone, which included an unspo-ken "but . . ." Something was wrong. "That's correct. We were in the process of completing adoption papers when . . . when this happened."

Bill and Terri Larsen raised their eyes and looked at him.

"But the fact is, Mr. Sloane, you did not legally adopt Jake, correct?"

"Are you cross-examining me, Mr. Harper?"

"I'm simply—"

"I just told you, Tina and I . . . and Jake, for that matter, agreed that I would adopt him." Sloane looked to the end of the table. "Frank, we talked to you about this. You agreed."

Now it was Frank Carter's turn to divert his eyes.

"What is this about?" Sloane said. "What's going on here?"

Harper cleared his throat but his voice quivered. "Legally, you do not have custody of Jake."

Sloane leaned forward, palms pressed on the wood. "Legally? Are you kidding me? As compared to whom, a man who abandoned his son when he was three?"

Harper leaned back, creating distance. "The parents were divorced. The mother obtained custody of the child and moved to Seattle. The father did not abandon the boy; he was given visitation rights."

"Which he never exercised," Sloane interjected, "even during all the years they lived here in San Francisco. Frank, what the hell is this?"

"To the contrary, he provided the child with birthday gifts—"

Sloane banged a fist on the table. Harper flinched. So did Bill and Terri Larsen.

"The boy's name is Jake. The 'parent' or 'deceased' was my wife. Her name was Tina. So do not refer to them again as if they were some hypothetical in a law school class, Mr. Harper. And do not insult me by trying to tell me how involved Frank was in Jake's life. I know exactly how involved he was; I lived with Jake for the past two years, and before that I worked with his mother for ten. So don't try to paint a picture of a doting father. I know better." Sloane turned. "So do you, Frank."

"There is no need for hostility, Mr. Sloane."

"Maybe not for you, but I've put up with just about all I'm going to put up with." Sloane directed his comment to the Larsens.

"Mr. Sloane, I asked you to direct—"

"I don't care what you asked me to do." He looked at Bill Larsen. "I tolerated your keeping Jake from me because I was in no condition to see him or to take care of him. I tolerated your cremating Tina and burying her without me. But I am not going to tolerate having a lawyer patronize me with legal jargon and a warped perception of reality."

"Wait a minute, Mr. Sloane. If—"

"We are discussing the well-being of a thirteen-year-old boy who just lost his mother. The last thing he needs is to have his life further disrupted by removing him from his home and placing him in a strange house, in a strange city, away from his friends and school and everything left in his life that provides him stability."

"We are all here in the best interests of the child . . . of Jake," Harper said.

"If we all had Jake's best interests at heart we wouldn't be having this discussion. Jake belongs with me; everyone in this room knows that."

"Legally, custody remains with Mr. Carter, his biological father."

"Did anyone talk to Jake about this? Did anyone ask him what he wanted?"

The silence was telling.

"He wants to live with me, doesn't he?"

"I don't think a thirteen-year-old boy can judge what is best for him," Harper said.

"How would you know? How many times have you talked to Jake? How many minutes, total, have you spent with him?" Harper did not respond. "I made him a promise. I made Tina a promise that if anything ever happened to her, I would take care of Jake."

"Well, you got your wish didn't you?" Terri Larsen spat the words at him, nostrils flared and eyes rimmed red by anger. "You couldn't even protect her. You couldn't protect my daughter, my baby. All of your celebrity and television appearances . . . all it did was bring the crazies into my daughter's life. You couldn't protect her. How are you going to protect Jake? Who's going to watch him while you're flying all over the country to mug for TV? Who's going to protect him when another one of the crazies comes to kill you? When the crazy who killed her comes back? You're responsible for her death." She sobbed. "You killed her. You killed my baby."

Bill Larsen put an arm around his wife's shoulder.

"I told him we were a family," Sloane said, almost slipping and telling them about Tina's pregnancy but recognizing it would only be cruel.

Terri Larsen flung her husband's arm off her shoulder. "Family? What would you know about family?"

"Jake loves me."

"Jake thinks you're the reason his mother is dead."

Bill Larsen pulled back his wife, and this time she allowed him, swiveling her chair to the side, away from Sloane.

"That's not true," Sloane said, feeling a cramp in his chest. "You're just saying that because you're in pain and you want to hurt me. You want to hurt me? Fine, go ahead, hurt me. Say anything you want to me, but don't hurt Jake; don't do something that is going to hurt him more than he's already been hurt. Maybe I don't know family the way you do. But I know what it's like to lose a mother. I lost everything; they took everything from me. They put me in a home with people I didn't know; people who didn't love me or care about me. All they cared about was the monthly check. I don't want that for Jake."

"Jake is not going to a home where no one loves him," Harper said. "He's going to live with his father."

Sloane would have laughed if he had thought Harper was joking, but the expression on the man's face indicated that he was serious. Sloane looked to Frank Carter. "You can't honestly think that it is in Jake's best interests to live with you."

Frank did not answer.

"Frank?"

"Jake's my son, David. I know I haven't been the best father, but I want a chance."

Maybe it was his comment about his foster parents and the monthly check, but suddenly Sloane put the pieces together, why the Larsens would seek to execute on the personal note when the money had already been placed in a trust for Jake.

"My God," he said. "They're paying you. They're paying you to take Jake." Nobody answered, their silence damning. "What kind of people are you?"

"There's no need for insults," Harper said.

"This is an insult," Sloane said. "It's an insult to me and it's an insult to Jake. And I'm not going to allow it. I won't let you buy your grandson. I'll seek custody. And I will win."

"You have no legal—" Harper said.

Sloane lifted himself from his chair, palms flat on the table. "I don't give a good goddamn what kind of legal basis you think I have. I will get Jake. And I guarantee this—it won't be you who stops me. Check it out, Mr. Harper. I usually win, and I've never been more motivated to win in my life."

No one answered.

"Where is he? I want to talk to my son."

"If you attempt to contact Jake my clients are prepared to take legal action—"

Sloane snapped, seeing only black. He stumbled forward on his bad leg and grabbed Harper by the lapels, lifting him from his seat. "Where is Jake?" Someone bear-hugged him from behind.

"David, don't."

Sloane swung an elbow, striking Frank Carter in the ribs and causing him to fall backward, toppling one of the conference room chairs on his way to the floor. Bill and Terri Larsen had retreated from the table to a corner near the windows, Bill using his body to shield his cowering wife.

Sloane pointed a finger at them, breathing heavily, feeling spent. "I would have been willing to work with you. Even after the way you've treated me, I would have done it, for Tina and for Jake. Not now. Not ever."

THE ART INSTITUTE
GEORGETOWN, WASHINGTON, D.C.

ANNE LEROY LOOKED up from her easel, initially thinking the hissing came from the old radiator at the front of the
room before realizing the insanity of a radiator being on this time
of year.

"Psssst."

Peggy Seeley stood in the hall outside the classroom door.
When LeRoy made eye contact, Seeley gave her a stern expression
and motioned her to the door, as if she held an urgent secret.

LeRoy sneaked a glance at the instructor standing at the front
of the room, hoping she hadn't heard or seen Seeley, but the
woman's frown indicated otherwise. She was clearly perturbed by
the intrusion. The instructor emphasized the need to maintain a
serene atmosphere to foster artistic creativity, playing soft classi-
cal music "to entice the inner artist." LeRoy wasn't convinced the
music was to inspire the students as much as it was to drown out
the drone of the fans used to disperse the nauseating paint odor.

Stuck between a disapproving frown and a stern expression,
LeRoy reluctantly rested her paintbrush on her easel and wiped
her hands on a rag. Though she stepped softly to the door, some
of the students exhaled and rolled their eyes, as if she had blown
a bugle. LeRoy had taken the class thinking it might be fun while
she sought employment, but that was quickly dispelled by the instructor's serious demeanor and the other students' self-indulgent
attitudes. From what LeRoy had been able to discern over the past
weeks, none were going to be the next Picasso or Rembrandt, but
God forbid she be the one to tell them.

She stepped into the hallway and spoke in a hushed voice.
"What are you doing here?"

"I need to talk to you," Seeley said, also whispering.

"I gathered that. Can it wait? Why didn't you call?"

"Your cell is off."

"Because I'm in class," she said.

"Well, I'm sorry but it's important. Payne came to my cubicle today."

"So?" LeRoy hadn't given Payne much thought since the day she left. "What did he want?"

"Oh nothing, he just asked how I was doing and wanted to make sure I was happy."

"You came here to tell me that?"

"No. What do you think he wanted? He knows you down-loaded the report on magnets."

"What?" LeRoy's raised voice drew the attention of several students closest to the door. She pulled Seeley farther down the hall. "How?"

"Probably when he had someone from IT check your computer," Seeley said.

LeRoy paced the drab white hallway, battered lockers on one side for students. "Have you ever heard of them doing that before?"

"No. But I also don't care. I don't want to get fired. I can't afford to get fired."

"Why would *you* get fired?"

She raised her voice again. "Because he obviously must think I'm a part of this, otherwise he wouldn't have told me to tell you that he wants the report back."

"Okay, okay, take it easy." LeRoy sighed, trying to think. "What if I just get rid of it? What if I just tell him I threw it out?"

"No," Seeley said, emphatic.

The art teacher stuck her head out the door. "Are we disturbing you?" she asked.

"I'm sorry," LeRoy said. "It's a family matter." She pulled Seeley still farther down the hall as the teacher shut the door to the room.

"That's exactly what you can't do," Seeley continued. "Payne said you had to return it."

"Why? I'll just tell him I never had it. How can he prove it?"

Seeley looked about to scream. "Hello! Have you been listening to anything I've said? The IT guys know you downloaded the file, that means Payne knows you have it. You can't just throw it out. You have to give it back."

"So how would he know that I didn't just copy it again?"

"Anne, are you looking to get in trouble?"

LeRoy groaned, frustrated. "Fine, I'll give the damn thing back. I hadn't even given it any thought since I left. But if you ask me, there's something else going on here, and he's pissing me off."

"Like what?"

"I don't know." She thought further. "But why is he so interested in a report that he told me not to finish? He pulled the funding; it isn't going anywhere. So why is he making such a big deal about it?"

"I don't know and I don't care," Seeley said. "All I know is I don't like being in the middle of it."

"Well, I'm sorry I ever gave you the memory stick, okay?"

"So, you're going to give it back, right?"

LeRoy scratched the top of her head, thinking.

"Anne?"

CHAPTER
SIX

Already barely hanging on, Sloane knew the thread holding him upright would snap if he lost Jake. He had initially refused to get on a plane back to Seattle, wanting to at least try to find Jake, which provoked a confrontation with Jenkins outside the building.

"We have no idea where he is, and even if we did, it won't do Jake any good to be part of a confrontation between you and his grandparents or his father."

"I'm his father."

"Then act like it. Do what's in the best interests of your son. You'll have your day in court. Until then, the last time I checked, taking a child by force across state lines would be a federal offense."

"He's my son. Jake will go willingly."

"Not legally, he isn't, and the Larsens will tell the police you kidnapped him."

It all added to Sloane's mounting frustration. Despite all the rational evidence that he had been more of a father to Jake than

Frank Carter had ever been, he knew it would be an uphill battle to gain custody of a child from his biological father. The law did not want parents to negotiate their legal and moral obligations to their children. So even though Tina's express wishes were for Sloane to take the boy, her will could not trump Frank Carter's legal right and obligation, especially if Carter sought custody. The court would be hard-pressed not to give him that opportunity. Sloane had also not helped his cause with his outburst; the Larsens would use it to obtain the temporary restraining order to which their attorney had alluded, prohibiting Sloane from initiating any contact with them, Frank Carter, or Jake. They would say Sloane was mentally unbalanced, that Tina's death had caused a breakdown, that he was too unstable to raise a young boy.

Maybe they weren't far from the truth.

As Jenkins drove from the Seattle-Tacoma Airport garage he instinctively followed the exit signs toward Burien but must have realized what Sloane had already come to know.

"Where to?"

Sloane had no idea. He knew only he could not go back to Three Tree Point. It was no longer his home or a place of comfort and warmth. The happy memories he and Tina and Jake had shared there had been shattered, replaced by one horrific nightmare.

"We'll go to Camano," Jenkins offered. "We have more room than I know what to do with."

Sloane declined. Jenkins and Alex had their own life with a new son, and while Sloane was happy for them, he feared the daily reminders of what he would never have would only make him bitter.

"Take me downtown."

"Alex understands, David."

"I know she does, but I need some time," he said.

"David—"

"Damn it, Charlie, just do what I ask, will you, please."

They drove the freeway in silence. When they reached downtown Seattle, Jenkins steered the car to the curb on Sixth Street and stopped just outside the front entrance to the Washington Athletic Club, which included a hotel with workout facilities and a restaurant. The club was within walking distance of Sloane's office. Sixth Street was deserted, enveloped in darkness but for the dull glow of the streetlamps.

"You want me to come in?" Jenkins asked.

"No. Go home to your wife and son."

"We're all hurting, you know. Alex loved Tina too. You don't have to go through this alone."

Sloane knew his friend meant well, but he also knew Jenkins was wrong. No one could go through this with him. He had to endure this pain alone.

He reached for the door handle. "I appreciate everything you've done."

Jenkins touched his shoulder, causing Sloane to stop, though he did not turn back.

"I know you don't want to hear this now, but I'm going to tell you anyway, as your friend."

Sloane didn't want to hear it, not from Jenkins or anyone else, but Charlie had earned the right to say what he had to say when he sat in the hospital room and bore the burden of delivering the news that Tina was dead. Sloane would listen, not because there was anything Jenkins could say to help him, but out of respect for their friendship.

He took his hand off the door handle but kept his gaze fixed out the windshield.

"When you leave the Nam they don't put you in a decompression chamber and wean you off the jungle the way they wean junkies off dope, but they should," Jenkins said, "because

Nam gets in your veins just as bad. It gets in and it won't let you go. But we didn't have that back then—detox and counseling. One minute I'm walking through foot-sucking muck, sweating my ass off in a rice paddy, wondering where the sniper is waiting to kill me, and the next I'm on a public bus on the streets of New Jersey."

That got Sloane's attention.

"They wouldn't even give my mother the day off to pick me up. How do you like that? And I'll tell you this. I was scared a lot over there but never as much as those last few hours waiting to step aboard the Big Bird to Paradise. I didn't close my eyes until the pilot said we were leaving Vietnam airspace, and even then I couldn't sleep. It seemed surreal, to actually be going home, because I had resigned myself to the fact that I never would. When I got there I used the key hidden under the ceramic cat to unlock the door. I didn't even have to think about it. It was still there. I just walked in and dropped my duffel bag in the front hall, made a sandwich, and lay on the couch, watching the news and smoking a cigarette. Next thing I knew I was choking on smoke. I'd finally fallen asleep, exhausted, and the cigarette had fallen on one of my mother's crocheted throw pillows. 'God Bless This Home.' I survived thirteen months over there and nearly burned to death on my mother's couch."

Sloane wasn't sure where his friend was going with the story, but he let him continue.

"My point is, it seemed as if nothing had changed," he said. "Nothing, except me. I went back to the same place, but it no longer felt like home and I no longer felt like I belonged there." Jenkins let out a breath. "I slept on the floor because I couldn't get comfortable in a bed. I kept beer in a cabinet because I couldn't drink it unless it was warm." He shook his head. "For the longest time over there I hadn't cared if I lived or died, because for the longest time nobody else cared either. I was just another grunt who was going home in a body bag. It was easier that way, not caring, not making plans, but then God went and played a cruel joke on me."

Sloane waited.

"He let me live." Jenkins shook his head. "For so long I felt so guilty knowing that so many of my brothers over there died. I mean, why me? Why did I get to go home and not them? I kept seeing all their faces. It got so bad one afternoon I pulled out my dad's revolver, loaded a bullet, and spun the chamber."

Sloane looked over at his friend, but now Jenkins had looked away.

"I never told anyone this, not even Alex. I made a deal with God right then and there. And I put that gun to my head and pulled the trigger."

"Jesus, Charlie."

"Yeah, I know. But you know what, I got my answer. I found out why I was alive."

"So what was the answer?"

A thin smile of irony creased his lips. "Dumb, blind luck." He shrugged. "It was just dumb, blind luck. It wasn't God who kept me alive. The bullets just missed me and hit someone else. After that I realized that I didn't have to feel guilty because it wasn't anything I'd done. It was just the luck of the draw, like spinning that chamber. Once I had accepted that, I could settle in to living again. I could move on. So when two guys showed up out of the blue and gave me a second chance with the CIA, I took it. I had a reason for getting up in the morning, a purpose. When I went to Mexico City everything seemed right with the world again."

Jenkins shook his head with a look of disgust. Sloane knew what was to come.

"Then I stumbled into that village in the mountains, your village, and saw the carnage, and I was right back in Nam again. I'd gone full circle to a place that made no sense and where I didn't want to be. And I couldn't deal with it. I couldn't go through it, not again. So I checked out and went to live on an island. The next thing I knew I'd lost thirty years of my life. I didn't deserve a third chance, David. I'd already had two, which was two more than my brothers in Nam got. But then Alex showed up. God knows I didn't deserve her, but she came into my life just the same."

Jenkins squeezed his arm.

"Don't do what I did. Don't lose thirty years of your life. Tina wouldn't want that. She loved you too much to see you suffer. There's another chance out there for you."

At the moment, Sloane didn't believe that to be true.

Jenkins's voice cracked with emotion. "I'm not going to insult you by telling you that I can imagine your pain, because I can't. And I'm not going to preach to you. I'm just telling you that if you go and live alone on an island you won't find any answers. You'll just find yourself alone. Don't go to that island."

The silence lingered. Sloane pulled the handle and pushed open the door, stepping out. He leaned back inside the car. "Get me what I asked for, and maybe I won't have to."

SLOANE FELT THE walls closing around him as soon as he entered his room on the twentieth floor and couldn't stand the thought of being confined. Leaving, he wandered the streets without destination or purpose, everything a blur, foreign, surreal, and inconsequential. At one point he found himself limping down the cobbled road of the Pike Place Market, the outdoor booths shuttered closed, the street deserted and quiet. He looked up at the arched windows of Matt's, which had been one of their favorite restaurants, and could still see her.

•   •   •

TINA STOOD BESIDE the table, gorgeous in a sleeveless white dress that hugged the curves of her body and accentuated the sheen of her dark hair and tanned skin. The arched window framed her like a portrait, and the red glow of the three-story neon sign outside it, PUBLIC MARKET CENTER *and its famous clock, bathed her in a soft crimson. This time she had outdone herself; the flowers he had purchased in the market no longer seemed worthy of her beauty.*

They kissed warmly, unconcerned about those seated nearby. When their lips parted neither pulled away and Tina's smile became an impish grin. "You're drooling, Mr. Sloane."

"New dress?"

"Do you like?"

Sloane's smile broadened.

Tina placed her elbows on the table and leaned across, whispering, "We could just skip dinner and go to our room." She opened her hand and dangled a hotel key from her finger.

But before Sloane could throw a glass of cold water in his face, or rush from the restaurant dragging Tina by the arm, the waiter appeared at the table with a bottle of wine and two glasses. He showed Tina the label.

"I'm sure it's fine," she said.

Neither spoke as the waiter opened the bottle and poured. When he had departed, Tina raised her glass. "Cheers."

Sloane laughed. "Not fair, Mrs. Sloane. This is not fair."

The summer night was warm enough that the multipane window, which pivoted in the middle, had been pushed open to allow a light breeze.

"Are we celebrating anything in particular?" Sloane asked.

"Do we need a reason to celebrate?"

"No. But I don't want to get in trouble for missing an anniversary or anything."

"In that case we're celebrating our eleven-month anniversary," she said. "And the fact that next week we'll be moving into our first home together."

"And our last home," Sloane said. "I don't plan on doing this again, so just cremate me and put my ashes on the mantel."

"Well we won't have to worry about those kinds of decisions for many, many years, will we?"

THE PAIN SHOT up and down his leg, nerve endings regenerating. Sloane turned his gaze from the window and walked to a railing overlooking the Alaska Freeway, taking a moment to rest. The lights from a passing ferry boat and the windows of homes on Bainbridge Island shimmered on the pitch-black water of Elliott Bay. Lying in a hospital bed for three weeks, Sloane had realized his life had come full circle—once again an orphan, but this time without a child's naïveté to blindly assume that everything would be all right, that his only option was to get up each morning and put one foot ahead of the other. The harsh reality of life had stolen that child's naïveté bit by bit. You realize there can be no Santa Claus, no matter how much you wish it were so, because it is simply impossible for one man to visit every house on the planet in one night. And you realize that you aren't going to become president of the United States, or walk on the moon, or become a famous Hollywood actor. You realize you are like 99.9 percent of the rest of the world, just a cog in the wheel trying to make some sense of where you belong in the incomprehensible grand design of it all. And you realize that people you trust are going to disappoint you, friends will come and go, and those you love will die.

Sloane had met people who coped with life's harsh reality by believing everything to be a part of God's divine plan, but Sloane had never found that comfort. He was not a religious man; he was no longer certain he even believed in a God. What kind of a God would take Tina?

Others found their peace in the families they cultivated, the children they nurtured, seeing in them the hope they once had for themselves. Tina and Jake had given Sloane a purpose in life. They had given him a reason to live. They had restored a bit of that lost naïveté. But now her death had plunged him back into the dark and harsh reality, and he had no idea what to do, how to cope, how to exist.

Turning from the railing, he steeled himself for the walk back to the Athletic Club, his leg throbbing, at times so bad he had to stop and look again for a taxi, seeing none. When he reached his hotel he collapsed in a chair by the window, uncertain how long he had been away. He felt even further adrift, alone and lost. He stared out at the lights of the downtown office buildings, wondering again how he was to go on, and saw his answer.

He slipped his jacket back on, swallowed two ibuprofen, and walked one block up Sixth Street to the only place that still had meaning, where he still had a purpose. The security guard dutifully checked his identification and unlocked the elevator in the lobby. On the twenty-fourth floor Sloane entered the six-digit code on the keypad on the wall, pulled open the security door, and stepped inside. He did not turn on the overhead lights, choosing instead to stand at the window in darkness, searching again until he found the man framed in the rectangular pane of one of those thousands of windows, seated at his desk, still working, alone.

It was how Sloane had survived all those years in San Francisco, working, allowing the hours to pass one at a time.

He pulled the chain on the antique desk lamp he rarely used, opened the McFarland and Gallegos files, and did what he did best, what he would need to do again to survive.

He went to work.

CHAPTER SEVEN

J ohn Kannin did a double take when he walked past Sloane's office the following morning, then stopped and peered in, as if seeing a ghost.

"What the hell are you doing here?"

"Working," Sloane said.

Kannin walked in and closed the door behind him. Though they were roughly the same age, Kannin had become a mentor for Sloane, perhaps because their relationship began with Sloane hiring Kannin as a consultant on military law, or because Kannin had run his own law practice for nearly twenty years before the two men agreed to become law partners.

"You're not even supposed to be out of the hospital until the end of the week. Get the hell out of here before I carry you out."

Sloane had no doubt the man could do it. A lineman when he played football for the Air Force Academy, Kannin had traded bulk for muscle. Sloane had lifted weights at the underground, windowless gym Kannin preferred to the swanky health clubs, so he knew Kannin was country strong.

"When's the last time you slept?" Kannin asked.

"I'm fine."

"You don't look fine. You need rest. You need time."

"Time is all I have, John."

Carolyn pushed open the door, nearly hitting Kannin with the edge.

"Good. I'm glad you're here. Will you please tell him to go home and get some rest," Kannin said.

Carolyn placed a cup of coffee on a coaster beside Sloane's computer screen, picked up the cassette tapes from the out-box on his desk, and continued like it was business as usual. Carolyn had never married, and Sloane suspected she knew exactly why he was at work.

As Carolyn departed Pendergrass rapped on the door and poked his head in. Looking from Sloane to Kannin, he asked, "Should I come back?"

"No," Sloane said. "Come on in."

Shaking his head, Kannin started to leave.

"John, this involves you too," Sloane said.

They settled into chairs at the round table near the plate glass windows. Sloane turned first to Pendergrass. "I want you to find out what I need to do to get custody of Jake."

Both Kannin and Pendergrass gave him perplexed looks.

"I just dictated a memo that Carolyn will give you shortly. Tina's parents have taken Jake to San Francisco. They want his biological father to raise him." He stared down Pendergrass. "I want my son back. Do whatever needs to be done to make that happen."

Pendergrass nodded. "I'll get right on it."

Sloane had never had the opportunity to tell Kannin or Pendergrass about his trip to Mossylog or his meetings with Manny Gallegos and Dayron Moore. After filling them in that morning, he handed Pendergrass the Gallegos file. "There isn't much there. But look into having the settlement agreement set aside for fraud in the inducement, misrepresentation, anything else you can think of."

He spent the next ten minutes explaining the results of Mateo Gallegos's autopsy report.

"Magnets?" Kannin asked.

"Apparently they are so powerful they link together through the intestinal walls. When they pinch together they cut off the blood supply to the area and eventually the intestine dies and the magnets corrode through, allowing bacteria to leak into the body cavity. It causes a toxic condition called peritonitis and sepsis."

"This child in Mossylog suffered similar symptoms?"

"High fevers, vomiting, chills, a lack of appetite, listlessness. Like Austin, eventually he lost consciousness."

"And his father confirmed the family had one of these Metamorphis dolls?" Kannin asked.

"Robots," Sloane corrected. "Gallegos works at the Kendall factory in town. They gave him one of the toys as a reward for being a good employee and paid the family fifty dollars to have their son Ricky play with it. Gallegos said his son flipped over it, but also that the plastic cracked, which would have freed the magnets."

"But we don't know that for certain."

"No, we don't, but it is exactly what Kyle Horgan warned about."

"And you think that's what Kendall doesn't want anyone to know?" Pendergrass asked. "That the plastic is defective?"

"There's a tremendous amount of money at stake, and based upon what I've been reading in the paper, Kendall can't afford to have anything go wrong."

Sloane had spent much of the night thinking through possible

scenarios and explained his theory that, at Dee Stroud's suggestion, Kyle Horgan had likely approached Malcolm Fitzgerald with
the toy and how, upon seeing it, or at least its design, Fitzgerald
must have realized that Horgan was sitting on the next "It" toy.

"Everything would have been fine until Horgan warned about
the defective plastic."

"And then when Mateo Gallegos died, Horgan became a huge
problem," Kannin said.

"Which hit a head when Horgan gave me the file. That's why
the man came. He wanted the file."

They sat listening to the hum of the computer beneath
Sloane's desk, no one wanting to relive what had happened next.

Kannin's dark eyes narrowed. "Do the police know about this,
David?"

"Without some evidence linking Fitzgerald to Horgan, I can't
link Horgan to the man who killed Tina."

"You're that link," Kannin said. "You have to tell them."

Sloane shook his head. "If I tell the police they'll go to Fitzgerald, and he'll simply deny everything as absurd. Without the file
I don't have anything to prove what relationship, if any, Horgan
and Fitzgerald had. Unless Charlie can find Horgan, and I think
we have to realistically conclude he never will, we have no way to
prove there was one."

"That's not for you to decide. You have a man out there that
has killed three people," Kannin said.

Sloane stood. "You don't think I know that?" He caught himself. "Look, John, this man is not an indiscriminate killer; he kills
the people he's paid to kill. The police are not going to catch him."

"So what do you propose we do?" Kannin asked.

"We do what we do best. We get Kendall Toys and Malcolm
Fitzgerald into a courtroom and put so much financial pressure on
the company that it will have to act."

Kannin shook his head. "How are you going to get them into a courtroom? You don't even have a plaintiff." He spoke to Pendergrass. "Unless this guy Moore was in collusion with Kendall, which would be next to impossible to prove, we won't get the settlement set aside."

"Did Moore give you any reason for settling so cheap?" Pendergrass asked.

To the contrary, when Sloane had accompanied Moore back to his office to retrieve the Gallegos file, Moore had defended his settlement. "He said the child could have died from the rusted nail, that they had no proof the magnets came from the Metamorphis toy. The family no longer had it, and since it was a prototype he had no ability to get one like it."

"He didn't even try?" Kannin asked.

Sloane shook his head. "He wasn't looking for a fight. I think he was afraid of the law firm."

"Who is it?" Kannin asked.

"Reid Matheson."

Kannin smirked. "He probably felt like Custer at Little Big Horn; he'd have been outnumbered five hundred to one."

"He never even filed a lawsuit," Pendergrass said, flipping through the file. "To settle that case for fifty thousand dollars without doing any discovery at all was criminal."

"Not if he couldn't prove the magnets came from the toy," Kannin said. "So we're right back to the same problem, no plaintiff."

Sloane paused. "Maybe not."

Kannin leaned forward. "The McFarlands? Come on, David, that case is over; a judgment's been entered. And other than that not-so-small legal hurdle, we don't even know whether the McFarlands ever came in contact with the toy. This is all just speculation."

"But if I can place the toy in both homes, with the boys suffering the same medical symptoms, then you'd agree that I have something, right?"

"Yeah, you'd have something, but again, the case is over. Have you even talked to them about any of this?"

Sloane shook his head. The McFarlands had left town for a vacation after the trial, and he had been in no condition to talk to them since.

Pendergrass stood from his chair and gathered his papers. "I'll run a search and see if I can find any other articles on any other kids dying or being hospitalized with flulike symptoms during the past four months. Who knows, maybe there's another one out there. And I'll see if there are any complaints about Kendall in general or about this particular toy."

"I don't mean to be the one always throwing cold water here," Kannin interjected, "but even if you can place the toy in the Mc-Farland home you still have to prove Austin ingested magnets. Until we know that, we're just spinning our wheels. And . . ." Kannin hesitated. They all knew there was only one way to find out. "Are you really sure you want to go down that road? Austin is dead, David. Nothing we do will change that. Do you want to run that family back through this?"

Sloane had thought about the implications of pursuing the matter and he didn't want Pendergrass or Kannin to think he was involving them or the two families in a personal crusade.

"I'm not going to sit here and tell you this isn't personal," he said. "It is for me, but not for you. For you it's a legal case. This company may be responsible for the deaths of two young boys, and if this toy gets mass-marketed, it could be a danger to millions of other children. I know we can't bring back Mateo Gallegos, or Austin McFarland, but don't we have a responsibility to try to save at least one more family from the grief and agony of having to bury their child? Don't we have an obligation to go after a company that would do something like this?" Sloane looked to Pendergrass. "And if I'm right, Dr. Douvalidis didn't deserve this. He wasn't responsible."

Pendergrass looked pale.

"Hey, you're preaching to the choir," Kannin interjected, breaking the tension. "But we're not the ones you have to convince. Even if you're right and you can somehow get the Gallegos settlement thrown out, you already obtained a judgment in the McFarland case. It's over."

"I think that could actually help us," Sloane said, one step ahead after a night mulling through the legal hurdles.

As Sloane explained his plan, Kannin sat back, smiling. When Sloane had finished Kannin said, "I don't know if it will work, but it's going to kick up one hell of a lot of dust."

Sloane stood. "Tom, see if you can find any precedent for it. I'll be back in a few hours."

"You want me to go with you?" Pendergrass asked.

Sloane shook his head. He would handle it alone.

GALAXY TOYS' HEADQUARTERS
PHOENIX, ARIZONA

WITH THE AMOUNT of stress in her life she should have had the figure of a freaking model, but Maxine Bolelli had spent all her life battling her weight, which was why she sat in her private dining room atop Two Arizona Center staring at bird-sized portions of grilled chicken, broccoli, and brown rice. Bolelli hadn't eaten a bite.

She pushed back from the table and walked to the windows, looking south to the duel spires of St. Mary's Basilica with its red tile roof. In 1987, Pope John Paul II visited the 130-year-old mission-style church and elevated it to a minor basilica. Two blocks over on Fifth were cathedrals of another kind, Chase Field, home to the Arizona Diamondbacks baseball team, and near it, U.S. Airways Center, where the Phoenix Suns played basketball. Galaxy kept a corporate suite at each facility and had its corporate name plastered inside nearly every civic facility in Phoenix. The expenditure was necessary advertising, but Bolelli wanted to retch each month when she saw the amount spent to keep the Galaxy name front and center in the community.

She turned from the window at the sound of Brandon Craft striding into the dining room. Craft had the smile of a kid bringing home an A on his report card.

"It's an action figure."

Bolelli rolled her eyes. "I assumed it was an action figure. Kendall makes action figures." Her tone conveyed what she did not verbally express: *Idiot.*

"There's more," Craft said, recovering from the initial blow. "It's an action figure the child builds on his own, using plastic pieces, anything they can imagine."

"I'm impressed, but not much."

"The figure can morph into other shapes the child chooses."

"Been there, done that."

"Not by remote control."

"That's not technically possible."

"Apparently it is."

"How?"

"Magnets." Craft sat, smiling again.

"Tell me."

"High-powered magnets act in concert after receiving an electrical pulse." Craft sounded giddy. "Can you imagine the potential? A child can design and create an action figure to his own specifications, whatever he wants, and then program it to change into whatever else he can imagine and build, a boat, plane, tank, helicopter. When he gets bored, he changes it. It transcends age limits. Hell, there are adults out there who would want one. Apparently the focus groups were off the charts."

Bolelli stepped forward. "Focus groups? How far along are they?"

"Already in production, and"—Craft paused for dramatic effect—"I'm told they're having the manufacturing done at a factory in China."

"China? Kendall doesn't use Chinese manufacturers."

"Apparently they do now," Craft said.

"Can we find out which one?"

"I already have somebody working on it."

"Why would Fitzgerald go to the trouble of using a Chinese manufacturer?"

"They're in financial trouble. They need to cut manufacturing costs or implement huge layoffs," Craft suggested.

Bolelli shook her head. "Sebastian Kendall has always been a hard nut to crack. I don't see him going to China for financial reasons."

"Maybe not, but Fitzgerald is the new regime."

"No. Not yet. Not with the old man still alive. This goes against everything Kendall has professed to stand for. Fitzgerald wouldn't do this unless he was concerned about something." She paced. "He's trying to keep this completely under wraps; he sent it overseas so no one would find out."

"He's hiding it?"

She stopped, turned. "Wouldn't you? Think about it. He keeps it completely under wraps and launches it right for Christmas. He'll create a run at the stores, like when Tickle Me Elmo came out of the blue. It will be the toy of the season."

"It *is* amazing," Craft said.

"Need I remind you, Brandon, that it is not our toy?"

The smile vanished.

"So where did it come from?" Bolelli asked.

"No one knows. No one recalls seeing anything like it in New York or Germany," Craft said, referring to the two biggest annual toy fairs. "Maybe Kendall's in-house design team came up with it."

"If that were the case then why didn't Santoro tell you about it?"

Bolelli knew Craft and Santoro had been talking since Galaxy first approached Kendall with an offer to buy the company. Not believing she'd get far with Fitzgerald, who had a perverse sense of loyalty to Sebastian Kendall, Bolelli had sought an advocate inside the company and didn't have to go far. Santoro was disgruntled after Kendall passed him over in favor of Fitzgerald. Since Santoro and Fitzgerald were roughly the same age, Santoro's prospects of ever running that company were slim at best. That meant he'd be looking for another opportunity, or more money. Not wanting a paper trail leading back to her, Bolelli arranged for Craft to attend a trade industry conference she knew Santoro was attending. Craft came back with his chest puffed, as if he were the next James Bond, advising that "someone" at Kendall was unhappy with his situation, might be looking for greener pastures, and with a little persuasion, might just be willing to provide Galaxy with inside information on a company Bolelli coveted. Bolelli had played along, telling Craft to pursue it. Once she had acquired Kendall she'd fire both Craft and Santoro. She knew from personal experience that if a man cheated once, he'd cheat again, and no one was ever going to cheat on her again. Besides, what could Craft or Santoro do, sue and have the information about their clandestine meetings come out in public? They'd never get another job.

"He said he didn't know about it until Fitzgerald broke it out at a board meeting. No one on the board had ever seen or heard of such an idea."

"Which means Fitzgerald must have suspected someone was leaking information and is keeping everything about this toy very close to the vest. That's why it's being produced in China." She thought for a moment. "That board meeting was weeks ago. Why didn't Santoro tell you about this sooner?"

Craft opened his mouth as if to speak, but instead his face twisted, as if considering a complex mathematics problem.

"He's getting cold feet," Bolelli said, starting to pace again. "If this thing is as good as projected, Kendall's revenues will go through the roof, and so will their stock. Santoro could sell and be worth three to four times what he'd get in salary here. He's playing you, Brandon." Before Craft could respond Bolelli changed gears. "Have you discussed the concept with our design people? Can we duplicate it?"

"They say it can't be done."

"Well, tell them someone has already done it, damn it." Bolelli stopped pacing. "Oh shit!"

"What?"

"Titan. If Ian gets wind of this he'll be on it like stink on shit. Why the hell did we go public with our offer?"

"I tried—"

"Kendall will need help with distribution and getting retailers to agree to prime shelf space right out of the gate. Damn it! Fitzgerald and Ian are probably already working on it together."

"What do you want to do?" Craft asked.

At the end of the table Bolelli gripped the back of a chair. "Start buying more Kendall stock."

"It will drive the price up even higher," Craft said, alarmed. "It's already inflated. We could create a feeding frenzy."

"What do you think will happen when this thing hits the store shelves?"

"How high do you want to go? We've already depleted most of our cash reserves."

"I don't care. Overpay if you have to. I want as much control over Fitzgerald as I can leverage. If he partners with anyone, it will be Galaxy, not Titan, and if he doesn't, we'll still stand to make a shitload when this thing hits the stores."

EMERALD PINES DEVELOPMENT
KENT, WASHINGTON

HIS STOMACH CHURNING, Sloane drove past the rock wall with silver letters identifying the development as Emerald Pines. It seemed every development built since the 1970s identified itself as if it were an exclusive gated community, but there was no gate at the entrance, and the homes were modest and unmemorable—between two and four thousand square feet with wood siding, trim, and wraparound porches. The developer had broken the uniformity by flipping the floor plans, placing the garage of some of the homes to the left of the front door rather than the right.

As Sloane stepped from the car his foot sank into the saturated thick lawn separating the curb from the sidewalk, the moisture seeping through his leather shoe and dampening his sock. A broken sprinkler head bubbled water, flooding the area. He pulled free his shoe and approached the house. The garage door was up, revealing a Toyota Camry beside an empty space for a second car. Michael McFarland had kept his job as a machinist at Boeing, but Eva, who had been employed at a local Costco, had been unable to work since Austin's death. Bicycles hung from hooks in the ceiling, and sporting equipment and household supplies filled storage racks. To the right the front door was beneath a pitched porch with a skylight that offered natural lighting.

Eva McFarland answered the door looking like she had recently put on makeup and tried to comb her hair before giving up and pulling it back in a clip.

"David," she said, trying not to sound rushed though he obviously had not given her enough advance warning. "Come on in."

"I better take off my shoes," he said. "Looks like you have a broken sprinkler."

She looked past him to the sidewalk. "The gardener runs over them with the lawn mower. Mike is not going to be happy."

He slipped off his shoes and left them on the porch. The tile entry was slick in his socks, and he felt a bit like a beginner ice-skater feeling his way, but the rubber stopper on the end of the cane gave him security as Eva led him toward the back of the house.

"I was just starting the wash," she said, slipping a hard *r* into the word, as was the case with some native Washingtonians.

As with her own appearance, the rooms showed signs that someone had tried to tidy quickly: a single tennis shoe stranded in the hall, dishes in the sink, bread crumbs on the tile counter. Eva tossed a brown stuffed rabbit onto a pile of toys overflowing from a toy box in a corner of the family room off the kitchen.

"The dog likes to use it as a chew toy," she said.

As if on cue, a small dog barked and scratched at the sliding glass door leading to a fenced-in backyard. More toys lay strewn on a rounded cement patio and lawn, along with a baseball contraption of some sort, a ball hanging at the end of a tethered string staked in the ground. Though the sun was out, the room faced north and was well shaded.

Eva turned off CNN. "I was tracking that storm in the Gulf.

Mike has relatives in Texas. They say they're going to lose every-thing."

"I'm sorry to hear that."

She crossed her arms, as if cold. "You don't really lose it if you can rebuild it or replace it. I look around the house now at all these things that were once so important, and, well, now I just see a bunch of stuff." She seemed to catch herself. "I'm so sorry about your wife, David. When we heard about it we just couldn't believe it. How horrible. I don't know what to say." And as if to empha-size the point they stood in an awkward silence. "We sent a card."

"I appreciate it," he said. "Thank you." Carolyn had placed the card on his chair that morning so he would have time to read it in case the subject came up.

"Can I get you anything, coffee?"

"No, I'm fine."

Another awkward pause.

"Please, sit down," she said.

Sloane sat on a leather sofa as Eva retrieved the newspaper from a matching chair and set it on a wood coffee table next to a *People* magazine, *US*, and *Sports Illustrated*. The room held the burnt smell of a recent fire in the fireplace. Eva continued to ask him the perfunctory questions, whether the police had arrested anyone and how he was doing recovering from his injuries. Sloane answered her questions patiently until, with nothing left to dis-cuss, she got to the reason for his visit.

"You said on the phone you wanted to talk about something about the case." Sloane heard the hesitation in her voice. "They're not going to appeal, are they?"

"No, they can't do that," Sloane said. "They've already paid the judgment."

"Thank God." She exhaled in relief.

Sloane hadn't known Eva McFarland before the death of

her son, but he had seen photographs. Whereas at one time she would have been considered perhaps ten pounds overweight, she was now rail thin, though she did not have the healthy, toned appearance of someone who had exercised and dieted to lose the weight. Despite the family's recent vacation Eva continued to look gaunt and pale and had dark circles beneath her eyes. Sloane wondered how many hours a night she slept, and how often her nightmares woke her.

"I wanted to ask you a few questions about something that has come up."

Her brow furrowed.

"It's actually about Mathew," he said, referring to their older son.

"Mathew? I don't understand."

"Was he ever part of a group of kids chosen to evaluate a toy made by Kendall Toys?"

"What?"

"Was he ever asked to play with a Kendall toy and tell them what he thought of it?"

Eva folded her hands in her lap and looked to the darkened television. "I'm sorry. Things are still a bit hazy. What is this about?"

Sloane took out a crude sketch he had made from memory and showed it to her. "The toy was an action figure called Metamorphis."

Eva considered the diagram and, after a moment, displayed the beginnings of a smile. "You know, I think I do remember this."

Sloane's pulse quickened.

Her smile widened. "Yeah. I do remember this. Mathew would take that thing all through the house yelling, 'Metamorphis,' and make it change. I think it became a boat, or an airplane or something. I can't remember."

Sloane tried not to sound impatient. "How did he get the toy, do you recall?"

Her nose scrunched. "I think it was through a friend of a friend type of thing. Mathew's best friend's father has a relative . . . someone who works at Kendall. I don't know, but they were looking for a few boys. I remember because Mathew couldn't tell his friends at school anything about the toy, or let them see it. And I seem to recall that we had to sign a document that said we wouldn't divulge anything about it— as if I were about to run out and talk to all my friends about a toy."

"You didn't keep a copy of that document, did you?"

"If I did, I've long since thrown it out. There's enough clutter around here without adding to it." Her head tilted. "How do you know about this?"

Sloane had debated whether it was best to tell Eva about the Gallegos family or let her read the articles. He decided that the articles would be too painful.

"How long did Mathew play with it?"

"A few days, maybe a week. Like I said, I don't really recall all the details."

"Did he have to go anywhere and be observed playing with it, or to answer any questions?"

She closed her eyes and rubbed her forehead. "I have a vague memory of something like that, a Saturday—I remember because Mike had to take him pretty early in the morning. He said it was a warehouse in the middle of nowhere. You'll have to ask Mike. Mathew was happy, though. I remember they paid him some-thing."

"Was it by check?"

"I assume, but I really don't know."

"What did Mathew think of the toy?"

"He loved it," she said without hesitation. Then she leaned forward, hands on knees, eyes narrowing. "But how do you know about this?" she asked again. "Why is this important?"

"I'm sorry. I don't mean to be cryptic. I had someone come and talk to me about the toy. He designed it."

"Okay."

"He gave me a file with some drawings and an article . . . an article about another boy in Southern Washington."

Eva's eyebrows knitted closer together.

"The boy died a few days before Austin."

She pulled back.

"He lived in a town with a Kendall manufacturing plant and his brother was also given one of the same toys to play with. The boy came down with flulike symptoms: high fever, vomiting, listless."

Eva covered her mouth with her hand.

"The parents didn't take him to the doctor right away because they're here in the country illegally. By the time they did the boy had slipped into a coma."

Tears pooled then overflowed the corners of her eyes, running down her cheeks. "What are you saying?"

"Did you ever notice any pieces of the toy around the house, anything at all?"

"You think Austin choked?"

Sloane shook his head. "No. Small black pieces, tiny rectangles."

She shook her head.

"The toy operates through the use of dozens of tiny, powerful magnets."

"No, nothing like that," she said.

"If the plastic cracks the magnets can become free, and if a child swallows more than one, the magnets will attract each other inside the intestines. With time the intestine starts to die in that area, and it can perforate. If that happens, bacteria can get in and poison the bloodstream and organs."

"No. Nothing like that," she said again. Then, "This other boy, he had . . . they found magnets in his body?"

"They did an autopsy; the medical examiner found six magnets."

Eva rubbed her face with both hands, mumbling. "Oh my God. Oh my God. This is a nightmare. This is such a nightmare." She looked at Sloane, wringing her hands. "You think the same thing happened to Austin, don't you? That's why you're here."

"The symptoms are remarkably similar. If the same toy was in the house . . ."

She raised her voice, upset. "Why haven't we heard anything about this before? Why wasn't it on the news?"

"The father works for Kendall. He was afraid of losing his job. The attorney they hired settled the matter out of court, without litigation."

"Can he do that? Isn't there some obligation to let someone know about it?"

"Only a moral one, I'm afraid."

She stood abruptly, turning away, one hand at the small of her back, the other alternately rubbing her forehead and the back of her neck.

"I'm sorry, Eva. I know this is hard."

"I thought this was over. I thought maybe we could . . ." She choked back tears. "At least try to have some semblance of a normal life, if not for Mike and me, then for the kids."

"If I'm right, Eva, Dr. Douvalidis is not responsible for Austin's death."

She closed her eyes, softly uttering, "God damn it. God damn it!"

Sloane couldn't think of any easy way to say what had to be said. "There's really only one way to find out for cert—"

"No!" She opened her eyes and put up her hands a foot apart, just below her chin, staring him down, emphasizing each word. "No. Do not even suggest it."

"Eva, it's not just about Dr. Douvalidis. The other children in that focus group had the same reaction to the toy as Mathew. They loved it. It's already in production. Millions will be in stores . . ."

She shook her head as Sloane spoke. "No. No, no, no."

" . . . for the holiday season, and those toys will be brought home to houses with children as young or younger than Austin—"

"No!" she yelled, cutting him off. Tears streamed down her cheeks, leaving a black trail of mascara. Her hands, clenched claws, looked as if she were strangling someone. "You can't ask me to do this. You can't ask me to dig up my son and have someone cut him open. I won't do that. I won't do that to him."

"I know it's difficult—"

"Don't you dare sit there and presume to know how I feel. Don't you do it! Do you know how many people have presumed to know how I feel? How many have offered their condolences and then left my house and gone right back to their lives? They don't know how I feel. They don't have a clue. They get to go home every day and see their babies sit across from them at the dinner table instead of an empty chair. They help them with their homework, see their naked little bodies get into their pajamas at night, kiss them, hear their soft little voices, angels." She wiped the moisture from her cheeks on her jeans. "Get out."

Sloane gathered his things. "I'm sorry," he said.

He got to the doorway leading to the hall before she spoke again.

"Could you?"

The question stopped him, but Sloane did not look back.

"Could you do what you're asking me to do?"

GEORGE BUSH CENTER FOR INTELLIGENCE
LANGLEY, VIRGINIA

THE BROWN SIGN with white lettering hidden amid the tree branches and foliage indicated he was nearing the George Bush Center for Intelligence. That sign had not existed the last time Charles Jenkins had been to the facility, George Bush Sr. having not yet been president. Jenkins suspected that more than one late-night comedian had recently used the words on that sign as the punch line to a joke.

Jenkins turned off the main road and soon thereafter approached a guard booth with a yellow metal gate extended across the road. In case a visitor still missed the point, a sign warned that he was entering a restricted government facility and overhead bubbles recorded every car coming and going. He slowed and lowered the window to speak into a box.

"Can I help you?" a male voice asked.

"I'm here to see Curley Wade?" Jenkins was about to correct himself; Wade's real name was Edward, but Jenkins had never known anyone to use it. Neither, apparently, did the faceless voice.

"Your name?"

"Charles Jenkins."

"Stand by for a second."

After a minute the voice directed Jenkins to drive through strategically placed barricades designed to prevent a vehicle from getting up a head of steam as it approached the entrance. He parked next to a white concrete barrier, and proceeded to a nearby building to obtain a visitor's pass.

Inside the building, uniformed guards sat behind what Jenkins assumed to be bulletproof glass. Jenkins provided his name and the nature of his business. One of the guards instructed that no photographs were to be taken on the property and directed Jenkins to lock his cell phone in a small locker in the lobby. That was also not a requirement the last time he had been at the facility, since cell phones were still only seen on the *Star Trek* television series. He clipped a visitor's pass to the lapel of his navy blue sport coat, and the guard advised him to take a seat in the waiting area for Wade's assistant to escort him onto the facility. At least that hadn't changed. Employees parked in lots a safe distance from the building and were shuttled to the campus.

Jenkins listened to the hum of vending machines while considering the assortment of magazines on the coffee table, and it struck him that he could have been waiting in any dentist's office in America instead of one of the government's most highly classified facilities. It served as a further reminder that much had changed in the thirty years he had been away.

AFTER RETURNING HOME from his tour in Nam, Jenkins had spent much of the next couple of months sleeping late, drinking beer with neighborhood friends, and ignoring his mother's inquiries about when he might find a job. When he got bored he put on his green army jacket and walked the streets or frequented questionable bars, hoping someone would say something derogatory. No one did. The military had transformed his body from soft body fat to ropelike muscle. At six five and 250 pounds with a scowl and an attitude, no one with a brain even looked in his direction.

One afternoon a knock on the front door awoke him from a nap on the couch, and Jenkins found two men in dark suits with crew cuts standing on the porch.

"Wasting your time, fellas, I don't believe in God."

The men shot each other a sideways glance. The shorter of the two did the talking. "We'd like to talk to you about being of further service to your country."

Military recruiters.

Jenkins started to laugh. "I was stupid enough to enlist once. I'm not stupid enough to do it again."

But they had not come to ask him to reenlist. They had another proposition for him, and it was quickly apparent they had already combed through his background.

"I don't think so," Jenkins said.

"Is that because you have so many other job offers rolling in?"

Jenkins stepped out onto the porch, sat in one of the wicker chairs, and lit up a cigarette, another bad habit he picked up in Nam. He blew smoke in the air and considered the Ford parked at the curb. "I'm on sabbatical."

"How long have you been home?"

"Not long enough."

"So are you going to just keep going out looking for fights in bars the rest of your life until someone puts a knife or bullet in you?"

Jenkins shrugged. "Just spent thirteen months in the jungle asking myself that same question. How come you weren't interested then?"

The stocky man nudged his partner. "Forget it. Davidson was wrong." The two men started from the porch.

Jenkins stood. "Major Davidson?"

Major Davidson had shown up in the jungle with Jenkins's Special Forces outfit. Everyone knew Davidson was CIA, though he never admitted it, and in between killing time and mosquitoes, Davidson and Jenkins had talked about things like what Jenkins intended to do when he left the jungle. Jenkins hadn't given it much thought, seeing no point, since he didn't believe he would leave,

not alive anyway. Davidson had seemed particularly interested in
the fact that Jenkins spoke fluent Spanish, but then he disappeared.

"I thought he was dead."

The stockier man handed Jenkins a business card, just a name
and a phone number. "When you're ready to stop doing the poor
veteran act and feeling sorry for yourself, call that number."

Jenkins threw the card in the waste can and grabbed a beer
from the refrigerator, but later he retrieved it and taped it to the
mirror in his bathroom. For a solid week he considered it each day
and night. He figured they wanted him for Cuba. With his dark
complexion, wiry hair, and a little work on the dialect, he could
pass as a native.

"MR. JENKINS?"

Curley Wade's assistant was an attractive brunette. She took
him by shuttle to the front of the building, which, with its cement
overhang and absolutely no redeeming architectural qualities, had
also not changed.

Like it or not, Jenkins was back.

KENDALL TOYS' CORPORATE HEADQUARTERS
RENTON, WASHINGTON

DURING THE WEEKS since leaving the hospital, Sloane
had forced himself to keep busy. He moved from one task to the
next, trying his best to keep his mind occupied, and had been seeing a physical therapist to strengthen his leg and shoulder. The
woman damn near killed him in the first visits, but he had worked
hard to rebuild his strength and stamina. He'd need both when the
time came.

Back inside the car, he turned his focus from reality to perception; what people perceived to be true was often more important than the truth. Malcolm Fitzgerald and Kendall Toys would not know that the McFarlands had refused Sloane's request, and like Sloane, they could not guarantee what a court would do with the Gallegos settlement. If Sloane was going to bluff and try to get Kendall to react, there was no time like the present.

As anticipated, Malcolm Fitzgerald's assistant was curt and protective on the phone. "What is this about?" she had asked.

"Tell Mr. Fitzgerald it's about Metamorphis," Sloane said and, after leaving his cell phone number, hung up.

The woman had called him back within minutes to advise that Fitzgerald would meet with him immediately.

Sloane had expected a high-rise facade of glass and steel, but Kendall's corporate headquarters resembled an industrial complex. As with the factory in Mossylog, the first thing Sloane encountered was a gated entrance with a guard shack. Because the guard did not find Sloane's name on an approved list of visitors he had to make a telephone call to confirm the appointment. Hanging up the phone, he asked to see Sloane's driver's license, wrote down the license plate of the car, provided Sloane a parking pass for the windshield, and directed him where to park. As Sloane drove through he saw a white placard attached to the fence in his rearview mirror urging departing employees to

KEEP KENDALL SECRETS SECRET
AND KENDALL'S TOYS
WILL REMAIN KENDALL'S

Inside a marbled lobby, near the bank of elevators, another guard sat behind a console and again requested Sloane's driver's license. Though he was tempted to say something like "I'm here to kidnap Sergeant Smash," Sloane had the impression it would provoke the same result as yelling "I have a gun in my bag" when passing through airport security.

The guard typed Sloane's name into a computer and handed him a visitor's badge, which Sloane peeled and stuck to his shirt pocket as the guard made a call. Hanging up, the guard advised that someone would be down to escort him into the building.

The wait would do Sloane good. He could feel the adrenaline pulsing through his body from the anticipated encounter with Malcolm Fitzgerald and he told himself that he could not lose his temper. Any chance of success depended upon Fitzgerald buying into Sloane's bluff. He walked about the lobby, a museum depicting the history of the company and its more famous toys. Inside a thick Plexiglas case stood an original eleven-inch-tall Captain Courageous action figure. The accompanying placard explained that Kendall first introduced Captain Courageous in 1934, well before Sloane's time, but since he recognized the name, it was likely one of the "It" toys Dee Stroud had talked about. Other versions of the doll, taller, more muscular, some dressed in camouflage, others in Hawaiian shirts and shorts, documented Captain Courageous's evolution through the years. In the glass case beside the toy, a similar display documented the evolution of Sergeant Smash from his introduction in 1966 during the height of the Vietnam War, to the present day.

Moving along, Sloane read placards mounted on the wall next to blown-up photographs of Constantine and Aristotle Kendall. The placards told the story of how the two brothers had immigrated to the United States with less than fifty cents, but with a love of toys. A grainy black-and-white photograph showed them at work in their toy booth in downtown Seattle, and others documented the subsequent moves to new buildings as well as the ascension of the son, Sebastian Kendall Senior, and grandson, Sebastian Junior. Junior had reigned the longest as chairman of the board and CEO. The date of the end of his reign had not even been engraved on his placard, but next to his picture hung the smiling portrait of his successor, Malcolm Fitzgerald. Fitzgerald had boyish features and sandy blond hair, but his sideburns, two blocks of gray, indicated he was in his midforties.

Though Sloane had seen pictures of the man while researching the company, something about the portrait, hung in the lobby of a heavily guarded building, made Sloane's hands clench in fists. In a dark blue jacket, white shirt, and light blue tie, Fitzgerald looked like a cocky and arrogant executive, someone who believed himself to be omnipotent, bulletproof.

That was about to change.

Sloane took a deep breath and again told himself that he had to play this out, that he couldn't allow his anger to cloud his judgment. If he did, Tina would have died in vain. He wasn't about to let that happen.

"Mr. Sloane?"

The young woman who escorted him to the elevator bank either had very little personality or had been instructed not to say much. Either way her reluctance to speak made for a silent elevator ride. Stepping from the car, the woman used an electronic card to access closed and locked doors as she led Sloane through several hallways. On their journey Sloane noticed two large vaults with television cameras mounted overhead. Glancing into open offices, he noted the same dark tinted glass as in the lobby, and shredders atop garbage cans. The precautions made him recall Dee Stroud's admonition about the prevalent threat of ideas being stolen. Kendall obviously took that threat very seriously.

The woman led Sloane into a conference room where Malcolm Fitzgerald stood near the windows. Sloane felt his entire body tense. The knuckles of his hand atop his cane turned white. When Fitzgerald extended his hand it was all Sloane could do not to drop his cane and grab the man around the throat. But that day of reckoning would come soon enough.

They migrated to chairs at a long table: the polished top of which reflected overhead recessed lights. Windows afforded a view of the south end of Lake Washington, shaped like a horse-shoe with Mercer Island in the center and spotted by tiny sails and the wakes of speedboats.

The pleasantries did not last long.

"You indicated you wished to discuss a Kendall toy in production," Fitzgerald said, not naming the toy.

"Is it in production?" Sloane asked.

Fitzgerald slid a piece of paper across the table along with a pen. "If that is the case, I will need you to execute an agreement that anything discussed today is confidential."

Sloane left the document and the pen on the table and maintained eye contact with Fitzgerald. "Given that I already know about Metamorphis, that it is in production, and that it has been the subject of at least two focus groups, I don't think it's very confidential."

Fitzgerald too kept a poker face. "Nevertheless, we won't have this meeting without a signed agreement."

Fitzgerald was posing as the alpha dog, pissing on trees; Sloane wasn't about to cede him the campground. "Then I guess we'll both read about it in the newspapers."

"And you should know that we will treat the dissemination of any proprietary information very seriously."

"You might, but I don't think a court will," Sloane said. "So let's stop with the threats and try to make this a productive meeting. I'm willing to agree that nothing you say in this room today is an admission of liability in any case I may file against Kendall."

Though Fitzgerald expressed no outward concern at the mention of a lawsuit, Sloane knew that the mere possibility of litigation, especially on the eve of what all signs indicated would be the biggest toy launch in Kendall history, was making him uncomfortable. Fitzgerald folded his hands on the table but looked like a man fighting the urge to scratch an itch.

"Do I have your word?" Fitzgerald asked.

"I just gave it."

Fitzgerald sat back. "Then I'm here to listen."

Beneath the table Sloane's hand continued to squeeze the cane handle. Fitzgerald was as arrogant as his picture depicted. "I know Kendall recently used focus groups to test a toy called Metamorphis."

"And how would you know that?"

"Pay attention. It will become apparent. I also know that Kyle Horgan, the designer of that toy, advised your company that he was concerned about the integrity of the plastic being manufactured in China, that it did not meet ASTM standards, that it was cheap, and that it had the potential to crack. He was concerned that if that occurred, it could release powerful magnets inside the plastic."

Fitzgerald did not react.

"Two families from Kendall focus groups, the Gallegos and McFarlands, had young boys in their homes. Both suffered high fevers, nausea, vomiting, diarrhea, and dehydration. Both died after slipping into comas. The medical examiner found six magnets inside Mateo Gallegos that perforated his intestines and allowed toxic bacteria to poison his body and ultimately caused his death."

Fitzgerald continued to play poker. "And you can prove these magnets came from some Kendall toy."

"I'll do one better, Mr. Fitzgerald. I'll prove they came from *a specific* Kendall toy, Metamorphis."

Fitzgerald unfolded his hands. "Your evidence, if it were accurate, would be circumstantial, at best."

"I'm not sure a jury would see it that way. I've been known to convince juries of many things."

"Would the McFarlands be the parents of the young boy on whose behalf you recently prosecuted a medical malpractice action against the boy's pediatrician?"

It was a good blow. Sloane struggled to deflect it. "They would."

"So we can conclude you weren't convinced by this circumstantial evidence."

"I obtained the evidence after the trial."

"And what evidence would that be?"

"A letter written by the toy's designer advising Kendall of the problems with the plastic."

Fitzgerald's eyebrows arched. "Do you have a copy of this letter?"

"Not with me."

"But you'd be willing to provide it?"

Sloane shrugged. "It would certainly be subject to a document request in litigation."

"Anything else?" Fitzgerald asked.

"I don't think I need more, but if you'd like me to depose you and your officers and directors I can arrange for that."

"I've been deposed, Mr. Sloane," Fitzgerald said with a shrug intended to convey that he was not concerned. "I'll tell you now what I would tell you under oath and save us both the time. I have no idea what you are talking about. Metamorphis was designed in-house here at Kendall. There was no independent toy designer, and I'm unfamiliar with any memorandum or letter such as the one you're describing."

Now it was Sloane's turn to shrug. "A court can sort that out as well, I guess," he said, inferring from Fitzgerald's explanation what he had suspected: Fitzgerald had likely stolen Horgan's design, which was why it became imperative that the man retrieve Horgan's file and prevent anyone from using it to prove Horgan had designed the toy.

"I'm sure it can. And we will prove that the toy in question has been product tested and meets all applicable government and industry regulations. Kendall has been in the toy business for more than a hundred years—"

"—I took the tour downstairs after I crossed the moat," Sloane said.

Fitzgerald gave Sloane a patronizing smile. "Then you know that Kendall has not stayed in business for more than a hundred years by putting dangerous products into the marketplace or ignoring legitimate concerns regarding one of our toys. Kendall complies with all federal regulations, and the toy of which you speak has received approval from the Product Safety Agency."

"But not from the man who designed it."

"The man who designed it works in Kendall's product development department."

"Then he stole the design."

"Can you prove that?" Fitzgerald asked.

"As I said, ask around. I've been known to prove a lot of things. Can you afford the bad publicity when I do?"

"Kendall's reputation is impeccable. The safety of children has always been Kendall's primary concern, which is why Kendall has never had a toy recalled, and why no toy has ever left the Kendall warehouse, and none ever will, that has not been tested and found to be completely safe for children."

"Yet you settled the Gallegos matter for fifty thousand dollars."

In their game of chicken, Fitzgerald blinked first. "That is a confidential settlement," he said, before catching himself and taking a moment to recover. The muscles of his jaw undulated and his nostrils flared.

"Nevertheless . . ." Sloane returned the patronizing smile.

Regaining his composure, Fitzgerald said, "The situation to which you refer was tragic. Despite the lack of evidence of liability, we made the decision that it was prudent to avoid the publicity that, as you have said, so often accompanies litigation. The settlement was against our attorney's advice, I might add."

Sloane wasn't buying that Kendall settled out of concern for bad publicity. He couldn't imagine Dayron Moore putting fear in anyone, let alone Kendall's attorney, Barclay Reid. It was clear that Reid had intimidated Moore so badly he wouldn't even file a complaint.

Fitzgerald sat back. "What is it you want, Mr. Sloane?"

"I want a prototype independently tested before Metamorphis is placed in the market. I would agree to keep any results of those tests confidential pursuant to ER 408 and would agree not to divulge the information to the media." He referenced the evidence code section that made any discussions of information obtained while engaged in settlement talks inadmissible in court. Without a plaintiff, that wouldn't be an issue. Sloane could not even file a complaint, let alone get to a trial, and without a complaint he couldn't initiate discovery to try to get one of the robots in production. But Fitzgerald did not know that. Perception. Sloane was bluffing and hoping Fitzgerald wouldn't call him on it.

Fitzgerald shook his head. "You're asking us to do your work for you."

"Not if I can't use the information, and not if the results of those tests, as you proclaimed earlier, will show that the product is completely safe."

"I've been sued enough to know that whatever the test results, you'll find some expert to spin it so that it warrants litigation against Kendall. As you said, Mr. Sloane, your reputation precedes you. As a compromise, I'd be willing to provide the results of the test by the PSA."

"And I'd be happy to receive those results, but not as a substitute for having one of the robots currently in production independently tested. The other option is I file the complaint and obtain one through discovery."

Fitzgerald sat forward. "Mr. Sloane, do you think I would commit this company's resources to design, market, and advertise a product if I had a concern it would be deemed unsafe and subject to a recall, not to mention the damage that would do to Kendall's reputation? Would that make sense from a business standpoint?"

Again Sloane pushed down the anger boiling inside. Both men knew they were already beyond that point; Fitzgerald had demonstrated, very clearly, that he would do anything for the prospects of Kendall making hundreds of millions, if not billions, of dollars, including sending a killer to retrieve Horgan's file. Besides, Sloane also knew from the newspaper articles that, given Kendall's precarious financial situation, if Metamorphis failed, the company would likely no longer need to protect its reputation. But Sloane bit back those potential comments because it was not the bluff he was playing. Instead, he said, "Would it make sense from a business standpoint to protect the design and development of a toy only to have that information become public just months before its release? I don't know a lot about the toy business, but I can't imagine that would be a good thing."

That pushed a button, as Sloane had intended it would. "Let me caution you, Mr. Sloane, that the release of any information pertaining to the design or development of Metamorphis is proprietary. To the extent you possess any such information it would have to have been illegally obtained."

"I agree," Sloane said, baiting him further, "by Kendall."

Fitzgerald's jaw clenched. "Consider this a demand that any such information be returned immediately, or the company will take legal action. You're not the only one with a winning record, Mr. Sloane. We've won on this issue in the past, and we will win again. Look that up."

Sloane pushed back his chair. He'd bluffed. The next play belonged to Kendall, and only time would reveal whether Fitzgerald would actually call him on it.

"I guess that's why they run the races," he said, "to see which horse actually wins."

GEORGE BUSH CENTER FOR INTELLIGENCE

LANGLEY, VIRGINIA

JENKINS'S ESCORT LEAD him through the glass doors beneath the concrete overhang into the drab marble foyer with the circular emblem of the CIA embedded in the floor. The entrance to the Old Headquarters Building, apparently so named because there was now a New Headquarters Building, hadn't changed, though there were more gold stars on the north wall, one for each CIA officer killed in the line of duty. Jenkins counted eighty-nine. As in the past, not all of the officers' names were revealed, since doing so might still jeopardize the lives of others. Inscribed on the south wall above the bronze bust of Major General William J. Donovan, the first director of the Office of Strategic Services, predecessor to the CIA, was a passage from scripture, John 8:32.

AND YE SHALL KNOW THE TRUTH,

AND THE TRUTH SHALL MAKE YOU FREE.

Curley Wade's assistant scanned Jenkins's visitor's badge through a computer and Jenkins was allowed entry through turnstiles like those found at a subway station. He walked down a hall bustling with people. Halfway down the hall his escort pushed open a glass door to the courtyard patio between the old and new buildings. No longer having security clearance, Jenkins could not meet Wade in his office, but the man was not difficult to find. He was one of only two black men in the courtyard, Jenkins being the other, the sun shining atop Wade's bald head. "Curley" was a nickname that had apparently been passed down multiple generations, regardless of the amount of hair atop that particular generation's head.

Wade stood from a red metal picnic table and removed his sunglasses, considering Jenkins with an uncertain stare. "Charles fucking Jenkins. I wouldn't believe it was actually you until I saw you in the flesh."

Jenkins smiled, shaking the man's hand. "Yeah, I guess it's been a while."

"'Been a while'? I thought you were dead. After Mexico City you dropped off the face of the earth."

Jenkins had first met Wade during his orientation to the Agency, studying its organization, and its history. It was likely that the Agency had paired the two men together, given they were both African American and racism and intolerance remained prevalent. After ten weeks Jenkins was sent to a remote training center in the West Virginia hills, where for six months he learned, in essence, how to become a "spook." The culmination was a six-week probationary period running twenty-four hours a day, seven days a week, in which he was to showcase what he had learned. When it concluded, a "murder board" gave Jenkins high marks. From there most of the case officers were sent for additional paramilitary training, but because Jenkins had received that training in the Special Forces, the Agency sent him to Mexico City.

"I needed to get away and deal with some of my demons."

"Well, you haven't changed much. Still built like a friggin' tank."

Jenkins patted his stomach. "I got a little bit more fuel in the tank I'm afraid."

"Don't we all? You want to get some chow? We got everything you could want, even a Starbucks."

"I get enough of that in Seattle. I'm good."

The operations officer at the Mexico City Station, Wade became Jenkins's case officer. It had been Wade who assigned Jenkins to work with Joe Branick to infiltrate the village in the mountains of Oaxaca, where a young boy was giving sermons so riveting the peasants had begun to rally around him and call him Mexico's "savior." At a time when the Saudis were threatening to cut off the flow of oil to the United States, or raise the price to be prohibitively expensive, Mexico, with its billions of barrels of oil offshore, had become a valuable alternative. The United States government could not risk any potential disruption to its relationship with the Mexican government in power, or to its ability to again gain access to Mexico's oil. The boy was deemed a threat to the stability of the government and an order was given to eliminate that threat. That boy turned out to be Ephraim Ybaron, who managed to survive and whom Joe Branick would hide in California's foster care system as David Sloane. Wade had sworn that he had no knowledge of the subsequent operation that had led to the massacre of the residents of that village, including Sloane's mother. At the time Jenkins wanted to believe him, but whether Wade knew or didn't know became irrelevant. Jenkins was done, finished with the whole business.

They sat across from each other. A breeze blew through the courtyard, rustling the leaves of an oak tree and giving a short reprieve from the humidity. Behind Wade water trickled down a stone sculpture that Jenkins had never seen before but looked like four encoded panels. Wade saw him considering the panels.

"Someone's figured out three of the four," he said. "But don't bother with the fourth. Someone else determined there's an error."

"That must have been fun."

"We had people pulling their hair out for weeks. Not me of course." He turned back to Jenkins, "So, what happened to you? Where'd you go?"

"Seattle," he said, as if he had just moved to a different city. "A little island about an hour to the north. A farm."

"You? The boy from New Jersey?"

Wade was no longer the young man with the unblemished skin and chiseled features that had been a thirty-year snapshot unchanged in Jenkins's memory. The years and twenty pounds had reshaped his features. His face was rounder, his nose more prominent. A scar remained partially hidden beneath his right eyebrow.

"I see you're still in recruiting," Jenkins said. Wade's office was in the Office of Personnel, which was under the auspices of the deputy director of operations.

"Not the kind of recruiting that you're thinking of. I'm a desk jockey now. I hire secretaries, though we can't call them that anymore. I'm a lot more familiar with ADA and the Department of Labor and Industry than I am with the shit you and I used to deal with."

Again, Jenkins didn't know if Wade was telling the truth, but again it didn't matter. "You still have connections in that world?" he asked.

Wade put his elbows on the table. His eyebrows inched together. "You interested in jumping back in?"

Jenkins laughed. "No. Nothing like that." He got serious. "I have a favor to ask. I might not have any right to ask it, given how I left, but I need to ask it anyway." The fact that Jenkins had just disappeared, rather than have his cover "rolled back," had probably caused Wade some headaches. But Jenkins had never breached his lifetime secrecy agreement.

"If I can help, I will. You know that."

Jenkins handed him a copy of the photograph Sloane had taken from the envelope when the two detectives came to the hospital.

"This is a bad guy, a sociopath. I need to know his name and how to find him."

"Why not the police?"

Jenkins had anticipated the question. "It's personal," he said. "And the police won't have the resources to find this guy."

"Mercenary?"

"Maybe. He's a professional, well trained, I have a hunch he served." Jenkins knew that no one kept records quite like the United States military and hoped his hunch was accurate.

Wade sat for a few moments, saying nothing. Then he asked, "How personal?"

"He killed a pregnant woman in cold blood."

"Not your wife . . ."

"No, but someone who meant a lot to me."

Wade nodded. "How long are you in town?

"As long as it takes, Curley."

ONE UNION SQUARE BUILDING
SEATTLE, WASHINGTON

SLOANE CLOSED HIS office door and threw the cane across the room, clenching and unclenching his fists as he paced the carpeting. The door pushed open, nearly hitting him. Carolyn entered, holding a mug of coffee. Sloane stopped his pacing but apparently not soon enough.

"Well, caffeine is definitely out of the question," she said. "You want something stronger."

Sloane made his way to his chair, falling into it. His leg throbbed.

"You okay?" she asked.

"My leg hurts," he said.

"I'll bring you some ibuprofen." She pulled the stack of documents from the out-box on his desk and left him alone, shutting the door behind her.

Sloane took out the prescription bottle from his top desk drawer, nearly pulled off the cap, then reconsidered. The pills would ease his pain but not his frustration; Fitzgerald had remained arrogant, and Sloane knew that without a plaintiff it was unlikely Kendall would react to his threats. If Barclay Reid was as competent as her reputation suggested, she would advise Fitzgerald that a barking dog was not to be feared until it actually bit someone. Without the McFarlands, Sloane was barking, but he had no bite.

Could you?

Eva McFarland's final question haunted him. That was always the issue when it came to doing the right thing. People often asked more of others than they asked of themselves, and in this instance Sloane had asked Eva McFarland a hell of a lot. He had not lost a child, but he understood what it meant to love someone so much you would rather die than lose them.

THE WAVE HIT the boat so fast Sloane never even saw it coming.

He and Jake had taken the boat out early that morning after Jake had read about a run on king salmon in the Sound, although farther out beyond Vashon Island, which had been the limit of Sloane's comfort zone driving the boat. He relented because he did not want to disappoint Jake, and only after checking the weather forecast, which called for overcast skies and a chance of light rain. At the time, Sloane was not yet educated on Northwest weather and did not know that, as with so many forecasts in the Pacific Northwest, the weatherman would be wrong. It seemed that with Seattle being located so far north, it was susceptible to the rapidly changing weather patterns coming down from Alaska, making forecasts often no better than a dart throw.

The weather began to change for the worse just after three in the afternoon. Dark clouds rolled in quickly, and the temperature dropped. Light rain became a steady downpour that turned to hail and strong winds, agitating the Sound into a froth of whitecaps and foam. As Sloane struggled to control the twenty-one-foot boat against the wind, the choppy waters, and the current, he never saw the large wave until too late. Though he tried to correct into its impact, he could not steer the boat quickly enough. The wave hit the bow of the boat at an angle and lifted it from the water. Sloane had remained upright only because he managed to hang on to the steering wheel. With trepidation, he turned his head to make sure Jake was okay but instead realized his worst fear. Jake was not in the boat.

His heart leapt in his throat, and he let go of the steering wheel, spinning around.

"Jake! Jake!"

An orange bob in the water was rapidly becoming smaller when another wave hit the boat and knocked Sloane off balance to the floor between the seats. By the time he got back to his feet the orange bob had become a speck.

His heart hammering in his chest, he turned the boat around quickly and hit the throttle, but with the surging waves tossing the propeller in and out of the water, steering the boat was nearly impossible. Jake had his hands raised over his head, waving frantically, the life vest pushed up under his chin. As Sloane approached he slowed, realizing another problem—getting the boy back into the boat would be no easy task. Sloane could not cut the engine entirely because he would lose all power and be at the mercy of not only the waves crashing against the boat but also the wind.

He pulled the boat alongside Jake and ripped off the seat cushions in search of rope. The wind caught one cushion and hurled it fifteen feet into the air before it fell and tumbled across the waves out of sight. Sloane pulled out a purple nylon ski rope and quickly untangled it while trying to keep the nose of the boat into the wind and the waves and not get pushed too far from Jake. He fastened one end of the rope around a cleat, then went back to the wheel and pressed down the throttle, making a horseshoe around Jake. He tossed the line, but the wind took it and pushed it well out of Jake's reach. Sloane left it in the water and this time made another pass so that the rope would come to Jake, as if he were a downed water-skier. But with the wind, rain, and whitecaps the rope was hard to distinguish. Sloane could see Jake frantically looking for it, slapping at the water.

"Get it, Jake. Grab it."

But the boy missed it.

Sloane had no choice but to circle again, all the while knowing that Jake was freezing in the forty-five-degree water. He could tell from the expression on Jake's face as he drove away that the boy was now panicked. He brought the boat around again, the waves tossing it up and down like a cork. This time he brought the rope closer and Jake snatched it. Sloane centered the throttle to neutral.

Afraid that Jake would not be able to hold on to the rope as Sloane pulled him through the water to the boat, Sloane shouted out to him, "Tie it around you," but the wind and the rain swallowed his voice.

Sloane mimicked the action of tying the rope around his waist while trying to remain upright with the waves jostling the boat.

"Tie it around you."

Jake tied the rope around his body and Sloane tested it with a yank. The rope held. He pulled hand over hand, Jake swimming for the boat as he did, but it was still like pulling a tire through mud. Making things worse, the waves continued to rock the boat, knocking Sloane off balance and dousing him with foam. He could get little traction, and the boat was taking on more and more water.

His arms ached by the time he pulled Jake to the side of the boat, reached down, and yanked him out of the water by his life vest. The boy was shivering from the cold and shock, but Sloane had little time to con-

sole him. The waves were growing ever bigger. He put him in the passenger seat and throttled forward, turning the boat back on course, praying they'd make it back to Three Tree Point.

When they got within site of their beach Sloane saw a tiny, solitary figure standing on the bulkhead. Tina looked out from under the hood of her blue Gore-Tex jacket, leaning into the wind and rain. She would later tell him that she had stood there for almost an hour, cell phone in hand, hoping to see them or the Coast Guard, whom she had called.

Sloane didn't bother to tie up at the buoy. He threw Tina the rope and beached the boat on the gravel, unconcerned about the damage that might cause. As Tina tied the rope to a ring cemented in the bulkhead, Sloane helped Jake to the shore. Tina rushed to them, hugging them both, crying, unable to speak, not having to do so. Clutching Tina and Jake tight, Sloane knew what he had almost lost and now realized what he could not live without. And with that knowledge he came to understand, for the first time, what it truly meant to love and to be loved.

THE FIRST NIGHT in the hospital after Charles Jenkins had told him Tina was dead had been the longest of his life. The succeeding nights did not get any shorter. People who said time heals all wounds were wrong. The days became a week, and the week an emotion-deadening month, but he still felt the pain as fresh as that first night, and every morning bore the same reality—there was nothing he could do to change it. For all his skill and talent, he had no control over the one thing that could bring color back into his world and make him feel again. He could not bring back Tina. Now he feared he was about to let her down all over again, unable to bring those responsible to justice, and the frustration that wrought was almost paralyzing.

Carolyn knocked and opened the door, looking perturbed. "Did you schedule an appointment you didn't tell me about?"

Sloane shook his head. He had no appointments, not today, not tomorrow, not for the rest of the month. He was focused on just two tasks, taking down Kendall Toys and exacting revenge on the man who had killed his wife.

"Well, Michael and Eva McFarland are in the lobby and they asked to speak to you."

Sloane sighed. Michael had probably come to give Sloane the remaining piece of mind that Eva had not unleashed on him. He deserved it. "Ask them to wait in the conference room," he said.

THE MCFARLANDS STOOD near the windows with their backs to the door. The two cups of coffee Carolyn had set on the conference table remained untouched, and the strap of Eva's purse remained around her forearm. They didn't intend to stay long, probably just long enough for Michael to ask Sloane where he got the nerve.

Sloane knocked to get their attention as he walked in. Michael stepped forward, though not with the assertiveness Sloane had anticipated. Eva hesitated, but her husband wrapped an arm around her shoulder. She looked as she had many days in court, eyes puffy red, skin pale. "We wanted to talk with you about the check."

It would have been standard procedure upon receiving the $3.2 million judgment from Dr. Douvalidis's insurance carrier for Carolyn to deposit the check in Sloane's trust account and cut the McFarlands a check, less Sloane's fee and costs. "Did Carolyn not send it?"

"No, we got it." Michael had trimmed his goatee since Sloane last saw him. It was a shade darker than his brown hair with strands of gray at the chin. "That's what we wanted to talk to you about."

Sloane gestured for them to take seats at the conference room table. Eva opened her purse and pulled out a white envelope

Sloane recognized to be his firm's stationery. Then she slid it across the polished surface.

Sloane considered it before looking back up at them. "I don't understand. Is there something wrong? Is it the wrong amount?"

Eva's voice cracked. She paused to clear her throat and let her emotions pass. Tears pooled again. "I'm so sorry, David. I'm so sorry for those things that I said to you about not having lost someone you love."

He put up a hand. "No. You have nothing to apologize for. I never should have put you in that position. It was wrong of me. You asked me if I could do it, and now . . . well, I know my answer."

"But that's really the point, isn't it," Michael said. He gestured to his wife. "I mean, that's what we talked about when I got home. Eva told you came to the house and what you told her, about that other family. No one should *have* to make that decision. No one should *have* to go through what we've gone through. Austin never had a chance. I mean, no one knew there could be a danger. You don't go to the store and buy your child a toy and think that it could kill him. You think that if it's there, if it's on the shelf, then it has to be safe, right? I mean there are agencies that are supposed to check those things, aren't there? So no one could have prevented what happened to Austin because no one knew." McFarland paused, as if to catch his breath. "But now it's different. Now we know that toy is dangerous. And, well, we couldn't live with ourselves if something happened to another child and we knew that we could have, maybe, prevented it."

Eva's chest shuddered. "I thought about what you said, about the other families; I don't want another mother to go through what I've gone through. I also thought of Dr. Douvalidis. Oh my God, David."

Sloane had no answer for her. He had no answer for himself. Douvalidis might still have been found negligent, but the doctor was not responsible for Austin's death. Kendall Toys was.

"We were thinking," Eva said. "Maybe, you know, in some way this could at least give some meaning to Austin's death."

Michael agreed. "That maybe Austin died so that other kids won't." He shrugged. "Maybe he wouldn't have died for no reason, you know."

"Do you know what we mean?" Eva asked.

Sloane nodded. "My wife was pregnant," he said, fighting back his own emotions. "I know what you mean."

Eva reached out and covered Sloane's hand with her own.

"When I found out, I was so happy," he said. "But then I felt something I never expected."

"Fear," Eva said, knowing.

He nodded. "I realized that this was going to be a very big responsibility for a lot of years, and I had no way of really knowing if I would be up to it. It killed me to think of anything happening to my child like what had happened to Austin."

For a moment no one spoke. Then Michael broke the silence. "So we'll sign whatever papers you need, you know, to find out for sure. But we don't want to be there. We can't be there."

"I understand," Sloane said, knowing Michael referred to the exhumation and autopsy. "I'll be there for you, and I'll make sure Austin is taken care of."

The McFarlands looked at each other with expressions of resigned relief, Eva exhaling, as if she had been holding her breath. They walked around the edge of the table to where Sloane stood, balanced on his cane. Their movements seemed lighter. Michael McFarland shook Sloane's hand but said nothing further, perhaps concerned that one further word would unleash the tears pooled in his eyes. He stepped to the side to compose himself as Eva hugged Sloane.

"Maybe she's up there with Austin," she said. "Maybe she's taking care of my baby for me. I'll bet she would have been a good mother."

"She was," Sloane said. "She was a very good mother."

LAURELHURST
WASHINGTON

FITZGERALD LEANED CLOSER, peering at the splotches on the peasant woman's face, admiring the individual strokes of the paint brush. Kneeling in what appeared to be a field of wheat, the woman wore a blue dress with red spots and a beige apron about her waist. A yellow sun hat covered her head, the underside of the brim nearly orange, to indicate shade. The painting was worth twice as much as everything Fitzgerald owned, and that included his stock in Kendall.

"Van Gogh." Sebastian Kendall spoke as his nurse wheeled him into the room. He looked to be sitting more upright than he had during Fitzgerald's prior visit.

"I remember when you bought it," Fitzgerald said.

"You mean when I overpaid for it," Kendall said, admiring the piece, "and yet it is worth twice as much today as the day I bought it."

"You were always a good judge of a wise investment."

"Hah!" Kendall barked. "I wanted it, and I let my personal desire cloud my business judgment. I was lucky."

"We should all be so lucky."

"Perhaps." Kendall wheeled closer. "He has always fascinated me, Van Gogh, so brilliant and yet so fragile. Did you know that his paintings are a public exhibition of his descent into madness?"

Fitzgerald nodded. "Erin and I attended a lecture at the UW that chronicled his illness through his paintings. It was quite fascinating. They say the line between genius and madness is razor thin."

Kendall's nurse wheeled him closer to a fire in the river rock fireplace, then left them.

"You look well today," Fitzgerald said, "stronger."

Kendall responded with a small shrug. "Today has been a good day, but to infer anything from it would be no less mad than Van Gogh. I have acknowledged the inevitable, Malcolm, and I do not fear it. Tell me, what brings you here late at night when you should be home with your family? No toys on this occasion?"

Fitzgerald sat in a leather chair, elbows on his knees, hands pressed together at an apex just beneath his nose, like an altar boy praying. He had debated bringing up the subject with Kendall. God knew the man had enough on his plate, and if Fitzgerald truly was to assume the mantle of control, he would have to make these decisions on his own soon enough. But Kendall had been Fitzgerald's safety net for many years and remained his mentor during the transition of power. With so much riding on the success of Metamorphis, Fitzgerald was not yet ready to fly without the net secure below him.

"I'm sorry to trouble you with this, Sebastian. I had intended on handling it myself . . ."

"Please, if it allows me to remain of some use . . ."

"We have a mole in the company. I've known of it for sometime, but I thought I could keep it under control by keeping the production of Metamorphis confidential, as we discussed. I'm afraid that is no longer the case."

"Who do you suspect?"

"Santoro."

Kendall tilted his head backward, and it looked as if it might roll completely off before it listed forward again. "He remains upset."

Fitzgerald rubbed his hands, as if to warm them. "He's been meeting with Brandon Craft."

"Then you can assume it is with Maxine Bolelli's blessing. Craft isn't savvy enough to do something like this on his own."

"It began shortly after Maxine and I met in Scottsdale to discuss Galaxy's proposal. I never should have included Santoro in the discussions, but I was hoping it would make him feel less insecure about his future at the company. Initially I believed he was only testing the waters, and I couldn't really blame him, nor would I have stopped him. I'm sure he sees his position now as a dead end, and I would prefer to be rid of him as we move forward."

"And something has made you now suspect there is more to his overtures?"

"I believe he's been playing Kendall and Galaxy against each other and I believe he's using Metamorphis to do it."

"How?"

"He knows that if Metamorphis succeeds, it eliminates any chance of Galaxy acquiring Kendall. If it fails, the chances of Kendall surviving the economic downturn or a hostile bid by Galaxy are equally as slim. If that happens, Bolelli does not need Santoro to get what she wants; she could just absorb Kendall's action figure department for pennies on the dollar. Why bother hiring Santoro?"

"It makes sense."

"So it is in Santoro's interest for Kendall to fail outright but for Metamorphis to succeed."

"He uses Metamorphis to entice Bolelli to hire him."

Fitzgerald nodded. "He takes a position as head of Galaxy's new action figure department, and he just so happens to bring with him the design of a toy that could very well be the toy of the decade. It's a win-win."

"How is he going to accomplish this?"

"He has apparently paid a low-level toy designer to take credit for the design of Metamorphis, and to allege that he placed Kendall on notice of a flaw in the design."

"We'll simply expose this man as an imposter."

Fitzgerald stood. "I wish it were that simple. It seems Santoro has sent this man to an attorney, and not just any attorney, but to David Sloane."

Kendall shook his head to indicate the name meant nothing to him.

"He's the attorney who brought suit against the government last year on behalf of that national guardsman's family. The attorney who never loses."

"Wasn't he just in the news?"

"His wife was murdered by an intruder in their home. Sloane was shot twice but lived and seems no worse for wear. I had a meeting with him this afternoon. He knows about Metamorphis and he's convinced that this Kyle Horgan designed it. He says he has a file with the design drawings to prove it, as well as a letter from Horgan warning of a flaw in the plastic. Only Santoro could have provided the design drawings. As careful as we've been, we can't deny that Santoro still has a lot of support at the company. Who knows what he's promised certain individuals if he takes a position at Galaxy, or what he's told them about Kendall's future. But our immediate problem is Sloane. We cannot let him disclose this design, and we cannot let him stand up in court and argue that Kendall has knowledge of a flaw but intends to put the toy to market."

"You indicated on your last visit that the toy has met all regulations and received PSA approval."

"It has, but there was that matter in Mossylog."

"An aberration, likely misuse of the product. Besides, there was insufficient evidence to confirm that the death was caused by the toy."

"Legal arguments, Sebastian, which are persuasive to other lawyers but not necessarily to the general public. You know that. Sloane would spin the child's death as evidence the toy design is flawed. He wants us to pull the plug until Metamorphis can be independently tested."

"Out of the question."

"He says he'll file suit and make this a very public matter."

"Did you talk to Barclay?"

"Not a minute after Sloane left my office. She says we can fight any attempt to set aside the Gallegos settlement, that the family was represented by counsel and signed an agreement, but that isn't my primary concern. My primary concern is Sloane making the design public during litigation."

"And what did Ms. Reid say?"

"She said that *if* Sloane has a plaintiff, and *if* he files suit, we can seek a court order preventing him from disclosing any information about the design. But that still does not prevent Santoro from taking the design to Galaxy and exploiting any delay caused by this litigation."

"A knockoff."

"And when Kendall goes under, Santoro shows up at Galaxy."

"Can we expose this imposter, Kyle Horgan?"

"We can't even locate him. I think Santoro has him hidden."

"Have you confronted Santoro?"

Fitzgerald shook his head. "Not yet. I don't have anything concrete to confront him with, and he would only deny it and become more guarded. I was hoping that he'd make a mistake and hang himself."

"You may be running out of time for that," Kendall said.

"That's why I'm here."

Kendall nodded. "Put a tap on his office and cell phone and monitor his e-mails. Use the people we've used in the past. Arian is smart. He'll be discreet. So see about putting something in his car as well and put him under twenty-four-hour surveillance. All you need is one phone call or e-mail or photograph to expose him."

Fitzgerald nodded.

"Santoro lost any expectation of privacy when he talked with Galaxy."

"What about Sloane?"

"Pay him what he wants and get rid of this before it gets in the media. You must fiercely protect the Kendall name. This toy could be to you what Sergeant Smash and Captain Courageous were to my father and my grandfather, a solid foundation upon which to build Kendall's, and your, future. Do not let anyone take that away from you."

CHAPTER
EIGHT

King County Superior Court Judge John Rudolph stared down at Sloane with a mixture of curiosity and confusion, like a man viewing a breed of animal he'd never seen but with which he was vaguely familiar. Two weeks after meeting the McFarlands in his conference room, Sloane was appearing ex parte in Rudolph's courtroom. Unlike other legal proceedings, in which the attorneys filed their papers days in advance, by appearing ex parte, Sloane had not given Rudolph the opportunity to read the papers before Rudolph's clerk handed him the copy Sloane brought with him. When Rudolph appeared in court from his chambers his robe was only partially zipped. His clerk, court reporter, and bailiff followed him, a clear indication Rudolph wanted every word spoken in his courtroom on the record. Sitting behind his elevated bench, Rudolph's already ruddy complexion was nearly as red as his hair.

"I've been on the bench for thirty years, Mr. Sloane, and in all those years I have never had anyone make a request like this."

Michael and Eva McFarland stood beside Sloane. They had

provided declarations in support of his motion to set aside the jury's verdict, but given the unusualness of the request—a winning plaintiff wanting to set aside a judgment—Sloane knew Rudolph would want them in court. Dr. Douvalidis's counsel was also present.

"I recognize this is unusual, Your Honor."

Rudolph interrupted him. "Not unusual, Mr. Sloane. Unprecedented. You're asking the court to throw out a favorable verdict; I've never heard or read of such a thing."

There had been some significant hoops Sloane had to jump through with the county prosecutor to have the body of Austin McFarland exhumed. Because the McFarlands had consented, it eased the paperwork but not necessarily the process. Sloane had to find a forensic pathologist and pay him to perform the autopsy, since the county wasn't about to foot the bill. But it had not been the procedural aspects that had caused Sloane the greatest angst. As he had promised the McFarlands, he remained present with Austin's casket from the moment it was exhumed to the moment it was reburied. As difficult as it was to watch the cemetery workers dig up the casket and lift it out of the ground, being present for the autopsy was far worse. But Sloane had kept his word and stayed through it all. And when the pathologist had finished, Sloane ensured that Austin was lowered back into the ground to his final resting place. He went back to the Athletic Club and, overcome by emotion, threw up. Then, after a hot shower, in which he scrubbed at his skin to rid it of the smell of the autopsy, he drank Scotch until he passed out.

Because he had been present, Sloane knew the results of the autopsy that very day, but the pathologist took another three days to complete his written report. Austin McFarland had swallowed five magnets. That fact could not be denied. What was problematic was the condition of the body. With the passage of time, the intestines had deteriorated to unrecognizable muck, and the forensic pathologist Sloane had hired, Dr. Leonard Desmond, the same pathologist who had performed the autopsy on Mateo Gallegos, could opine only that he found the magnets in the abdominal cavity. He could not, even through microscopic analysis, conclude that there had been magnet-induced bowel necrosis or ischemia followed by perforation of the bowel. In short, he could not testify that the magnets were the cause of death. Any such opinion would be based on circumstantial evidence and maybe not even that, if Sloane could not get the Gallegos settlement set aside.

"Children explore the world at this age through their fingertips and their mouths," Dr. Desmond had said. "It isn't aberrant behavior. It's typical. The tendency tapers off at age three, but clinical studies have found that children of all ages put things in their mouths that they shouldn't. Moreover, because they are told not to put things in their mouths, if the child is asked whether they swallowed something, they will usually deny it." He held up the small bottle encasing the magnets. "And look at the size and shape of these. They look like pieces of candy."

With the report in hand, Sloane personally delivered a copy to Dr. Douvalidis's attorney. Though he also sought to talk to Douvalidis's wife, she had declined all overtures.

Rudolph spoke to the McFarlands. "Is this your intent? Do you want me to throw out the verdict?"

Michael McFarland answered, "Yes, Your Honor."

"And you recognize that by throwing out the verdict, you will be required to return all of the money awarded to you in the judgment."

"We brought the check with us, Judge," McFarland said.

Rudolph raised a hand. "That won't be necessary. You can give that to your attorney to handle." He addressed Douvalidis's counsel. "And I guess for the record I better ask if you also consent."

"Yes, Your Honor. I appreciate the McFarlands' honesty and their integrity. Like you, I've been at this for a long time and I've never seen anything like this. I must say it renews my faith in the legal system, and in people. What has transpired is tragic and nothing can change that. I have spoken to Mrs. Douvalidis, and she would like the McFarlands to know that she also respects what they are doing here today."

Rudolph nodded his head. "Mr. and Mrs. McFarland, I sat through the trial of this matter with you for three weeks, and while I was not allowed to express any of my feelings during that proceeding, nothing prevents me from doing so now. There is never anything more tragic than for a parent to bury their child. We spend our lives trying to protect the ones we love, but we can't protect them against every potential danger out there. What happened to your son is a tragedy that should never befall a family."

"That's why we did it, Judge," Michael McFarland said. "So maybe no other family has to go through it, so that maybe Austin's death might help prevent it from happening again."

"It's very admirable." Rudolph turned his attention to Sloane. "Mr. Sloane, my hat is off to you as well. The court is well aware of the recent events that befell you, and I offer my sincerest condolences."

Sloane thanked him.

"So be it," Rudolph said. He took a pen and signed the order Sloane had prepared. "The judgment is vacated."

SLOANE LED THE McFarlands to microphones set up on the courthouse steps where Dr. Douvalidis's attorney, Manny and Rosa-Maria Gallegos, and several reporters waited beneath one of those glorious Seattle September skies unblemished by even a single cloud, and the temperature hovered in the midseventies with a light breeze. Birds sang in the surrounding trees. The Gallegoses had found courage in the McFarlands' unselfish act and Sloane's assurances that he would represent them and ensure they would never be deported.

Sloane had accurately predicted that the local and national media contacts he had made from his work as a legal commentator would deem newsworthy his motion to set aside a favorable verdict, which, as Rudolph had confirmed, was "unprecedented." To further ensure a crowd, he had remained coy about the legal basis for the motion, saying only that he would reveal recently discovered information at a press conference following the hearing.

Sloane stepped to the microphones, the McFarlands at his side.

"This morning, Michael and Eva McFarland did something extraordinary. They asked Judge John Rudolph to throw out the favorable verdict we obtained against Dr. Peter Douvalidis more than a month ago. Recent information has come to our attention that Dr. Douvalidis's actions were not directly responsible for the death of the McFarlands' son Austin. I have in my hand and will disseminate to the media a report from forensic medical examiner Leonard Desmond of a recent autopsy performed on Austin. That autopsy revealed that Austin ingested five very small, but very powerful, magnets, and it is Dr. Desmond's belief that those magnets, manufactured in China, attracted one another, causing the thin intestines to eventually perforate and allow bacteria to seep into the body cavity and bloodstream. Austin died as a result of that poisoning."

"How did the child come in contact with the magnets?" a reporter asked.

"It is our belief, and it will be our allegation, that the magnets that killed Austin McFarland came from the prototype of a toy created by Kendall Toys, a toy that Kendall is close to putting on the market. My office will be filing a lawsuit today on behalf of the McFarlands, as well as Manny and Rosa-Maria Gallegos, whose son, Mateo, also died from the ingestion of these magnets."

"How did you learn about this?" another reporter asked.

"The information of a possible connection between the deaths and these magnets, as well as the defective design of the toy, came from a source I cannot identify at this time." Sloane turned and motioned Michael McFarland forward. "Michael Mc-Farland would like to make a brief statement."

McFarland wore dark glasses to shield the bright sun and to hide his red, puffy eyes. He thanked Sloane and apologized publicly to Dr. Douvalidis. "Raising children always comes with risks. Parents expect skinned knees, even the occasional broken bone from a fall off a bike or jungle gym. They don't expect pieces from a broken toy to rip holes through their child's gut. I hope that our actions today, if nothing else, keep another family from having to suffer through what we have gone through for more than a year. I hope it means that Austin's death will not be in vain."

McFarland folded his piece of paper and stepped back. The questions flew. Sloane did his best to answer them. The reporters wanted to know more about the toy. Strategically, Sloane did not provide it. He cited confidentiality agreements signed by the two families preventing them from releasing the name of, or any specifics about, the prototype.

"However, I expect all of that information will be made public through discovery," he said, purposefully.

After several more minutes answering questions, Sloane thanked the media and started to step away from the microphones. One of the reporters shouted a final question, and it stabbed Sloane like a sharp knife.

"Has there been any further information on the man who killed your wife?"

Sloane took a moment. "No," he said. "Her killer is still out there."

KENDALL TOYS' CORPORATE HEADQUARTERS
RENTON, WASHINGTON

THIS WAS HIS worst nightmare. Malcolm Fitzgerald watched David Sloane's press conference on the flat-screen television beside framed awards Kendall Toys had received from the Toy Manufacturer's Association and other industry organizations. Sloane had not been bluffing; he had a plaintiff. A simple phone call had confirmed that Mathew McFarland had been a member of one of the Metamorphis focus groups. Fitzgerald wouldn't need to create wall space for any more awards if Metamorphis did not make it to the market, and at the moment, Sloane appeared a formidable impediment to that happening.

"You should not have met with him without me present." Barclay Reid turned off the television and walked to the conference table where Fitzgerald sat running a finger over his lips, a nervous habit. Though he had loosened the knot of his tie and unbuttoned the top button of his shirt he felt anything but comfortable.

"Hindsight is twenty-twenty," Fitzgerald said. "What do we do now?"

Reid walked to Fitzgerald's end of the table and fixed him with her green eyes. "Is there any evidence of any other complaints, anything that would have put the company on notice that the toy could be problematic?"

"Nothing."

"I need to know everything, Malcolm. I can't have any surprises when I stand up in court. If there is anything out there, tell me now."

"There's nothing."

"What about Sloane's allegation of an independent designer?" She flipped through a pad of notes. "Kyle Horgan?"

"I told you, I have no idea who the guy is. Metamorphis was designed in-house. This guy is a liar."

"What about someone else in the office, one of your designers?"

"I've already asked. No one knows anything about him. Metamorphis passed inspection by the PSA, and the factory in China manufacturing the plastic has been independently certified."

"He'll depose you. What you knew will come out."

Fitzgerald walked to the marble counter in the corner and poured a drink, adding two chunks of ice. What the hell, he was going to miss his racquetball workout anyway. "I'm not worried about being deposed. I'm worried about Sloane disclosing anything about the design. If we can keep Metamorphis under wraps for just a bit longer, I'll do more than save this company. I'll take it to a level even Sebastian Kendall never dreamed of."

Arms crossed, Reid said, "I'd still prefer that Sloane make the first move."

Fitzgerald scoffed, pointing at the darkened television screen. "I think he just did."

"Filing a temporary restraining order could be tricky. It gets Sloane into court and before a judge a lot sooner than would otherwise be the case. If you wait—"

"I can't afford to wait. I can't afford the possibility of Sloane leaking the design. You know as well as I that it would take another company no time at all to rush a knockoff to the market. We'd lose our window of opportunity, not to mention the millions I've invested in production, marketing, and advertising. We'd be done. I don't have a choice."

Reid nodded. "Okay. Then we'll serve Sloane's office with the TRO this afternoon and seek a hearing for tomorrow. I already have half a dozen people working on it."

Fitzgerald sipped his drink. "What are the chances the court will grant the TRO?"

"The TRO should be a slam dunk."

"I hate it when you say that."

"Have I ever been wrong?"

"There's always a first time."

"Then let me put it this way. If everything you are telling me is as you say, there is a strong likelihood we will succeed on the merits given that all of Sloane's evidence is circumstantial. This isn't a class action. Sloane represents one family, maybe two depending on how the judge rules on the settlement agreement, and there is no chance of irreparable harm to his clients since the children are already dead. Their remedy is monetary damages. The likelihood of irreparable harm to Kendall if Sloane discloses anything about the design is equally clear. It would be reversible error for a court not to grant the restraining order."

"I liked it better when you called it a slam dunk."

Reid gathered her suit jacket from the back of a chair and picked up her briefcase. "I want you at the hearing tomorrow. I want the court to understand that Kendall is taking these allegations very seriously. Two children are dead. I want the judge to see the face of a toy maker, not a big corporation."

ONE UNION SQUARE BUILDING

SEATTLE, WASHINGTON

SLOANE HUDDLED IN a conference room with John Kannin and Tom Pendergrass. Each had arrived with a mug of coffee, anticipating a long night. Carolyn had stayed late to field calls from the media, and it had not taken long for the telephone to start ringing. The major news networks had picked up the story, as had Internet news outlets. Some had begun to introduce the story as "an honest act," and others quickly picked up this tagline.

Barclay Reid had acted nearly as quickly. Late that afternoon, as Sloane had predicted, Reid tried to bury him in paper. The motion for a temporary restraining order was classic big-firm overkill. With declarations and exhibits, it was a 176-page tome that Sloane hoped would only serve to piss off a judge and his clerks, who would be forced to work late to read it and prepare for the hearing. Besides, the introduction of computers into the legal profession had effectively leveled the battlefield between big firms and small. Every law office kept forms on their computers along with legal research on a variety of topics as well as previously filed motions. With the click of a few keys, a lawyer could fashion together the basics for almost any pleading in a matter of minutes, then go to work on the specific facts.

"It would make a good doorstop," Kannin said, weighing the stack of paper in his hand. "I have to give you your kudos, you played Reid like a drum, and that's no easy task."

Sloane had thought of the strategy after Kannin reminded him that he had no plaintiff, and even if he did, it would take months before the matter ever reached trial, far too late to keep Kendall from releasing Metamorphis. What Sloane needed was a temporary restraining order preventing Kendall from releasing the toy until it had been independently tested, but Sloane had little chance of getting a TRO, even if he had a plaintiff. A court would not grant a TRO without Sloane showing irreparable harm to his clients. As tragic as the deaths of two boys remained, there was nothing the court could do to change that. The court would deny Sloane's request because his clients' recourse was to obtain a money judgment against Kendall. That had been the reason for Sloane's meeting with Malcolm Fitzgerald. If he could get Fitzgerald to believe he still had the design from Horgan's file, and that he intended to make that information public, he might just force

Kendall to move for a temporary restraining order. If so, Sloane could get his concerns about the toy's safety before a judge in a matter of days, rather than months.

And even if Kendall won at the TRO stage, Sloane would have another shot at a subsequent hearing on whether the court should enter a permanent injunction, which was an equitable remedy fashioned by the judge using his or her discretion on how best to balance the competing interests of the two parties. If Sloane could get a sympathetic judge he might, at a minimum, get her to order that Kendall submit Metamorphis for independent testing to ensure its safety. The question was whether Fitzgerald would fall for Sloane's bluff. There was no guarantee he would, not with Barclay Reid as Kendall's attorney.

Sloane's investigation revealed Reid to be a graduate of Harvard Law School, where she had been editor of the *Law Review*. She hit the ground running upon graduation and had her own office up and running within two years, growing that office to nearly five hundred attorneys in multiple cities during the next fifteen years. "High energy" and "motivated" were two descriptions reporters often used to describe her. In her early forties, with a teenage daughter from a failed marriage, Reid had served as president of the Washington Bar Association in between putting the fear of God in those she litigated against. An article in the *Bar News* written as her term of office ended quoted her as saying she "missed the litigation trenches."

"Who's our judge?" Kannin asked.

"Rudolph."

Kannin's eyebrows nearly blended into his hairline. "You're kidding?"

"I just found out myself, and I don't think it was the luck of the draw. I think he has an interest in how all of this is going to play out," Sloane said.

Kannin tapped the pleading. "Rudolph hates this kind of stuff.

He doesn't mind working hard, but it throws off his entire staff's calendar, and he's protective of their time."

"My inclination is to take the opposite approach." Sloane directed his comments to Pendergrass, who would draft the initial response. "I want to file something lean and to the point. Insinuate from our response that this is overkill, this is a company worried because it has something to be worried about. If there wasn't any truth to the allegations they wouldn't be going to this extreme."

"We definitely have the better story," Pendergrass said. "I'll argue the death of two children over the potential loss of corporate profits any day."

"Just one child at this point," Sloane said. "After the hearing on the TRO we'll file the motion to have the settlement in Gallegos set aside. If we succeed, we'll add them to the lawsuit."

"We'll succeed," Pendergrass said. "You have Dayron so scared he'll sign a declaration saying just about anything. The fact that he told the Gallegoses they'd be deported if they didn't agree, and that they don't read English, provides a solid basis for getting the settlement thrown out."

"What about the money?" Kannin asked.

"Moore says he doesn't have it. He's sending me a check for three thousand dollars and a note to repay it," Pendergrass said.

"We'll advance it, and we'll pay the Gallegoses' share," Sloane said. "I don't want it taken out of their pocket."

Anticipating that Sloane would focus on children's lives over corporate profits, Reid had tried to soften that argument in her moving papers by including a sworn statement from Malcolm Fitzgerald in which he declared that he was a father himself and would never allow a Kendall toy to injure a child if he could prevent it. It came off sounding stilted and forced, but it also let Sloane know that Kendall would argue it had no knowledge the toy could be dangerous, and that if Sloane could somehow prove it was, Kendall would argue that the toy was not intended for children under the age of seven and that the two deaths were more the product of parental neglect than product defect.

"I'm on it," Pendergrass said, getting to his feet and leaving the office.

"You got what you wished for," Kannin said.

Sloane nodded but couldn't help but consider the adage that having got what he wished for might not be such a good thing.

CHAPTER NINE

The following morning, still limping but no longer using a cane, Sloane again entered Judge John Rudolph's courtroom, this time with both John Kannin and Tom Pendergrass accompanying him. Sloane would argue the matter, but he wanted to send a message to Barclay Reid and Kendall that he could and would staff the case. Kannin also had a prior relationship with Rudolph, who had presided over the criminal calendar for many years and, as Kannin put it, "appreciated my brand of practice," which Sloane interpreted to mean fighting until, and sometimes after, the bell.

Sloane recognized Reid from photographs in the various legal periodicals. But she was more attractive in person, her hair more auburn than brown and her eyes nearly jade. She met Sloane in the courtroom head-on, like a semitrailer driving a one-lane highway. That, and a firm handshake, indicated she was not intimidated by Sloane's record. Reid had brought a team of lawyers with her, as well as Malcolm Fitzgerald, and they set up at the table closest to the empty jury box.

The fire again burned when Sloane saw Fitzgerald, and he turned and took a moment to calm down, admonishing himself to stay on course.

"You okay?" Kannin asked.

Sloane now had a responsibility to the Gallegoses and McFarlands, who all had sacrificed much. His first obligation was to find justice for them. In the process he would obtain his own revenge, destroying Kendall Toys and ruining Malcolm Fitzgerald before putting the man in jail.

Rudolph's staff entered first and sat in the well beneath the judge's desk. Rudolph followed his bailiff and seemed to make a production of dropping Reid's tome with a thud on his desk before sitting and rearranging papers. He looked up at Sloane over bifocal glasses but it was Reid who spoke first.

"Your Honor, before we get started I want to be sure that the courtroom is closed to the public and that the participants be forbidden to talk about these matters outside of these proceedings."

Reid sought a gag order.

Rudolph looked to the back of the courtroom, where several people sat. "I'm going to have to ask you all to leave," he said, turning to his bailiff. "Quinn, clear the courtroom."

After the bailiff had escorted out all spectators, Rudolph turned back to Sloane's table, wasting no time.

"Who'll argue?" he asked.

"I will, Your Honor." Sloane stood.

"Then tell me why I shouldn't grant this order. The design of this toy is trademarked and proprietary, and Kendall has demonstrated a substantial risk of harm if you were to disclose that design in court papers or otherwise to the public."

"They certainly have met that element of their burden, Your Honor, but as the court recognizes, irreparable harm is only one of four elements they are required to meet. First, they won't succeed on the merits because we will prove that the design is defective, that the plastic components do not meet ASTM standards, and that Kendall was given notice of this potential danger before it gave these toys to these children as part of focus groups. They also cannot reasonably argue that the financial harm the company might suffer from a delay in production outweighs the potential injuries that will result to children if they put a defective toy in the marketplace. The public interest in this instance clearly does not weigh in favor of the moving party."

"Can you show that Kendall had reason to know the toy was dangerous?"

"Your Honor, under a strict liability theory, if I show that Kendall placed a defective and dangerous product into the marketplace, it is responsible for all injuries caused by that product regardless of its knowledge or fault."

"Then let's answer that question. What evidence do you have that the product is dangerous? Or that these magnets did not come from some other source?"

Sloane knew Rudolph was testing him, and that he was not achieving a passing grade. But this hearing was not about winning; it was about educating the judge. "Austin McFarland's older brother, Mathew, and Mateo Gallegos's older brother, Ricky, were both members of Kendall focus groups for the toy Metamorphis. The toy was in their homes. The parents' declarations establish that fact. Metamorphis is a product in which the magnets are encased in plastic. Austin McFarland and Mateo Gallegos both died from the ingestion of tiny but powerful magnets that eroded their intestines."

"But can you prove the magnets came from the toy, as opposed to some other product? Don't misunderstand my question." He looked to Reid and her associates, who until that point had been sitting fat and happy. "I think the evidence I've read here would certainly be enough to go to a jury, if this matter were to get that far. But the standard before me this morning is different. I need to balance the equities here. Can you prove that element?"

"Without a sample of the toy or its component parts, I can't, Your Honor. But I intend to obtain one through discovery."

Reid stood. "As Your Honor has correctly pointed out, the issue here is irreparable harm. Kendall is prepared to release this product for the holidays. Preventing Kendall from doing so, based on speculation and innuendo, would result in the loss of millions of dollars, not to mention dozens of lawsuits by retailers. It would cripple the company."

"I think he has more than speculation and innuendo, Ms. Reid, quite a bit more."

If the shot hit its mark, Reid did not show it. She continued without a pause. "First, Your Honor, Mr. Sloane represents a single family. He may claim to represent the Gallegoses, but his pleadings do not reflect that he does. Their declaration must be stricken as irrelevant. So we are really talking about evidence of a single child, and up until a few days ago, I don't need to remind this court that Mr. Sloane was convinced, and convinced a jury, that medical malpractice was responsible for that child's death. Moreover, even if Mr. Sloane could prove that a Kendall product was responsible for that child's death, which Kendall vehemently denies, the plaintiff's remedy is monetary damages. As callous as this may sound, no irreparable harm will befall the McFarlands. The harm has already occurred."

Reid was correct, of course, and she had stated Kendall's case eloquently, as Sloane expected, which was why Rudolph's next question surprised Sloane.

"If we are talking about the potential safety of children, what harm would it be to Kendall if I were to order it to submit a prototype for independent testing?"

Reid remained poised, apparently having anticipated this question. "Your Honor, there is no hard evidence to require such a drastic measure, and anything that caused a delay in the production of this toy would result in millions of dollars in losses. Kendall has timed the release of this product very carefully with the holiday season. It has contractual obligations with its retailers, and anything that might delay or impede production would cause it to breach those contractual obligations. I have provided you with a declaration from an industry analyst attesting to the fact that nearly seventy-two percent of toys are purchased immediately before the Christmas holiday. In light of this substantial harm, and the lack of any solid evidence that the product is defective, the drastic remedy of delaying production to test the toy is not warranted."

Sloane said, "If the company has no worries, as it professes, there would be no reason for it to shut down manufacturing or be in any jeopardy of breaching its contracts with its retailers while a prototype is inspected."

"But there is no need or legal obligation that Kendall do so," Reid shot back. "We have submitted within our packet of materials evidence that the product meets all applicable ASTM standards and, I will add, voluntary compliance with all federal regulations. The product was also tested and approved by the Product Safety Agency. There is no need for the product to be retested and, I must emphasize, there is no regulation that requires Kendall, or any other manufacturer, for that matter, to have their product independently inspected. Mr. Sloane is asking something of Kendall that no manufacturer is required to undertake."

"No other manufacturer produced a toy that killed my clients' child," Sloane shot back.

"Enough," Rudolph said, putting a quick end to the bickering. "Both of you will direct your comments to the bench. Do not test my patience. I'll fine you both." He sat back, contemplating his options.

Sloane was about to speak when Kannin touched his arm to indicate he'd said enough.

"Here's what we are going to do," Rudolph said. "I'm going to grant the motion for a temporary restraining order preventing plaintiffs from disclosing any information pertaining to the design of this product, and I am going to set this matter for further hearing on whether a permanent injunction should issue. At that time I will consider again plaintiffs' request for an independent inspection of the toy. At the moment I don't have enough information before me to order that be done. Mr. Sloane, how much time will you need to conduct your discovery on that limited issue?"

"Two weeks," Sloane said. "We'd like to depose certain individuals and would request that defendant agree to produce its witnesses on shortened notice."

"We have no objection," Reid said, "so long as plaintiffs agree to the same."

"I will put it in the order that the two sides are to cooperate. If you don't, you'll feel it in your wallets."

Rudolph made some handwritten notations, signed the document on his desk, and handed it down to his clerk in the well, who handed it to Reid.

"I'll see you all back here in two weeks," Rudolph said.

CAMELBACK MOUNTAIN
PHOENIX, ARIZONA

MAXINE BOLELLI PUSHED on, her tanned legs pumping like pistons up the mountain, her back and stomach glistening. The robin's-egg blue bandana wrapped around her head dripped sweat, turning it navy blue. She wore a matching sports bra and shorts. Bolelli loved to prove people wrong. So anyone who assumed from her plumpish figure that she was out of shape was in for a rude awakening. She liked nothing better than to walk onto a racquetball court looking like the big girl who didn't know which end of the racquet to hold and proceed to kick the crap out of some unsuspecting foe.

"So we have a name, Metamorphis," she said, her breathing only slightly labored despite an increase in the incline. "I like it."

"Kendall must be really concerned to have filed for a TRO," said Galaxy's president, Brandon Craft, his breathing strained as he spoke.

Craft was just a shade taller than Bolelli but a good twenty pounds overweight and clearly struggling. Bolelli had no sympathy for him. Lazy, Craft was not a hiker, or a walker for that matter. Had there been a moving sidewalk from the parking lot to the front of the building he would have taken it. It disgusted Bolelli. Still, Craft was doing better than Elizabeth Meyers. Galaxy's chief financial officer lagged three yards behind them, and the last time Bolelli checked, Meyers looked like an overripe tomato about to explode. The rest of Galaxy's executive team trudged along, some with heads bowed, as if on a death march, either struggling to keep up, or smart enough to realize they shouldn't pass their bosses.

A few years back a board member suggested that Galaxy hold "team-building retreats" to promote morale and foster an attitude of sharing and cooperation among the various departments. Other board members, thinking it a splendid idea, quickly approved the suggestion. What a crock of bullshit. Bolelli knew there would be no sharing among departments because everyone was too busy kissing her ass in search of the next promotion. What the board members really wanted was a boondoggle at the shareholders' expense. The word *retreat* conjured images of expensive hotels in exotic locales with golf courses, five-star restaurants, spas, and everyone sitting around the pool sipping mai tais and piña coladas while some team leader spewed psychobabble bullshit and asked everyone, "How do you feel about that?"

Ka-ching!

Lest anyone think Bolelli wasn't sympathetic to their wants and needs, she came up with her own morale-building retreats. She asked her administrative assistant to pick various spots around the Phoenix area for exercise. In the hotter months she moved the "retreats" indoors for racquetball tournaments and squash. Since today the weather was a balmy 102 degrees, she had taken everyone to Camelback Mountain. The hike was known to be arduous and had a reputation of leaving inexperienced hikers in positions where they had to be rescued. Still, no one had bowed out. No one dared.

"They don't want any information about the design becoming public," she said. "Can we get the pleadings?"

"Already have," Craft gasped. He used a water bottle to spray his face. "The pleadings are online. Nothing of use, though. The complaint is vague."

"What about the TRO papers?"

"They've been sealed by the court at Kendall's request."

"What about the theory that the toy could be dangerous?"

"Again, vague. No specifics."

"Give me the details," Bolelli said.

Craft took several deep breaths. "It indicates the children had siblings in a Kendall focus group. Kendall denies any liability. They say it's a publicity stunt to force a settlement."

"Can we get the names of the other children in the groups, talk to their parents?"

"Santoro doesn't have it. He says Fitzgerald must have it under lock and key. The parents of the children named in the lawsuit declined to talk to us."

"Keep an eye on it." Bolelli dug in for the final incline before the summit.

"What about the stock?" Craft asked.

"What about it? Fitzgerald is no dummy. He wouldn't be wasting his time filing a TRO unless he knew he was sitting on something huge, something that has never been done before. This just confirms everything we've already learned. Buy it."

"Our cash reserves are taking a hit."

"Sometimes you have to pay to play," she said, "and I intend to play."

At the summit, Bolelli stood king of the mountain. She sucked the warm desert air through her nostrils, feeling it burn, then wasted no time before beginning her march down the hill even before the others had reached the top.

"We're moving, people," she barked.

ONE UNION SQUARE BUILDING
SEATTLE, WASHINGTON

FOLLOWING THE HEARING, Sloane returned to his office and debriefed the McFarlands and Gallegoses in a conference room. Despite their demographic and socioeconomic differences, the two families had been bonded by one shared horrific experience. He sent the McFarlands home and the Gallegoses to a room at the Athletic Club so they would not have to travel back and forth to Mossylog each night. Manny's cousin would watch their children. Then Sloane returned to his office to see what fires burned.

Carolyn greeted him with a grim expression and handed him a document. "We were just served," she said. "I'm sorry."

The motion on behalf of Bill and Terri Larsen and Frank

Carter sought a temporary restraining order from San Francisco Superior Court prohibiting Sloane from coming within a hundred yards of the Larsens, Frank Carter, or Jake. Attached to the pleading was a declaration from Bill Larsen providing vivid details of Sloane's "assault" on Frank Carter. Bill Larsen also said Sloane had been menacing toward him and his wife in the meeting, and that he believed Sloane was mentally unbalanced and unfit in his present condition to care for Jake. Conspicuously missing was a declaration from Frank Carter, which Sloane found to be of particular interest. The motion sought a date for a hearing to determine custody of Jake.

Sloane had no intention of physically confronting the Larsens, or Frank, and, practically, he couldn't get to Jake either. What he did care about was the custody hearing.

"The hearing is in San Francisco Superior Court tomorrow," Carolyn said. "The judge's clerk said the custody hearing has not yet been set."

"Where's Tom?"

"In his office."

Pendergrass sat at his desk. Sloane handed him the papers.

"I saw them earlier," Pendergrass said. "How do you want to handle it?"

"File a pleading stating I have no objection to implementation of the temporary restraining order, but that I will contest custody and wish to be present and put on evidence. Ask to appear at the TRO hearing tomorrow telephonically. Make it clear, Tom. I want the court to know that I will contest custody, and I want Tina's parents to know that I have no intention of giving up Jake."

"I understand," Pendergrass said.

As soon as Sloane stepped into the hallway Carolyn barked at him again. "David, Barclay Reid is on the phone."

CONSTITUTION GARDENS
WASHINGTON, D.C.

CHARLES JENKINS WALKED the dirt and gravel path beneath the canopy of oak, maple, and dogwood trees parallel to the Reflecting Pool that stretched from the Washington Monument to the Lincoln Memorial. The leaves showed early signs of fall, faint hints of what would become the glorious reds, oranges, and yellows. A few had fallen, scattered by government employees passing him in business attire and tourists strolling the paths. Three men and a woman jogged past, their running shoes crunching the gravel beneath their feet in pounding unison.

Jenkins paused at the Lincoln Memorial before following a path to the bronze sculpture of three young men dressed in jungle attire and carrying weapons. Their faces were unknown to him, and yet so familiar; they could have been any of the men with whom he had served. The artist had been racially sensitive, but their varied ethnicities—white, black, and Hispanic—were of no matter. Nam was color-blind. So were the Vietcong bullets.

Jenkins continued down the path to the vertex of the black wall and the first name carved in stone. The dead were inscribed not in alphabetical but in chronological order, by date of their deaths. As the wall rose from the ground like a huge tombstone, he soon was running his fingers along thousands and thousands of the etched letters. The immensity and length of the granite, and the sheer number of names it held, overwhelmed him. Jenkins had never even seen pictures of the memorial in a magazine or newspaper. He'd avoided reading anything about Nam. He now realized that in so doing, he had abandoned these men, these brothers, while for thirty years he hid on Camano Island not to live, but to die. He'd been wrong. He'd been so wrong. What would each of the men and their families give to have been in his shoes, to have left the jungle alive, to be standing here at this moment, staring at someone else's name? He thought of the years he had served, and the names of the men, and he was tempted to look for them but knew that finding them now, thirty years removed, would only bring him back to a place he did not want to go.

"Unbelievable, isn't it?" Curley Wade stood to Jenkins's immediate right but facing the wall. Jenkins had not heard or seen him approach. "No matter how many times I come here it never gets any easier." Wade faced Jenkins. "But I come. I walk this way every chance I get—so I don't forget. I've heard that the graveyard in Normandy is like this, the magnitude of the sacrifice almost too immense to comprehend. I get a kick out of those people who say we live free. They need to come here and see this."

Jenkins followed Wade to the end of the wall and eventually down a path with black metal park benches. The early evening sky revealed the faint hint of a half moon, and the temperature had cooled, though it remained humid. They sat opposite the women's memorial, and as Wade opened a satchel, Jenkins watched a gray squirrel claw its way down a tree trunk, seeming to defy the laws of gravity. A breeze scattered leaves on the ground and rustled the branches. Overhead he heard the engines of a plane and behind them the rush of traffic on Constitution Avenue.

Wade removed a plain white envelope, handing it to him. "It isn't much."

Jenkins opened the flap and pulled out a grainy photograph of a man in a long black coat and slacks. The photograph had been taken with a telephoto lens, but the features of the man's face were clear enough that Jenkins could confirm it to be the same man in the photograph he had provided Wade. Judging from the other men and women in the photograph, and knowing that the average male was just over five nine and the average female just under five four, Jenkins estimated the man to be several inches over six feet.

The next photo was a blowup of the first. The man wore his hair combed back off his forehead in a ponytail.

"Arab?" Jenkins asked.

"American." Wade nodded to the envelope. Jenkins pulled out the remaining photograph. It depicted a group of men dressed in desert cammies holding automatic weapons. Perspiration had caused their face paint to smudge, a black and beige mask that made the whites of their eyes bulge at the camera.

Wade pointed to the third man from the right. "Anthony Stenopolis."

Jenkins had a name.

He studied the photograph more closely, his interest no longer the face but the uniform. He saw no patches on the fatigues: no American flags, no insignias. He saw no dog tags or even chains wrapped around the men's necks. In Vietnam there had been missions where men like Major Davidson showed up and Jenkins's squad was instructed to remove everything that could in any way associate them with the United States. That meant no cigarettes, no chewing gum, no dog tags, no flags, no insignias of any kind. Nothing. These excursions usually took them into Cambodia, though no one ever said so, and no records of the missions existed. When Jenkins later joined the Agency he learned that the missions were referred to as "counterinsurgency." In Nam, the men had called them something else: suicide runs.

"Very early after nine-eleven, U.S. intelligence agencies launched a series of operations that enabled them to locate and target key individuals in groups such as al-Qaeda in Iraq, the Sunni insurgency, and renegade Shia militias, or so-called special groups," Wade said. "The operations relied upon some of the most highly classified information in the U.S. government."

"What's his background?"

"Parents immigrated from Greece. He enlisted in the army and was identified as a candidate for further training. Apparently he showed a propensity for learning foreign languages—Spanish, Portuguese, German, French—and was assigned to the Defense Language Institute. He later served during Desert Storm. Honorably discharged and went to work for a private security contractor in the Middle East, Afghanistan, and Northern Africa."

"And we brought him back after nine-eleven."

Wade nodded. "He also speaks Farsi and several other Arab dialects."

Jenkins knew that this skill would have made Stenopolis a valuable asset. "Then what?"

Wade shrugged. "Based on what you've told me, he apparently went out on his own."

Jenkins reconsidered the blowup of the man's face. "If he's independent, there has to be a way for people to get in contact with him."

"This is where it gets tricky."

Jenkins waited.

"There's a name on a card in the file, someone who might know how to contact him but who won't be eager to talk to you about it."

Jenkins did not recognize the name on the card, but he knew why the man would be reluctant to discuss any association with someone like Stenopolis. "I appreciate it, Curley," he said. Then he asked the question that had been on his mind since he saw the photo of Stenopolis in uniform.

"How long did he work for the Agency?"

It was the only way Anthony Stenopolis could have been brought back into the fold so quickly after 9/11, given that the Agency had sent officers to Afghanistan just eight days after the planes crashed into the Twin Towers and had boots on the ground within fifteen. It was also the only way Wade could have obtained the information on Stenopolis so fast. He either had been, or remained, on the Agency's radar.

Wade did not immediately answer the question. Measuring his response, he said, "If he's done what you say, somewhere along the way he suffered a break. It could have been something during the war or something after, but he's gone down a very dark path."

Jenkins slipped the photos back into the envelope. "That path is about to come to an end, Curley."

THE SORRENTO HOTEL
SEATTLE, WASHINGTON

SLOANE ENTERED THE Sorrento Hotel from Madison Street still pondering his strategy. He pushed through a draped entrance that separated the hotel lobby from the Fireside Room and saw Barclay Reid sitting in a leather wing chair near a green tiled fireplace. Built in 1908, the hotel had been renovated but retained the original decor and furnishings. Shaped like an octagon, the Fireside Room was as ornate as a set from *Titanic*, with beaded lampshades, tasseled and overstuffed leather and cloth upholstery, potted palms, and dark mahogany walls. Crown molding gleamed beneath recessed ceiling lights, one of which lit Barclay as she stepped around the leather ottoman.

"Thank you for agreeing to meet with me." Her handshake remained firm, but her tone was much more conciliatory than it had been in the courtroom earlier that day.

"Not a problem," Sloane said. "I've always wanted to see this place."

"Let me first express my condolences. I'm very sorry for your loss. I haven't had the chance to tell you that."

"Thank you," Sloane said, believing her genuine. He sat in one of the wing chairs across the ottoman. The flames from the fire flickered shadows, and a piano player filled the room with soft jazz.

"What did you think of the hearing today?" Reid asked.

"About what I expected. You?"

"I wasn't thrilled that he's still considering the independent testing, but I agree, about what I expected."

A waiter in tuxedo attire, absent the jacket, approached. Reid already had a martini set on the table by her chair. "Would you like a drink?" she asked.

"Scotch, rocks," Sloane said.

"A Scotch man." Reid smiled. "Also what I would have expected."

"Am I that transparent?"

"You're in the news a lot."

"So are you, but I wouldn't have guessed martini."

"What would you have guessed?"

"Cosmopolitan."

She made a face. "Too sweet. Truth is, I'd rather have a beer, but it didn't seem an appropriate choice given the decor." She picked up her glass. "I think when push comes to shove, Judge Rudolph will deny your request for independent testing. There's no legal basis for him to order it."

"My experience is Judge Rudolph doesn't get too hung up on the law," Sloane said.

"We'll take a writ." Reid pulled an olive off a stick with her teeth. She referred to an immediate appeal to an appellate court to get a decision on a particular legal issue before the final resolution of the case.

"You could do that," Sloane said. "But tell me, why would Kendall? As I've said, if the product is safe and not susceptible to defects, why not just get the independent testing performed and be done with it?"

"Because it sets a bad precedent, and the law does not allow for it."

"How is making sure a product is safe a bad precedent? What about a moral reason? This is the same company that professes to put the safety of children first and foremost."

"And they have, for over one hundred years. But they don't want the government or the courts ordering them to do what the current law and regulations do not require."

"So tell them to do it voluntarily. Be a trailblazer. They can use the positive publicity."

The waiter set Sloane's drink on a coaster on the table beside him. Sloane took a sip, keeping the glass in his hand and letting the Scotch stimulate his taste buds before swallowing.

"You also have no evidence that Kendall was aware of the alleged defect."

"I beg to differ," Sloane said, hoping to provoke some response.

"And what would that be?"

"Kyle Horgan."

"Malcolm mentioned something about that. He'll state under oath that he never saw any letter and does not know the man," Reid said.

"Then we'll let a jury decide who's telling the truth."

Reid tucked her hair behind one ear, looking girlish. "Who is this guy anyway?"

"He designed Metamorphis."

She smiled. "Metamorphis was designed in-house at Kendall."

"Then someone stole Horgan's design."

"You can prove that?"

"I'm working on it."

"We'll want to depose Horgan."

"That's one of the things I'm working on. He's disappeared. I don't know where he is." Sloane saw no reason to hide that ball. Reid would learn of it soon enough.

Reid contemplated that piece of information for a moment, undoubtedly wondering if Sloane truly didn't know where Horgan was, or if he was just keeping the information from her.

"We'll find him," she said, confirming his deduction.

"If you do, let me know, would you?" Sloane took another sip. "I don't need to show knowledge if the product is defective and injured two children."

"One child," she countered. "We intend to file a motion to enforce the settlement agreement with the Gallegoses. Given that they were represented by counsel, Rudolph will have to enforce its terms."

"You've met Dayron, have you?"

"Not in person, no."

"I have. You might want to meet him before you conclude the Gallegoses were represented by anybody."

"The law doesn't look into how competent the attorney is."

"Actually it does, and it does require that the attorney be licensed. Dayron's in a bit of trouble with the bar, Barclay, and it isn't the first time. He had his license suspended two years ago. My clients don't read English, he never told them about the magnets, he threatened them with deportation, and he kept two-thirds of the settlement." Sloane shrugged. "So, one child with magnets in his intestines might be an accident, but two is a problem for your client. It will be very difficult for a court to dismiss, or the media for that matter. But let's forget all that for a moment. How is it going to look if six months from now Metamorphis is recalled because another child has died? How's it going to look when the public learns that Kendall had knowledge of even the possibility of a defect but chose to go to market anyway? Is that the image your client wants portrayed to the media? Is that the image your client wants for a company that has proudly made safe toys for children for more than a hundred years?"

"My client is confident there will be no recall."

"I hope for the children of the families who buy the toy that he's right."

Reid sipped her martini. "But you do raise a good point."

"I did?" Sloane said. "It didn't sound like it. Which one?"

"Kendall has built a reputation in the community over the past hundred years and doesn't want to see that reputation dragged through the media."

A settlement. Sloane had suspected it to be the purpose for the meeting. He didn't think Reid had called to get better acquainted. "I'm all ears."

"I've been authorized to offer each of your clients a million dollars."

That number surprised him, by a wide margin. He was glad he had not been sipping his drink because he might have choked. In an instant Reid had pulled the rug out from beneath Sloane's feet. A settlement would keep him from getting to Fitzgerald.

"But they both have to agree," she said.

"You can't link the two together."

"I can and I am. If one declines, the offer is off the table and Katie bar the door. Kendall is not admitting liability. It's protecting its reputation. Both families must agree to full confidentiality of the settlement, and abide by the temporary restraining order. You agree to return any documents in your possession that make any mention of Metamorphis."

"And will Kendall agree to have the toy independently tested?" Sloane asked.

Reid spoke over the rim of her martini glass. "That," she said, "is a deal breaker."

HE ADMIRED THE ebb and flow of muscles in the full-length mirrored walls. Attired in spandex pants and tennis shoes,

Anthony Stenopolis followed a droplet of sweat over the ridges of his stomach as he pulled himself up and placed his chin over the bar. Around his waist he had strapped a leather belt, and hanging from it, a forty-five-pound weight. His personal best at this weight was twenty-eight pull-ups. He was halfway to that goal and felt no fatigue.

The fitness club frowned on patrons displaying flesh, but it was open twenty-four hours, and nearing midnight, Stenopolis had the weight room almost to himself. Besides, the woman doing a set of lunges on the opposite side of the floor didn't seem to mind, sneaking peeks at him in the mirror and giving him a flirtatious smile. He ignored her, maintaining his focus despite the annoying heavy beat of music thumping the room.

When he had completed a set of thirty-four he dropped to the rubber mat and quickly counted out fifty push-ups, rolling a small medicine ball back and forth between his hands to add difficulty. His forty-five-minute workout focused on core muscles, balance, and stamina. He smirked at the muscle heads who threw three hundred pounds on a bar and bench-pressed it once to their chest, then flexed in the mirror, as if it were an incredible act of strength. Most couldn't run up a flight of stairs without becoming winded.

He used fitness clubs in the various cities he frequented, buying one-day guest passes. He kept no permanent memberships because he kept no permanent address, both of which could be traced. Since he also discarded most of his clothing after each job, his wardrobe came from a suitcase, replenished in the cities where he worked around the world. It further eliminated any trail of identification.

After his push-ups he found an isolated corner and went through each of his martial arts movements, concentrating on exact precision. When done, he would conclude his workout with five three-minute rounds of kickboxing on the heavy bag. It was more than he had intended to do, but he remained disturbed after a client called to express displeasure with his recent performance. It seemed that the attorney, David Sloane, remained a nuisance, and the client opined that Stenopolis should have killed Sloane when he had the chance. Stenopolis hated it when clients sought more than they had bargained for, or questioned his integrity. He politely reminded his client that his assignment had been to retrieve Kyle Horgan's file, and that he had accomplished that task. If the client had wanted Sloane dead, Stenopolis would have put a bullet in his skull and ensured it. In fact, had the kid not called 911 that's exactly what he would have done. Stenopolis was not in the habit of leaving anyone alive who could identify him, and he had assumed, wrongly, that Sloane's wounds were also fatal. Once he'd heard the sirens his priority became retrieving Horgan's file. Stenopolis had never failed to complete an assignment. Still, he was more than willing to accommodate his client—for a further fee, a sum they agreed upon after minimal bartering.

During his workout Stenopolis focused his attention on how best to accomplish the task of killing David Sloane, which would now be more difficult, since Sloane would be guarded and could visually identify him. Sloane was also obviously bright and would likely be more attentive to anything out of the norm. What Stenopolis found most intriguing, however, was the information he had obtained about the police investigation into the death of Sloane's wife. The police had not directed any inquiry to Kendall Toys, which surely would have been the case if Sloane had advised them about Kyle Horgan's file. The lack of inquiry could only mean that Sloane was holding back information, and the only reason Stenopolis could fathom that Sloane would do so was Sloane did not want the police talking to Kendall. Sloane apparently thought he could exact revenge for his wife's death. Stenopolis smiled at his reflection in the mirror. Sloane had convinced himself that he was a physical and intellectual match. It was a typical marine mentality and Stenopolis had encountered it many times during and after his military service. Their arrogance—unwilling even to refer to themselves as a "former marine"—was usually their downfall. Most still saw themselves as the lean, muscular recruits brainwashed out of boot camp to believe they could run through brick walls and that bullets would bounce off their chests. In reality civilian life made them soft. They lost their edge. Sloane was about to find that out firsthand.

The veins of Stenopolis's biceps bulged with the flow of blood pumping through his body. The thought of Sloane fueled him until his arms trembled from the exertion and he could barely lift them above his shoulders. Sitting and wiping the sweat dripping down his chest with a towel, he heard the cell phone in his gym bag ring, barely audible over the coarse music pumping through the overhead speakers. Cell phones were also prohibited in the club. Stenopolis answered.

"Someone pulled your file."

Stenopolis did not have to ask the caller his name, or the meaning of his statement. He recognized the voice, though he had not heard it in some years.

"Do we know who?"

"Former operative. Has a desk job now. Curley Wade."

"When?"

"Yesterday."

Stenopolis disconnected the call, grabbed his gym bag, and walked toward the locker room and showers. Mr. Sloane had been granted a temporary reprieve.

CHAPTER
TEN

The following day, Sloane separated the McFarlands and Gallegoses in two conference rooms, not wanting either to feel pressured by the other's decision. He knew Kendall's motivation to settle was to avoid the media, and he couldn't blame them for making it an all-or-nothing deal. It had, however, placed him in a difficult situation. It was reasonable to assume, given that they had already returned more than three million dollars, that the McFarlands would turn down Kendall's offer. The Gallegos situation, however, was completely different. For them a million dollars could substantially change their lives and the lives of their children.

As Sloane walked down the hall to where the Gallegoses waited, Tom Pendergrass intercepted him. "The court in San Francisco granted the TRO, David."

Sloane had expected as much, given his decision not to contest it. "What about the custody hearing?"

"Two weeks from today. The court ordered briefs filed by the end of this week. I'm going to need some time to talk with you.

The court looks at the child's living situation, school, finances. There are a lot of factors."

Sloane looked at his watch. "Okay, let's catch up this afternoon."

The Gallegoses sat at the conference room table still wearing their coats and looking concerned and uncomfortable. Sloane greeted them in Spanish to try to ease their anxiety. It only partially worked. Manny smiled, but Rosa-Maria continued to fidget with an oval-shaped medal around her neck.

"It's beautiful," Sloane said of the blue and silver medallion at the end of the chain.

She moved her hand so that he could better see it. "It is Our Lady of Guadalupe," she said, still speaking Spanish. "Are you familiar with her?"

"I'm afraid not." Sloane knew Mary was considered to be the mother of Jesus Christ, and he had learned somewhere that 90 percent of the households in Mexico had an image of Our Lady of Guadalupe in their homes, a higher percentage than the population of Catholics in the country.

"I'm sorry," she said, replacing the medallion beneath her shirt.

"No," Sloane said, sensing that the medal gave her comfort. "Tell me."

Rosa-Maria explained that the Lady had appeared to Juan Diego, a Native American, on a hilltop outside of Mexico City during the fifteenth century and told him to instruct the bishop to build a church on that site. When the bishop resisted, demanding some sign, Diego returned in mid-December with his cloak filled with roses. Upon spilling them at the bishop's feet he revealed the image of the Lady imprinted on the fabric. Five hundred years later that image remained behind glass on a church wall and showed no signs of decay.

"My mother named me Rosa for the roses and Maria for Our Lady," she said. "We pray to her every night that she will take care of our Mateo and now, that she will look after your wife as well."

Sloane was moved by her comment and thanked them both. He also sensed that her telling the story had relaxed her, and it made him again wish that he had that same kind of faith, but if he had ever had that gift as the young boy preaching in the mountains of Oaxaca, the ensuing years of loneliness and isolation had stolen it from him.

It was time to get to it. "I received a telephone call yesterday from Kendall's attorney."

"The woman?" Manny asked.

"She asked to meet with me following the hearing. Kendall wants to settle this matter."

"Settle? How?" Manny asked.

"They want to pay you one million dollars." The number caused Manny and Rosa-Maria to sit back.

"And the McFarlands?" Manny asked.

"Yes, both of you." Sloane did not tell them they both had to agree.

"What did the McFarlands say?" Manny asked.

"This is your decision," Sloane said. "I want you to make your decision independently before we talk further. I know it's a lot of money. Why don't I give you some time to think about it?"

"That is not necessary," Rosa-Maria said. "Since you came to our home we have prayed every night to Our Lady. We believe that she sent you to us, for Mateo and the other children."

Sloane deflected the statement. "I'm no angel," he said.

"We have talked to the McFarlands. We know they gave back the money they received from the doctor and that you did too. We know that you are a man of principle, a good man. Your wife has died and yet you are here, trying to help us."

Sloane felt a twinge of guilt, knowing his motives were not completely altruistic.

"If you can do it, so can we," Rosa said.

"I'm here for my own reasons, but they are not your reasons, and I don't want them to influence you in any manner. You need to make the decision that is best for you and your family. A million dollars would do a lot to change your lives and your children's lives."

"But we told you," Rosa-Maria said. "This is not about the money. We have never had much, but we were happy. No money will ever bring back our Mateo. We will be happy only when we know that other families will not suffer. We don't want their money. We want you to stop the toy."

"I can't promise you I can do that."

"But you will try."

"Yes, I will try," Sloane said. "But I might not succeed, and then Kendall will not make this settlement offer again."

"Then we will pray to Our Lady to help you win."

Sloane didn't know what to say. He knew what a million dollars would mean to them, and yet here they sat, not even considering it. It was a remarkable sacrifice, and he could only hope that he would be able to justify the depth of their faith in him.

THE KETTLE

GEORGETOWN, WASHINGTON, D.C.

ANNE LEROY WALKED down steep concrete steps that smelled of mold despite what looked like a fresh coat of paint. She pushed through Dutch doors into hazy, yellow-tinted light. As with the rest of the country, smoking had been prohibited in most drinking establishments in Georgetown, including the Kettle, but the smell of tobacco, smoked in the below ground bar for more than two hundred years, still seeped from the heavy wooden beams across the ceiling.

The plank floor was scattered with sawdust, and LeRoy circled the bar, glancing behind the wood-and-glass dividers separating the booths. No neon signs hung on the wall advertising beer, nor were there any metal street signs or posters of athletes. No televisions blasted out the evening's sporting events, though she knew the Nationals were playing a night game. The Kettle sought to remain as it had been in the late 1700s, when it was rumored to be a drinking establishment of George Washington, Thomas Jefferson, and a few other of the nation's founding fathers. And yet, despite its aversion to modern technology, the bar still maintained a steady and faithful clientele, mostly from the nearby Georgetown campus.

LeRoy liked it because it was a quiet place to get a beer and an inexpensive bite to eat within walking distance of her apartment where she didn't have to worry about some jerk trying to hit on her.

Not seeing Peggy Seeley, LeRoy slipped off her backpack, shook the water from her hair from the unexpected late-afternoon thunder shower, and took a seat in an empty booth. When the waitress did not descend on her like a bird of prey she unzipped her pack and took out her latest Kevin O'Brien novel, opening to the dog-eared page. Three pages later the waitress stood beside her table, and LeRoy contemplated ordering the macaroni and cheese but decided instead on her usual, a Sam Adams and a cheeseburger. The waitress didn't ask her how she wanted it cooked. The cook didn't care. It would come with a heaping of grease-dripping French fries, the oil saturating a paper-lined wooden basket.

When the waitress departed, LeRoy watched Peggy Seeley

step through the doors and turn a corner, peering into the booths. She leaned out and flagged her down.

Seeley slipped in the other side of the booth, sounding exasperated. "I walked by this place three times," she said. "I was about to call your cell."

It was no wonder, given the amount of dust and particulates on the lenses of Seeley's wire-rimmed glasses. "Didn't you see the lantern above the door?"

"Obviously not. You didn't tell me the door was below ground." Seeley looked at the fire burning in a brick fireplace. "I feel like I'm in a Harry Potter novel. Do these walls open up into Diagon Alley?"

The waitress approached, pen on pad, but didn't say a word.

"You want something to drink or eat?" LeRoy asked.

"What do you have?" Seeley asked.

The waitress leaned across the nicked and scarred table to grab a rectangular menu about twice the width of a bookmark and handed it to Seeley. Seeley considered it with a frown. "Could I get a salad and a glass of white wine?"

"Oil and vinegar?" the waitress asked.

"Do you have ranch?"

"Nope."

"Then I guess so."

Seeley opened her briefcase, pulled out a section of the newspaper folded in half, and slid it across the table to LeRoy. The headline indicated the article was about a lawsuit in Washington State against a toy company. Beneath it was a photo of a good-looking, dark-haired man in a suit and tie, an attorney named David Sloane.

"Tell me he's your rich uncle and he's single," LeRoy said.

"You wish. Read," Seeley said.

LeRoy did.

Associated Press

SEATTLE—Attorney David Sloane is back at it. Yesterday, on the steps of the King County courthouse
in Seattle, Sloane announced a product liability action against a local landmark, Kendall Toys, Inc.

Sloane's complaint alleges that two children, Austin McFarland (6) and Mateo Gallegos (4), died from
the ingestion of tiny magnets embedded in a toy that
were freed when pieces of the toy broke. Yesterday
the company struck back, filing for a temporary restraining order to prevent Sloane and the two families from disclosing any information concerning the
design of the as yet unreleased toy. A spokesperson
for the company denied the allegations, calling the
press conference "a publicity stunt."

"Holy shit," LeRoy said. "This is exactly what my research
warned against."

"I know," Seeley said.

"What did Payne say?"

"What do you mean what did he say?"

"You didn't show this to him?"

"God, no. I'm not supposed to have anything to do with you
or your report."

"But this changes everything. This is exactly why I was doing
the investigation."

"It changes nothing."

"What are you talking about? I should call him, maybe—"

"Maybe what? It isn't going to happen, Anne."

LeRoy sat back, not because she was deflated, but because a
thought struck her. A flame sizzled and flickered over the counter

separating the bar from the small kitchen, illuminating the chef in a burst of light.

"Anne?"

"What if he knew?"

"What if who knew? What are you talking about?"

"This story, this, the magnets, what if Payne knew?"

"I'm not following you."

LeRoy leaned forward and lowered her voice. "Remember I said that none of this made any sense: Payne shutting down an investigation that he asked me to pursue, how excited he was about the initial findings and telling me that he was going to take it to Senator Wallace."

"Yeah."

"What if this is the reason he shut it down? What if this company somehow knew about the report and . . ." LeRoy couldn't finish.

"And what, Albert Payne took a bribe?" Seeley laughed. "Come on, Anne, the man won't take an extra cookie at a party until he knows everyone has had one."

LeRoy sat back, frustrated. "It's just . . . The timing is an odd coincidence, you have to admit that."

"Timing has nothing to do with it. We never even would have given the article a second glance if you hadn't been doing the investigation. We're just sensitive to it, that's all."

"Maybe you're right."

"Of course I'm right. Besides, you sent it back, didn't you?"

"What?"

"The report. You sent back the memory stick, right?"

"Yeah, yeah, I'm going to."

"Going to?" Seeley asked with alarm. "You haven't done it yet?"

"I've been busy."

"What, painting? Are you looking for trouble?"

"But don't you see?" She tapped on the article, her finger hitting the attorney directly between the eyes. "This vindicates my research. It vindicates what I was doing. Payne can't pull the funding now. He can't."

"He already did. Besides, Anne, he's still acting bizarre. I saw him the other afternoon coming out of the bathroom, and he looked like he had just thrown up. He left and didn't come back. He doesn't look well. He still has that rash."

LeRoy studied the article further. "Maybe it's Maggie Powers."

"What?" Seeley said, sounding more exasperated.

"Maybe she told Payne to pull the funding. Maybe she knows something about this. She was in the toy industry. Maybe somebody just didn't want a report about magnets coming out because of something like this." She tapped the article again. "Maybe she's pressuring Payne because someone is pressuring her."

"Like who?"

"I don't know. Maybe this company." She searched the article. "Kendall Toys. It says they're coming out with a new toy that uses magnets that will revolutionize the industry. If there's a report out there that says these magnets could be harmful . . ."

"I think you've been inhaling the smoke in here too long or the chemicals from your painting class have got to you. How would that company have even known you were doing a report?"

LeRoy put down the newspaper. "All I'm saying is the whole thing is weird, and this just makes it even weirder."

"Which is exactly why you need to get rid of that report; you need to send back that zip drive. You need this like you need a hole in the head. Why would you want anything to do with this?"

LeRoy kept reading the article.

"Anne?"

"I know. I know."

The waitress put a basket with a hamburger half-wrapped in paper and a mug of Sam Adams in front of LeRoy and the glass of wine and a salad in a wooden bowl on Seeley's side of the table.

"So you're going to mail back the zip drive, right?" Seeley asked.

"Yeah, I'll give it back," LeRoy said, but then she ignored her hamburger, focusing on the picture and the caption beneath it.

THE RENAISSANCE MAYFLOWER HOTEL
DUPONT CIRCLE, WASHINGTON, D.C.

HE COULD SPOT them from across the room, the subtle ways they carried themselves, shoulders pulled back, posture perfect, the way they tilted their heads, flirtatious, but subtle. The hemline of her dress, which carried a four-figure price tag, was an inch or two higher than necessary, the neckline an inch or two lower.

God she was delicious to look at!

Auburn hair folded behind her ears and rested against the peach-colored flesh of her back. She crossed one long, toned leg over the other, sitting at an angle, her open-toe, three-inch heel dangling from her foot. The subtle eye contact confirmed it, holding his gaze a fraction longer than necessary before diverting. Still, these things needed to be handled delicately. He couldn't rush over like a bull elephant in heat. He had to be discerning. He watched the room to determine if anyone else had caught sight of her. Men glanced in her direction, but none looked to have the cojones to approach.

And that was part of the thrill.

He signaled to his waiter, paid his bill, and walked as if to leave, stopping at her booth, which she had selected in a discreet area of the lounge. She looked up at him with bored indifference, but he could see the hint of a smile curl the corner of her lips.

"How does a beautiful young lady such as yourself end up alone?" he asked.

She shrugged, her cleavage heaving gently. "I have bad taste in men," she said.

"And what type of men is that?" he asked.

She ran a painted fingernail across her chin. "Bad men."

TEN MINUTES LATER, he walked through the ornate lobby past the registration desk to the elevators, fidgeting like a schoolboy on his first date, almost unable to wait for those in the elevator to get out before he stepped in. He hit the close button three times. On the eighth floor he followed the arrows on the wall to room 827 and considered the hallway in each direction. Seeing no one, he removed the breath mint from his tongue and tossed it aside, then knocked three times. Seconds passed and he panicked, thinking perhaps he'd gotten the room number wrong, but then he heard the latch turn and the door pulled open. She was even more beautiful standing, tall and elegant. He couldn't wait to see what she looked like on her back.

"No trouble finding me?" she asked.

He smiled. "I could find you anywhere."

He moved forward and she let him in, pushing the door shut behind them and tilting back her head to allow his lips to slide past her cheek to her neck. He grabbed her hard about the waist, his lips moving down the contours of her dress to her breasts. He slid one strap off a shoulder. She shrugged her arm free. The other strap followed. His hands moved lower, gripping her below the waist. He felt no panty lines.

She pushed him back. "It's a thousand," she said. "I pay for the room. You pay for the room service."

He liked this one. She had spirit. He pulled his billfold from his jacket pocket, counting out ten hundred-dollar bills, letting each flutter to the bed. "I hope you take cash," he said.

She smiled. "Doesn't everyone."

She unbuttoned his shirt, somehow managing to remove it without removing the tie, which she tugged playfully, pulling him toward the windows. In the near distance shined the dome of the Capitol Building.

"So you're a bad boy," she said.

"Very bad," he said.

She undid the buckle of his pants, then the button, and let her hand slide down his hairless flesh.

"I thought you might like a view," she said, lowering to her knees.

Screw the view, he saw it every day. He closed his eyes. After a moment, when he had felt nothing, he opened them. She had pulled the straps of her dress back onto her shoulders.

"Hey, what gives?" he asked.

The answer came from behind him. "You, apparently."

APPALACHIAN MOUNTAINS
VIRGINIA

HE CROSSED INTO Virginia driving exactly five miles over the speed limit. With the bars closing, officers looked for cars driving suspiciously slow, as well as those maneuvering erratically. Driving the speed limit could attract police attention as much as speeding. A full moon and a blanket of stars painted the two-lane interstate a bleak white, only the shadows of the dense trees and foliage along each side visible. But for an occasional car passing in the opposite direction, the road was deserted.

After thirty minutes he exited the interstate, continuing

southwest, through a thick forest. Another twenty minutes passed before he approached the unmarked turnoff. Unless a driver were searching for it, they would not likely detect it. He checked his rearview mirror for headlights. Seeing none, he killed the lights and turned, driving blind until certain he was clear of the road, then switched the lights back on. The pavement ascended a gradual slope for another mile and a quarter before coming to a rusted metal bar and, attached to it, a white sign, rusted around the edges and where the two bolts held it in place.

NO TRESPASSING

PRIVATE PROPERTY

He exited the rental car, not bothering to turn off the headlights. There was no longer a need. The property had been abandoned for more than twenty years, since the discovery that asbestos could be fatal to one's health. The acreage surrounding the mine had been contaminated with tons of asbestos particulates and would remain that way for many decades. The cost to remediate was exorbitant, and the company had long since filed for bankruptcy. The good people of Virginia weren't about to spend their hard-earned tax dollars to do it, and the government had dozens of other Superfund sites of higher priority.

Stenopolis had been to the property before. On the first occasion he had considered the heavy lock that secured a chain to a post cemented into the ground. From the rust he could tell that it had not been opened in years. On his second visit he had snapped the lock with a pair of bolt cutters and replaced it with an identical, though brand-new, lock and set it to his personal combination.

He now entered the four digits and pulled the heavy chain from the gate. After driving through he stopped just clear of the gate's swing and resecured the lock.

The sagebrush continued to intrude upon the road, branches brushing against the car's side mirrors and windows. Heavy rains had washed out the untended road, and snow and freezing temperatures left deep potholes that caused the tires to pitch and bounce. Stenopolis took his time, in no hurry and not wanting to get stuck, though he had rented a four-wheel-drive vehicle and had bought a winch with a fifty-foot steel cable. He couldn't very well call AAA for roadside assistance.

A quarter of a mile up the unpaved road the headlights shone upon the weathered metal siding of one of the abandoned structures and reflected in windowpanes that had been cracked and broken. He drove into a dirt area that had, at one time, served as the mining company's parking lot. The beams revealed a white, snowlike material that carpeted the soil and clung to the rusted metal piping and the equipment like Spanish moss hanging from the branches in a Louisiana bayou. In the foreground sat a large metal Quonset hut. Pipes and troughs pierced its sides, entering and exiting at odd angles. Rail spurs behind the building continued past mounds of dirt that nearly reached the roofline, and rusted metal drums, some cut in half, littered the ground. Stenopolis drove slowly up another slope and entered the facade of a metal building at the top of the ascent into the mine. Boxcars sat idly on tracks that led from the headlights' beams into darkness. The cars had at one time carried the dirt out of the mine and dumped it into the Quonset hut for processing of the vermiculite from the stone.

Stenopolis turned off the headlights and the engine and enjoyed the utter darkness and silence. He could see nothing in front of him or behind; even the reflection of the moon stopped at the mine entrance, as if fearful to enter.

He grabbed the flashlight from the seat as he stepped out and used it to find the metal bar he had left on a prior visit. When he opened the trunk the man inside moaned, but the cloth in his mouth, secured with duct tape, prevented him from speaking or shouting for help. Not that it was needed any longer. Several additional strands of the tape wrapped around the man's head prevented him from seeing. Stenopolis had read somewhere that enough duct tape was sold every year to circumnavigate Earth several times. He didn't doubt it. He had found it to be a product he could put to any number of uses.

He pulled the six-inch serrated blade from its sheath and with a single flick cut through the cord that secured the man's bound wrists to his ankles, grabbed his hostage under the arms, and pulled him from the trunk. The man continued to thrash but was more than manageable.

Stenopolis shoved the metal bar beneath the man's left armpit and pushed it through the other side. Grabbing the pole on each extended end, he kicked the man's legs out from underneath him, and he fell back. The man groaned in pain as the metal bar caught his body weight beneath his armpits. Stenopolis dragged him deeper into the mine, like pulling a wheelbarrow backward, the heels of the man's shoes carving a path in the dirt that Stenopolis would erase when he had finished.

Twenty feet farther down the shaft he came to the snap hook that extended from the metal chain he had secured to a ceiling beam. He fastened the hook to the bar in the center of the man's back, pulled the chain through the eye hook in the ceiling beam until taut, then hooked a link of the chain on one of the teeth of a gear train attached to a crank handle. He turned the handle until the chain lifted the man onto his toes and the teeth of the gear train caught, locking it in place and freeing Stenopolis to use his hands for other tasks.

The man swayed, as if pushed by a light breeze, the creaking chain against the wood beam and the wind whistling deep within the mine shaft the only sounds. The man turned his head, moaning, but this time it had less to do with the pain and more to do with his confusion as to his captor, and his fate.

Stenopolis stepped forward and used the knife to cut the tape across the man's mouth, drawing a line of blood. He pulled the tape free and yanked the rag from the man's mouth.

Gasping, the man desperately tried to lift his chest to suck oxygen into his lungs.

"You might not want to breathe too deeply," Stenopolis said. "They say the stuff around here can kill you."

"Who are you?" the man asked between gasps for air.

Stenopolis had once watched a special on the Discovery Channel about the ancient practice of crucifixions and was fascinated to learn that the victims usually did not die from their wounds or beatings. They suffocated. Their bound or pierced arms weakened until they were no longer strong enough to lift their bodies to allow their chest to expand and bring oxygen into their lungs.

"Who are you?" his guest asked again. "What do you want?"

Stenopolis flicked the knife again and pulled free the tape across the man's eyes as he placed the stream of light beneath his chin. "Boo."

The man jerked away. "What the . . . ?"

"Good evening, Mr. Wade."

"Who are you?"

"I believe you already know my name, which is why we're here."

"I don't know you."

"Oh, but you do. You pulled my file just the other day."

Curley Wade's brow furrowed. "I don't know what you're talking about. What file?"

"Mr. Wade, I assure you that this will go a lot more efficiently if you don't play games with me. I'm not a patient man. It's late and I would still like to get a few hours of sleep tonight."

"Maybe there was a mistake. I work in Human Resources. Maybe your file was pulled by someone else."

Stenopolis cranked the handle half a turn. The chain raised Wade another inch, enough so that his toes no longer reached the ground and the muscles of his shoulders and chest now bore his full weight. Wade grimaced.

"For an Agency man, you are not a convincing liar, but then I always did think your training lacking. I never felt you pushed your candidates far enough to find out if they would break. I'm betting you will. Now, tell me why you pulled my file."

"Go to hell."

Stenopolis stepped forward and put the beam of light back beneath his chin. "I'm about to show you why you can be very certain of that."

THE RENAISSANCE MAYFLOWER HOTEL
DUPONT CIRCLE, WASHINGTON, D.C.

THE MAN SPUN. "What the hell? Who are you?"

Charles Jenkins emerged from the bathroom holding the small portable video camera that, as the salesclerk had promised, had no problem filming in the room's limited lighting.

"Who I am is irrelevant. Who you are, Mr. Secretary of Labor, is very, very relevant." He nodded to the woman. "You can go."

She grabbed her jacket and small purse from the bed, along with the hundred-dollar bills.

The man stepped forward, but Jenkins stepped between them. "Hey, that's my money."

Amazing, Jenkins thought, but then, like many politicians, it was Hotchkin's arrogance that had got him in trouble in the first place.

"Here's the problem, Ed. I promised the young lady fifteen hundred dollars and I'm about a thousand short."

Hotchkin fumed as the woman retrieved the money and continued to the door, looking back over her shoulder with a smile before stepping out.

"Who do you work for?" Hotchkin asked.

"Again, not relevant. Who *you* work for, very relevant. You work for the people of the United States of America. That makes you a public figure. I'm not sure the new administration needs this embarrassment, do you?"

Hotchkin sighed. "What is it you want? Money? I can get you some."

"If I had wanted any more of your wife's money, Ed, I would have taken the grand off the bed. Does she know how you spend her inheritance? I guess the fact that you managed to get your current appointment, despite your past indiscretions, makes that doubtful."

Hotchkin stewed but did not respond.

Jenkins sat in the chair by the window. "Now, I'm not looking to break up a happy home or even to embarrass you, so neither your wife nor anybody else needs to know anything about what happened tonight."

Hotchkin continued to sound skeptical. "Then what do you want?"

"I want to know how I can get in touch with Anthony Stenopolis."

"Who?"

Jenkins took out the photograph taken by the security camera at Kyle Horgan's apartment building and showed it to Hotchkin. In the dim light it took Hotchkin a moment for his eyes to adjust.

"I don't know him," he said.

Jenkins smiled. "Then tell me how you got in touch with him."

"Are you with the FBI?"

"I'm an independent contractor with independent business with Mr. Stenopolis."

"I don't know how to get in touch with him."

"About a year ago he took care of a messy problem for you. I believe you were caught in similar circumstances but the individuals involved that night weren't as reasonable as I am. You got in touch with Stenopolis and the problem disappeared, along with the prostitute and lowlife trying to blackmail you. So did someone arrange a meeting? How did it happen?"

Hotchkin didn't immediately answer.

"Once I get the information, you're out of this, Ed. I'm trying to be reasonable here. Don't force me to do something I don't want to do."

Hotchkin sat on the edge of the bed looking defeated. "I was given a number to call. No one answered, but I was told to leave a message."

"What kind of message?"

"Just my telephone number. I had to answer a question when he called back."

"What was the question?"

Hotchkin lowered his head. "'What comes but once, can't be avoided, and ends as soon as it begins.'"

"And the answer?"

"'Death.'" Hotchkin said.

"I want the number."

Hotchkin shook his head. "I don't have it anymore. I threw it away."

"I don't believe you. A guy like you who can't keep his pecker in his pants isn't about to throw away his lifeline."

"I did. I don't have it anymore."

Jenkins stood and started for the door. "Then I guess we're done here. Sorry we couldn't do business. Make sure you check out the front page of the *Washington Post* tomorrow, and You-Tube. The Internet can really get those videos out there fast."

Jenkins got halfway to the door, which was a lot farther than he thought Hotchkin's game of chicken would last.

"Wait."

Jenkins turned. "You have something you want to say?"

"If I give you his number you have to be certain he does not trace it back to me. You're wrong about my ever calling him again. I won't. I don't want anything more to do with him, and if you were smart, you wouldn't either."

"Agreed. Here's how this will work. I'll give you a number to call. You will call and leave the telephone number after the message. If I find out you gave me a fake number, Ed, you'll have a bigger problem than him."

Hotchkin smirked. "You have no idea who you're dealing with."

"To the contrary, I now know exactly who I'm dealing with. He's the one who's going to be in the dark this time."

THE WASHINGTON ATHLETIC CLUB

SEATTLE, WASHINGTON

MENTALLY EXHAUSTED, SLOANE returned to his hotel room and sat by the window, the ambient light casting half his face in shadows. He had still not been back to Three Tree Point. He had relied on Jenkins to retrieve needed clothes, and now that Jenkins was back east, he had bought what he needed.

Nights and mornings remained the most difficult. He filled the days with the only thing he knew, the only thing he had ever known before Tina and Jake—his work. His resolve to take down Kendall Toys and Malcolm Fitzgerald kept his mind occupied until the point of exhaustion, usually well past midnight. But by the time he finished the short walk back to his hotel room the memories of Tina and Jake swirled in his head, and the depth of his pain, and guilt, kept him from sleep.

IT WAS STILL dark out. Sloane slid from bed and slipped on running shorts, a T-shirt, and sweatshirt. He closed the bedroom door behind him and walked softly downstairs. In the kitchen, Bud jumped onto the counter to greet him. It wasn't love. Bud wanted to be fed. Bud always wanted to be fed. It was a bad habit Sloane began when he first rescued the cat, feeding him at all hours of the day and night, not knowing he was establishing a pattern.

"Sorry, Bud, but Tina says you're too fat. This is her domain. Have to put you on a diet. One meal a day."

The cat mewed.

"Don't I know it, brother. She's got me eating almonds and flax-seed."

He made himself a cup of tea and sipped it while allowing his body to wake. After ten minutes he had put off the inevitable as long as he could, slipped on his running shoes and pulled open the door, stepping out into the morning cold and dew.

He was not one of those people who looked forward to getting up at the crack of dawn for a crisp five-mile run. He had yet to ever get the adrenaline high runners claimed kicked in. His was a five-mile slog that took every ounce of discipline to keep him from turning around and heading back to bed. He forced himself to do it because his ego would not allow him to be fat. Tina was five years younger with the metabolism of a teenager. Tall and fit, she could still eat just about whatever she wanted, with minimal consequences. That was no lon-

ger the case for him. He worked out at the Washington Athletic Club downtown, but the treadmill became monotonous, and he couldn't even think about a basketball game or racquetball match without twisting an ankle or pulling a muscle. Running the streets of Burien was his next best option.

The dampness cut through his clothing and he shivered, as if someone had dumped an ice cube down his shirt. Pulling a stocking cap over his head and a pair of thin gloves over his hands, he did windmills with his arms to generate body heat as he pulled open the gate, stepping through to the easement.

"About time you got here."

Sloane startled and immediately balled his hands into fists. Jake stood in the easement.

"Jake? You scared the hell out of me; what are you doing up so early?"

"I've been waiting since six."

"For what?"

"For you. You said you were running at six. It's now six-ten."

Sloane noticed the boy wore sweats and running shoes. "You want to go running?"

"You said I could."

Jake had brought up the subject the night before, but Sloane hadn't taken him seriously. "I thought you were kidding."

Jake started back for the gate. "It's okay, never mind."

"Whoa, whoa, whoa. Hang on there. I didn't say I didn't want the company. I'd love to have you join me."

They started down the block at a slow pace and ran along the street parallel to the Puget Sound, their feet slapping the pavement in unison.

"So why the sudden interest in running?" Sloane asked, breathing hard and waiting for his wind to kick in.

"I thought I might go out for the cross-country team," Jake said, not sounding at all winded. Nearly thirteen, Jake was not the most co-ordinated kid, and athletics did not come easy. He was tall for his age, *already five nine with feet nearly as big as Sloane's. It was taking time for his skills to catch up to his growth. Junior high had been a transition, and Sloane sensed that Jake wanted desperately to play sports but was anxious about trying out.*

"No kidding? I thought you wanted to try basketball?"

"I don't know," Jake said.

"Something bothering you?"

"I'm not very good. Mom has taken me to play a few times but . . ."

"You like to play?"

The boy's face lit up. "Yeah."

"Well, I know a pretty good coach. He played in high school. Started on the varsity and once scored twenty-two points in a game."

"Really? Who?"

Sloane laughed. "Me."

"No kidding?"

"Is that so hard to believe?"

Jake shrugged, smiling.

"What do you say we go to the gym tonight and get started?"

"That would be awesome."

Sloane looked up. They were coming to one of two very big hills. "Race you to the top," he said, but Jake was already three steps ahead of him.

SLOANE WOULD GIVE anything to have just one of those mornings again. He'd give anything to turn back the clock and simply decline Kyle Horgan's file. Nothing that had transpired from that one simple act had been what he intended, but had he been blind to the unintended consequences? Had he dismissed them because, as Tina said, he felt the need to try to help everyone?

But even as he thought it, he knew he had not been wrong to

take Horgan's file. The autopsy of Austin McFarland proved it. The toy was dangerous. Children were at risk. Tina would have told him to take the case. He knew it in his heart.

So if he had done nothing wrong, why then did she have to die? Why was it always someone he loved? First his mother, then Melda Demanjuck, his Ukranian neighbor when he lived in Pacifica, and now Tina. Why had every woman he had ever loved died a violent death?

Tina had told him that he was her soul mate, that nothing would ever separate them.

She was wrong.

His cell phone rang. In a daze from fatigue and grief, Sloane found it on the floor by the chair and answered without considering the time or the caller. It didn't matter anymore. The hours and the days bled together without distinction.

"David?"

His heart skipped a beat, and for a moment he could not speak. Was it a dream? Had he fallen asleep in the chair?

"Jake?"

"Hey, David, I just wanted to call. I had to wait until everyone went to bed. They won't let me call you."

He didn't know what to say. "How are you, son?"

"I miss you, Dad."

He fought back the tears. His voice choked. "I miss you too, Jake, more than you can imagine."

"I want to come home. Can I come home?"

His hands shook. As much as he wanted to get on a plane and bring the boy home that night he knew he could not. He knew he had to do it the right way or risk losing Jake forever. He needed to be strong and he needed Jake to be strong. "Yes. I'm going to get you home, Jake."

"When?"

"As soon as I can, son. We have to go through the court system now."

"Why? I don't understand. I want to come back. Why can't I just come home?"

As much as he wanted to, Sloane would not bad-mouth the Larsens. They were and always would be the boy's grandparents and Tina's parents. "We both have to be patient, okay? Can you do that for me?"

Sloane heard the boy sniffle.

"Jake, you trust me, right? You trust that I'll do everything I can to make sure you're okay, right?"

"Someone's coming. I have to go."

"Jake?"

"I have to go."

"Jake, I love—"

The call had disconnected.

Sloane stared at the phone, the word *disconnected* shouting at him. He tossed it onto the bed and threw back his head, the grief so overwhelming it physically pained him. Short of breath, he stood and tried to force air into his lungs as he paced and ran a hand through his hair.

The phone rang again.

"Jake?"

"David? Are you all right?"

Sloane closed his eyes.

"David?" Charles Jenkins sounded wide awake.

"Yeah. I'm here."

"Bad dream?"

"I don't think so. No." Sloane checked the call log and confirmed the prior area code to be for San Francisco.

Mentally, he switched gears and realized it was late, after midnight. Sloane had told Charles Jenkins to call him the minute he found out anything about Tina's killer, no matter the time. "Have you found him?"

Jenkins paused. "No. But I know who he is, and I have a way to get him to come to me."

Sloane pondered the information. "Then I'm coming to you."

APPALACHIAN MOUNTAINS

VIRGINIA

STENOPOLIS HOOKED THE jumper cables to the car battery and flipped the switch. The metal chain pulled taut, and the cars on the rail spurs lurched and creaked, creating a cacophony of echoing noise inside the mine before inching forward with a grinding hum. The car in front, which contained the body of Curley Wade, would travel down the shaft a quarter of a mile and spill its load. Wade's body would plummet farther, into a black hole, how deep Stenopolis did not know, but certainly deep enough never to be found.

Stenopolis pulled off his perspiration-soaked T-shirt and replaced it with a clean shirt. Wade had been more resilient than Stenopolis had expected; the man was clearly not working in Human Resources. He had displayed impressive stamina and resolve, more than most.

As the car disappeared into the darkness, Stenopolis retrieved his laptop computer and sat on a metal drum outside the mine, considering the evening sky while the machine powered up. A low blanket of millions of stars stretched to the trace glow of artificial light on the eastern horizon. He loved this time of day, often the only time he found peace.

He entered the site for a familiar search engine and typed the name Curley Wade had provided, confident that Wade had told him the truth. Once he broke a man, he did not worry about lies.

Wade had advised that Charles Jenkins had served in Vietnam and had been recruited by the Agency because he was fluent in Spanish. Jenkins had been sent to Mexico City to monitor the activities of Marxist guerrillas during a time when the United States thought it might need Mexico's oil. However, Jenkins abruptly left the Agency, for reasons Wade clearly did not know, and disappeared before resurfacing thirty years later to ask Wade to help him identify Stenopolis from a photograph. Stenopolis was upset at being so sloppy. Ordinarily it was a mistake he would not make.

So who was this Charles Jenkins, and how did he get a photograph? Those were the ultimate questions, but others intrigued Stenopolis as well. Where had this Charles Jenkins been for the past thirty years, and what had he been doing? Could Stenopolis and Jenkins be in the same line of work? If so, Stenopolis could expect the man to be highly trained and skilled. He would have to be extremely cautious.

Over the next thirty-five minutes Stenopolis visited a number of trusted sites but found nothing on the man, and for the first time he began to wonder if he had underestimated Wade. Then he caught a break. The information was limited and did not explain where Jenkins had been for the past thirty years, but it did reveal what he was currently doing, and that was more than enough to put the rest of the pieces of the puzzle together. Two years earlier, a Charles Jenkins had applied for a license to work as a private investigator in the State of Washington.

"My my," Stenopolis said, staring at a photograph of a light-skinned African American. "A private investigator. Mr. Sloane, you are proving to be quite resilient."

CHAPTER
ELEVEN

Anne LeRoy stepped from the elevator and strode down the hall, key in hand, backpack slung over one shoulder, and utterly exhausted and disheartened. Maybe Peggy had been right. Maybe quitting had not been the smartest thing to do in the current economy. LeRoy unlocked the dead bolt, and then the lock embedded in the handle while Matilda mewed from behind the door.

"I'm coming. I'm coming," she said.

She pushed in, using her foot to keep her orange-and-white tabby from darting down the hall. Inside, she dropped her backpack on the carpet. Matilda weaved in and out of her legs as she crossed the small living area to the even smaller kitchen—more of a nook. As LeRoy pulled open the refrigerator Matilda jumped up onto the bar counter. Neither had many options; LeRoy had the choice of milk or the last can of Fresca. Matilda's choices were better, chicken and rice or salmon and rice. She chose the salmon for Matilda and the Fresca for herself. Something was wrong when the cat was eating better than the owner. But after another day of failed interviews, that didn't look like it was about to change anytime soon.

After feeding Matilda, LeRoy took the Fresca to the living room, popped open the can, and drank in gulps. The effervescence shot a beeline to her nose, and she grimaced while allowing the sensation to pass. Too bad the Fresca wasn't something stronger. Three job interviews, three polite handshakes, and three dismissive remarks like "Thank you for coming in."

Another day like today and she'd have to move. That was the least of her problems. She wasn't exactly wedded to her tiny apartment, and living in Georgetown hadn't exactly suited her budget when she was working for the PSA. On her current salary, which was zero, it would be even less manageable. She could tap into her trust fund, but living with the guilt of having done so would be worse than moving. She had sworn to her grandmother she would not use the funds unless absolutely necessary. She wondered if eating was an absolute necessity.

LeRoy placed the soda can on the counter and walked to the shelving unit in the corner of the living area opposite the couch and weathered coffee table she had inherited from her college roommate, who had moved back home to Nebraska and didn't want to pay to ship it. The shelves held a small television, a couple of potted plants, paperbacks, and tiny speakers. LeRoy plugged her iPod into the speakers and hit the ON button. The band Coldplay had barely sung its first lyric when Mrs. Garibaldi banged on the adjoining wall.

"All right, Mrs. Garibaldi," she shouted as she lowered the volume, adding under her breath, "you old bitch."

LeRoy walked to her bedroom to change. "Bedroom" was never a more fitting name for a room, given that her queen-size bed was the *only* thing that fit in the space. She had to put her dresser in the closet.

She traded her interview suit, a traditional blue jacket and matching skirt—hemline below the knee—for sweatpants and a sweatshirt, and tossed her white blouse in the bathroom sink, filling the bowl with cold water and a squirt of Woolite. Dry cleaning was not in the budget for a while.

After filling the sink and soaking the shirt, she turned on the hot water in the combo shower and tub, shut the drain, and poured a capful of the bubble bath powder under the splash. She owed herself this much. As the room filled with a fragrant aroma, LeRoy retrieved her latest novel from her backpack and also found the newspaper article Peggy Seeley had given her at dinner the night before. LeRoy sat on the edge of the bed, reconsidering the photograph of the good-looking attorney. "Why couldn't you live in Virginia? You are GU," she said, meaning geographically undesirable. "Not to mention too old. What would Grandma say if I brought you home?"

As she reread the article, LeRoy experienced the same sense of dread that had been haunting her for two days. She just couldn't shake the thought that there was more to Albert Payne's pulling the plug on her report than a lack of funding. What were the odds of him killing her project and shortly thereafter two children dying from the very hazard LeRoy had been investigating? It just couldn't be coincidence, no matter what Peggy Seeley thought. Payne would not be pressing so hard to get back the report unless there was something else going on, and that realization had made LeRoy a wreck. She spent the last two days looking over her shoulder, certain that people were following her.

Reading further than she had the night before, LeRoy learned that Sloane had recently been in the news himself when his wife was murdered in their home.

LeRoy stood. "Oh my God."

She flipped to the jump on an inside page and bit her fingernail as she continued reading. Sloane had been wounded in the attack but survived, and police had no leads on a suspect. Feeling sick to her stomach, LeRoy paced her apartment, taking deep breaths and telling herself to calm down. "Don't let your imagination run wild."

She'd return the report to Payne in the morning. She'd deliver it personally and be done with it. Seeley was right. She couldn't very well afford to get in a legal battle over it.

She dropped the article on her comforter and retrieved the Fresca from the counter in the kitchen, drinking as she went back to the bathroom and used a toe to test the water temperature in the tub, now half full. Not hot enough, she cranked the hot water handle another turn, walked back to her bedroom, and sat on the edge of the bed while the tub continued to fill. She told herself she would feel better after she'd soaked for half an hour.

She looked down at the article. Her report was solid. She had worked her ass off talking with experts and pulling past investigations of manufacturing plants in China. And now there was confirmation. The magnets were dangerous. How could they just bury the report?

How can you?

LeRoy suddenly realized what had been bothering her. Maybe her report couldn't have saved the two kids in the article, but what if maybe it could save other kids? This was no longer just a hypothetical situation. There was proof, solid proof that the concerns she had investigated were very real. Payne certainly couldn't dispute that now, could he? And what could the agency really do to her? Would it risk punishing her for a report that could save children's lives? Did they really want to start down that path? And she found it hard to believe the Justice Department didn't have better things to do with its time than go after a low-level ex–federal employee for releasing a report on a very real problem.

But did she really want to spend her grandmother's trust hiring a lawyer to defend her?

LeRoy reconsidered David Sloane's picture beside the article. The idea and the smile formed together.

Maybe she wouldn't have to.

REAGAN NATIONAL AIRPORT

ARLINGTON, VIRGINIA

AS HE DISCONNECTED his call with Charles Jenkins to coordinate where to meet, Sloane's phone rang, the screen indicating his office. He'd left them in a lurch after advising Barclay Reid that his clients had declined Kendall's settlement offer and would not be making a counteroffer. Reid wasted little time serving an onerous document request, interrogatories, and notices of depositions for both sets of parents. Sloane felt guilty about leaving, but Kannin had nearly pushed him out the door.

"You know me; this is the kind of stuff that gets me out of bed in the morning," he had said. "Bring it on."

"How was the flight?" Carolyn asked. Since Tina's death, Carolyn had mellowed. Her comments had been far less caustic and at times even maternal.

"The way I like it, boring."

"That might change."

"How so?"

"You just got a phone call. A young woman wants to speak to you."

"Can John handle it?"

"Probably, he's walking around here like MacArthur on the deck of the *Missouri*, but this is one I think you'll want to take yourself. She said she read an article in the *Washington Post* about the lawsuit and that she had some information for you about magnets."

"I really think John can handle it, Carolyn."

"So did I, but then she said she used to work at the Product Safety Agency."

Sloane stopped his progress down the battered hallway to the airport exit. Travelers veered to avoid him. "Did she leave a number?"

"I thought that might interest you. She did, and I checked it. The area code is for Washington, D.C. She's legit."

Retrieving a pen and piece of paper from his briefcase, Sloane wrote down the name and number. Ten minutes later, he hurried outside into a muggy evening and found Jenkins talking with a police officer who held a book of tickets and a pen in his hand.

"Here he is." Jenkins hurried inside the car as Sloane slid into the passenger seat. "What took you so long?"

"Change of plans," Sloane said. "We need to get to an apartment in Georgetown."

HE CONSIDERED EACH assortment inside the refrigerated glass cases, seeking something large, but not ostentatious. His goal was to distract, not to cause suspicion. Finally he came upon what he was looking for.

"Did you find one you like?" the woman asked.

He pointed. "I'll take that one."

"Excellent choice."

She took the bundle to the front of the store, speaking as she cut the stems and wrapped them in paper. Stenopolis had chosen a spring mix of purple, white, yellow, and lavender hydrangea with spray roses and chrysanthemums. He picked out a small card from a stand on the counter to accompany the arrangement.

Earlier that evening, after a call from his client, he had popped the door lock on a white van and hot-wired the ignition. It took less than sixty seconds. When he returned the van later that evening he would smash the driver's-side window to make it look like an amateur had failed in an attempt to steal the vehicle. The owner might make a police report, but since the insurance company would pay for the repairs the owner wouldn't pursue it, and the police had better things to do with their time. After stealing the van he had purchased a pair of blue coveralls and nondescript matching hat.

This would be his last stop.

He regretted having to further postpone his inevitable confrontation with David Sloane and his private investigator, but business was business, and his client emphasized that the current task took priority.

"There you go." The woman behind the counter handed him the bouquet, which she had adorned with baby's breath and fern leaves and wrapped in a purple paper. "These are going to make someone very happy," she said.

Stenopolis slipped the card in the small plastic pitchfork sticking out from the flowers. "She'll be surprised," he said.

BLUES ALLEY APARTMENTS
GEORGETOWN, WASHINGTON, D.C.

LEROY STEPPED FROM the bathwater with one towel wrapped around her head like a turban, and another covering her body. It had not been the relaxing soak she had hoped for, barely ten minutes, but it was all the time she could afford. Ten minutes after she had called the law offices of David Sloane and had lowered herself into the soothing bubbles, her cell phone rang.

The caller ID indicated a private number, and she almost didn't answer, but her intuition told her to do so. She was glad she did. David Sloane said he had received her message and was calling her back. That Sloane called so quickly was surprising in and of itself, but what shocked LeRoy was when Sloane advised that he was in D.C. on an "unrelated matter" and anxious to meet with her.

"My secretary indicated you had some information on magnets," Sloane had said.

LeRoy explained her former position at the PSA as well as the contents of the report she had been preparing, which definitely caught Sloane's interest, but not as much as when she told him that her boss, Albert Payne, had suddenly pulled the plug on her investigation. She told Sloane how Payne had initially been excited about her report and that he had intended to present it to Senator Joe Wallace, who had called for a congressional hearing on the rash of product recalls and the potential danger of Chinese manufactured products to American consumers. When LeRoy told Sloane that she had kept a copy of the report he asked to meet with her immediately.

Though eager to find an ally, LeRoy was more eager to find an attorney. "Listen, I don't want to get in any trouble. The agency said they'll press criminal charges if I don't return the report. I really can't afford to be sued."

"I understand."

"But I also spent a lot of time on the research, and it's a good investigation. There are some real problems with these magnets, like what happened to the two children in the article. I just felt like this is something I had to do. The thing is, I don't have a lot of money, so I was thinking that maybe, you know, if I give you the report and I get in trouble, maybe you could represent me."

Sloane asked for her address and said he would be right over.

LeRoy used her fingertips to wipe a hole in the steam on the mirror and studied her face. Unzipping her cosmetic bag, she ran the tiny mascara brush over her lashes then traced the contours of her eyelids with the liner. She spotted her cheeks with blusher and wiped away the excess with a piece of tissue. Satisfied, she put a dab of perfume on each wrist and touched her wrists to her neck. As with the contents of her refrigerator, the options in her closet were limited, especially with her interview shirt in the sink, but if she didn't pick out something soon she'd be meeting David Sloane in her bra and underwear.

AS HE DROVE, Jenkins advised Sloane on what he had learned about Stenopolis, and how they might be able to contact him.

"He's been at this for a while, which means he pays attention to the details and is thorough. He's not likely to make a mistake, and he'll be suspicious of any new client calling him out of the blue."

"So how do we do it?"

"Hotchkin said he never met Stenopolis; he gave him the name of the target, and the target disappeared. His payment was made to a drop box. That means we need a target. And that would be me."

Sloane shook his head. "No. You have a wife and child at home."

"This guy operates by surprise. He attacks people who are not expecting him. That's his advantage. He doesn't have that advantage with me. He'll do his research, so we'll have to play it straight. I'm a private investigator from Washington who's been retained to get a compromising video of a powerful member of the president's cabinet, which I just happen to have. That particularly powerful member will make a call and request Stenopolis's help in rectifying the problem. Since they have a past relationship, Stenopolis will feel comfortable with the contact and the likelihood he will be well compensated."

"I thought you said Hotchkin wanted nothing to do with this guy?"

"He doesn't." Jenkins held up a phone. "But I stole his cell phone."

"He'll report it stolen."

"I already did. Then I bought another one and restored the service. I figure it's good for at least a couple of days. I only have to leave a message, so I don't need to say much on the phone, but I can do a fairly good impersonation of Hotchkin from studying the videotape."

Sloane considered the scenery. "We do it your way with one exception. I'll be the one waiting when Stenopolis arrives."

Jenkins shook his head.

"It isn't negotiable," Sloane said.

"This is personal for you, but not for him. For Stenopolis it's simply business. If you call him to settle things mano a mano, he won't take the bait, and then we lose the element of surprise."

Red taillights flashed as they approached the Frances Scott Key Bridge. Jenkins hit the brakes. "Damn. Washington traffic."

"How far away are we?"

"Not far. Georgetown is just on the other side."

Thunder rumbled overhead, a loud boom. Sloane pulled the cell phone from the clip on his belt. "I'd better give her a call and tell her we'll be late. She sounded anxious on the phone."

LEROY FINISHED BRUSHING her hair, checked her makeup for the twentieth time, and shrugged. So be it. She had chosen a pair of blue jeans and a powder blue cashmere sweater, which lay on the bed. It was casual, but classy.

She checked her watch. She had five minutes. She picked up the jeans, then remembered she had promised to copy her report to a disc for Sloane. "Darn."

Still in her underwear, she went into the living room, pulled the memory stick from her backpack, and stuck it into the UBS port on the side of the computer. As she did, she realized she didn't have any discs on which to copy the report. She hurried into her bedroom, pulled down the first of two storage boxes on the shelf in her closet, and rummaged through what had been the contents of her college desk.

She found no disc, pulled down the second box, and found an unmarked silver disc in a light green plastic sleeve. Hurrying back into the living room, she placed the disc into the computer and waited for it to boot. She hoped it didn't contain the contents of the hard drive she had used in college, but that hope was dashed when the database pulled up a list of files, mostly papers she had written. She'd likely never use them again, but nostalgia made deleting seem somehow wrong. Anal retentive, she decided to copy the documents from the disc onto her laptop hard drive. Then she'd clear the disc and copy the report to it. Whatever she did, she'd need to do it in a hurry.

She highlighted the list of documents and used the arrow to click COPY. The computer reported an error.

She checked her watch, becoming more anxious.

She logged out of the program and tried a different one, repeating the process, this time without an error message popping onto the screen. But as the tiny file folders flew across the screen some stopped, and the computer indicated that the particular papers were so old the Word program had changed to a different version and the computer would have to convert them before saving them to the hard drive. She checked her watch again as the computer transferred the files one at a time, taking several minutes to complete. LeRoy then checked to be sure that the files had copied onto the hard drive, which took still more time, and finally highlighted the list on the disc and hit DELETE. The computer asked her if she was certain she wanted to delete all of the files.

"Yes, yes," she said, pressing the key.

The disc clear, LeRoy opened up the files on the memory stick and found her report on magnets. She directed the computer to save the document to the disc and watched as miniature manila folders again flew across the screen to confirm transfer of the file.

Her doorbell rang.

LeRoy looked from the screen, surprised. The building had a security system at the front door requiring visitors to be buzzed in, but at this time of day, with people coming home from work and leaving for dinner it was common for the door to be open. Still, she could have used the extra warning, and minutes.

Still in her underwear, LeRoy called out, "Just a minute."

She started for the bedroom but the doorbell rang again. Rather than try to throw on her jeans and sweater she pulled on her bathrobe, intending to open the door a crack to apologize that she needed another moment. Sloane could wait in the living room while she got dressed and the computer continued to copy the report.

At the door, she unlocked the dead bolt.

JENKINS LEANED FORWARD to look out the windshield as he inched the car down the street while Sloane searched for addresses on the buildings. The wipers hummed, sweeping away the splatter of rain on the glass, but the water, darkness, and foliage from the occasional tree planted in a patch of dirt in the sidewalk made it difficult to see.

"Even numbers on your side," Jenkins said.

Sloane saw the green lettering on a metal awning over the sidewalk. "Blues Alley Apartments."

Jenkins jerked the car to a stop in front of a multistoried building. The driver behind honked and sped around him, middle finger extended. Up and down the block, cars lined the curb in each direction.

"Double-park and I'll run up," Sloane said.

Jenkins pulled alongside a white van. "Keep your cell phone on," he said. "If it looks like it might be awhile, call me. I'll go grab a cup of coffee down the street and come back."

Sloane stepped from the car and jogged for cover beneath the overhang. A strong wind rustled the branches of the tree in front of the entry. He found the entry keypad where Anne LeRoy had described it, but despite the incandescent lights in the overhang it was difficult to see the numbers. Sloane bent down and punched 602 on the keypad.

A phone rang several times, but LeRoy did not answer. He hit the * button and hung up, then entered the number again. Again she did not respond.

He pulled the scrap of paper from his pocket to confirm the apartment number and looked back to the car. Jenkins leaned across the car with his hands extended in the universal sign for "what gives?"

Sloane shrugged, and Jenkins powered down the passenger-side window.

Sloane shouted to him, "She's not answering." LeRoy had indicated she was jumping into the bath. "She could still be in the bath."

Jenkins considered his watch. "If she's like Alex this could be hours. Try again."

Sloane punched in the numbers. Again LeRoy did not answer.

Jenkins shouted. "Look for a building manager. These apartment complexes usually have someone to accept deliveries."

Sloane reconsidered the list of names then noticed the sign below the box. NO SOLICITORS. FOR DELIVERIES RING 407. He punched in the numbers.

A man's voice squawked at him. "Yeah?"

"I have an appointment to see Anne LeRoy."

"Hang on."

"Wait." But the man was gone. A moment later he came back. "She's in six-oh-two."

"I know. There's no answer."

"I can't help you with that."

"Can you let me in?"

"Not without the tenant's approval."

Sloane heard a click. End of conversation.

ANNE LEROY PULLED open the door. "Mr. . . . ?" Her voice caught at the sight of a large bouquet of flowers.

"Anne LeRoy?"

"Yes."

He smiled. "I have a delivery for you."

"For me?"

"Apparently."

"Who could they be from?"

"There's a card."

LeRoy pulled the door open farther and reached for the bouquet. When she grabbed it, the man's hand clamped suddenly about her throat, choking her windpipe, preventing her from calling out. She felt her feet leave the ground, her body propelled backward into the apartment as the door slammed close.

Behind her, somewhere, she heard her phone ring.

. . .

AS SLOANE FLIPPED CLOSED his phone Jenkins pushed open the car door and walked around the back of the car, the collar of his black leather jacket turned up against the rain. Alex might have had Jenkins on a diet, but Sloane couldn't help but think that it didn't take away from the sheer immensity of the man.

Jenkins pushed a series of three numbers on the keypad. A man's voice answered, "Yeah?"

Jenkins bent to get closer to the voice box. "Sorry. I hit the wrong button."

He ran a finger down the list of tenants and pressed three different digits. This time a woman with a twinge of a southern accent answered.

"Wrong button," Jenkins repeated, scrolling farther down the list and repeating the process. When no one answered he entered the same numbers.

"We have a winner," he said, and rang the superintendent's apartment.

"Yeah?" The man sounded more annoyed than when Sloane called.

"I have a delivery for apartment five-one-five," Jenkins said in an affected Boston accent.

"Hold on." A moment later the box clicked. "No one's home."

"Can someone else accept it?"

"What is it?"

"Luggage delayed at the airport. The woman wasn't too happy about it and I ain't exactly excited about coming back."

There was an audible groan. "Bring it to four-oh-seven."

The lock buzzed. Jenkins pulled open the door and they stepped into a marbled entry with a mirrored wall that created the illusion that the lobby was twice its actual size. The decor was spartan, just an entry table with two potted ferns. Two elevator doors were to the left. One opened as soon as Sloane hit the button.

They stepped from the elevator onto the sixth floor, looking at their mirror images and the back of a man stepping into the adjacent elevator carrying a bag of trash. Wall sconces offered muted light as Sloane and Jenkins started down the hall looking for Apartment 602. When they realized the apartment numbers were ascending they had to backtrack. Apartment 602 was the last door on the left. Sloane knocked three times. No one answered.

Leaning closer he shouted through the door. "Ms. LeRoy? Ms. LeRoy?" He pressed his ear to the door, heard muffled music and a cat mewing, and knocked again. "Ms. LeRoy?"

A dead bolt turned, but the sound did not come from inside the apartment. It came from the adjacent door, which pulled open a crack, revealing half the face of an elderly woman. At her feet a small dog yapped up at them, fighting to get out.

"I'm sorry," Sloane said. "Do you know if Anne is home?"

The woman gave Sloane a disapproving frown. "She probably can't hear you over the music. I've asked her to turn it down, but she just ignores me."

"So she's home?"

"First thing she does is turn on the music. She could have left I guess. I had to take Percy out. I don't sit here spying on her," she said. "It's just that the walls are paper thin. I have my name in to move when a vacancy opens."

Sloane pulled out his cell phone and dialed LeRoy's number while putting his ear to the door, but he did not hear the phone ring. He tried the handle and shook the door. From the play in the jamb, the dead bolt was not secured.

"She had a delivery a while ago," the woman said. "Flowers."

Jenkins was looking down the hall, then to the woman. "Is there a garbage chute on this floor?"

"What?"

"A garbage chute. Is there one on this floor?"

"Every floor," the woman said.

"Break it down." Jenkins turned and ran down the hall, jacket splaying, the hall floor vibrating with each pounding boot. He disappeared through a door beneath a green illuminated sign indicating EXIT.

Sloane stepped back and lunged forward, putting his right shoulder into the door.

The old woman quickly slammed shut her door.

Pain radiated across Sloane's chest from the wound in his shoulder. It wouldn't take another blow. Panting, trying to catch his breath, he stepped back, transferred his weight onto his bad leg, and crashed the sole of his shoe into the door. It flexed but did not give. He took a moment to recover, then stepped back and kicked the door again. This time he heard a crack. Mustering what energy he had left, he kicked it a third time, springing the door open. An orange-and-white cat skirted past and ran down the hallway. Feeling light-headed, Sloane gripped the doorframe and stumbled into the apartment, panning the small living area while trying to regain his balance and clear his vision, which had blurred. He stumbled farther in and through another doorframe to his right: the bedroom. Empty.

He pushed open another door and stepped in. The shower curtain was closed. Water had pooled on the tile floor. Sloane reached for the curtain and noticed the electrical cord, his eyes following it from the socket above the sink until it disappeared behind the curtain.

JENKINS GRIPPED THE tubular metal hand railing, propelled himself around the horseshoe turn, and started down another flight of dusty concrete stairs. He tried to maintain a delicate balance between hurrying and falling flat on his face. The goal was to beat the elevator carrying the man with the garbage bag to the ground floor. The car had been empty when the man stepped on. Jenkins could only hope it had made at least one stop on its descent.

At the third floor landing he gained a rhythm—seven stairs, grip railing, spin. Seven stairs, grip railing, spin. Second floor. He repeated the process, descended to the first floor, spun one more time, and came to a door stenciled LOBBY. He pulled the Smith & Wesson from its holster, grabbed the handle, and yanked open the door, surveying a short hall, perhaps eight feet long, leading to the lobby. The bell for the elevator rang. Jenkins took aim as the doors pulled open.

The man in a Washington Nationals baseball cap still held the black bag and gestured politely for a woman on the elevator to step out ahead of him. Jenkins waited for the woman to clear and then yelled, "Freeze!"

Unfortunately only the woman froze. Before Jenkins could get off a shot, Anthony Stenopolis had dropped the plastic bag and snatched the woman by her collar, locking an arm around her throat, a gun in his free hand. He fired twice, forcing Jenkins to duck back into the stairwell.

"Pick up the bag," Stenopolis yelled.

Jenkins swung his head out from behind the jamb. The woman had bent to retrieve the garbage bag but Stenopolis had kept his aim focused on the stairwell. The bullet skipped along the wall, spraying Jenkins with wallboard dust as he pulled back.

"Hand it to me," Stenopolis instructed. "Hand it to me."

Jenkins took several short breaths, trying to relax. He could do little as long as Stenopolis continued to use the woman as a human shield, but no other options were popping into his head. He had nowhere to go, trapped in the small stairwell with the closest safe exit up to the second floor. By that time, Stenopolis would be long gone.

"Now move! Move!"

Jenkins peered out from behind the wall, but again it was brief. Another shot forced him to pull back.

"Reach behind me and open the door."

"I can't," the woman cried, her voice shrill, hysterical.

"Do it!"

"Let her go," Jenkins yelled.

He peered out. Stenopolis had retreated to the front door. Jenkins could no longer see him because of the angle of the wall. He rushed from the stairwell and pressed his back against the wall, sliding toward the lobby. At the corner he crouched and stuck his head around the corner. Stenopolis had his back to the entry door, his arm, now holding the garbage bag, still wrapped around the woman's throat. She struggled to reach behind him and find the door handle. Jenkins saw a blur of blue outside the entry just as the door pulled open. A young woman in a coat walked in wearing earbuds, completely oblivious to everything around her.

Stenopolis shoved the young woman from behind and she stumbled to the ground at the edge of the wall where Jenkins crouched. Her eyes widened at the sight of the gun and she started to push away, but Jenkins managed to grab her and drag her behind the wall. She scrambled from her knees to her feet and ran down the hall.

Jenkins swung the gun around the corner. Stenopolis had used the diversion to get out the door to the van. People on the sidewalk scattered, some seeking refuge behind a tree.

Stenopolis fired back into the building, one bullet shattering the glass door into tiny crystals, the second exploding the mirrored wall near Jenkins's head. When Jenkins looked again, Stenopolis had maneuvered around the back of the van to the driver's side and forced his hostage inside.

Jenkins rushed out, staying low to the ground, the sound of glass crunching beneath his shoes. He pressed his back against a parked car. The van's red taillights glowed and the engine roared to life. Because Jenkins had double-parked beside the van, Stenopolis could not easily pull from the space. Jenkins stood, intending to shoot out the van's tires, saw Stenopolis's reflection watching him in the side mirror, and ducked back behind the parked car just as more bullets shattered the van's two rear windows and pierced its metal door, leaving a puckered hole.

The van jerked from the curb and smashed into the bumper of his rental car, the rear lights cracking and metal crunching as the van pushed it forward. Two more shots kept Jenkins pinned down. Stenopolis put the van in reverse and backed into the car parked behind him, crunching its fender and setting off the car alarm. Having cleared sufficient space, he clipped the rental car again before speeding down the street.

Halfway down the block the van slowed and the passenger door flew open. The woman tumbled out onto the street, the van's tires spinning on the rain-slicked pavement before the vehicle lurched forward. Jenkins hurried to the woman and redirected a car around her. She had a cut on her forehead and was shaking. Jenkins lifted her to her feet and helped guide her toward the sidewalk, looking back over his shoulder as the van's taillights disappeared around a corner.

SHE LAY IN the bathtub, her body submerged, eyes open, hair floating about her head like a halo. Tiny bubbles clung to her lips, and Sloane's instincts propelled him toward the porcelain basin, stopping short when he saw the hair dryer in the water.

Anne LeRoy looked to be not much older than her early twenties, just a kid with her whole life ahead of her. Not anymore. The weight of another death weighed like an anvil on Sloane's chest and shoulders.

"David!" Jenkins appeared in the bathroom doorway. "Shit!" He reached in and grabbed Sloane by the arm, dragging him from the room.

"We have to do something," Sloane said.

"Nothing we can do." Jenkins pulled him out the apartment door. "And the police will have too many questions we can't answer."

INSIDE THE HOTEL room to which he and Jenkins had retreated, Sloane was supposed to be watching the television for news reports on the shoot-out at the Georgetown apartment building and the death of a young woman in that building, but his attention wandered and he could not focus. LeRoy's death pushed him closer to the darkness, a place into which Sloane had so often felt himself slipping before he met Tina, a place to which he had hoped to never again return. It was a place void of all light, pitch-black, and cold. When he did fall, he felt like a man plunged into a deep, cylindrical hole, the walls sheer and impossible to climb.

Sloane stood and walked to the hotel-room window, looking out on a dimly lit parking lot. He felt the walls and the darkness inching closer. When he closed his eyes, struggling to relax, he saw Anne LeRoy floating in her bathtub, her eyes gazing up at him from beneath the water, lifeless. Then the face changed; Tina, lying on the staircase, staring up at him but not at him, past him, her eyes already losing focus, the life within her fading. And it made him again confront what he had tried not to acknowledge, that as LeRoy lay dead, Sloane's first concern had been for the information she had possessed and that he would not get, just as his first concern as Tina lay dying had been that he would again be alone. And he hated himself for it. He didn't know how, or why, but he had never fully allowed himself to believe that he had made it completely out of that dark hole, that he had found a life and a purpose to go with it. All along, the darkness had lingered behind, waiting to envelop him, and he should have known, somehow, that if it could not have him, it would take that which meant the most to him. It always did. His mother. Melda. Now Tina.

COOL AIR BRUSHED *the spot on his chest where a moment before she had been resting her cheek, fast asleep. Tina propped her chin in the palm of her hand and peered down at him, her lips inching into an impish grin. Was it too much of a cliché or just too much of his ego that he thought she did indeed look radiant after an afternoon spent making love in their room?*

"A penny for your thoughts," she said.

"Am I that cheap?"

The breeze fluttered the thin curtain of the patio doors, allowing another glimpse of the view from their terrazzo tile patio—the palm trees and tiled roofs of Santa Margherita and the colorful fishing vessels in the harbor and the yachts anchored in the deep blue waters of the Mediterranean Sea. The breeze brought the sweet smell of the bougainvillea overwhelming the trestle and climbing the stucco onto the tiled roof. Somewhere in the distance a rooster crowed.

"Actually, since Washington is a community property state, your thoughts are now only worth half a penny."

"I don't know if it's scarier to think that you knew that, or to think that you might have looked it up," he said.

She smiled. "You keep being this quiet and you won't have to worry about it. Anything on your mind you would like to share?"

He shrugged. "I've been a bit overwhelmed by the view."

She turned her head to look out the patio doors. "It is beautiful, isn't it?"

"I meant you."

She inched up the bed to kiss him.

Their lips parting, she whispered, "For a moment there I thought you went someplace else."

"I'm just enjoying the moment," he said, half honest.

He had left the room, not physically, but in his mind. Ever since the wedding he'd had moments where he felt as if he were a spectator, watching a man who looked much like himself interact with Tina. He had dismissed it, but the feeling had persisted. Upon further reflection, he came to realize that he was simply having difficulty grasping that he had found someone so good and that he was, for the first time in his life, no longer alone. It was almost too good to be true, too good to believe it could be happening to him.

And that terrified him.

"Well, get used to it, Mr. Sloane, because I expect there will be many more just like it."

"Then I better step up my workout routine, Mrs. Sloane."

Her auburn hair, which she had allowed to grow nearly to her shoulders, draped his face and fell across his chest. When she pulled back her eyes sparkled down at him, as blue as the sky, darkening with the setting of the sun.

She rolled onto her back, her head resting on his shoulder. "Do you think about that?" she asked.

"Think about what?"

"The future, what it's going to be like?"

"I'm happy now," he said.

She glimpsed him out of the corner of her eye. "I could tell. But don't you wonder what we'll be like? Where we'll be living? What our kids will be like?"

When he didn't answer she lifted again onto her elbow, the thin sheet falling across her breast. "What's the matter?"

"Nothing."

Her eyes narrowed. "You do realize of course that with the wedding vow comes the right to not accept that for an answer."

"Funny, I don't remember that part."

"Oh yes, if you're arrested you have the right to remain silent. Once you're married you lose that right. 'Do you promise to honor, cherish, and tell her everything on your mind, till death shall you part'?"

"It's nothing." He moved to kiss her, but she pulled away suddenly.

"Ah-hah! You said 'it'; that means there is something."

He laughed. "Maybe you should have been the lawyer."

"Tell me."

Sloane turned his head and considered the pale orange plaster walls adorned with paintings of the Italian countryside. A price tag hung from each, painted by the owner of the bed and breakfast. "Have you ever had a moment where you suddenly feel as though you're watching someone else living your life?"

"Huh?"

He thought how best to express it. "Have you ever had a moment where you feel like maybe you're in a painting, looking out, and everything is so perfect, you wonder if it could possibly be real?"

Her eyebrows inched closer. "I suppose."

"I don't want to think about the future because I don't think I could ever be happier than I am at this moment, and I'm afraid to let it go."

For a moment she didn't speak. She put a hand to his cheek, caressing it. "You don't have to be afraid anymore, David. I know you've lost so much that you must feel like you have to hold on to everything with both hands. But you don't. You're not going to lose me. I'm not going anywhere."

"Before I met you I never knew how alone I really was. I mean, I sensed there was something more to life than getting up and going to work and maybe having an occasional date, but that's what I knew, what I thought life was. So I just came to accept it as the norm. And now I realize it's nothing about what life is supposed to be. I mean, work is supposed to be what we do, not who we are. I just had one of those moments where I looked around and suddenly felt like I had to be someone *else to be lying here in a room in Italy having just made love to someone so beautiful. This couldn't possibly be real. It couldn't be my life. This isn't the kind of thing that is supposed to happen to someone like me."*

Tears pooled in her eyes. "Someone like you? What does that mean?"

And therein was the source of his frustration. "I don't know."

"It's real," she whispered. "I'm real. We're real."

"I know," he said, but did not finish his thought aloud. And that's what scares me so much. I've never had so much to lose.

She sighed. "Then we won't think about the future; we'll just enjoy each moment."

She flipped her hair from her face and placed her cheek back against his chest, her fingers caressing his skin.

For a moment he felt content again; then he turned to the side, seeing the image in the oval antique mirror in the corner of the room, the image at which he had been staring before she sought his thoughts for a penny.

The man in the mirror remained foreign to him.

THE DOOR TO the hotel room opened and Charles Jenkins stepped in. "Hey. You all right?"

Sloane turned from the window, nodded.

"Anything on the news?"

Sloane looked to the television. He had no idea. "Nothing yet. You find out anything?"

Jenkins had walked to a coffee shop down the block with Internet access. He held up a piece of paper. "An address, but we're going to need to be careful and play this just right. We'll likely only get one shot. We spook him and that could be the end."

CHAPTER
TWELVE

A lbert Payne exited the Express Dry Cleaners with a finger full of hangers, the clothes dangling over his shoulder, the plastic wrap rustling in the breeze. His hand shook as he set a tall cup of coffee atop a garbage bin to maneuver his glasses over his eyes. Though early in the morning, his button-down, powder blue shirt already showed rings of perspiration beneath each armpit.

Retrieving the cup, Payne sipped from the slit in the white plastic top while he waited for a silver Mercedes to back away from a parking spot. Then he stepped across the asphalt to the cars parked perpendicular to the businesses.

He thought again about the argument earlier that morning. His wife was fed up with what she called his "moodiness and surly attitude." She said he was short-tempered with the kids and went off to "la-la land" even when he was home and if he didn't snap out of it she wanted him to move out. Most nights he'd fallen asleep in the leather recliner in the family room, watching television, mentally exhausted from another day wondering if, and when the man from China would return. He usually awoke in his chair and spent the evenings listening to the sounds inside the house and the voices in his head, some urging him to go to the police or perhaps to Larry Triplett, or maybe even Maggie Powers. Hell, they were directors of a government agency, they had to have connections that could help him, didn't they?

But those thoughts did not persist, pushed aside by his vivid recollection of the man's cool detachment as the back of the Chinese woman's head exploded and the spray of blood splattered Payne across the face and arms. The man had made it clear he would think nothing of killing Payne's wife and children in similar fashion and leave enough evidence to link Payne to their murders as well as the murder of the Chinese prostitute. The police would assume Payne had gone off his rocker, gone absolutely crazy, and there would certainly be enough witnesses to confirm his recent erratic behavior to make that scenario plausible.

The only thing that got him out the door in the morning was the hope that it would all be over soon. He would provide Powers with a favorable report on the Chinese manufacturing facilities and profess no knowledge of any dangers from new technology. Powers would testify similarly before Congress, Joe Wallace's bill calling for more stringent safeguards on products and more funding to the agency would be defeated, and Payne could get on with his life and get back to his family.

Anne LeRoy would not have that opportunity.

He squeezed between two parked cars but came to a sudden stop when a man walking in the opposite direction blocked his path. A hanger slid from his grasp to the ground, his wife's tan vest. He would have also spilled his coffee but for the white plastic lid.

"I'm sorry." Payne crouched to retrieve the hanger.

"Let me help." The man bent to help pick up the dry cleaning. Payne raised his eyes. "Thank you, but I think I can . . ."

Behind him Payne heard a car stop, though he did not take his eyes off the barrel of the gun, only partially concealed by the man's leather jacket.

"You are going to stand and get into the backseat of the car behind you. You're not going to yell, or say a word. Do you understand?"

Payne nodded.

"Good. Now, slowly."

When Payne did as instructed the man slid into the backseat beside him and pulled the door shut as the driver exited the parking lot.

SLOANE CONSIDERED ALBERT PAYNE in the rearview mirror. Two mornings after Anne LeRoy's death, Sloane and Jenkins had tracked Payne from his home in Bethesda to the strip mall. They had dismissed the thought of walking into his office to talk to the man, uncertain whether Payne had pulled the plug on LeRoy's investigation as part of a scheme to conceal the information. If so, Payne could alert others involved that Jenkins and Sloane were in Washington, D.C., and asking questions. They decided to surprise Payne instead, but where? Not at his home; Payne had a wife and children. They also couldn't very well do it at his place of business, where Payne would have the comfort of dozens of coworkers, not to mention security guards and video surveillance cameras. That meant following Payne until the right opportunity presented itself. The opportunity had come that morning, when Payne stopped at the strip mall to pick up the dry cleaning. Sloane and Jenkins had discussed the need to avoid a confrontation in a public place, but Payne had been surprisingly compliant. He had slid quietly into the back of the car, where he now sat looking like a man resigned to his fate and not interested in trying to fight or even negotiate.

As Sloane drove, Payne spoke barely above a whisper. "Do you work for him?"

Sloane and Jenkins made eye contact in the mirror. Albert Payne was not calm. He was paralyzed by fear.

"Relax, Mr. Payne," Sloane said. "We're not going to hurt you; we might even be able to help you."

Despite the reassuring words, Payne continued to bite at his lower lip, and his eyes remained unfocused, a vacuous gaze.

Sloane pulled off the road into the gravel parking lot of a nearby sports complex with multiple soccer and baseball fields. At the back of the lot he parked near two baseball fields built side by side. Jenkins motioned for Payne to exit the back door. Payne left the dry cleaning on the seat but still held the cup of coffee. They climbed a row of metal bleachers and sat, a breeze blowing the tall, thin trees planted alongside the third base line. The baseball field was empty.

"What is this about?" Payne asked.

"Anne LeRoy," Sloane said.

The lenses of Payne's glasses were flecked with dry skin. He looked to have a rash all about his neck and face, which still had remnants of a white cream recently applied. "You know Anne?"

"No. But she called me," Sloane said. "She said she had done an investigation on magnets in toys. She said you pulled the plug on her investigation. I need to know why."

"Who are you?" Payne asked.

"I'm an attorney."

"An attorney?" Payne exhaled, as if he'd been holding his breath. "I don't understand."

Sloane handed Payne a copy of the article in the *Washington Post*.

"I have a case against Kendall Toys. I represent two families with children who died ingesting magnets that came from one of their toys. Kendall is about to bring that toy to market for the Christmas holiday, and all indications are that it will fly off shelves and into the homes of millions of children."

Payne read several paragraphs before putting the article down on the bench and staring out at the empty ball field. Another breeze silently rustled the branches of the trees.

"I don't know anything about that."

Sloane knew fear was the cause of Payne's reticence, but he also did not have the time or inclination to play games. LeRoy's death meant Stenopolis was close. "Yes, you do, Mr. Payne. Anne LeRoy told me all about it."

He shook his head. "She shouldn't have done that," he said, still staring straight ahead.

"Why not?"

Payne just shook his head.

"Anne LeRoy is dead." Payne turned and looked at Sloane. "I found her electrocuted in her bathtub."

Payne dropped his head and began to retch, gagging at first before bending over and throwing up between the bleachers the coffee and whatever else he had eaten for breakfast. When he had finished he used a brown paper napkin with the same logo as on the coffee cup to wipe his mouth. Perspiration had beaded on his forehead.

"You've met him, haven't you?" Sloane asked.

"Who?"

"Dark-haired man. Ponytail, maybe six foot two, well built."

Payne nodded.

"So have I."

Payne's eyes narrowed. "I don't understand. What would he want with you?"

"The designer of the toy had given me a file warning about the dangers of the magnets, not unlike the report Anne LeRoy gave you."

"I can't," Payne said, his voice a whisper, "I have a wife and kids."

"I had a wife too," Sloane said. "Anthony Stenopolis killed her because she saw his face."

Payne paled a ghostly white.

"So I know you're scared, but if you think this is just going to go away, you're wrong. It's not going to end, whatever he might have told you. Once you do whatever it is he's forcing you to do, he'll come for you, just like he came for me and for Anne LeRoy."

Payne shook his head. "How could he have known? I didn't tell anyone. I tried to protect her. I tried to get her to drop it, but she . . ." He choked back tears.

"It has to be someone who knew about that report."

"How did she get in touch with you?"

"She saw the article and called my office. She was going to give me a copy of the report."

"I told her not to," Payne whispered. "I tried to . . . Oh God." He began to retch again. When he had finished, Sloane continued his questions.

"Explain it to me. Tell me why you shut down her investigation."

"He told me to," Payne said. "He knew about it . . . somehow. Anne didn't take it well. She had worked very hard on the investigation and was upset. She said she would take it to the media and . . . I yelled at her. I told her that I would take legal action; I was trying to protect her. I was concerned . . ." Again Payne's voice drifted.

"I need to know how you first came in contact with Stenopolis. I need to know all of the ways that he could have learned of Anne's investigation."

A young boy and his father walked onto the outfield grass carrying baseball mitts and began to play catch, the sound of the ball smacking the leather gloves as Albert Payne explained his ill-fated trip to China to inspect manufacturing plants being used by American companies, including the plant with which Kendall Toys had contracted. He told Sloane that Larry Triplett, one of the agency directors, had been insistent that Payne be included on the trip, that Triplett was incensed at how the former administration had gutted the PSA in its quest to deregulate the toy industry. He said Triplett was working with Senator Joe Wallace, from Indiana, who was sponsoring a bill that would provide the agency with more power and more money, and Wallace had called for a congressional hearing into the recent spate of toy recalls with the hope that the inquiry would cause enough consumer outrage to put political pressure on the members of the House and Senate to pass the bill.

"Maggie Powers was supposed to go on the trip as well, but she canceled because her son was getting engaged. She also was eager to have me go."

"What happened over there?" Sloane asked.

"The factories were as I suspected. The manufacturers had worked hard to clean them up, but it was clear they were not following the regulations we try to impose on American companies. The workers were overworked and underpaid, and most of the products did not meet the quality control standards we seek to impose. In China if the regulation is voluntary, they ignore it. Following the inspections the government officials and owners insisted I attend a reception." Payne blew out a breath. "After one of the receptions I woke up in the morning with what I thought was a horrible hangover. He was there."

"Stenopolis?"

"I don't know his name. There was an Asian woman asleep

in bed beside me. I had no idea how I got there or who she was. I thought he was going to blackmail me, maybe try to bribe me but . . ."

Payne broke down, sobbing, his body shaking. He began to wipe at his face and chest, as if he had suddenly been sprayed. Sloane looked to Jenkins who wrote on a notebook and showed him the page. PTSD. Post-traumatic stress disorder.

Sloane could only guess at what horror was coming next.

Payne closed his eyes, grimacing, choking back tears as he said the words. "He shot her in the head. There was blood . . ."

Sloane put a hand on the man's back, giving him time to regain his composure. Payne blew his nose into the napkin, took several deep breaths, and looked out at the ball field. "He said that if I didn't do what he wanted he would make sure the Chinese had all the evidence they needed to convict me. Then he would kill my family."

"What exactly did he tell you to do besides drop the investigation into magnets?"

Payne's eyebrows inched together, surprised by the question. "He didn't tell me to drop the investigation."

"But you told Anne LeRoy . . ."

"I told Anne to drop it because I was trying to protect her. But he didn't want the investigation dropped. He wanted the report changed. He wanted me to ensure that the report concluded there was no reasonable likelihood of any danger and that the Chinese manufacturers met U.S. regulations."

"And the acting director would give that report at the congressional hearing," Sloane said.

"Yes. Maggie Powers."

"And you can't think of who else knew about Anne's investigation besides you?"

Payne shook his head, but then he stopped. His eyes widened.

PRODUCT SAFETY AGENCY

BETHESDA, MARYLAND

THREE SOFT KNOCKS, but the door did not push open.

"Come in," Payne said.

Peggy Seeley inched her head into his office like a kid sent to the principal's office. "You wanted to see me?"

"Yes. Come on in and shut the door."

Seeley hesitated before doing as instructed. She sat in one of two chairs across from Payne's desk and folded her hands in her lap, kneading her fingers and squinting, as if looking into a glare. Payne thought that she resembled a mouse.

"I'm afraid I have some bad news, Peggy."

Seeley lowered her gaze. "I suspected it was only a matter of time with the budget problems."

Payne raised a hand. "No, it's not that. It's not your job. I'm afraid it's worse than that."

Seeley slumped in her seat, her shoulders narrow, and her chest nearly concave. The squint became more pronounced.

"It's about Anne LeRoy."

"Is it the file? I told her to give the file back, like you asked. She said she was going to do it. I'm sure it just slipped her mind. She's been interviewing, and well, that hasn't been going too well—"

"Anne's dead, Peggy."

Seeley stared at him. "What?"

"There was some kind of accident in her home."

Seeley covered her mouth with the fingers of both hands, her eyes wide behind her glasses.

"The police found her in the bathtub. It appears that she dropped the hair dryer. She was electrocuted."

"Oh my God," Seeley said, openly weeping. "Oh my God."

He placed a box of tissue on the edge of the desk and she grabbed a handful.

"I'm very sorry. I know the two of you were good friends."

"When did this happen?"

"Just a few days ago. The police just called to advise me."

"The police?" Seeley stopped blotting the tears rolling down her cheeks. "Why did the police call you?"

"I'm not certain. They said that with an unattended death they have to follow through . . ."

"On what?"

"I don't know. They're reasonably certain it was an accident."

"Reasonably certain?"

"That's what they said."

Seeley sat back, hands in her lap, no doubt contemplating Payne's bizarre behavior during the past weeks, his insistence that LeRoy return the file, and now the police were asking him questions.

"I know that the two of you were close; I didn't want you to read about it in the paper or be shocked when the police called you."

"Me? Why would the police call me?"

"I'm sure it's just routine. They wanted the names of Anne's family and friends. Had you seen her recently?"

"Just the other . . ." Seeley caught herself. "No. Not recently."

"So you didn't note any bizarre behavior?"

"Bizarre behavior?"

"Anne didn't say she was alarmed by . . . anything?"

Seeley shook her head. "No. Nothing."

"She didn't discuss anything about her report with you?"

Seeley shook her head, more emphatic. "No. I don't know anything about it. Just that you didn't have the funding. I mean . . . she told me that, but nothing specific. No."

Payne nodded. "Well, I know this must come as a horrible shock. Why don't you take the rest of the day off? Go home and try to relax. I'll be letting everyone here know when I learn the details about the service."

Seeley nodded and stood from her chair, making her way to the door, this time without hesitation.

"Oh, and Peggy." Seeley turned. "You don't happen to know if Anne still had a copy of her report, do you?"

Seeley shook her head, pulled open the door, and walked out, closing it behind her.

Payne waited a beat, then took out his cell phone and punched the numbers as he walked to the plate glass windows that overlooked the front entrance to the building and the employee parking lot. "She's on her way down now," he said. Within minutes Seeley burst out the front door in a fast walk, nearly jogging. "That's her," Payne said. "Light blue sweater."

DAVID SLOANE SAT in the passenger seat, speaking into his cell phone. "I see her."

Seeley fumbled in her purse, first for her keys, then for her cell phone. She dropped her purse in the process, nearly stumbled over it, and retrieved it before climbing into a green Subaru Outback. She had the phone pressed to her ear as she maneuvered from the parking space, the car coming to a jarring stop just inches before hitting the car parked in the space kitty-corner to it. She pulled forward, nearly clipping the bumper of another car, and sped from the parking lot.

Jenkins and Sloane followed her at a safe distance, hopeful that Payne had scared Seeley sufficiently that she would seek help, or at least let whoever she was working with know what had happened to Anne LeRoy. According to Payne, Seeley had every reason to be afraid of him. He had been acting bizarre ever since his return from China, prone to emotional bursts and obsessive about getting LeRoy to return the copy of the report she had down-loaded. He said that making Seeley believe that the police were asking him questions, and therefore that he was a suspect, would not be difficult and should be sufficient to put her over the edge. Sloane hoped he was right.

Seeley drove northwest on River Road past homes and shop-ping malls, Sloane charting her on a map and trying to decipher where she might be going. He figured she might head home, but if so, it would not be for a while. The homes in this area were large and spread out. It was unlikely Seeley owned one on a gov-ernment salary. She turned west on Falls Road, and the landscape did not change much: large homes and lots of lush acreage. In be-tween the groves of trees Sloane saw swimming pools and private tennis courts.

"Any idea yet where she's going?" Jenkins asked just as Seeley came to a T in the road and turned right. Jenkins slowed.

"Why? You think she's worried someone's following her?" He repositioned the map in his lap and traced his finger along MacArthur Boulevard.

"Doesn't give any indication," Jenkins said, turning right and following.

The scenery became more rural, trees on both sides of the two-lane road. Sloane could no longer see any houses between the foliage. "The road ends," he said. "She's going to Great Falls Park."

"How far?"

"Maybe a mile."

"Any turnoffs between here and there?"

"Not that appear on the map. You can slow down."

Jenkins checked his rearview mirror. With no one behind him, he slowed considerably. In the distance they watched Seeley turn right.

"That's the park," Sloane said. "She's meeting someone."

Before the roundabout to the entrance to the park Jenkins stopped. "Get out. Take your cell phone with you."

Sloane exited the car wearing sunglasses and slipped on a Washington, D.C., tourist's ball cap. He walked the road to a paved footpath as Jenkins turned right and followed Seeley's car into a parking lot. A moment later his cell phone rang. He pressed his earpiece to answer.

"She's getting out of the car. Headed in your direction."

Sloane continued down the path to a visitor's center and plucked an information pamphlet from a plastic container near a window. He positioned himself near the Potomac River, which ran parallel to the footpath. It still being tourist season, Sloane stepped closer to a group, hoping to blend in. People milled about the grounds and stood on a footbridge overlooking the blue-green tinted water. It was warm out. Most wore shorts and tank tops and carried cameras.

After several minutes he spotted Seeley walking down the path toward him and held up his cell phone, as if to take a picture of the water. "I got her," he said.

Seeley walked briskly past the visitor's center and continued down the footpath. Still considering his pamphlet, which included the trails along the Potomac, Sloane followed at a safe distance and watched Seeley use a footbridge to cross over the river to a path on the other side, continuing south. The rush of the water became more pronounced as it funneled over a series of steep jagged rocks and through a narrowing gorge. Tourists passed Sloane on the path, walking in the opposite direction.

"You there?" Jenkins asked.

"I'm here," Sloane said, talking over the rush of the water. "She's still walking."

"I think we have a winner," Jenkins said. "Silver Mercedes

with government-issued plates just pulled into the parking lot. Driver looks to be talking on a cell phone."

Sloane looked up as Seeley stopped and reached into her purse. She pulled out her cell phone and pressed it to her ear.

"She's getting a call," he confirmed.

Jenkins described the person getting out of the car as Sloane watched Seeley turn right at a fork in the path. When he reached the fork he saw that the path led to a second footbridge overlooking a spot where the water cascaded over a short falls. Sloane went straight, then left the road for a less worn, unpaved footpath through the trees that emerged downriver and provided a view of the footbridge on which Seeley stood waiting.

Ten minutes later Seeley's contact arrived. They stood on the bridge talking as Sloane pretended to take photographs of the falls with his cell phone. They spoke for less than fifteen minutes. Seeley's contact left first, leaving her alone on the bridge. Sloane followed the trail back to the walking path and hurried over to the fork in the road, turning toward the bridge where Seeley remained standing, looking out over the brown water and falls.

Sloane removed his sunglasses and his hat as he approached. "Peggy Seeley?"

Seeley's head snapped in his direction. Her eyes registered fear. For a moment Sloane worried that she might scream.

"I'm David Sloane," he said, offering her his business card. "I'm the attorney in the article you gave to Anne LeRoy." Seeley's facial expression softened from concern to confusion. "Anne called me. We were supposed to meet the other night. I know what happened."

"It wasn't an accident," she said.

"No, it wasn't," Sloane said.

Seeley's eyes narrowed.

"Things are not what they appear to be, Peggy, but you need to trust that what I'm about to tell you is the truth, because your life is now in danger."

MCLEAN, VIRGINIA

ALBERT PAYNE KEPT one eye on the road while trying to read the directions he had downloaded from the Internet. Large oaks lined the streets, but the sidewalks and gutters were pristine; not a single leaf dared to have fallen. A lifelong resident of Bethesda, Payne knew that John Roll McLean, the former owner and publisher of the *Washington Post*, had built a railway to link the outlying areas to Washington, D.C., and named one of those train depots after himself. McLean probably never imagined the impressive roll call of residents who would someday live in the multi-million-dollar homes built on wooded lots with manicured lawns and gardens. Just eleven miles from Washington, D.C., McLean's residents included diplomats, members of Congress, and high-ranking government officials, as well as executives of the three *Fortune* 500 companies that maintained corporate headquarters nearby.

Payne slowed, confirmed the address, and turned just past a six-foot brick post adorned with an ornate light fixture. The driveway inclined and veered to the left, the lawn outlined by subtle Japanese garden lamps, and proceeded past the front entrance to a three-story, Colonial-style brick home with three white dormer windows protruding from the roof and leaded-glass windows. He parked in an area to the side of the home and took a moment to compose himself before stepping from the car. At the front door he pushed the illuminated doorbell and didn't wait long before a teenage boy in a T-shirt and baggy shorts answered.

"Hi. Is your—"

"Albert?"

Joe Wallace approached from down a hall, eyebrows knitted together. The boy stepped to the side and disappeared. Dressed in an Indiana basketball T-shirt and sweatpants, Wallace looked as if he was about to leave for a workout.

"I'm sorry to bother you at home," Payne said.

"You don't look well. Are you all right?"

"I need to talk to you. It's important."

Wallace stepped aside and welcomed Payne into a marbled entry with an ornate crystal chandelier. Payne smelled chocolate—as when his daughter baked double fudge brownies—and heard the chatter of a baseball game from a television in another room.

Wallace led Payne to a room just to the right of the front door adorned in white—white carpeting, two white sofas and a matching chair, white drapes. The only color in the room was a black baby grand piano near the bay window and a vase of flowers atop it. Wallace started to sit.

"Is there someplace more private?" Payne asked.

Wallace's brow furrowed, but he asked no questions, leading Payne through two sliding wooden doors to a library with a desk and built-in bookshelves. Wallace slid the doors closed behind them and offered Payne one of two high-back leather chairs opposite the desk. He sat in the adjacent chair and pulled the chain on a lamp between them, the bulb's wattage muted by a leather shade.

"You look terrible," Wallace said. "Have you seen a doctor?"

"Anne LeRoy is dead."

"Who? Albert, calm down and start over."

"She worked in my office. She was preparing a report on the use of powerful magnets in consumer goods, children's toys, and their potential danger. She's dead. Someone killed her."

Wallace frowned and looked at Payne as if he were speaking a foreign language. "Slow down, Albert, I'm not following you. Are you talking about the report you recently gave me for the hearing? I just read it."

"The report I gave you is not her report."

"I don't understand."

"I changed it."

Wallace leaned forward into the light. "What?"

Payne opened his briefcase and handed Wallace a multiple-page document. "This is Anne's actual report."

Wallace took it and sat back, flipping through the pages. After several minutes his fingers stopped, and he sat staring at the books on the shelves, lips pressed tight.

"I'm sorry," Payne said.

"Why would you do this? Why would you give me a bogus report?"

"The report on the factories in China complying with U.S. regulations is also false."

For a moment Wallace did not speak. He stood and paced the Oriental throw rug. "Why would you do this?"

"I had to."

"Had to?" Wallace stopped and faced him. "Why would you *have* to do this?"

For the next several minutes Payne explained what had happened in China and about the man and his demands. "And now Anne LeRoy is dead. He electrocuted her in her bathtub."

"That sounds like an accident."

"No."

"How do you know?"

"There's a lawyer pursuing this named David Sloane. He's filed a lawsuit in Seattle against Kendall Toys for the deaths of two children who swallowed magnets from a Kendall toy. The *Post* ran an article and Anne saw it and called him. He was supposed to meet with her, but this man beat him to her."

"How would this man know about her report?"

"Someone had to tell him about it."

"Who? Who else knew about the report?"

"Anne had a friend at the agency, Peggy Seeley. She knew about it, but it can't be her. It has to be someone with power, someone who could also be sure I was included on that trip to China."

"Triplett wanted you to go," Wallace said. "He was insistent."

"So did Maggie Powers. It has to be one of them. They must have promised Seeley something, a promotion to keep them apprised of what my department was doing."

Wallace took a deep breath. "So you don't know who this man is working for?"

"Not for certain, no, but if I had to guess, I'd guess Maggie Powers."

"Why her and not Triplett?"

Payne handed Wallace a copy of the *Washington Post* article on Sloane. As Wallace read, Payne continued. "Maggie Powers worked for the Toy Manufacturer's Association, and Kendall is in financial trouble. They need this new toy to hit big to stay afloat. A report like Anne's would kill the project. Under the circumstances we would have to initiate an enforcement action and delay production. And if the attorney is right, the toy won't pass an inspection. It's a danger to kids."

"What do you mean 'if the attorney is right'?"

"I spoke to this guy, Sloane."

"On the phone?"

"No. He's here in Washington."

"Why is he here?"

"I told you. Anne called him. He was supposed to meet with her."

"Did she give him a copy of the report?"

"No. She was dead by the time he got there, but they spoke on the phone about it. Apparently Anne told him I'd pulled the plug on her investigation, and he wanted to know why. He said that a boy in each of the families in that article died when the plastic on two Kendall toys cracked and the magnets fell out. They swallowed them, and the magnets attracted one another through the intestines, creating a hole that allowed bacteria into the body cavity and organs."

Wallace stared through the thin curtain covering the leaded-glass window, seemingly deep in thought.

"Have you told anyone else?"

"I couldn't. The man said he'd kill my family. I didn't know where to go, who to talk to."

Wallace paced, rubbing his forehead. "We'll have to bring in the Department of Justice and the FBI."

"What will happen to me?"

"I don't know for certain, but under the circumstances anyone would have done what you did." Wallace paced again. "Since we can't be certain it's Powers and not Triplett, don't tell anyone else until we know who's behind this."

"I wasn't going to."

"In the morning we'll go to the Justice Department together. Where are you staying?"

"At home. Why?"

"Do you think it's safe?"

"This man doesn't know I'm here. He doesn't know that I know anything about Anne. He said as long as I do what he told me to do, nothing would happen." Payne thought for a moment. "My wife has been upset with me. I haven't been myself since this began. I can suggest she take the kids to her mother's."

"That would probably be a good idea." Wallace exhaled. "All

right. Go home and try to relax. I'll call you in the morning and arrange a meeting with the Justice Department in my office. I'll keep this as quiet as I can, Albert. For now, don't do anything with the actual reports; if Powers is involved, we'll let her hang herself at the hearing."

AMERICAN INN
BETHESDA, MARYLAND

CHARLES JENKINS PACED the carpet, cell phone pressed to his ear. The cabinet doors of the entertainment console hung open, the television on, though he had muted the sound. Alex had called as he watched the local news for any further stories about Anne LeRoy's death or gunmen at the Georgetown apartment complex. He was worried the lobby had a camera, though he had not recalled seeing one.

"How's David?" Alex asked.

Jenkins heard the water in the shower through the thin motel walls. The furnishings were equally cheap: a small desk to the right of the television, a cushioned chair and lamp in the corner near the curtained window, two queen-size beds separated by a dresser.

"I'm worried about him." Jenkins pulled back both the heavy blue curtain and the thinner drape to look out the window into the parking lot. "He's detached, somber, like the first time I met him on that bluff in West Virginia. He's lost again, I'm afraid. "

"You think he could be suicidal?"

"I think he could be, but at the moment he's focused on something he needs to do. We'll need to keep a closer eye on him after this is over." One way or another, Jenkins thought, but he did not say it. "You're safe?"

"We're fine. It's you I'm worried about," Alex replied. Jenkins heard his son mewl through the speaker.

"How is he?"

"He misses his daddy," she said. "So do I."

"Tell him Daddy will be home soon." He heard the shower turn off.

"Be careful. I love you," she said.

"I love you too." He disconnected and sat on the edge of the bed, pressing the mute button and listening to the newscast. After several more minutes the bathroom door opened.

"You feel better?" Jenkins asked.

He wore a pullover polo shirt and blue jeans. His feet were bare. "Yes, thank you," Albert Payne said.

ALBERT PAYNE'S HOME
BETHESDA, MARYLAND

SLOANE DROVE ALBERT PAYNE'S four-wheel drive up the inclined driveway and pressed the button for the automatic garage door on the box clipped to the visor next to a picture of Payne's wife and two children. He slowed his approach as the paneled door rolled up. Ordinarily the door would have triggered an inside light, but Payne had disabled it earlier when he convinced his wife to take the children to his mother's.

Sloane turned off the headlights and pulled forward until a green tennis ball hanging from a string touched the windshield. He pressed the button again and waited for the door to roll closed before getting out of the car.

Jenkins had not agreed with Sloane's plan. In fact, he had been dead set against it, but they both knew that Stenopolis would need to get to Payne quickly, before the morning. Payne could not be the bait, and Jenkins was out of the question because of his size. Sloane told Jenkins he was not looking to die, not with Stenopolis at large and unfinished business with Malcolm Fitzgerald and Kendall Toys. Jenkins had relented and taken a hotel room within minutes of Payne's home. While Jenkins wanted to be physically closer to the property, they agreed that it was another risk if Stenopolis were watching. At the moment, they held the element of surprise. Stenopolis would be expecting to find an unprepared, out-of-shape, frightened bureaucrat. What he would encounter was one alert, armed, and determined marine.

Sloane stepped from the garage to a covered causeway leading to the house. A light in the center illuminated the path, but they had decided not to disable it, concerned it would be too conspicuous. Sloane wore a button-down shirt and brown slacks he had purchased in a mall to match those Albert Payne had worn earlier that evening as well as Payne's olive green London Fog jacket, padded with newspaper for additional girth, and a pair of glasses without lenses. They picked up a beard at a theater costume shop and applied it with rubber glue that was making Sloane's skin itch. Jenkins had trimmed the beard and added gray. Sloane turned his head as he walked beneath the light, as if considering the keys in his hand.

He slipped the key into the lock and pushed open the door into the kitchen. Inside, he closed it before flipping the wall switch just to the right, exactly where Payne had diagrammed it. He removed the Sig Sauer 9 mm from beneath the jacket, walked from the kitchen into the family room, and flipped another wall switch, which caused the blades of a combination ceiling fan and light to spin overhead. Brown leather furniture arranged in an L pattern faced a flat-screen television positioned in the center of an entertainment console with books and framed family photographs. A green potted plant dominated a corner of the room.

Going over the layout of the house with Payne, Sloane and Jenkins decided the family room was the best place for Sloane to wait, providing him a clear view of the entry from the kitchen, as well as the open archway that led to the front hall. It also gave him two avenues of escape, if that became necessary.

A family portrait of Payne with his wife and two children hung over the mantel. Payne looked different, and not just because he had more hair and no beard, making his face appear thinner. The most striking difference was the expression on Payne's face.

He was smiling.

"Just one big happy family," the voice said.

AMERICAN INN

BETHESDA, MARYLAND

JENKINS POINTED THE remote at the television, about to change the channel when his cell phone rang, the number indicating David Sloane.

"Everything all right?"

"Everything is fine. I presume this is Charles Jenkins?"

The adrenaline rush brought Jenkins to his feet.

"Cat's got your tongue? I'm looking forward to making your acquaintance, Mr. Jenkins."

Jenkins felt numb.

"Let me explain how this is going to work. First, you will bring Albert Payne to me. Why? Because I have never left an assignment unfinished, and I have no intention of beginning now. If you fail, I will kill Mr. Sloane—"

"I want to talk to David."

"Do not interrupt me again, Mr. Jenkins. It's rude." Stenopolis paused. "If you fail, I will kill Mr. Sloane, and we both know that I will eventually find and kill Mr. Payne, anyway."

"I want to talk to David," Jenkins repeated. "How do I know you haven't killed him already?"

"A fair request."

There was a pause. Jenkins heard a voice, though it did not sound like Sloane. It sounded tired and slurred. "Don't come. Don't give him the satis—"

Jenkins heard a thump followed by a groan.

"David!"

The voice remained calm. "You don't have much time, Mr. Jenkins. I know you're in a nearby motel and I timed the distance. I'm not a patient man. Any delay and I'll assume you have breached our understanding and I will kill your friend and disappear. Time is running out."

THE ROOM WAS a blur of black-and-white flashes. As his vision cleared, Sloane was looking up at the blades of an overhead fan. His head snapped forward, further startling his senses. He tried to move but found his arms bound behind him, the pressure around his wrists making his fingers cold and numb. He felt the same pressure around his ankles, though he could not see them either. His legs had been pulled behind him, bound to the back legs of a sturdy chair. The right half of his face tingled numb; his right eye was swollen shut. Searching the room through his one eye, he saw orange and yellow flames wick and dance in the fireplace and flicker shadows across the furniture and the portrait of Albert Payne and his family. Stenopolis sat, legs crossed, elbows propped on the arms of the leather chair, hands forming a pyramid just beneath his chin.

"We meet again, Mr. Sloane. I've never had the pleasure of saying that to one of my targets. You are resilient." Stenopolis uncrossed his legs, smiling. "I must admit I made a mistake not killing you when I had the chance. I normally don't make mistakes."

The Sig Sauer lay on the glass, circular coffee table between them, taunting him.

"You made another big mistake." His tongue felt too big in his mouth. He tasted blood.

"And what is that?"

"You killed my wife."

Stenopolis unclasped his hands and calmly pulled the poker from the fireplace. Wisps of smoke spiraled toward the overhead light fixture, dissipating before reaching the rotating blades. Sloane felt the heat of the fire on his bare arms and smelled freshly cut pine. The sap from the wood crackled and popped.

"You should be grateful," Stenopolis said.

"Yeah? How's that?" Sloane felt the anger welling inside of him. The wrist and ankle restraints tightened.

"Because she did not suffer." Stenopolis shoved the tip of the poker back into the glowing orange embers and rotated it. "Your wife's death was quick and painless. We should all be so lucky. I find it fascinating that so many people fear death, when death is not what should be feared. Death is the end. It brings peace and comfort. I've read many books on the subject."

"And here I was betting you couldn't read, Anthony."

Stenopolis ignored the use of his name. "It is what happens before death that people should fear. You've heard the saying 'a fate worse than death'?" Without taking his eyes from Sloane,

Stenopolis reached behind him and gripped the handle of the poker, turning it. A glowing orange ember tumbled onto the brick hearth. "Imagine having your tongue cut out while you are still alive, or your eyes burned from their sockets, being forced to live in total darkness. Imagine living with no thumbs. Have you never considered such things?"

Sloane didn't respond.

"I have."

"That's because you're a sociopath, Anthony. Do you know the meaning of the term 'sociopath'?"

Stenopolis burst from the chair, his face just inches from Sloane's. He smiled. "A person who engages in antisocial behavior, I believe. Though I do think the term is overused." He stepped back, waving his hands in the air. "Everyone is 'crazy' now. Everyone who does something out of the ordinary is a 'sociopath.' It really detracts from those who are truly crazy, don't you think?"

"Not you."

Stenopolis did not respond.

"Why kill her?" Sloane asked. "She couldn't have stopped you."

Stenopolis stepped closer to the fireplace, one arm leaning on the mantel, the flicker of the flames casting shadows across his body, seemingly impervious to the heat. "You're feeling guilt." He turned and looked at Sloane. "You tested my acumen. Now I will test yours. Do you know the meaning of the word *machismo*?"

Sloane did not answer.

"No? It means an exaggerated awareness of one's masculinity. Tell me, do you feel guilty because your wife is dead, or because, as a man, you could not protect her?"

Sloane had been but a boy when his mother was killed, and rationally he knew there was nothing he could have done to save her. But he could not use that rationalization to shake the guilt that his first instinct had been to dive behind his desk, even if it had been to get his gun. He had been over that moment a thousand times, wondering what would have happened if he had rushed Stenopolis immediately, and he knew it would continue to haunt him for the rest of his life, however long that may be.

"Allow me to alleviate your guilt. I killed her because she was there." Stenopolis shrugged. "Once she came down those steps, I had very little choice in the matter. It really wasn't personal, Mr. Sloane."

"Maybe not for you."

"We're not that different, you and I. People come to you with a problem and you solve it for them for a price. I provide the same type of service. I just employ a different means to the end."

"You kill innocent men and women."

"Do I? I kill blackmailers, thieves, adulterers, pedophiles, and corrupt government officials. I kill people who refuse to live by the rules of society that govern all of us."

"My wife was not one of those. Nor am I."

"You meddled where you shouldn't have."

"You're just trying to justify your actions."

Stenopolis advanced, his face again inches from Sloane's. "You're wrong. I told you, I need no justification. Unlike you, I feel no guilt."

WHAT JENKINS NEEDED was time, and he was anything but certain he would get it. Once he delivered Albert Payne it was highly probable Stenopolis would shoot Jenkins and eliminate him as a threat. Jenkins would do the same. But not bringing Payne was also not an option. Jenkins would be playing Russian roulette with Sloane's life, and, as Stenopolis had made abundantly clear, he would kill Sloane and hunt Payne down eventually. The only thing Jenkins possessed that Stenopolis might find of value was the name of the man who Stenopolis would believe had given him up, the secretary of labor, Ed Hotchkin. A guy like Stenopolis didn't stay in business long if his clients talked; his business was dependent upon fear and intimidation that fostered a code of silence.

Jenkins entered the house through the back door off the kitchen, Albert Payne behind him. Payne started for the family room, but Jenkins grabbed him by the arm and pulled him back, stepping in front. Payne had been acting odd since Jenkins told him their plan had gone awry, as if he had known from the start that it was his fate to die and he was resigned to the outcome.

Sloane sat slumped in a chair. At the sound of Jenkins's entering the room, Sloane raised his head.

"Oh my God."

Sloane peered out of one eye, the other swollen shut. Blood, nearly black in the muted light, streaked his face, flowing from a cut along his forehead over his right eye. The right side of his mouth was equally swollen, and his hands and ankles were bound behind him. An empty chair had been placed beside him, and on it a thin rope.

Stenopolis entered from the opposite side of the room, gun directed at Jenkins. "Alive, just as I promised," he said. "You made good time, Mr. Jenkins. Please remove your coat and drop it on the floor."

Jenkins slipped the long black coat from his shoulders and let it drop to the floor.

"Step forward."

Jenkins did.

"Don't stand in the doorway, Albert. Come in. A man's home is his castle."

Payne remained off to the side.

"Turn around, Mr. Jenkins."

Jenkins complied.

Jenkins heard Stenopolis approach from behind and thought again of trying to disarm him, but that thought passed when the hard steel pressed against the back of his skull. Stenopolis ran his hands over Jenkins's body, searching for weapons.

"Turn around."

Again Jenkins complied.

"Excuse my manners," Stenopolis said, gesturing to the empty chair beside Sloane. "Please, take a seat."

Jenkins sat. "If you think I'm going to tell you which one of your clients gave you up, Anthony, forget it," he said purposefully.

"Actually, Mr. Jenkins, I had no such interest, but I appreciate the information. You, perhaps, should be wondering who gave you up. Your friend Mr. Wade was equally recalcitrant."

Jenkins's jaw clenched at the sound of Curley Wade's name, but he tried to display no emotion. He had been right that Stenopolis had once had CIA connections and apparently still did.

"He told me to kill him because he would never break. A mistake, I'm afraid. He broke. I killed him. What he failed to comprehend is that a man who enjoys his work can keep at a task for a very long time, and I very much enjoy my work, as you are about to find out."

Jenkins gripped the chair arms. "We all have to die sometime, Anthony."

"How perceptive."

Stenopolis kept a safe distance. "You will do the honors, Albert." He pointed to the strand of cord. "The lengths of rope are sufficient to go around the arms and legs of the chair six times if you maintain proper tightness. I would suggest you do."

Payne did not move.

Stenopolis shot at the floor, just missing Jenkins's shoe. "Do not test my patience again, Albert."

"Just do what he says," Jenkins said.

Payne stepped forward and took the rope, kneeling and binding one of Jenkins's arms.

"I'm disappointed in you, Albert. I gave you specific instructions and you breached those instructions."

"He didn't breach them," Jenkins said. "I told you. We already knew all about you. One of your clients gave you up."

Payne tied the second of Jenkins's wrists.

"I doubt that very much, Mr. Jenkins, but we'll determine that soon enough. I'll reward your silence by allowing you to watch Mr. Sloane and Mr. Jenkins die, Albert. I believe you will find it fascinating."

Payne finished tying Jenkins's ankles and stepped back. Stenopolis checked the wrist restraints. Satisfied, he removed the poker from the fireplace. The end glowed orange. He approached Jenkins with the tip extended. "Now, Mr. Jenkins, the first piece of business, since you brought it up. Who told you how to contact me?"

Jenkins laughed. "Go to hell, Anthony."

Stenopolis shook his head. "Mr. Wade made the same suggestion. But as you can see, I'm still here."

He moved the tip of the poker toward Jenkins's left eye.

The front doorbell rang.

No one moved.

It rang again, a repeated chime of bells followed by a loud male voice. "Al? Hey Al? You home?"

Stenopolis turned to Payne.

"It's my neighbor," Payne said.

The bell rang again. "Al?"

"Do not say a word," Stenopolis said.

"He has a key," Payne said.

Stenopolis's nostrils flared. He shoved the tip of the poker back into the flames, grabbed Payne by the back of his shirt, and shoved him out of the room. "Get rid of him or I will kill him too." He turned to Jenkins and Sloane. "If either of you make a sound I will shoot them both."

The front door was already opening, the neighbor struggling to pull the key from the lock. He startled when he looked up and saw Payne. "Al? Hell, you scared me. Didn't you hear me yelling out there? Why are you standing in the dark?"

"I'm sorry. I was upstairs."

"No worries. I figured you were home; I saw your car drive up and the lights go on. Mary and the kids at soccer?"

Stenopolis stepped into the entry.

"Sorry, I didn't know you had company."

"Albert's my cousin," Stenopolis said.

The neighbor extended a hand. "Cousin? Nice to meet you."

"Pleasure," Stenopolis said.

The neighbor addressed Payne. "Well, then. I won't keep you. I was just hoping I could borrow your ride mower. I wanted to catch you tonight in case you left early for work in the morning."

"Sure," Payne said.

"The wife's been after me for about a week to cut the lawn. You know how that is. I won't enjoy a minute until it's done." He turned to Stenopolis. "Are you married?"

"No."

"Lucky you. Al here knows what I'm talking about though, don't you Al? The wife keeps me busier than a one-legged man in a butt-kicking contest."

"Let me get you the key," Payne said.

The neighbor waved him off. "Don't trouble yourself. I know where it is: top drawer in the kitchen. I'll be out of your hair in a minute; sorry to have interrupted." He spoke to Stenopolis. "Nice to have met you."

Stenopolis nodded. He and Payne followed the neighbor into the kitchen, where he rummaged through a drawer beneath the tiled counter. "Did you move it?" he shouted over his shoulder. "Ah nope, here it is."

In one quick motion, the neighbor spun. Just as quickly, Payne dropped to the ground.

Stenopolis made a play for his gun but never got his hand behind his back.

Detective Tom Molia had the barrel of his gun aimed directly between Stenopolis's eyes. "Go ahead. I can pick a flea off the ass of a white-tailed deer, shithead. So give me a reason."

Stenopolis raised both hands.

"With your left hand I want you to very slowly reach behind your back, pull that gun from your pants, and let me hear it hit the floor."

The gun hit the tiled floor with a thud and clatter.

"Now, take three giant steps back," Molia said.

Stenopolis did.

Molia maintained ten feet between himself and Stenopolis. "Mr. Payne, pick that up and bring it to me."

Payne approached cautiously, retrieved the gun, and brought it to Molia.

Stenopolis grinned. "Clever. Can I assume you are not the neighbor?"

Molia spoke to Payne but kept his eyes and the gun trained on Stenopolis. "Where's David and Goliath?"

Payne pointed to the family room. "He has them tied up."

"Take a knife and cut them free."

Payne stepped to a drawer and pulled out a serrated knife.

"You're well trained," Stenopolis said. "I'm presuming you are an officer of the law, and perhaps a thespian; that was quite the performance."

"Wait until you see me play the part of a pissed-off detective. I'm good at that. Put your hands on top of your head and interlock your fingers."

Stenopolis continued to do as Molia asked.

"Now let's you and me walk into that room."

Jenkins stood rubbing his wrist as Payne cut the twine binding Sloane's ankles.

"Jesus," Molia said, seeing Sloane's face. "You all right?"

Sloane retrieved Stenopolis's gun from Molia, turned, and pointed it in the man's face.

"David," Molia said.

Stenopolis smiled. "Do you have it in you, Mr. Sloane? I told you we aren't that different."

"I want to know who you're working for."

Stenopolis shook his head, amused. "Let me tell you how this will work, Mr. Sloane. I will tell you nothing, no matter how much you torture me. This officer will then 'take me in' in the parlance of law enforcement, where I'll be allowed to make one phone call. When I do, within the hour two gentlemen will come to the police station and advise the good officer that they are taking jurisdiction of the suspect out of national security concerns. After several more phone calls and much hand-wringing and profanity by others, I will walk out of jail a free man and disappear, seemingly never to be seen or heard from again."

Sloane turned to Jenkins, disbelieving.

Jenkins nodded. "Someone tipped him that Curley Wade had pulled his file. It had to be someone at the Agency."

Payne stepped forward, shell-shocked. "Is that true? He's going to get away with this?"

"He's just trying to antagonize us," Jenkins said. "He's not going to get away with anything."

"You know that's not true," Stenopolis said. "Your friend Mr. Wade told you that we were all once kindred spirits, the three of us. I had my reasons for disappearing, Mr. Jenkins. What were yours?"

"Shut up," Sloane said.

"It's not going to be over, is it?" Payne asked.

"To the contrary, Albert, we're just getting started."

"Shut up," Sloane said, rage building.

"Oh my God," Payne said, stepping away. "It's not going to end."

"I did warn you, Albert."

"Shut up!" Sloane smashed the gun across Stenopolis's face, the blow knocking him to the floor. He lifted himself to an elbow and flicked his tongue at the stream of blood trickling from the corner of his mouth.

Molia stepped forward, but Jenkins gripped his arm and held him back.

"Who are you working for?" Sloane asked.

"Trade secret, Mr. Sloane, I'm afraid I can't divulge that information."

Sloane kicked Stenopolis in the face, knocking him onto his back. He grabbed the poker handle, pulled the tip from the fire, and pressed a foot across Stenopolis's neck. Standing over him, he lowered the smoldering tip to within an inch of his face.

Stenopolis grunted at him. "The problem you have, Mr. Sloane, is that while most people fear death, I don't."

"Who said anything about death, Anthony? Like you said, we're just getting started. We're going to find out about that fate worse than death. Now, who hired you?"

"David!" Molia again started forward, but Jenkins kept him back.

Stenopolis spit blood through a grin. His voice choked. "You can't do it. You don't have it in you."

"Wrong." Sloane stared down at the man who had stood over Tina and watched her suffocate on her own blood. "That changed the moment you killed my wife." He pressed the tip of the poker against Stenopolis's cheek, flesh burning. Stenopolis grimaced, growling between clenched teeth, but he did not yell.

"David?" Molia said, more forceful.

"The next time I aim two inches higher," Sloane said. "You don't answer, and I take out an eye. Who are you working for?"

Stenopolis smiled, but for the first time it was tentative and unsure.

Sloane inched the poker closer to his eye.

"David!" Molia yelled.

Stenopolis's eyes widened then instinctively closed. Adrenaline pulsed through Sloane's body, causing the poker tip to shake. He screamed and pushed it down, diverting it, the fibers of the carpet melting and emitting a strong chemical odor. He took his foot from Stenopolis's throat and stepped back, throwing the poker across the room, his body continuing to shake with rage.

Stenopolis rolled onto his stomach, choking and wheezing. Molia freed himself of Jenkins's grasp and stepped forward, handcuffs out. He knelt and grabbed one of Stenopolis's wrists, yanking it behind his back and snapping the cuff. As he did, Stenopolis's right hand reached behind and gripped the detective's wrist. Stenopolis then spun onto his back. Hips arched, knees bent, his body uncoiled like a spring, he landed on his feet, bending Molia's arm behind his back while his free hand grabbed the butt of the detective's gun.

"No!" Jenkins yelled.

Sloane turned at the sound of Jenkins's voice. Too late. Stenopolis had taken aim and the retort echoed as the dark blur crossed Sloane's peripheral vision.

Before Sloane could refocus he heard another shot and watched as Stenopolis spun, letting go of the detective. Three more shots exploded in succession, a string of firecrackers. The bullets drove Stenopolis backward, his body impacting violently against the brick fireplace. Legs quivering, he remained upright, gun at his side, then slumped to the hearth.

Albert Payne advanced, hand outstretched, gun extended.

Stenopolis put a hand to his chest and held it up, staring at the crimson red staining his fingertips, as if not comprehending the sight of his own blood. He looked up at Albert Payne with an expression that was part bemusement, part disbelief. His jaw opened, as if he were about to speak.

Apparently not interested, Payne fired again. Stenopolis's head snapped back. Then his body listed to the side.

Tom Molia approached slowly. Payne's arm lowered, as if too fatigued to hold it outstretched any longer. The gun slid from his palm to his fingertips where it lingered a moment before falling to the rug. When Molia touched his shoulder Payne did not react, continuing to stare down at Stenopolis's lifeless body.

"Charlie!" Sloane yelled.

His friend lay on the floor, a hand pressed against his stomach, blood seeping through his fingers.

Sloane crouched over him, shouting over his shoulder. "Call an ambulance! Oh shit, I'm sorry, Charlie, I'm so sorry."

"Don't." Jenkins grimaced, his voice angry. "Do not blame yourself for this. I don't want that on my conscience."

"Just hang on. We're going to get you help."

"Pure dumb luck."

"What?"

"That's all it is. What happens just happens," he said, though in this case Sloane knew that wasn't the case. Jenkins had deliberately taken the bullet for him. "You're not responsible for this any more than you were responsible for what happened to Tina. Do you understand?"

Jenkins grimaced again and shut his eyes.

"Charlie?"

His breathing labored.

Sloane grabbed Jenkins's hand. "Come on, stay with me, Charlie."

DESPITE HIS PROTESTATIONS, the paramedics would not allow Sloane to ride in the back of the ambulance. He followed in a police car, refusing medical attention for his own injuries, unwilling to let Jenkins out of his sight.

Tom Molia remained at the house with Albert Payne to answer the questions of the Bethesda police officers who had arrived with the ambulance.

When the paramedics pulled the stretcher from the back of the ambulance and wheeled Jenkins through the emergency room doors he lay unconscious, an oxygen mask covering his nose and mouth. Sloane followed as far as the doors leading to an operating room before a nurse and two security guards convinced him to step back and allow the doctors to do their job.

The nurse led Sloane back down the hall to a bed in the emergency room, where he sat while she cleaned his wounds. A doctor put four stitches in the cut above Sloane's eye and three more inside his upper lip. He told Sloane that his right eye was too swollen to examine, and therefore he could not yet be certain whether the injury would cause any permanent impairment to Sloane's vision. When the doctor had finished his examination, the nurse led Sloane to a waiting area where he sat until he decided he could not wait any longer before calling Alex.

Though upset, she took the news stoically and did not panic. She made Sloane promise to call the second he heard anything further. Hanging up, Sloane sat feeling more alone than he ever had.

An hour passed before he heard the sound of dress shoes slapping the hospital linoleum. Tom Molia turned a corner and entered the waiting room. "Have you heard anything?"

Sloane shook his head. "He's in surgery."

Molia sat beside him and exhaled a long breath.

"How's Payne?" Sloane asked.

Molia frowned and shook his head. "I don't know. It's going to take awhile. He's pretty shook up, though I think maybe he's seeing some light at the end of what has been a very dark tunnel." He turned his head, looked at Sloane. "He said to say thank you."

"For what?"

Molia shrugged.

Sloane leaned his head back against the wall. "Maybe Stenopolis was right; maybe we do all have it in us."

"I don't know about that, but he was right about one thing: higher authorities came to take possession of his body. I called both the Department of Justice and the FBI."

For a moment neither spoke, then Molia said, "I keep thinking of that Springsteen song. You know, the one about the dog being beat too much and spending its life covering up? Then there are others that just get tired of getting beat and one day just bite back. I think Payne just snapped when he heard Stenopolis say he was going to walk away, that it might never be over, that he might spend the rest of his life looking over his shoulder and worrying about his wife and kids. He just wanted it to end."

"Where'd he get the gun?"

"Jenkins. He knew Stenopolis would search him for a weapon when he got to the house, but he was hoping he wouldn't consider Payne a threat."

"What about the media?" Sloane asked.

"Given his skill and the extent to which Stenopolis went to remain anonymous, nobody will be releasing his name anytime soon. The Department of Justice and the FBI are on board, though they have a lot of questions for you."

Sloane figured as much, and had hoped that the relationships he had established with attorneys at the Justice Department, as well as with agents at the FBI during the Beverly Ford matter, would give him credibility with both agencies.

"You know," Molia said, "J. Rayburn Franklin isn't going to be real happy with me. He'll want to know what the hell I was doing so far out of my jurisdiction."

Sloane couldn't help but smile at the thought of Molia running circles around his bespectacled, hyperactive boss. "I thought you said he was retiring?"

"He was, until the stock market crashed and he lost most of his retirement. Just my luck." They sat quietly for a while. Then Molia said, "Listen, I'm not going to sit here and presume to tell you that I have the slightest clue what you're going through. I couldn't imagine losing my Maggie, but I also know that if something were to happen to her because I was out there doing my job, God forbid, she wouldn't want me to blame myself for what happened. I know that she loves me too much to think of me being in so much pain. I'm sure your wife would feel the same."

"The hardest part," Sloane said, "was I couldn't save her."

"No one could have, David."

"I should have rushed him. I should have gone for his gun."

"Maybe. But you didn't. And you'll never know what would have happened if you had. Hell, I never should have let him get my gun."

"This isn't your fault."

"It's nobody's fault, that's my point. We can speculate till the cows come home, but we'll never really know. What I do know is I didn't make a mistake. I did it by the book. I did my job the way I was trained, but something bad still happened because the guy was intent on something bad happening. You understand what I'm saying?"

Jenkins had told Sloane much the same thing. He put his head back against the wall and closed his eyes, physically and emotionally drained.

Molia stood. "Why don't I get us some coffee?"

"Tom." Molia stopped, turned. "This is the second time you've saved my life."

"Maybe next time you visit you can just stop by and have dinner like a normal person."

Sloane smiled.

"Do you like pot roast? Maggie makes a mean pot roast."

"I remember," Sloane said.

"Mr. Sloane?" The doctor from the operating room stood in the doorway.

CHAPTER
THIRTEEN

KING COUNTY COURTHOUSE
SEATTLE, WASHINGTON

At the hearing for a permanent injunction, Barclay Reid used much of the morning to introduce documents showing that the Metamorphis prototype passed inspection by the PSA. Sloane had refused to stipulate to their admissibility, forcing Reid to call a witness from the PSA to authenticate them. It gave Sloane the chance to cross-examine the woman and establish that the test by the PSA was extremely limited and performed in an outdated and understaffed lab.

"In fact it's just one man, isn't it?"

"Yes." An administrative type, conservative in appearance, the woman spoke in a monotone, without any inflection in her voice.

"And the lab tests some fifteen-thousand products a year?"

"Yes."

The stitches that had closed the cut over Sloane's eye had been removed, the scar nearly invisible beneath his eyebrow. The swelling and bruises to his face had also faded, only noticeable upon close inspection. "You testified that you checked the agency's records and did not find any complaints concerning Kendall or the toy Metamorphis, is that correct?"

"Our records do not reflect any, correct."

"But the agency does not record every consumer complaint, does it?"

"No, we don't."

"In fact, isn't it true that the new acting director ordered that records of complaints be disposed of?"

"Yes, she did." The woman seemed almost happy to answer.

"So there could have been a complaint that was expunged."

Reid objected. "It calls for speculation."

"I'll let her answer," Judge Rudolph said. "I take it you're not asking if there was such a record, only that such records did at one time exist?"

"Exactly, Your Honor," Sloane said.

"It is possible," the woman agreed.

"And you testified that you are not aware of any reports by your agency on the dangerous propensities of magnets?"

"I'm not, no."

"And you checked the agency's database thoroughly to determine if there existed such a report?"

"I did, and I did not find any."

"If there had been such a report, it would have been in the databases you searched."

"It would have been, yes."

These were small gains, but Sloane felt he needed every inch he could get.

Following the testimony Rudolph recessed for a short break, and Sloane took the opportunity to step into the hall and call Alex.

"How's the patient?"

Sloane had spent much of the prior week preparing for the hearing while helping Alex care for Jenkins at the Camano Island farm. When the surgeon appeared in the waiting room, it had been to tell Sloane that though they had removed the bullet, Jenkins had lost a lot of blood.

"But he'll be okay, right?" Sloane had asked.

"He's stable, but he's not out of the woods. The next twenty-four hours will be critical. I'll keep you posted."

After the doctor had departed, Sloane remained standing, staring out the door.

Molia put a hand on his shoulder. "He'll be okay. He's like a buffalo. He's too damn big to kill with one bullet."

The detective had been right: one bullet would not kill Jenkins, though it was several very long days before Jenkins's vital signs stabilized and several more before the doctors would allow him to fly home. Sloane had hired a nurse and rented a private jet. Their roles reversed, he had never left Jenkins's side until they reached Camano and Alex stepped in.

Kannin stepped out from the courtroom to the hall. "Judge is back."

Sloane rejoined him at counsel table along with the McFarlands and the Gallegoses.

Reid called a product expert to testify that the toy met or exceeded the Toy Manufacturer's Association safety mandates, but on cross Sloane got the expert to admit that the TMA safety requirements were voluntary, that the TMA strongly opposed regulation of the toy industry by the government, and that it had no enforcement powers should a company choose not to abide by the voluntary regulations. Again it was a minimal gain, but it was the safest course of attack.

The only surprise that morning was when Reid rested her case without calling Malcolm Fitzgerald. Sloane wasn't sure whether she would put him on the stand, since all she really needed to do to get an injunction preventing Sloane from disclosing the design of Metamorphis was show that Kendall had designed the toy and kept that design confidential. It was Sloane's burden to prove extraordinary circumstances existed to justify an order that the Metamorphis action figure be independently inspected. Reid was like a boxer ahead on points in the late rounds of a fight; she just needed to avoid being knocked out. A skilled lawyer, she had yet to make a mistake and apparently decided not to risk one with Fitzgerald.

Sloane, however, wasted no time calling Fitzgerald as a hostile witness, though he realized that at this point there was little to be gained. Predictably, Fitzgerald denied knowing Kyle Horgan and testified that Metamorphis had been designed by the Kendall design team. Without Horgan, or his file, Sloane had nothing to rebut that testimony, or to show that Fitzgerald had knowledge of the dangerous propensities of magnets in general, or the toy in particular.

Sloane decided not to call Albert Payne as a witness. Payne could not testify as to what Kendall knew or did not know, and while Anne LeRoy's report discussed the dangerous propensities of magnets, the information in it did not directly relate to Metamorphis or Kendall. Reid would have rightly objected that it was irrelevant, and Sloane would do nothing except educate those involved in burying the report. The opportunity to disclose that report would be better served in a more public forum to be held that same week.

Instead, Sloane called Dr. Leonard Desmond and waited at the lectern while the forensic pathologist settled into the witness chair, opened a file, and placed it on his lap while slipping on half-lens reading glasses. With bushy silver hair, eyebrows as thick as an untended lawn, and a beige suit, Desmond looked like a cross between Albert Einstein and Mark Twain.

As Sloane adjusted the lectern to a spot where the linoleum floor had not been worn, Judge Rudolph directed his gaze over the top of his bifocals to Barclay Reid. "I think we can dispense with Dr. Desmond's qualifications," he said.

Reid smartly agreed so as not to irritate Rudolph; Desmond had performed more than five hundred autopsies, including the only two that mattered that afternoon, the autopsies of Mateo Gallegos and Austin McFarland.

"Dr. Desmond, let's get right to it," Sloane said. "You performed the autopsy on Mateo Gallegos as part of your duties as the Lewis County coroner, correct?"

"I did. With the child under the age of five, an autopsy is mandatory."

"And you also performed the autopsy on Austin McFarland?"

"At your request, yes."

"What is a forensic pathologist?"

"Simply stated, a forensic pathologist determines the cause of death by examining the cadaver."

"Dr. Desmond, let's start with the autopsy you performed on Austin McFarland." Sloane took Desmond through the series of questions concluding with Desmond advising that he had located five magnets within the body cavity.

"And are you able to opine, based upon the physical evidence, what impact those magnets had on Austin McFarland in particular?"

"I'm afraid not. By the time the autopsy was performed, the intestines had deteriorated to the point that they offered no real independent source of information."

Eva McFarland moaned.

"The best I can do is state that the child had five magnets in the area where his intestines would have been and provide an educated hypothesis based upon my findings with respect to Mateo Gallegos."

Reid stood to object but Sloane headed her off. "We'll get

there, doctor. Let's go ahead and discuss your findings with respect to Mateo Gallegos."

Reid sat.

After walking Desmond through the preliminary questions
Sloane considered another multipage document. "Let me hand
you what has previously been marked as Exhibit Twenty-seven
and ask that you review it."

Desmond did as instructed, though there was little need,
given that he had written the report. He flipped to the last page.
"Yes, this is my report."

"You signed it?"

"Yes, that's my signature."

"Would you tell the court your findings?"

"I found that the decedent had also ingested multiple magnets."

"Can you explain to the court how it would be physically possible for a child to swallow six magnets?"

Desmond displayed the magnets inside of a jar, which Rudolph inspected. "The magnets are very small. A child would have
no physical problem ingesting them."

"So you would not expect a child to display any signs of choking after swallowing one of these magnets?"

"No, I would not. The size of the magnets makes it unlikely the
child's airway would be obstructed, so I would not expect that the
child's complexion or physical response would give a parent any
reason to suspect the child had swallowed anything hazardous."

"So other than actually witnessing a child swallow the magnets, a parent would not have any immediate indication that their
child had done so?"

"Unless the child told them, no, they would not. The child
would be able to breathe, talk, cry."

"What happens when these magnets remain in a child's system?"

Reid stood. "I'm going to object, Your Honor. Dr. Desmond is here to provide a report of his findings with respect to Mateo Gallegos. He has not been disclosed or introduced as an expert witness on the effect of magnets on the body in general."

"Sustained. Rephrase the question."

Sloane did.

"In this case, because the child swallowed more than one magnet, the magnets attracted one another while inside the intestines."

"They just bunched together?"

"No. Because they were likely swallowed at different times, they were in different areas of the intestine and attracted one another through the intestinal walls."

Sloane had the doctor use a diagram of the intestines to identify where he had located the magnets. Desmond then clenched his hands into fists and pressed the knuckles together. "The magnets are so powerful they attach through the intestine and strangle blood flow to the affected portion. Once the blood supply is cut off, the clock is ticking."

"What do you mean 'the clock is ticking'?"

"Without blood supply that particular area of the bowel begins to die. The magnets erode through the intestinal wall, or make the bowel more susceptible to perforating in general."

"What happens if the intestinal wall is perforated?"

"If the intestinal wall is perforated, bacteria will spill into the abdominal cavity."

"Deadly bacteria?"

"It can be. It's essentially like a gunshot or stab wound in that it can result in septic poisoning of the child's blood supply and carry that poison to other organs."

"And in this particular instance did you reach a specific conclusion about what occurred with respect to Mateo Gallegos?"

"I concluded that the child died as a result of septic poisoning to his system caused by the factors I just described."

"And did you find anything further to indicate that the ingestion of these magnets might not have been the cause of death in this instance?"

"No, I'm quite certain they were the cause."

"Doctor, I noted in your report that you also indicate a puncture wound to the abdomen, is that right?"

"Yes it is."

"And did you reach any conclusions as to what might have caused that wound?"

"I concluded it was a nail. I'd estimate a sixteen-penny nail, though it isn't really possible to say so with certainty."

"For the record, that's the size of the nail?" Rudolph interjected.

"It is," Desmond said. "But again, I can't be certain."

Sloane would have preferred not to bring up the subject, but he knew if he didn't, Barclay Reid would. In legal parlance, Sloane was stealing the wind from Reid's sail, bringing up an unfavorable piece of evidence and allowing his witness to explain it before she could make a bigger deal of it on cross-examination.

"Is there any indication the nail was rusted?"

"There is some indication in the subcutaneous tissue of an infection that could be consistent with the type of infection one might experience from a rusted nail, yes."

"And in your opinion, is it likely that this perforation could have caused the septic poisoning you believe led to Mateo Gallegos's illness and ultimately his death?"

"In my opinion it is not likely. Given the presence of the magnets, they represented a far more acute cause of the symptoms leading to death."

"Now, as a result of your findings with respect to Mateo Gallegos, Dr. Desmond, did you draw any conclusions with respect to your autopsy of Austin McFarland that you could not have previously drawn based on the available physical evidence?"

"I did. Having reviewed the doctor's notations in the medical file identifying the symptoms that the McFarland child suffered, and given their remarkable similarity to the symptoms that the Gallegos child presented, as well as, of course, the undeniable presence of the magnets within the McFarland child's body, it is my educated opinion that the McFarland child died as a result of the ingestion of magnets that resulted in a similar septic reaction caused by perforations to his intestines."

Sloane checked his notes. Satisfied, he addressed Judge Rudolph. "I have nothing further on direct."

Reid strode to the podium. "But you don't know that for certain, do you, doctor. As you've just said, that's a guess."

"It's an educated deduction from the evidence."

"But not the physical evidence as you've described with respect to the condition of the McFarland child's body, correct?"

"Correct."

"You cannot state with certainty that the magnets caused perforations to the child's intestines."

"I cannot."

"And you could not conclude that the magnets caused any transient bacterial infection that occurred just before death."

"I could not. The body was too badly decomposed."

"Doctor, in giving you your assignment, did Mr. Sloane advise you that he obtained a medical malpractice judgment against the doctor who treated Austin McFarland?"

Sloane stood. "Objection, Your Honor, it's irrelevant."

"Sustained."

"Dr. Desmond, did you inspect these magnets that you removed from Austin's body closely?"

"I did."

"And did they have any markings on them of any kind?"

"No, they did not."

"And is the same true with respect to the magnets found in the Gallegos child?"

"That's correct."

"Nothing that would indicate to you a serial number or anything of that sort?"

"No, nothing like that."

"And you are not here to render any conclusions as to the source of these magnets."

"I don't have any such knowledge."

"You don't really care?"

Sloane stood. "Objection, Your Honor. It's irrelevant."

"Sustained."

"The source of the magnets is not significant to the conclusions you've shared here today," Reid said.

"No, it is not."

"So you don't know if the magnets came from a toy, or an electric toothbrush, or any other of a number of household appliances that the child could potentially have gotten hold of. In fact, the magnets might not necessarily have even been in the child's home. They could have come from school or any number of other locations."

Sloane stood again. "Objection. Counsel's testifying at this point, Your Honor. Dr. Desmond has already answered that he doesn't have such knowledge."

"Sustained."

Reid's strategy was simple. She would not dispute that which was indisputable—that Mateo Gallegos and Austin McFarland had ingested magnets. Instead she would emphasize that which Sloane could not prove, that the magnets had come from a

Metamorphis action figure. Unless Sloane could do that, or otherwise offer a different knockout punch, Judge Rudolph would be hard-pressed to issue an injunction or order that the toy be independently tested.

"Doctor, I'm assuming that if you noted something in your report you considered it significant, is that a fair assessment?"

"Yes, I'd say it is."

"And you testified that you noted in your report that the Gallegos child appeared to have a puncture wound to his abdomen. So we can assume that you considered that puncture wound to have been significant at the time you performed the autopsy, correct?"

Desmond smiled, recognizing the lawyer's trap. "Well . . . it was significant in the sense that I noted it."

"Noted it while attempting to determine the cause of the septic poisoning that you believe killed this child, correct?"

"Yes. I was—"

"And a potential cause of that poisoning was this rusted nail, correct?"

Desmond shook his head, eyes closed, looking almost amused. "It isn't likely."

"But it is possible, isn't it?"

He sighed, resigned. "It's possible, yes, but—"

"So although you indicated you were quite certain the child's poisoning came from these magnets of unknown origin, you could not rule out *conclusively* this prior puncture wound, could you?"

"One hundred percent?"

"That would be conclusive, wouldn't it?"

"I suppose I couldn't, not one hundred percent."

Like a magician, Reid produced a nail, holding the head between her thumb and index finger, so that it looked as long as a spear. Since she had deposed Desmond and had a copy of his report, she knew before the hearing his opinion regarding the size of the nail. "You identified the puncture wound as likely having been caused by a sixteen-penny nail, correct?"

"I said likely. I can't be certain."

"I don't think I've pounded a nail in my life, Doctor, except to hang a picture frame, but I suspect you're familiar enough with nails to correct me if I misrepresent that this is a sixteen-penny nail." She handed Desmond the nail.

"It appears to be, yes."

"How deep did the nail penetrate Mateo Gallegos's body?"

"I don't recall making that notation on my report."

She handed him the report. "Please consider it."

Desmond did. "No. I did not note it."

"Would the depth of penetration be significant to a conclusion as to whether the nail could have caused a septic-type reaction?"

"In theory it could be, yes."

"The deeper the penetration, the greater the potential for poisoning?"

"Yes, that's right."

"A sixteen-penny nail is three and a half inches." Reid made it sound like three and a half feet. "And if the nail penetrated up to, say, the head, then it would have penetrated through the subcutaneous tissue to the lining of the stomach, correct?"

"Correct."

"It could also have punctured the intestine, could it not?"

Desmond hesitated.

"Doctor?"

"I can't rule it out, no. But again, it isn't likely."

"And if it punctured through the tissue to the stomach cavity I would assume that any infection would, remembering my very brief anatomy class, eventually find its way into the small intestine. Am I correct in that assumption?"

"You are."

"And the stomach has a rich blood supply, which, if infected, could result in the circulation of that contaminated blood throughout the body."

"Correct."

Reid let Judge Rudolph ponder that information for a moment as she flipped through her notes. Then, as if stumbling on her next line of questioning, she asked, "And would whether or not the child had a recent tetanus shot also be significant as to whether the rusted nail could cause an infection?"

"Yes, but—"

"Thank you, doctor. I have nothing further."

Sloane was on his feet before Judge Rudolph asked if he had any redirect.

"Doctor, it appeared to me that you wanted to explain your last answer before you were cut off. Would you like to do so?"

"Yes, I would. Tetanus shots protect against *clostridium Tetani*, which is a cause of tetanus. It is not usually a cause of sepsis. What I was attempting to explain was that all of the factors counsel mentioned—the nail, the rust, the depth of penetration of the nail, and the date of the deceased's last tetanus shot—could be of import in theory, but not with respect to the evidence that was before me."

"And what specific evidence are you referring to?"

Desmond's voice grew more adamant. "There were six magnets in the child's intestines," he said. Sloane thought he might add, "Good God, are you people stupid?" but the doctor refrained. "There is no doubt those magnets had perforated the child's intestines. It was very clear to me where the septic poisoning had originated."

Reid declined to recross. There was no need. She had scored what points she could and was abiding by the lawyer's well-known adage: if you've scored a few points on cross-examination be grateful, sit down, and shut up.

The court took its afternoon recess following Dr. Desmond's testimony. Before leaving the courthouse for lunch Sloane and John Kannin slipped into the men's room. After making sure they were alone, Kannin said, "She didn't get any mileage out of the rusted nail with Rudolph. Maybe with a jury, but Rudolph isn't going to buy it."

Sloane wasn't so sure. "We're asking him for extraordinary relief. Any doubt Reid can introduce isn't going to help. Besides, without some better evidence that the magnets came from the prototype, we can't win. We both know that."

ALTHOUGH SLOANE HAD gone over Rosa-Maria Gallegos's testimony the day before, she still looked apprehensive as she took the witness stand that afternoon, opening and closing the clip in her hair. They had rehearsed the questions and answers, but it was more difficult to simulate the anxiety a courtroom produced for the average person.

Sloane eased Gallegos into the examination by having her talk about her family and Mateo. When he felt she had settled in and relaxed a bit, he began in earnest.

"Are you a legal resident of the United States, Rosa-Maria?"

She shook her head. "No."

"Then how is it that your husband works for a company like Kendall Toys?"

"He uses a different Social Security number, from his cousin."

"His real name is not Manuel Gallegos?"

"Here he is Manny Gallegos."

"How long has your husband been employed at the Kendall Toy manufacturing plant?"

"Four years."

"And during that time his employer never questioned him about his residency or Social Security number?"

Reid objected. "The question is irrelevant."

Rudolph nodded his head. "Sustained. Mr. Sloane, move on."

Sloane knew that Manny Gallegos's illegal status and use of a false identity was largely irrelevant to the hearing for an injunction, but getting Reid to object that the information was irrelevant would prevent her from bringing it up on cross-examination to imply that the Gallegoses were dishonest.

"At some point, Mrs. Gallegos, did your son Ricky come into possession of a Metamorphis action figure?"

"Yes. My husband's boss gives it to him for being a good employee and asked to have Ricky play with it. They paid us fifty dollars."

"And for how long did your son Ricky play with the toy?"

"It was about one week."

"And where did he play with it?"

"In our home."

"How big is your home, Mrs. Gallegos?"

Reid looked about to stand but caught herself.

"It is not very big."

"How many bedrooms?"

"Ricky and Mateo share a room," she said, still speaking as if her youngest were alive. "My husband and I sleep in the other room."

"Your two sons shared a room. Is there another room to keep things like toys?"

She smiled. "No. There is no room."

"During that period of time when the toy was in your home,

did your son Mateo play with it, or was he with his brother when Ricky played with it?"

Gallegos lowered her head to compose herself, wringing her hands in her lap. Tears rolled down her cheeks. "We try to tell Ricky not to let Mateo play with it because the box warns about choking, but Mateo, he wanted to. He was always, you know, 'Me, me. I want to play.'"

"And do you know if your son Ricky ever let Mateo play with the toy?"

"We did not think so, but he told us later that he did."

Reid stood. "Objection, Your Honor, hearsay."

"I can bring Ricky here and put him on the stand, Your Honor, but I question whether that is really necessary."

"I'll allow it," Rudolph said.

"Did Ricky ever tell you that any pieces of the Metamorphis broke?"

"He said that some did."

"And did Ricky ever mention seeing any magnets from the toy?"

She shook her head. "No."

"So he did not tell you that he thought Mateo swallowed any magnets?"

"He did not say that, no."

"And did you ever find any magnets in your house?"

She shrugged. "I don't remember seeing them, no."

Again, Sloane had no choice but to bring up the unfavorable testimony. He would have preferred something else, like Ricky having seen Mateo putting the magnets in his mouth, but that had not been the case. Sloane changed gears.

"Could you talk a bit about when you first realized Mateo was sick?"

Reid again objected. "We're not contesting that the boy became ill," she said. "We'll stipulate to the medical records, which document his symptoms. To go through it is irrelevant."

It was a good objection and Rudolph sustained it. Reid did not want Rosa-Maria discussing the emotional trauma of watching her son grow more and more ill. Not wanting to end on a sustained objection, Sloane asked a few additional questions before sitting. To his surprise, Reid pushed back her chair. Cross-examining a mother who had lost a child was risky on a number of levels, but by the time she reached the lectern, Reid seemed to have undergone a transformation. The attack dog was gone.

"Mrs. Gallegos, you testified that you never saw a magnet in your house, did you?"

She shook her head, wiping at her tears. "No."

"Aside from your son telling you that pieces of the plastic cracked, you have no information that the toy was defective or broken in any way, do you?"

"I saw the pieces."

"And boys being boys, you don't know if the plastic cracked because your son might have played too roughly with the toy, for instance."

"No, I do not know."

"And it is true, is it not, that three weeks before he became ill, Mateo fell while playing outside and landed on a rusted nail."

"Yes," she said.

"And you never had your son treated for that wound, did you?"

"No," she said.

"And your son Mateo had never had a tetanus shot, had he?"

"No. Ricky got one at school, but Mateo is too young."

"Nothing further, Your Honor."

Rudolph excused Rosa-Maria Gallegos.

Sloane stood and called Eva McFarland to the stand.

As with Rosa-Maria Gallegos, Eva fidgeted when she sat and her voice cracked when she answered Sloane's initial questions.

Sloane again took his time, hoping to calm her. When she seemed to relax, he led her through the same series of questions to establish that Mathew McFarland had been part of a Kendall focus group, and had received the Metamorphis toy and played with it in the McFarland home. He also established that Austin had been in contact with the toy and had played with it with his brother and by himself, and that pieces of the plastic had cracked.

"Did you ever find any of the magnets within those pieces?" Sloane asked.

She nodded. "I did. I found one stuck to the small piece of metal at the bottom of a leg of one of the kitchen chairs. The chair was wobbling like it was uneven and when I looked, there it was. It was very strong. I had to pull it off."

"Did you look for others?"

She nodded. "I did, but I didn't find any but that one."

After several additional question, Sloane switched gears. "Eva, I'd like to ask you about the symptoms that Austin suffered when he became ill," he said, but Reid was on her feet, objecting.

"Kendall will stipulate to the contents of the autopsy report and to the medical records, which document Austin McFarland's symptoms." Reid would again take her chances with the autopsy report, particularly since Dr. Desmond could not definitively conclude the magnets were the cause of the septic reaction; she did not want another grieving mother on the stand talking about her dying child.

Sloane argued to the contrary, but nearing the end of the day, Rudolph agreed with Reid.

"While I am certainly sympathetic, I am well aware of the McFarlands' prior testimony on the subject and I agree with counsel. I don't think that Mrs. McFarland could add to the evidence already before the court," he said, an ominous comment that did not bode well for Sloane or his clients.

CHAPTER
FOURTEEN

Back in his office, Sloane felt the fatigue of the day. He rubbed his eyes to clear his vision and massaged the stiffness in the muscles of his neck. His limbs begged for exercise but were not going to be appeased anytime soon. He had sent the Gallegoses back to their hotel and sent the Mc-Farlands home. Eva had expressed disappointment that she was not allowed to testify about Austin. After days battling anxiety caused by the anticipation of returning to the witness stand, she felt cheated out of the opportunity to talk about her son't illness. Sloane tried to pacify her with the knowledge that he had submitted a comprehensive brief detailing Austin's symptoms, but it was little consolation, and he knew words on a page were a poor substitute for a mother's testimony. He feared Rudolph's decision was a further indication he had already made up his mind.

John Kannin knocked on Sloane's partially opened door. He held a bottle of Corona and a can of Diet Coke. "Thought you might need a beer."

The bottle felt cold in Sloane's hand and the beer a welcome respite for his throat. As Kannin sat across the desk, Sloane thought back to an evening when he and Tina had shared Chinese food and Tsingtao beer in his San Francisco office. For ten years she had been his assistant, but firm protocol had prevented him from pursuing her. Now he saw those years as lost time they might have shared but never would. When he witnessed his mother's murder, Sloane had been just a child and his mind had eased his loss by burying the memory. Even when it resurfaced as a nightmare thirty years later, Sloane could not mourn her death. The years had tempered his memory and blunted his emotions.

Not so with Tina.

Her death remained as painful as the bullets that had pierced and torn his flesh, and Stenopolis's death had not eased that pain, as Sloane had known it would not. Revenge was a poor substitute for love.

Sloane took a slug of beer as Kannin placed his size thirteen black wing tips on the corner of the desk, crossing his feet.

"Am I missing anything, John?"

Kannin shook his head. "If you are, I'm missing it too. It is what it is, David. You can't conjure up facts that don't exist. We knew that going in."

"The thought of Fitzgerald getting away with this makes me sick."

"Nobody gets away with anything; we all have to own up to our mistakes eventually."

"I'd like to see it in a courtroom."

"Don't underestimate Rudolph. He has an amazing power to grasp the truth, even when it's obscured."

"He'll follow the law, and he'll be right in doing so."

Sloane used his thumb to wipe at the condensation on the outside of the bottle, and it brought another memory, of a game Jake had liked to play. He'd ask Sloane and Tina what they would wish for if they had three wishes. "Have you ever thought about what you'd wish for if you could?"

"You mean like the genie in the lamp?" Kannin smiled. "Not for a long time. But I remember I would always save the last wish for three more wishes."

"You can't do that."

"Who are you, the genie police?"

"Jake's rule, not mine."

"Yeah, but back when I was a kid I made the rules. Doesn't matter, I blew the last wish anyway."

"On what?"

"I was fifteen, sitting in the bleachers at Wrigley Field watching the Cubs with my old man, and I got caught up in the moment and wished that the Cubs would win a World Series. And just like that"—Kannin snapped his fingers—"I realized I had used my last wish. I had kept it for years, and I remember initially thinking, man, I've blown it. But then I thought, what the hell; it would sure make me and my old man happy to see them win one. Hasn't quite worked out that way yet, but when you're a Cubs fan hope is eternal." He sipped his Diet Coke. "How about you, what did you wish for?"

"Nothing."

"You're boring."

"All I ever wanted as a kid was a family. I got that with Jake and Tina. I'd use all three wishes to have her back."

It was the finality of her death that haunted him. In law, Sloane had found no absolutes. Nothing was black and white, and he was adept at finding the gray area and exploiting it. Not so with Tina's death. She was gone, and no lawyer's trick or anything else would ever bring her back.

Kannin flexed the can in his thick hand, making the aluminum crinkle and pop. "She'd want you to be happy."

"I think the thing I fear most isn't losing this case, it's having it end. What do I do when it's over? How do I go on without her?"

Kannin shook his head. "I'd give my last wish, if I still had it, for the answer to that question for you."

"I just wish I knew she was okay," he said, but what he truly meant was that he wished he knew that she had forgiven him.

Kannin finished the remnants, crushed the can, and held it up over his head, as if to shoot a basketball, aiming at the garbage can across the room. "How much?" he asked.

In the two years Sloane had known him, Kannin had tried innumerable times to shoot an empty can or wad of paper into Sloane's wastebasket. He'd never made one.

"A buck," Sloane said, offering their usual bet. He removed a dollar from his pocket and slapped it on the desk.

Kannin stood, pretended to dribble a moment, then turned and arched the can across the room. Sloane judged the shot to be long, but the can hit the back wall with a clang and banked directly into the basket.

"Hey!" Kannin raised his arms in triumph and danced around the office. Then he leaned forward and took the dollar bill off the desk, snapping it twice. "I think I'm going to tack this on my wall and call it my lucky buck."

"Luck is right," Sloane said. "A bank shot? Please."

"I'll take it." Kannin put the dollar in his pocket. "You need anything before I head out?"

"No. Go home to your family."

Kannin started for the door, stopped, and turned back, grinning as if struck by a thought.

"What?" Sloane asked.

He glanced over at the garbage can. "I just had one of those déjà vu moments."

"About what?"

"That day in the bleachers with my dad. You want to know the best part of the story? The best part was when I told him, he didn't just laugh or dismiss it like he could have. He put an arm around my shoulders and said, 'Anything's possible if you have hope.' I don't think I ever really considered how prophetic that was until just now."

He knocked twice on the wall as he left, leaving Sloane alone.

Sloane picked up the phone and called Charles Jenkins, but Alex said he was asleep and she would have him call Sloane when he awoke.

Not eager to go back to his hotel room, which had taken on the feeling of a prison cell, Sloane lingered, going through the day's mail, then making notes to prepare a closing statement. It was not usual for a hearing, but Rudolph had indicated he would allow both sides a brief summation. Sloane wasn't overly optimistic it would change anything; his closing would have far less impact on a judge than a jury. But it gave him something to do.

He stood and stretched his back as he looked out the tinted windows, but this time he found no one working in the offices of the adjacent buildings. He was alone. On nights he had worked late Tina used to call to ask when he would be home, but like so many things, he had to accept that also would never again happen.

Then the phone on his desk rang.

CHAPTER
FIFTEEN

The following morning, Sloane rushed into the courtroom three minutes late. John Kannin had his back to the door, addressing Judge Rudolph, who was already seated on the bench as Sloane entered out of breath.

"I haven't been able to—" Kannin was saying.

"I'm sorry I'm late, Your Honor." Sloane stepped up to counsel's table.

"We were about to get started without you, Mr. Sloane," Rudolph said.

"I apologize for keeping the court waiting."

Sloane nodded to the Gallegoses and McFarlands and gave them an "everything's okay" smile as he pulled materials out of his trial bag and arranged them on the table. Kannin leaned close. "Where were you? I couldn't reach you on your cell."

"I was running around this morning. I worked late last night."

Kannin's eyebrows arched. "On what?"

Sloane smiled. "That hope you talked about found me."

Kannin pulled back and looked at Sloane as if he'd gone crazy, but before he could ask another question Rudolph spoke. "Are you prepared to give your summation, Mr. Sloane?"

"Your Honor, I would request the court's indulgence in allowing us to call Malcolm Fitzgerald back to the witness stand."

Reid shot from her chair. "We object, Your Honor. Mr. Fitzgerald was on the stand yesterday and dismissed."

"Mr. Sloane?"

"We desire to call him in rebuttal, Your Honor."

"On what subject?" Rudolph asked.

"Mr. Fitzgerald's personal knowledge concerning the dangerous propensities of Metamorphis."

Reid was having none of it. "There's no evidence to justify any further inquiry into that subject, Your Honor."

"I would be brief," Sloane said. "And there is new evidence. A letter."

"We object to the introduction of any document not previously produced in discovery as the parties stipulated, or identified as an exhibit for this hearing," Reid said.

"So would I, Your Honor," Sloane replied, "but the letter was not in my clients' possession."

"Who possessed it?" Rudolph asked.

"Kendall."

Reid sounded indignant. "If such a memorandum existed I would have produced it as an officer of the court."

"I don't question Ms. Reid's integrity," Sloane said, "but I don't believe she ever had the memorandum."

"Where did you obtain it, Mr. Sloane?" Rudolph asked.

"From the individual who designed the Metamorphis toy."

Reid looked to Fitzgerald, who shrugged to indicate he had no idea who Sloane was talking about.

"Can you authenticate it?"

"It's addressed to Kendall. I'm hoping Mr. Fitzgerald can."

Reid shook her head. "Your Honor, it seems a bit suspicious that a letter would suddenly materialize."

"The admissibility and weight of any piece of evidence is for the court to decide," Sloane countered.

"Why didn't you ask Mr. Fitzgerald about it yesterday?" Rudolph asked.

"I didn't have a copy yesterday. I just obtained it late last night."

Sloane handed a copy to Reid, who immediately showed it to Fitzgerald as Sloane provided Rudolph his own copy.

Rudolph tapped his finger on the desk as he considered the document, then raised his eyes and seemed to ponder the back wall. After several moments he said, "All right, I'll allow you to question Mr. Fitzgerald, but the document will not be admitted into evidence until it is authenticated. Mr. Fitzgerald, please retake the witness stand."

Fitzgerald's chair scraped the linoleum and he strode back to the stand. If he was perturbed, he hid it well. He unbuttoned his navy blue suit jacket and sat.

"You understand you're still under oath?" Judge Rudolph asked.

"I do." Fitzgerald nodded. He crossed his legs, his head slightly tilted, as if challenging Sloane to bring it on.

"Mr. Fitzgerald, you testified yesterday on direct examination that you had no knowledge that the Metamorphis toy was potentially defective or that such a defect could result in the release of magnets contained within its component parts. Is that a correct summary of your testimony?"

"It is. I had no such knowledge."

"So we can assume from your answer that no one in the design phase raised such a concern?"

"Not to me."

"Or anyone else to your knowledge."

"Or anyone else to my knowledge."

"No one in the manufacturing phase has raised such a concern."

"They have not."

"And no one during the testing phase, be it in-house at Kendall or by an independent testing lab like the PSA, advised you of such a potential concern."

"No one," Fitzgerald said, emphasizing the words, "raised any concerns of any kind."

"Verbally or in writing?" Sloane persisted.

"Verbally, or in writing."

"Given your position as CEO of Kendall Toys you would have expected any such concern to have been brought to your attention, correct?"

"Absolutely."

"And how long have you been CEO of Kendall Toys?"

"A little more than four months."

"Kyle Horgan designed the Metamorphis action figure, did he not?"

Fitzgerald smiled, smug. "No, he did not. The Kendall design team produced the design." His hands remained folded in his lap. "And has patented that design, as Ms. Reid demonstrated yesterday."

"You have never met Mr. Horgan?"

"Never."

"So you never would have paid him any money for the design of a toy, such as Metamorphis."

"I did not."

"If someone outside of the Kendall design team had designed Metamorphis, he or she would stand to benefit financially from its success, would they not?"

Reid stood. "It's speculative and irrelevant, Your Honor."

"I'll allow it."

Sloane repeated the question.

"They may. Typically an independent designer receives an advance and a percentage of the sales of each toy."

"And that can be quite lucrative, can it not?"

"It can be, yes."

"And for that to occur Kendall would have to sell a lot of toys, and if so would stand to make a lot of money, correct?"

Fitzgerald smiled. "One can only hope."

"And, conversely, Kendall would suffer financially if a product in which it heavily invested failed."

"Depending on the amount of money invested, it is a possibility."

Sloane retrieved the document from his table and asked the clerk to mark his copy, which he then handed to Fitzgerald.

"For the record, Mr. Fitzgerald, I'm handing you what's been marked as Exhibit Thirty-two to this hearing. Do you recognize this document?"

Fitzgerald considered the document front to back and placed it in his lap. "No, I don't."

"It is addressed to Kendall, is it not?"

Reid objected. "Your Honor, I'm going to renew my objection that this document was not produced during discovery. Moreover, since Mr. Fitzgerald has testified that he has never seen the document, and since it is not even addressed to him, its contents are irrelevant. He cannot authenticate it. It is inadmissible. Until it is moved into evidence it would be improper for Mr. Sloane, Mr. Fitzgerald, or anyone else to read from it. I would therefore move that the document be stricken."

"Can you authenticate the document, Mr. Sloane?" Rudolph asked.

"Apparently not with this witness," Sloane said, maintaining eye contact with Fitzgerald.

Rudolph put the document facedown on his desk, looking and sounding perturbed. "Then we're not going to consider it. Do you have any further questions of Mr. Fitzgerald?"

Sloane bowed his head. "No."

His cheeks turning red, Rudolph addressed Fitzgerald. "Mr. Fitzgerald, you may step down."

"I assume we're finished, Mr. Sloane?" Rudolph asked.

"Actually, Your Honor, we would beg the court's indulgence to call one additional witness."

Reid sounded exasperated. "Your Honor!"

"Since Mr. Fitzgerald could not authenticate the document, Your Honor, we need to call someone who can."

"And who is that?" Rudolph asked.

"Kyle Horgan."

WHEN SLOANE ANSWERED the phone in his office the prior evening he did not immediately recognize the voice, but the name made his heart race.

"Mr. Sloane? This is Kyle Horgan."

No words came.

After the pause Horgan said, "We met in the lobby of your building. I—"

"Where are you?" Sloane asked.

"I'm staying with a friend. She says you're looking for me."

"Who? Who are you staying with?"

"Dee Stroud. She owns a—"

"Dee's House of Toys," Sloane said, recalling the attractive brunette who had explained to him much about the toy business.

"Dee said there is some kind of trial going on; she read about it in the paper."

It took Sloane twenty minutes to get to Stroud's house in Kirkland. Horgan sat in Stroud's modest living room drinking a

Coke, a blue tin of butter cookies open on the table. He scarcely resembled the young man who had accosted Sloane in the lobby of his building. His hair, which had been wild and unkempt, had been cut business short and parted on the side, and he had lost weight, his facial features more angular and pronounced.

"He walked into my shop last night as I was closing," Stroud explained.

"The landlord evicted me and put everything in storage. I didn't have anyplace else to go. Dee told me about your case, about the two young boys. So you believed me?"

"Not initially," Sloane said, sitting on the edge of a chair across the table from Horgan. "And I'm sorry for that. But yes, I believe you, Kyle." Sloane shook his head, dismayed. With all of his skills and contacts, Charles Jenkins had been unable to find the young man. There had not been any activity on Horgan's bank account. Jenkins found no relatives. It was as if Horgan had vanished.

"Where did you go? We couldn't find you."

"California," he said. "I needed to get some help."

"He checked himself into a rehab center," Stroud said, coming back into the room and putting a cup of tea on the table in front of Sloane.

Sloane didn't tell the young man, but Horgan's decision to get help had also probably saved his life.

"Everything is anonymous," Horgan explained. "I knew I had a problem, and it was getting worse."

Sloane knew treatment centers were not cheap. "How did you afford it?"

"I used the money Kendall paid me. That's why I sold them the design."

Sloane tried not to let his emotions rush his questions, to remain analytical.

"The design of Metamorphis?"

Horgan spoke matter-of-factly. "Yes."

"How did they pay you, was it a check?"

Horgan shook his head. "No. He gave me cash. He called it a retainer so that I wouldn't take the design to anyone else."

"An option."

Horgan shrugged and nibbled on a butter cookie. "Something like that."

For the next forty-five minutes Sloane advised Horgan of what had transpired and continued to ask him questions.

"Can you stop them from releasing Metamorphis?" Horgan asked.

"I didn't think so," Sloane said, "but I do now."

KYLE HORGAN STEPPED through the back door into the courtroom as if on cue, Dee Stroud and Tom Pendergrass walking in with him. Horgan wore pressed tan slacks, a collared shirt, and a charcoal gray cardigan sweater. Pendergrass had bought him the clothes.

"We object," Reid said, finding her voice. "Mr. Horgan was not identified on the list of intended witnesses. He has not been deposed and . . . and this is highly prejudicial."

"Mr. Horgan is a rebuttal witness. He is being called to authenticate the document now marked as Exhibit Thirty-two. Furthermore, Mr. Horgan will explain that he was not previously available and could not have been previously disclosed."

"Your Honor, there are three people here," Reid said. "These proceedings are closed to protect the confidentiality of the Metamorphis design."

"The gentleman in the suit is my associate, Tom Pendergrass. The woman is Dee Stroud, the owner of Dee's House of Toys. She will also be a witness, if necessary."

"For what purpose?" Rudolph asked.

"To establish that Mr. Horgan designed the toy in question."

It had struck Sloane as he sat in Stroud's living room that Stroud could independently verify that Horgan had walked into her toy store and showed her the design of Metamorphis long before Kendall ever put the toy into production. That being the case, he could establish that Kendall must have stolen the design. Sloane had orchestrated her entrance with Horgan.

"If she is going to be a witness, she'll need to wait outside until called," Rudolph said. Sloane nodded to Pendergrass, who escorted Stroud back outside. After she departed, Rudolph looked to Sloane. "Mr. Sloane, why wasn't this witness disclosed previously?"

"Your Honor, I will establish that Mr. Horgan has been out of the state for the past six weeks and that he only called my office late last night to advise me that he had returned. My investigator could not locate him, and I daresay that neither could Ms. Reid's."

Sloane looked to Reid. When they had met to discuss the settlement he had deliberately given Reid Kyle Horgan's name, knowing that she would seek to have him found.

"Ms. Reid?" Rudolph asked.

"Mr. Sloane is correct," she said. "We were not able to locate Mr. Horgan."

"So he *was* disclosed."

"Not on the witness list, Judge, but Mr. Sloane did tell me his name and the allegation that Mr. Horgan had designed the toy."

"Then I see no prejudice." Rudolph looked to Horgan, who stood in the gallery with Pendergrass. "Mr. Horgan, please take the stand."

After Horgan settled into the witness chair, Sloane established where Horgan had been and why Sloane could not have disclosed him as a witness. Satisfied, Rudolph instructed Sloane to continue.

Sloane gestured to Fitzgerald, who sat forward in his chair, one hand covering his mouth and contemplating Horgan as if he were a rare artifact. "Have you ever met Mr. Fitzgerald?"

Horgan shook his head. "No."

"Have you ever sent him any correspondence?"

"No."

Reid stood. "Your Honor, this is really perplexing. Didn't we just go through this exercise with Mr. Fitzgerald on the witness stand? Mr. Sloane said this man would impeach Mr. Fitzgerald and authenticate the letter. Instead he's corroborated the testimony. This isn't rebuttal. Mr. Horgan says he's never met or corresponded with my client."

"Mr. Sloane?" Rudolph asked.

"If I could ask just one more question, Your Honor?"

"It better be a good one," Rudolph said.

But before Sloane could ask the question, the hand that had been covering Malcolm Fitzgerald's mouth lowered.

"Oh my God," Fitzgerald said, his voice a hushed whisper, though loud enough for everyone in the courtroom to hear.

CHAPTER
SIXTEEN

S enator Joe Wallace sought to smile, but it came off as a grimace, as if he were squinting from the glare of the lights from the multiple television cameras carrying the hearing live. Wallace was no doubt perplexed. He had two reports on his desk, the first of which concluded that Chinese manufacturing plants met or exceeded the voluntary regulations enforced in the United States, and the second of which concluded that there existed no imminent threat to American consumers. Yet the contents of those two reports differed 180 degrees from the testimony a solemn Maggie Powers had just provided to California Senator Morgan Tovey, who was presiding over the hearing.

Powers had reluctantly told Tovey that a recent investigation of Chinese manufacturing facilities by a delegation from the PSA, led by its director of compliance, Albert Payne, concluded that the plants remained woefully inadequate in meeting those regulations, that most plant owners were recalcitrant toward spending the money to do so, and that corruption of government officials within the various provinces made it unlikely that any change would take place soon. Powers had also testified that one specific problem arising in China was the use of powerful magnets in a variety of household appliances and toys that could pose a danger to American consumers, particularly children.

Powers's report should have pleased Wallace, as it had obviously pleased Tovey. It gave the senator more than enough ammunition to ensure that the House would pass his proposed bill calling for greater funding to the PSA and stronger penalties against American manufacturers who put defective products into the stream of commerce. But Albert Payne knew that Wallace's grimace was not from the glare of the lights.

"Are you ready?"

Payne nodded to the attorney from the Department of Justice, who sat alongside him in a room outside the hearing chambers, watching the telecast on a flat-screen television. Payne had spent the better part of his time since the night he shot Anthony Stenopolis working with the Justice Department fraud and corruption unit and with the FBI.

David Sloane had been right. Maggie Powers had not orchestrated Payne's participation in the trip to China and ill-fated introduction to Stenopolis. Nor had Powers been responsible for getting Payne to pull the plug on Anne LeRoy's investigation. Powers had never known about LeRoy's report. Payne had never told her because he was concerned she would shut down the investigation. The only person Payne had confided in had been Senator Joe Wallace, who also happened to be the person instrumental in ensuring that Payne made the trip to China. When Sloane sent Payne to the senator's home it had not been to seek his help. It had been to further flush out a snake. If Wallace was involved, as Sloane suspected, and as Wallace's meeting with Peggy Seeley confirmed, then he would have no choice but to have Stenopolis kill Payne before Payne could take the matter to the Justice Department. When Stenopolis showed up at Payne's home it confirmed Wallace's involvement.

"Pretty ingenious," the attorney for the Justice Department said, watching the television as Wallace ran his fingers through strands of blond hair. "Coauthor a bill to make it look like you're a proponent of the agency so no one suspects you're the guy actually behind the efforts to ensure the bill is killed."

Payne stood and buttoned the jacket of his new suit. He had shaved his beard and cut his hair. The rash was also gone, and his wife had commented when she kissed him that morning that he looked ten years younger.

The attorney held the door open, and Payne walked down the marbled hall. Outside the heavy wooden door to the congressional chamber he paused and took a deep breath before pulling open the door and stepping in. He stood in the entry, not moving, waiting where Wallace would have no trouble seeing him. When Wallace did, Payne took great pleasure in watching the color drain from the senator's face.

GALAXY TOYS' HEADQUARTERS

PHOENIX, ARIZONA

MAXINE BOLELLI CLOSED her eyes, hands clenched in fists.

"How much?" she uttered.

Beth Meyers, Galaxy's chief financial officer, cleared her throat. "We don't have final numbers at the moment. Kendall's stock is continuing to . . . decline."

"How much?"

"At present? Several hundred million dollars, pretty much all of our cash reserves."

"Can we unload it? Make up our losses anywhere?"

Brandon Craft, Galaxy's president, shook his head but otherwise did not speak. He had been grimacing since being summoned to Bolelli's office, and his grimace became more pronounced with each question. Kendall's stock plummeted with the announcement that a Seattle judge had issued a temporary injunction barring Kendall from distributing the Metamorphis action figure until further testing. Reports were circulating that Kendall had cut manufacturing corners by shipping the process to China, a decision that would save the company millions in production costs but that had resulted in defects in the plastic encasing the magnets, and that Kendall had sought to hide the defect so as not to cut into the product's profit margin. The news had pretty much wiped out a hundred years of goodwill the company had fostered. CNN had also reported that PSA Acting Director Maggie Powers had testified at a Senate hearing on Capitol Hill late that afternoon that a report by a staff investigator, Anne LeRoy, had concluded that magnets being imported from China and used in products such as the toy in question could be dangerous to American consumers and required additional study.

"How much more do we stand to lose?"

"If the banks call in our line of credit, which is highly probable in this economy, Chapter Eleven reorganization is a distinct possibility," Meyers said.

The intercom on Bolelli's desk buzzed. She had asked her assistant to track down Arian Santoro.

"Put him through," Bolelli said.

"Maxine?" The voice was pleasant, friendly, and easily recognizable. "It's Ian Hansen from Titan Toys in Chicago. I understand you're having a difficult afternoon."

BATHED IN THE soft light from an overhead antique chandelier, Sloane and Malcolm Fitzgerald stood side by side in a den the size of a basketball court. A Persian rug covered the parquet floor corner to corner, and large paintings in ornate frames hung on the dark mahogany walls and above a river rock fireplace from which emanated the smell of burnt oak. The servant who had led them into the room invited them to sit in the plush leather chairs. Sloane and Fitzgerald had declined.

The servant returned pushing a wheelchair, the man in it bent, old, and frail. Sebastian Kendall wore a dark bathrobe covering green-and-white-striped pajamas. Slippers rested on the metal footrests. But despite his physical appearance, there was something in the man's stoic, almost defiant expression that indicated to David Sloane that Sebastian Kendall was not as frail in mind as he was in body.

Fitzgerald waited until the nurse had departed, sliding paneled doors closed behind him.

"What have you done?" Fitzgerald asked. "For God's sake, Sebastian, what have you done?"

Earlier that afternoon, Judge John Rudolph had advised Sloane that his next question had better be a good one, and Sloane did not disappoint.

Sloane left the podium, standing in the center of the courtroom. "Kyle, have you ever met Sebastian Kendall?"

Horgan nodded. "Several times."

Fitzgerald had slumped in his chair, chin nearly touching his chest, his complexion blending with the white courtroom walls around him.

"And when did you first meet Mr. Kendall?"

"It was about six months ago; I showed him my design for Metamorphis."

"You just walked into the company and showed it to him?"

Horgan shook his head. "I showed it to Dee first. She told me she thought it was fantastic. She was the one who suggested that I take it to Kendall."

"And you took her advice."

"I tried."

"What do you mean?" Having been to the company, Sloane knew what Horgan meant, but every detail Horgan could provide would add to the young man's credibility.

"Kendall has a fence around the building and a guard. I couldn't get in without an appointment. I called a few times, but they wouldn't let me speak to anyone."

"So what did you do?"

"I sent Mr. Kendall a copy of my design."

"Then what happened?"

"Mr. Kendall called and said he wanted to meet me."

"Did you meet at his office?"

"No. We met at a restaurant in Pioneer Square near where I live. Mr. Kendall bought me lunch and told me he was very excited about my design. He said he wanted his design team to make a prototype to ensure the design worked. He said if it worked, Kendall would buy it."

"Did Sebastian Kendall ask you anything else, Kyle?"

"He wanted to know if I had shown the design to anyone."

"Had you?"

"Just Dee, but I had forgotten about that."

"What else did Mr. Kendall say?"

"He said he would pay me two thousand five hundred dollars if I agreed not to show anyone else the design."

"Did you sign a document agreeing to that?"

"No. Mr. Kendall said he didn't do business that way. He said he liked to look a man in the eye and shake his hand."

"And did you do that?"

"Yes."

"What happened next?"

"About a month later Mr. Kendall called me and asked for another meeting."

"Where did this meeting take place? Was it at Kendall?"

"No. None of the meetings were at Kendall. This one was at a warehouse in Renton."

"A Kendall warehouse?"

"I don't think so. There was no name on it."

"And what happened at that meeting?"

Horgan smiled, a boy's grin. "Well, Mr. Kendall paid me the money."

"And how did he pay you? Did he write you a check?"

"No. He gave me cash."

"Twenty-five hundred dollars in cash?"

"Actually, it was five thousand."

Again Sloane tried to act surprised, but everyone in the room knew this had been scripted. "Five thousand? Why five thousand?"

"Mr. Kendall said he wanted to retain me as a consultant to help with the design."

"Was anyone else present at that meeting?"

"A man trying to build the prototype, but he was having trouble with some of my calculations. Mr. Kendall wanted him to ask me questions."

"Did you work with the man on that prototype?"

"For about three weeks."

"What happened next?"

"Mr. Kendall said they were going to have some kids play with the prototypes and ask them what they thought. I was pretty excited about that."

"Did something happen to curb your excitement, Kyle?"

Horgan nodded. "When I got home I went through the design again, the one the man and I had worked on, and that's when I noticed the problem."

"What problem?"

"The plastic Kendall wanted to use wasn't strong enough. I was afraid it could crack when stressed."

"Did you tell anyone about your concern?"

"I called Mr. Kendall."

"What was his response?"

"He said he wanted to meet with me, that we would work it out together."

Sloane went through the steps of establishing the next meeting. Then he asked, "Tell the court what you and Mr. Kendall discussed."

"Well, first I gave him my letter."

Sloane approached the clerk and asked again for Exhibit Thirty-two. Taking it, he handed it to Horgan. "Do you recognize this document?"

"That's the letter I wrote to Mr. Kendall."

When Horgan had left for rehab he had taken his laptop, on which he kept many of his precious designs, as well as a draft of the letter.

Sloane asked, "Is this the original?"

"No. I gave the original to Mr. Kendall when we met."

"You didn't mail it?"

"No."

"Did you discuss the letter?"

"I told him I had done the calculations and I believed the plastic would be too brittle and crack too easily. I was worried that the toy wouldn't work."

"And what was Mr. Kendall's response?"

"He said he appreciated my concerns and would bring the issue to the attention of Kendall's design team. He said they would take care of it. He said it wouldn't be a problem. He said that I had to be flexible, that the toy would cost a lot to manufacture and that they were going to do it in China to keep it affordable. He said, 'You want children to play with your toy, don't you? It is the greatest feeling in the world to see a child play with one of your toys. You want that feeling, don't you?'" Horgan lowered his head, struggling to compose himself. When he looked up tears had moistened his cheeks. "I wanted kids to love my toy. I didn't mean for it to hurt anyone."

"What happened next, Kyle?"

"I met with the man at the lab. He wanted to know if I had any ideas on how to fix the problem."

"Did you?"

"I told him that they would have to go to a stronger base material. It would be more expensive, but it was the only way."

"And you thought they had followed your advice?"

"I did until I read that article about that boy in Mossylog who died. And then I knew they hadn't."

"Did you talk to Mr. Kendall about it?"

Horgan shook his head. "I couldn't get through to him. I heard he was sick and had left the company. I tried to call Mr. Fitzgerald, but I couldn't get through to him either. Then I read the article in the paper about the McFarlands' boy. That's when I went to talk to you, to give you my file. I had to go away. I felt so bad about those two boys, I couldn't handle it. I started drinking more and I had to go away."

Sloane nodded. Horgan had done well. "I have nothing further," he said.

When Sloane sat, Reid stood, perhaps knowing she was duty bound to cross-examine Horgan, though she seemed to have lost her edge. She approached with a yellow pad of scribbled notes and a copy of the article reporting the death of Mateo Gallegos.

"Mr. Horgan, your tale is rather fantastic in many ways. Let's start with your testimony that you read an article in the newspaper about Mateo Gallegos. Did that article mention that the boy had died from the ingestion of magnets?"

Horgan shook his head. "No."

"Did it mention the toy Metamorphis?"

"No."

"Did it mention Kendall Toys or Sebastian Kendall or Malcolm Fitzgerald?"

Again Horgan responded no.

One hand cocked on her hip, Reid held up the article and said, "You're right, it doesn't." Then she made her first mistake in two days. She asked a question to which she did not know the answer, but to which Sloane did. He had asked the question of Horgan the night before, and he had strategically led Reid to it.

"How then, Mr. Horgan, could you have possibly deduced from an article about the death of a young boy in Southern Washington that it was somehow related to the toy you now allege to have designed?"

"His brother's name was on the list."

Reid paused, wary, but already in the water up to her knees, she could not easily back out now. "What list?"

"The list with the names of the kids who were going to play with the toy."

Reid turned and looked to Fitzgerald, but he simply shook his head. "You have a copy of the list?"

"No—I asked the man at the warehouse how many of the prototypes had a problem with the plastic cracking so I could evaluate if it was due to the design or maybe just an anomaly in the manufacturing process. The man didn't know for certain, so he pulled out the list to count the names."

"And he gave you a copy of the list?"

"No. He couldn't. He said it was confidential, but he said they would follow through and find out if anyone else on the list had a problem with the plastic cracking."

"How long did you look at the list?"

"Just a few seconds."

Reid smiled. She paced a small area, faced Horgan, and asked her next question, her voice incredulous.

"Are you asking this court to believe that months after this man briefly showed you a list of names on a sheet of paper that you remembered one of those names?"

Horgan shook his head. "No."

Reid paused, her face twisted in confusion. "So you didn't re-member Ricky Gallegos's name."

"No. I mean, yes, I remembered his name."

"Didn't you just testify that you didn't remember his name? So what is it, Mr. Horgan? Did you or didn't you remember the name?"

"You asked, 'Are you asking this court to believe that months after this man briefly showed you an entire list of names on a sheet of paper that you remembered one of those names?'"

Reid glanced at the court reporter, who was taking down every word spoken in the room verbatim. The woman had arched her eyebrows, an indication that Horgan had parroted back the question exactly.

"And?" Reid asked.

"But I didn't just remember a single name," Horgan said. "I remember them all."

Reid froze, looking horrified at what was certain to come next. Horgan, the young man Dee Stroud described to Sloane as "brilliant," began to systematically rattle off names, one after the next. His eyes shifted, as if reading the names from a document only he could see, doing so with such authority that no one in the room questioned whether not only each name was on the list, but also whether Horgan was reciting them in order.

The day before, Eva McFarland had been denied the opportunity to address the court, but that morning her stifled sobs, the only noise in an otherwise silent courtroom, spoke louder than words ever could.

"WHAT HAVE YOU done?" Fitzgerald asked Sebastian Kendall again.

Kendall responded with an uninterested stare. "I have no idea what you're talking about."

"Kyle Horgan is alive, Sebastian."

"I don't know anyone by that name."

"Really? Well, a young man just walked into a courtroom in Seattle and testified that he knows you very well." Fitzgerald shook his head. "You said we designed Metamorphis; you said Kendall designed it."

"We did design it." Kendall's voice grew more adamant. "The man is lying."

Fitzgerald turned to Sloane. "He provided me the design when he chose me as his successor. He said Metamorphis would be his lasting gift to the company, that it would ease my transition into power. He said he had kept everything confidential, even having the prototypes manufactured off-site, because he wanted to take no chances that someone might leak the design, that another company might beat us to the market." Fitzgerald took a step closer to Kendall. "But that wasn't the reason at all. You didn't want anyone to know about your meetings with Kyle Horgan."

Kendall did not respond.

Fitzgerald looked to Sloane. "Once in production, I saw another benefit to keeping everything confidential. I knew Santoro was feeding information to Galaxy, and the more we kept everything cloaked in secrecy, the more Galaxy would speculate that the toy must be something special. The buzz Galaxy created by trying to acquire us was immeasurable. The stock soared, and every indication was that it would continue to do so when Metamorphis flew off the store shelves. It would have put Kendall in a position it had not been in since the release of Sergeant Smash." Fitzgerald again looked to Kendall. "But it was all smoke and mirrors, wasn't it, Sebastian? The toy couldn't be safely manufactured at that price; that's why you recommended we settle that case in Mossylog. It wasn't an aberration. The toy was dangerous."

Fitzgerald shook his head. "I could have sold out to Bolelli. I could have taken the money and betrayed you. Why do this?"

"I did it . . ." Kendall's voice cracked, not from emotion, but from the disease that had ravaged his vocal cords and made each word sound as if it were passing over sandpaper. He cleared his throat. "Because I knew you would not."

"I don't understand," Fitzgerald said.

"Did you think I was about to leave sixty years of my life, my legacy, to chance? My grandfather and father built this company from nothing, and I built it beyond anything they could have ever imagined. I sacrificed everything for it. You don't think I could have married, that I could have had children?" He thumped his chest, fist clenched. "Kendall Toys was my child. I gave it my blood, my sweat, my tears. I stayed up nights worrying when it was sick, and I nursed it back to health. It was the only thing in my life that ever mattered, the only thing I ever loved. It is my lasting legacy."

"You had people killed," Fitzgerald said.

"You must have the will to survive," Kendall said, "to do anything, anything to defeat your opponents."

"My wife was not your opponent," Sloane said.

Kendall's eyes burned up at him. "But you were. You would have ruined everything. You, the lawyer who doesn't 'lose.' You should have let it go."

"Joe Wallace has been arrested," Fitzgerald said, "and he's already looking to cut a deal. You owned his father when he was a senator, and that gave you the power to own the son as well, didn't it?"

The old man's shrug was nearly imperceptible but ever defiant. "Have them take me to jail; I'll be dead within weeks."

Fitzgerald straightened his jacket and fixed the cuffs of his sleeves. "No, Sebastian. You're not going to jail. But I've called another meeting of the board of directors and I'm going to recommend that we accept an offer from Ian Hansen to merge with Titan Toys. It's pennies on the dollar, but then the company isn't worth anything anyway. All that we had was the Kendall name, but you ruined that as well. Ian will simply absorb us and eliminate the name Kendall altogether."

"I won't allow it," Kendall said, for the first time looking grief-stricken.

Fitzgerald smiled. "As you said, drastic times require drastic measures. You made me chairman of the board and CEO, remember? Without my loyalty, you don't have enough ownership interest to stop me. Ironic, isn't it, Sebastian? You sought to preserve your legacy, but you'll go to your grave knowing that it was you who destroyed it."

CAMANO ISLAND
WASHINGTON

SLOANE SAT IN his car finishing a phone conversation. The light from a fading sun trickled through the limbs of the trees, causing mottled shadows inside the car and streaking the field of tall grass orange and yellow. Overhead, a rainbow arched across the sky, seeming to stop just above a grain silo on the adjacent dairy farm. Carolyn had called to tell him they had received Judge Rudolph's signed order and he had parked to allow her to read it to him.

"He provided a case management schedule for the trial on the issues of liability and damages." The case management schedule was the court's calendar of deadlines leading up to trial.

Sloane knew he could prove Kendall strictly liable for putting a defective toy on the market. He knew he could obtain a jury award of several million dollars in damages for both the McFarlands and the Gallegoses, and perhaps ten times that amount in punitive damages when he proved Sebastian Kendall knew of the defect and tried to conceal it. But a trial would not be necessary. Fitzgerald had authorized a settlement and it would be a debt Titan and Kendall's insurers would pay. Kendall's other significant creditors would be reimbursed from the sale of everything Sebastian Kendall owned, the proceeds of which he had specified in his will were to be used for the benefit of the company. The company, and the man, would soon cease to exist.

"Have John call the McFarlands and Gallegoses. He did the work. He deserves to make that call."

"When will you be back?"

"I have the preliminary hearing in Jake's custody case in San Francisco day after tomorrow," he said, referring to the initial hearing in which the judge would try to resolve the matter short of a trial. "I'm not thinking much beyond that."

"I made your plane reservation. Is there anything else I can do?"

"You do enough," he said. "I couldn't have got through these past six weeks without you."

The usual retort stalled. "Why is it you say things like that before I can turn on the tape recorder and use it at my performance review?"

"Are we having performance reviews?"

"I'm told it's wise when you have more than a certain number of employees."

Sloane smiled. "All right, here's your performance review: you're doing great and can expect a substantial bonus this Christmas."

"A bonus would be nice," she said. Then she surprised him. "But I like my job better. Just promise me you'll be back."

"I'll call in a few days."

He hung up and took another moment before driving down the gravel road leading to Alex and Charlie's home. Sam, the golden retriever, and Razz, the pit bull terrier Jenkins had picked up two years earlier, ran alongside the car, tails wagging and barking to announce his arrival.

Sloane stepped from the car, trying to appease both dogs. "Shh! Quiet now. You'll wake the baby and then I'll be in trouble."

Alex greeted Sloane at the front door. He handed her a wrapped package. "For the baby," he said.

She rolled her eyes. "Which one?"

He laughed. "The one still in diapers."

She kissed him on the cheek. "Thank you. It's sweet of you, but Tina . . ." Her voice trailed.

"I know Tina already got him one. This is from me." Inside the house she took his jacket. "I take it the patient is being difficult."

"He'll be happy to see you," she said. "I was just about to bring him dinner. Enchiladas. Are you hungry?"

For the first time since Tina's death, Sloane felt hungry. "Sounds great."

He heard the television from halfway up the stairs. When he stepped into the room, carrying the tray of food, Jenkins hit the mute button and turned in the bed. Charles Junior lay beside him, drinking a bottle.

"Let me tell you how this friendship thing works," Jenkins said. "I take a bullet for you, and you call me and ask how I'm doing."

Sloane put the tray down on the bed and removed one of the two plates. "I've called three times. You've been asleep."

He helped Jenkins into a sitting position, putting pillows behind him, and put the food tray in his lap.

"I saw the news about Kendall."

Sloane nodded.

"How do you feel?"

"Numb."

"You did a good thing, David. You should feel good about what you did."

But he didn't. It was over. He had done what he had set out to do, yet he found no joy in any of it.

"When's the custody hearing for Jake?"

"Day after tomorrow."

"Have you hired a lawyer yet?"

"I'm going to handle it myself."

"Isn't there a saying about a lawyer who represents himself having a fool for a client?"

The baby dropped the bottle and cried out. Jenkins repositioned it and held the end. "He's getting big," Sloane said.

"You want to hold him?"

Sloane shook his head. "Maybe in a little while."

"We're going to raise him Catholic."

It seemed an odd comment. "When did you make that decision?"

"Pretty much when Alex told me; it was part of the package if I wanted to marry her. So, we're looking for a godfather."

Sloane took a bite of enchilada, fighting back his emotions. "I'm not Catholic," he said.

"No, but you're the best man we know. I think that qualifies." Jenkins paused. "Remember that night I dropped you off at the hotel?"

Sloane did.

"Don't go to that island, David."

"Only to visit you," he said.

CHAPTER
SEVENTEEN

Sloane found the family law department and pulled open the door to a modern courtroom. He wondered about Jenkins's admonition of having a fool for a client. Maybe—but he also knew that no attorney would be more motivated than he to get Jake back. Jake was all Sloane had left. Lose him, and Sloane lost his only remaining connection with Tina.

Brightly lit from recessed incandescent lighting, the windowless room resembled a courtroom only by its furnishings: a gallery of pews behind a wood railing, and two tables facing an elevated bench. Modern technology provided not only the light, but also a climate-controlled temperature for everyone's comfort.

Sloane pulled out his notepad and pen and thumbed through the pleadings filed by the attorney for Frank Carter, which, as he had assumed, was not going to be Jeff Harper. He then read the responsive pleadings prepared by Tom Pendergrass, who had done a good job. Legally, Frank Carter had an advantage, being the boy's biological father, but Sloane would present evidence that it was only genetics. For thirteen years Carter had divorced himself from his son, rarely visiting Jake in San Francisco and never traveling to Seattle. He had rarely attended any of the boy's school or athletic functions, and had never financially supported Jake. Tina's will, in which she expressed her desire for Sloane to raise Jake, would confirm Frank was not a fit parent, and Sloane would leave no doubt Frank Carter did not love his son and only sought custody because the Larsens were paying him.

"Mr. Sloane?"

A bear of a man introduced himself as Dean Flannigan, which was the name on the pleadings. With a shock of dirty blond hair and a beard that covered the knot of his tie, Flannigan resembled Kenny Rogers before the plastic surgery. The man was so big Sloane did not immediately see Frank Carter, who stood off to the side dressed like a kid going for a prep school interview in his navy blue suit, white shirt, and tie.

Flannigan had a thick and calloused hand. "Do you have counsel?"

"I'll be handling the hearing myself."

Together, Sloane and Flannigan advised the judge's clerk that both sides were present. The clerk asked them to wait at the bench.

"Where are the Larsens?" Sloane asked. "I subpoenaed them."

"I don't know," Flannigan said. "I represent Mr. Carter. Their attorney did, however, leave me a message this morning indicating they will be here."

Sloane wanted to call bullshit; he knew very well who was paying Flannigan's bill, but he decided to let it go. Besides, Judge Marianne Zelinsky had glided into her courtroom.

"Counsel," she said, "our goal here today is the health and well-being of the child. It is my job, and it is my intention, to find the best living situation for Jake." With short gray hair and thick black-framed glasses, Zelinsky furrowed her brow frequently.

"That's everyone's goal, Judge," Flannigan said.

Sloane refrained from comment. There would be no need for a hearing if everyone had Jake's best interests at heart, but he would prove that soon enough. He also suspected that Flannigan, a local practitioner, had previously appeared before Zelinsky.

"You have complied with the temporary restraining order, Mr. Sloane?" Zelinsky asked.

"I have, Your Honor," Sloane said.

"Mr. Flannigan?"

"I am unaware of any violation of that order, Judge."

"Good. Then we'll get started."

Sloane returned to counsel table, and Flannigan retrieved Carter from the back of the courtroom, whispering final instructions before leading him to his seat beside him. Shortly after nine the judge's staff filed into the courtroom and Zelinsky took the bench.

"Who will testify today?"

Sloane and Frank Carter both indicated they would testify. Zelinsky asked them to raise their hands and swore them in.

"All right, Mr. Flannigan, you may proceed."

Flannigan pushed back his chair and stood. The fabric of his suit stretched to cover his ample girth. "Judge, I'd like to ask questions of Mr. Sloane if I may?"

Sloane was surprised. He had thought that Flannigan would open with Frank Carter.

"Mr. Sloane, please come forward and take the stand," Zelinsky said.

Sloane complied, feeling odd to be at the other end of an attorney's questions. Flannigan stepped forward, a paper in hand. He established that Sloane had moved to Seattle with Tina and Jake when she took a job at an architecture firm and that they had subsequently married.

"You otherwise have no other connection to that city."

"Define connection," Sloane said.

Flannigan nodded, as if it was a legitimate clarification, but Sloane knew where the lawyer was going with his questions. "You have no relatives in Seattle, no mother or father, no brothers or sisters, uncles, aunts, cousins, connections. Is that right?"

"Yes, that's correct."

"In fact, you have no relatives to speak of anywhere, do you?"

"No," Sloane said.

"You were raised in foster homes, several of them, were you not?"

"I was."

"Four to be exact."

The Larsens were pulling no punches. Sloane didn't answer, and Flannigan didn't push him.

"You own a home in Seattle?"

"Yes."

"And that is where you lived with the deceased and Jake since moving there?"

"Except for a brief time before we bought the home, that's correct."

"That is the home that your wife was murdered in."

Sloane paused. "Yes, it is."

"Have you been back to that home since that night?"

Damn. The Larsens must have hired a private investigator; Sloane hadn't considered that. "No, I have not."

"You haven't been back to the home at all, not once?"

"No."

"I see." Flannigan paced for a moment with a concerned expression. "And have you avoided returning to the home because to do so would be emotionally painful?"

Again Sloane knew where Flannigan was going with his questions but he could not redirect it and he could not avoid it. "Yes, I thought that it might be."

"And do you think returning would be emotionally painful for a thirteen-year-old boy who watched his mother die in that house?"

Sloane fought to not sound combative. "I know it would be difficult for Jake, and for me. But we would get through that together. We could also sell the house and find another place."

"And perhaps another school, another set of friends."

"I didn't say that."

Flannigan had made his point. "You have been providing for both Jake and Mrs. Sloane since moving to Seattle. In fact, you make a very good living as an attorney."

"I could care for Jake very well."

"Financially I'm sure you could."

"And emotionally," Sloane offered.

"You also do quite a bit of legal commentary on television, don't you?"

"I have."

"Chicago, New York, Los Angeles. I imagine that takes up quite a bit of your time, in addition to the full-time practice of law. Tell me, Mr. Sloane, how is it you plan on taking care of a thirteen-year-old boy while running a highly successful legal practice and flying around the country as a legal commentator?"

"I've hired two attorneys so I could cut back on my hours at the office and I would stop being a legal commentator."

"And who would watch Jake while you were at work?"

"Jake is in school. He participates in after-school activities. There were many nights I arrived home before him."

"You try cases, do you not?"

"I do."

"What would you do if you were in the midst of a trial and couldn't get home until very late?"

"I would work more at home."

"But you have no relatives to help you out, to help care for the boy, isn't that true?"

"We've already established that, counselor."

"Just answer the question," Judge Zelinsky admonished.

"No, I don't," Sloane said.

"So Jake could find himself alone in this house that you your-self have refused to return to because it is emotionally too upset-ting, is that right?"

"It would be very rare, and I would take some time off until we both became acclimated."

Flannigan let it go. "Prior to living with the deceased and Jake for a relatively short period of time—"

"It was two years. More than two years," Sloane interjected.

"That's right. Prior to living with Jake and his mother you lived alone, correct?"

"I did."

"And we've already established that you grew up without a father or mother. Is that a fair assessment? I mean you did not establish a parental relationship with any of the foster parents, did you?"

"No, I didn't, but Jake and I didn't have that kind of relation-ship." Sloane directed his next comments to Frank Carter. "No one was paying me to care for the boy. I love Jake. I love being his father. It's the reason I intended to adopt him. It's the reason Tina's will specified me as his legal guardian should anything happen to her."

"Yes, well, let's take a look at that adoption paperwork that you submitted with your briefing, shall we?" Flannigan flipped through a binder at counsel table and produced the paperwork. "I noticed it wasn't filled out."

"We hadn't had a chance."

"Too busy?"

Sloane bit his lip.

Flannigan said, "I also noticed that Mrs. Sloane never signed the document."

"We discussed it as a family just before she died."

"And I noticed that Mrs. Sloane's will left all of her personal estate in a trust for Jake, is that correct?"

Sloane struggled to remain composed. "Tina and I made that decision when she sold her flat in San Francisco. Since I was well off financially, I told her to put it in a trust for Jake."

The examination continued for nearly an hour. When Sloane stepped down he felt drained and was seriously reconsidering his decision to handle the hearing himself. After a brief recess, Flannigan called Frank Carter to the stand.

Flannigan wasted little time painting a contrast between Carter's and Sloane's backgrounds.

"How long have you been in the commercial brokerage business?"

"About three years," Carter said. "I went back to school."

"How much do you earn?"

"It depends. The last couple of years weren't very good for anyone."

"Say on average."

"Between sixty-five and a hundred thousand."

"What hours do you normally work?"

"Well, that's kind of the beauty of the job. I don't have set hours. I can pretty much make my own. So I'm home when Jake leaves in the morning and when he gets home."

"Do you drive him to school?"

"Sometimes, but the house is close enough he can ride his bike. There are a couple of other kids in the neighborhood he's become friends with. They ride together, and I'm encouraging it, you know, so he can make new friends."

"Do you own your own home?"

"I just bought one."

"You lived in an apartment before that?"

"Yes, but I thought a house would be a better environment for Jake. He has his own room and a yard. We just got a dog. Plus it's a better school district."

The news that Jake had a dog stabbed Sloane in the chest.

"Do you take Jake to school?"

"And pick him up."

"What happens if something unexpected comes up?"

"I have a lot of help. My parents are close by. I also have three brothers and sisters in the area."

"Does Jake have any cousins?"

"Seven. A couple his age."

"And has he spent time with them?"

"Lately he has. It's been good for him, having a family around."

The testimony was as positive as Sloane's was negative, but Sloane simply bided his time. Flannigan could orchestrate Carter's direct testimony to make him look like father of the year, but he couldn't protect him once Sloane began his cross-examination. In fact, Sloane thought it a mistake for Flannigan to go to such lengths to paint Carter as the doting father; it would make it that much easier for Sloane to tear down the facade and reveal the man for who he truly was.

After another half hour, Flannigan nodded to Zelinsky. "I think I'm finished, Judge."

Zelinsky addressed Sloane. "Mr. Sloane, do you have questions of Mr. Carter?"

"I do, Your Honor."

At the podium Sloane leveled his gaze at Carter, and Frank squirmed in his seat, as if anticipating a punch to the gut. The impact was going to be painful, but knowing it was coming and there was nothing he could do about it must have made it that much worse.

"Mr. Carter, why did you live in an apartment for so many years?" Sloane asked.

"It was just me then."

"Finances, or a lack thereof, didn't play into that decision?"

"I don't understand," Carter said, though Sloane was certain he did.

"Who provided you with the down payment to buy a $784,000 home in a development in the East Bay?"

Carter twisted his head, as if the knot of the tie had become tight. "My in-laws loaned me the money."

"The Larsens gave you the money?"

"It's a loan. I'm paying it back."

"Just out of the blue they gave you more than two hundred thousand dollars?"

"It was part of Jake's inheritance. They wanted Jake to have a stable place to live."

"And the monthly mortgage payment, you're making that payment?"

Carter squirmed. "Not yet, but I'm going to be."

"Well, who is now?"

"The Larsens."

"Is that also part of this loan?"

"I guess. I don't really know."

"Do you know whose name is on the title to the house?" Sloane knew the answer, having pulled the title report for the property.

"The Larsens'."

"So when you say you bought a house, that's really just a figure of speech, isn't it? I mean, it's not really your house at all; the Larsens made the initial down payment and they are paying the monthly mortgage. It's their house, isn't it?"

"Like I said, it's a loan."

"At what interest?"

"What?"

"Most banks charge interest on a loan, Frank. Surely you know that in your line of work. What interest are the Larsens charging you?"

"I don't really know," he said.

"You don't know?"

"They have all the paperwork."

"Then I'll have to ask them. But you seem to have done pretty well in this deal. A new house, no mortgage payment, no rent. Did you get anything else, a car, boat?"

Flannigan stood, speaking as calmly as a country lawyer. "Objection, Your Honor, counsel is badgering the witness."

"Sustained."

Sloane returned to counsel table to consider his notes. He was about to take Frank Carter apart for his lack of interest in Jake over the past thirteen years when the door to the courtroom opened and the Larsens entered, Jeff Harper at their side. Bill Larsen glared at Sloane, but Terri looked away. Sloane was about to turn his attention back to Frank Carter when another figure stepped through the doorway, giving him pause and bringing a lump to his throat.

Jake wore a pair of khaki pants and a blue button-down shirt, the tail only partially tucked in at the waist. It used to drive Tina crazy when he wouldn't fully tuck in his shirt. Hands thrust in his pants' pockets, Jake had his head down. His hair had grown long enough to cover his eyes. But as he entered the courtroom Jake looked up at Sloane. For a brief moment, his face was a blank mask. Then the corner of his mouth inched into an impish, "I'm not supposed to do this but I can't help it" grin.

Sloane felt his heart skip a beat. He fought to retain his composure, taking a deep breath.

"Mr. Sloane?"

Sloane took a drink of water from a cup on the table. "Yes, Your Honor, I'm sorry." He returned to the lectern, took another moment, and continued his cross-examination. "How large is this house that you live in, Frank?"

"It's three bedrooms. Jake has his own room."

His throat still dry, Sloane turned to pick up the glass of water and his eyes again found Jake, now seated between the Larsens in a pew, and this time it brought a different recollection—that of a six-year-old boy sitting next to his father in a San Francisco courtroom staring up at a photograph of his mother's battered and beaten body. The trial had been Sloane's last before moving to Seattle. Emily Scott had been raped and murdered in her office when Sloane's client failed to provide proper security. Like Emily Scott's young son, Jake's lasting image of his mother would be a horrific snapshot of her lying on her back, choking on her own blood.

"Mr. Sloane?" Sloane turned back to Judge Zelinsky, who looked down at him with a wrinkled brow. "Do you have more questions of Mr. Carter?"

Sloane had planned a forty-five-minute cross-examination that would expose Frank Carter for what he was, a lousy father who had never showed any love for his son and who was now only interested in Jake because the Larsens were paying him to take the boy. Sloane had no doubt he could do it; he had been fixated on getting Jake back, at all costs, since the confrontation in Jeff Harper's office. Now, all he could think of was that Jake had already lost his mother, and Sloane was about to take his father from him as well.

"Mr. Sloane?"

Sloane turned back to the judge. "Just one more question, Your Honor."

Frank Carter looked first to the judge, then to Dean Flannigan, seemingly uncertain and confused about this unforeseen development.

Sloane left the podium, stepping closer to the railing, obstructing Carter's view of his attorney. When he leveled his gaze, Carter leaned back.

"Do you love your son?" Sloane asked.

Carter's eyes narrowed, as if considering whether it could be a trick question. He searched Sloane's face for any hidden malice.

"Do you love your son, Frank?" Sloane asked again, his voice soft.

Carter looked past Sloane to where Jake sat. "Yes. I love Jake very much."

Sloane did not have to turn to know Jake was smiling. He could see it in the smile on Frank Carter's face and the tears pooling in the man's eyes. He knew it intuitively, as a father.

"I know I haven't been much of a father in the past. But I hope to change that," Carter said, looking up at Judge Zelinsky. "I hope to have a second chance. I wasn't expecting one, but here it is, and I intend to make the most of it. I intend to do better."

Sloane nodded. "I have nothing further, Your Honor."

AFTER DISMISSING FRANK CARTER, Judge Zelinsky sat back, surveying her courtroom, no doubt pondering what had just transpired. After nearly a minute she sat forward. "I'd like to talk with Jake. Young man, would you join me for a moment?"

Jake looked to his grandparents, who encouraged him out of the pew, then stood to follow. Judge Zelinsky stopped them with an outstretched palm. "Just Jake," she said. "Alone."

At the front of the room she put a robed arm around the boy's shoulders, and together they walked through the door to the left of the bench.

Thirty minutes passed before the door reopened. When it did, Jake emerged with his head bowed, but Sloane could see from his red and swollen eyes that the boy had been crying. Jake removed a hand from his pocket long enough to wipe his nose as he shuffled between the two tables, never raising his head or taking his gaze from the floor. Sloane pressed his lips together and squeezed shut his eyes, teeth clenched.

Then he felt him.

Jake wrapped his arm around Sloane's shoulders and buried his face in Sloane's neck. Sloane held him tight, feeling Jake's tears on his cheek and neck.

"I love you, Dad," he whispered.

"I love you too, son."

Judge Zelinsky gave them a moment. Then she said, "Mr. Sloane, Mr. Carter, I'd like to see you both."

Flannigan did not protest being left out.

Jake released his grip and stepped back. Sloane held him by the shoulders. "Remember my promise? I'll always be there for you. I'll always do what's best. Now go on back with your grandparents," he whispered. Then he followed Carter into the judge's chambers.

Judge Zelinsky's furnishings were modest, a leather couch along one wall beneath a nondescript print, a functional desk, two chairs. Nobody sat. The judge waited near windows that framed City Hall's glittering golden dome, brilliant in the bright sun. Sloane and Carter stood just feet apart.

"I think you both probably know what Jake would prefer," she said, looking to Sloane. "And I have no doubt, Mr. Sloane, that you love that child as much as any father and would do a tremendous job raising him. What just transpired in my courtroom this morning was one of the most selfless acts I have ever witnessed. Anyone who would do what you just did . . . Well, your love cannot be questioned."

Sloane could only nod.

"Too often I watch families tear themselves apart," Zelinsky counseled. "Parents belittle and degrade each other, then wonder why their children don't respect them. So while I know you would raise Jake just as selflessly, I have to look at all of the circumstances, including the boy's living situation, relatives, the disruption to his life. You are a successful attorney, Mr. Sloane, and I know what it takes to maintain a law practice."

"Judge," Sloane interrupted. "I'm withdrawing my request for custody. I recognize that what Jake needs now more than ever is stability. He needs a family. I can't give Jake what I don't have. I can't conjure up grandparents and aunts and uncles and cousins." He smiled. "Maybe a dog, but . . . While I have issues with the motivation behind much of this, I can't deny there is a group of people out there who love Jake and want him. That's all I've ever wanted for him, to be in a place where he knows he is loved." Sloane faced Frank Carter. "Did you mean it, what you said in that courtroom?"

Frank Carter nodded. "I was young, David. And the longer I stayed away, the more embarrassed I became. I saw that Tina loved you and that Jake loves you. So I stayed away. It was wrong of me, and I realized it these past weeks living with Jake. I've been given a second chance and I intend to do better."

In his head, Sloane heard Jenkins talking about second chances, even when it isn't deserved. He spoke to Judge Zelinsky. "If it's all right with you, Judge, I'll say my good-byes to Jake and be going."

"David?" Frank Carter extended his hand. "Anytime you want to see Jake you let me know and I'll put him on a plane to Seattle. That's a promise."

"What about the Larsens?"

Frank Carter shrugged. "They don't think much of me,

David, but they love their grandson. They're not going to do anything to hurt their chances of seeing him. That's why I hired my
own attorney. I've filled out the paperwork for a loan to pay them
back. My parents will help. I'm not going to let them dictate how
I raise Jake."

Maybe Carter had grown into a man after all. Sloane hoped
so, for Jake's sake.

"How about tomorrow?" Sloane asked. "Jake and I have something we need to do."

EPILOGUE

HOLY CROSS CEMETERY
DALY CITY, CALIFORNIA

The other headstones were mostly gray concrete, some blackened and chipped with age. A few were marble, but none were blue, Tina's favorite color. Sloane had wanted a headstone that would stand out and be easily found. He had succeeded.

CHRISTINA ANNE SLOANE

Seeing her name etched in the stone brought a finality he could not ignore, a proclamation for everyone to see. Tina had not left for the store. She was not on a trip. She was not coming home after a long day at the office.

She was not coming back, ever.

Sloane pulled tight the collar of his jacket, feeling the chill of the damp, overcast day. The sky seemed to mourn with him, emitting a persistent, light mist. Overhead he heard the hushed engine of a plane hidden somewhere in the fog, and the sky reminded him of so many of the mornings at Three Tree Point when they would walk along the beach in the marine fog.

It was time to go home. As hard as it would be to go back to the house that he and Tina loved, the house in which they had intended to grow old together, Sloane would not run from the memories. To do so would dishonor Tina.

He stood at her grave uncertain of what to say. Not having learned any prayers, he spoke from his heart.

"I miss you," he said. "I really miss you. I miss holding you and seeing you smile. I miss the smell of your hair and the softness of your skin, and the way you used to giggle just before we made love. I miss feeling completely lost in you, and sitting on the porch holding hands watching the sunset. I still imagine us sitting there, old and gray. You told me once you had always loved me and always would. I didn't understand what that meant, not completely, but I do now. You taught me to love selflessly." He paused, catching his breath. "I couldn't destroy Frank in court. I couldn't do that to Jake. I love him too much to hurt him. Frank seems to have changed. He says he loves Jake, and Jake seems happy. He'll have a family. I couldn't give him that, not without you."

He took a deep breath and pushed his hands deeper inside his jacket pockets. "It should never have been you. You were too good to die. It should have been me.

"I think about you and I wonder . . . if there is a heaven, whether you're happy. I hope you are. I know that I have to stop blaming myself, Tina, not because I don't still feel guilty, but because I have to be there for Jake. He still has his whole life ahead of him, and I have to make sure it's as good as it can possibly be. I promised you that. I just wish I knew that you understood, that you forgive me."

A noise drew his attention. Beside him an old woman had knelt on a wool shawl spread on the lawn and was brushing away leaves and picking at elongated strands of grass at the base of the stone where the blades of the gardener's lawn mower could not reach. Perhaps sensing Sloane's silence, she sat back on her heels. "I'm sorry. I hope I didn't disturb you."

At her side, hidden when she had been tending to the grave, Sloane saw a bundle of red roses. Some of the buds had bloomed wide, others were just beginning to open. Thorns traced the stems.

The woman considered the dates beneath the name on Tina's headstone. "So young. So recent." She got up from her knees. "Your wife?"

Sloane nodded.

"I'm sorry. I know how painful it is."

The dates on the tombstone that the woman had been tending revealed that the man buried there had been dead more than thirty years.

"When does it stop hurting?" he asked.

A breeze swayed the branches of the oak tree, causing them to creak and click against one another. The woman brushed a strand of white hair from her face, revealing cobalt blue eyes. "The ache in your heart each morning when you wake to realize she's really gone?" She held out her hand. When Sloane took it her touch caused his chest to radiate, despite the chilled weather. "It doesn't," she said. "Time doesn't heal all wounds. But it does deaden the pain so that we can go on."

"How?" Sloane asked. "How do you go on?"

She gave his hand a gentle squeeze. "The only way we can, dear. Moment to moment. Hour by hour. Because, what else are you going to do?"

They stood in silence, the breeze picking up. Sloane saw Frank Carter's car winding through the cemetery. He slipped free his hand, thanked the woman for her words of comfort, and walked toward the curb. The passenger door pushed open almost before Carter had pulled over and stopped, and Jake was out of the car, running toward Sloane with a huge grin on his face. Frank Carter had kept his word.

Sloane's arms engulfed the boy, the impact nearly knocking him over.

Frank Carter had stepped from the car but did not approach, the two men exchanging a nod.

"Are you ready to do this?" Sloane asked.

Jake stepped back, no longer smiling, the weight of their task sobering.

As they walked back toward her grave, Sloane searched for but did not see the woman standing amid the rows of rounded stones and assumed she had knelt again to tend to her husband's grave. But when he reached the proper row she did not kneel there. The woman was gone, though the roses remained, the red a beautiful contrast against the blue marble.

"You remembered," Jake said.

Sloane looked at him, uncertain.

"Roses. You always bought them for Mom after your trials."

In his mind Sloane saw Tina standing on the outdoor patio at the Tin Room, hand on her hip, smiling up at him, coy.

"Roses? For me?"

And all was forgiven.

"She's not here, you know," Jake said, looking down at the grave. He pointed to his heart. "She's in here, with us."

"I think you're right," Sloane said.

"Frank says I can visit over Christmas."

"I know. What do you say we go skiing up at Whistler?"

Jake nodded. "That might be fun," he said. "But I think I'd rather just go home, Dad, you know? Do you think we could do that?"

Sloane nodded. "I do now."

ACKNOWLEDGMENTS

ON FATHER'S DAY, June 15, 2008, I lost my dad after a three-year battle with cancer. That he would die on Father's Day was particularly appropriate given that my father raised ten children. But then, my father always had great timing, as any great comedian does. Born on Christmas Day, 1931, he was one of the funniest men you would ever meet. Truly larger than life, he commanded a room not by being loud or outspoken, but rather through his intimate and quiet demeanor. My father had a way of standing back, taking everything in, and smiling knowingly at it all. I always said he should have been a writer because he lived his life by the writer's mantra—show don't tell. I don't recall him ever yelling at me, even raising his voice, and I don't recall any father-son chats about not cheating or stealing or lying. And yet he taught me all those lessons and more through the way he lived his own life. He was the hardest working, most honest man I've ever met and I regard him now as simply the best man I have ever known. My greatest concern, living in Seattle, was that I would not get to say good-bye when my father died. But again, Dad's timing was impeccable. I went to the Bay Area to visit with my father the Thursday before Father's Day and spent three days and nights with him. I was in the house that Sunday morning when he left this world. He is now buried at Holy Cross Cemetery in Daly City beneath a blue marble headstone. He had wanted to redo the kitchen counters but died before he could. My mother got him the marble anyway.

I wouldn't be writing books had it not been for my father. His only goal in life, it seemed, was to give his children every chance to follow their dreams. This is mine. I owe him and my mother my career.

I've dedicated this book to my brothers and sisters. Growing up in a family of ten was remarkable in so many respects it is hard to put it down in words, but I hope to someday. I was never lonely, that's for sure, and I was surrounded by more love than one person has a right to have. My older sisters, Aileen, Susie, and Bonnie helped to raise me, and didn't let me get away with much. Thanks to them I know how to cook, clean, do the laundry, and raise my own children. My older brother, Bill, once my tormentor, has become my best friend. My baby sister Joann will always occupy that place in my heart reserved for baby sisters, and my younger brothers, Tom, Larry, Sean, and Michael, are all good men and good friends whom I admire, respect, and love. Thanks for making growing up so much fun.

I also dedicated this novel to Sam Goldman. Sam is a character in an as yet unpublished novel, though I am confident it will be published soon. I could never capture the true spirit of Sam Goldman, however. Sam taught me journalism and to love to write. More importantly, he taught me to love every minute of every day. No matter the circumstances, Sam always has a smile on his face and a twinkle in his eye and greets everyone with such expressions as, "Hello, great hero," and "Keep smiling, chief." He has more optimism than ten men. In many respects, Sam became the grandfather I never had. Though he is not that old, he is certainly that wise.

To Dr. Shane Macaulay, who has his hands full with his career and family but always finds the time to help me with medicine, weapons, and common sense. Thanks to my brother, Tom, a surgeon who helped me to make the emergency-room chapter real.

Thanks to my father-in-law, Robert Kapela, M.D., who helped with the issues about autopsies and provided articles on magnets. Thanks also to all of those who were willing to read the manuscript and provide me their insight but who wish to remain anonymous. You all made it better.

And a special thanks to Sim Osborne, attorney and friend. David Sloane is a fictitious character, as are the events portrayed in this book. But the issues concerning toys and child safety, as well as the potential dangers of magnets, are real. Sim fought the battles in the trenches and was willing to share some of his experiences with me to bring this book to life. Along the way he never broke a client confidence. I am grateful for his help.

There are also a number of books and articles out there on the toy industry and the Consumer Product Safety Commission, particularly its downsizing under prior administrations. I read everything I could get my hands on, but I'm sure despite all the research and my best efforts, that I have made some mistakes. Any mistakes in this book are mine and mine alone. If you find one, let me know. I'm always interested in learning.

Thanks to Meg Ruley of the Jane Rotrosen Agency, my agent. Meg has never wavered in her confidence for my career and remains a beacon of light. I am indebted to her for so much. Thanks also to the rest of the Rotrosen team for their support. I couldn't do it without you.

Thanks to Touchstone/Simon & Schuster for believing in *Bodily Harm* and in me. To my editor, Trish Lande Grader, thanks for your insight and kindness. Thanks to publisher Stacy Creamer and to Trish Todd, Stacy Lasner, Marcia Burch, Megan Clancy, Tyler LeBleu, art director Cherlynne Li, production editor Josh Karpf, and assistant editor Lauren Spiegel. If I missed anyone, you know you have my thanks.

To Louise Burke, Pocket Books publisher, and Pocket Books associate publisher Anthony Ziccari, as well as editor Abby Zidle, for great insight and support. And thanks to all on the Touchstone and Pocket Books sales forces. I wouldn't be writing this without you.

Thank you also to the loyal readers who e-mail me to tell me how much they enjoy my books and await the next. You are the reason I keep looking for the next David Sloane adventure, and beyond.

And always, first in my heart, my wife and my kids; you bring me more joy than one man has a right to experience. I love you all.

Finally, to Nick, our fifteen-year-old Rhodesian Ridgeback who also lost his battle with melanoma last July and now rests in peace on the family farm nearby. He was much loved by us all, but loved us all more in return, especially my wife. For a dog, he had great taste in women. You were a good dog, my first, and you taught me much about myself. We will miss you. I will miss you.